UNHOLY GODS

RECLAIMING HER

STACY RUSH

NYTE'S HALL SERIES
BY
STACY RUSH

Reclaiming Her

Copyright © 2024 by Stacy Rush

All rights reserved. Printed in the United States of America. No part of this book may be used or reproduced in any manner whatsoever without written permission except in the case of a brief quotations embodied in critical articles or reviews.

This book is a work of fiction. Names, characters, businesses, organizations, places, events, and incidents either are the product of the author's imagination or are used fictitiously. Any resemblance to actual persons, living or dead, events, or locales is entirely coincidental.

Cover Design by Stacy Rush
Proofread by 'Sky'
Formatting by Stacy Rush
Previously published as a Kindle Vella story.

ISBNs:
eBook ISBN 9798990324633
Paperback ISBN 9798990324640
SE Paperback ISBN 9798990324657

DEDICATION

To all the little smut lovelies who need the anti-hero in their life...

This one will devour you...

DISCLAIMER

No part of this book may be reproduced or transmitted in any form or by any means, electronic or mechanical, including photocopying, recording, or by any information storage and retrieval system without written permission of the author.

This is a work of fiction. Unless otherwise stated, all names, characters, businesses, places, events, and incidents in this book are either the product of the author's imagination or used in a fictitious manner. Any resemblance to actual persons, living or dead, or actual events is purely coincidental.

Please do not try any of the sexual practices found in this book without the guidance of an experienced professional. Author is not responsible for any harm, loss, injury and/or death resulting from the use of the information in this

WARNINGS

Your Mental Health Matters

This book has dark themes and matter. If you are sensitive to forced proximity, Dub/Con, Graphic Violence and Sexual Situations, Touch Her and Die, Drug Trafficking, and poisoning, just to name a few, I suggest you pass on reading this book. Please view the FULL LIST on my website at www.authorstacyrush.com...you have been warned....

PROLOGUE

Nyx

"We need to figure out how to go about getting the Kappels to move on to another town. I'd hate to have to get rid of Jarod and Jax; I'm rather fond of those fuckers." Zilas lines his pool cue up and takes his shot, putting his last two balls in their own corner pocket.

I sit in the armchair watching the game between the Carlson and Donovan Heirs, as I consider the alternative if the Kappel twins decide not to accept our conditions about moving their drugs to another town. Zilas and Craydon, Cray for short, are two of my four best friends. I know what Zilas means by liking the twins; we all grew up together. Granted, *our* families ruled this town, but they aren't too far behind us when it comes to being the richest.

Unfortunately, my father, along with Zilas, Cray, and Adrik's fathers, allowed the Kappels too much leniency when it came to running their drugs. We four Heirs, who live at Nyte's Hall, have never been too fond of the heavy drug trafficking coming and going through our town. Last year when the damn Feds closed in on the drug ring happening right under our noses, my friends and I rallied together and voted our fathers out, taking over their seats as the Gods of Nyte's Hall.

"Has Amara paid them a visit yet?" I ask my two friends.

"Not that we know of," Zilas replies as they both shake their heads.

Speaking of the she-devil, her stiletto boots click on the marbled floor as she walks into the room and over to the bar, reaching over the counter to grab her choice of poison. I watch as she stretches her petite frame over the top of the bar, her full leather body jumpsuit hugging every curve she's got. Amara's ass looks fucking delicious in it. I know what it feels like to be in that tight ass, and just the thought is making me harder than I already am.

Gripping the hair of the woman on her knees in front of me, I push her head down, holding her there; the length of my cock reaching past her gag reflex and into her throat. Not wanting her to pass out from lack of air, I pull back. I can feel the eight pack rippling my midsection as it contracts while I thrust my hips fast and hard until I'm releasing in her mouth. Biting my lower lip, I focus my gaze on the woman as she swallows everything I give her. She's a new hire, so I'm not sure how well she takes the cock, but she's done a pretty good job so far.

"That a girl, sweetie," Amara says to the woman as she walks over and caresses her head. "Don't get any on the rug; otherwise, I'll have no choice but to clean the whole floor with your tongue."

"Where the fuck have you been?" I ask our little housemate as I carefully extract the woman from my cock and tuck myself back into my pants.

Amara ignores my question as she watches me with amusement, and I know exactly what she's thinking. I shake my head no. She pretends to pout before saying, "Fine, maybe Zilas and Adrik will entertain me later." She tips the eighteen-hundred-dollar bottle of my favorite Johnnie Walker Blue Label Ghost, and I roll my eyes as I stand up.

Reaching down, I help the woman up off the floor, offering, "I'll walk you out."

"Oh." The pretty blonde says, "I thought I'd be staying for a while longer. You know, so I can have mine, too."

Amara snickers but then I watch her as she walks over to the pool table before giving the blonde my full attention. "Sugar..."

"Emily," she offers.

I loathe being interrupted, but instead of lecturing her, I give her a strained smile and say, "Okay, *Emily*. This was part of your audition. I need to ensure you know how to please the club's clientele. We have never had anyone leave dissatisfied."

I hold her firmly by the elbow as I walk us out of the billiard room and down the dimly lit hall. Each family has its own wing that we live in here at Nyte's Hall, but we tend to gravitate toward the center of the massive mansion in our downtime. Amara has her own portion at the center of the Hall, only one floor down.

"Who was that woman that came in?" Emily asks with a hint of jealousy.

"Amara lives here." I don't feel she needs anymore explanation.

"Have you fucked her?"

I smirk. "Of course. She's a beautiful woman, and I fuck beautiful things."

I hear her slight scoff at my little hint, but she doesn't say anything until we are almost at the front door. She must have been working up the nerve to ask me, because she stammers a bit as she asks, "Can I see you again, Nyx?"

My jaw tightens at her use of my name. Only my friends and those I allow to use it call me by my name. "It's Mr. Beckam to you, and no, you may not. I don't date my employees, Emily. I'm sure we will scene together at the club at some point, but if you keep acting like a needy whore, I'll make sure you get edged for a whole week."

"I-I'm sorry, Mr. Beckam. I meant no disrespect." The fear in her eyes when she looks up at me just as we get to the door has me softening just a little.

"It's fine. You didn't know, so I'll let it slide this time." I open the front door and am about to let go of Emily's elbow when it hits me. The scent of jasmine and lavender. I remember that scent well, and with it being accompanied by the hairs on the back of my neck standing up, I know she is nearby. Grinning inwardly, I turn to the woman still being held by my hand, and say, "Goodnight, Emily. You were amazing." I tilt her chin up and take her lips, but only briefly.

"Goodnight, I will see you at the club," she says and then walks away.

Waiting until she is out of sight, I step out onto the stoop and look to my right. She's there, sitting on the bench in the shadows. A suitcase is by her feet, causing me to raise my eyebrow.

"Why are you here, Saraya?" I ask in my deep baritone voice, the same one I use on the submissives at the club.

Her small form stands, and she steps somewhat into the light. She's visibly shaking, which sets alarm bells going off in my head. "I need your help, Phoenyx."

My eyes peruse her from head to toe, but then they come back up and latch on to the big, dark red stain on the front of her shirt. "Pray tell, Lil' Sis, what have you been up to?"

ONE

The sight of my stepsister standing there before me has my cock stirring at first until the blood stain on her shirt catches my attention. Now, my blood is boiling over at just the thought of it dirtying her person, but I don't let it show. *What trouble has she gotten herself into?* The last time Saraya and I had talked, it ended with me leaving Nyte's Hall until after college. That was the day she destroyed Phoenyx Beckam.

I wait for her response, lifting my brow as I do. She opens her mouth and then closes it again. Her hands are clasped in front of her, one gripping the other as she stares at the center of my chest.

"Saraya, look at me."

Her doe-like eyes meet my hard, gray ones, and a memory of a time when she was the sun, the moon, and the stars in my life float through my head. She was the air I needed to breathe and live each day. She was my fucking life. It didn't matter that we were teenagers or stepsiblings; I knew that Saraya Abbott was my future. At least that was the case until she reached in and yanked out the only thing keeping my humanity in place.

"Um...I..." Saraya fumbles a little bit before clearing her throat and trying again, "Ken tried to..." Saraya's lip trembles, and she turns her head to the side.

That's when I see the damage; a gash just above her temple and a bruise starting by her eye. It takes me two strides to get to her before I grab her chin and pull her face into the light so I can see the damage better. I see fucking red instantly.

"Did Kenneth fucking hit you?" I growl out as I examine the extent of the injury. She nods. "What other marks did he leave on you?"

Her hands shake as they approach the scarf she's wearing and pull it from her neck. The bruising around her neck has me releasing her immediately so I don't cause her any more injury. I pivot on my heel and put distance between us, but I don't go too far.

"Phoenyx..."

I close my eyes, loving the sound of my name on her lips, but I only allow myself to soak it up for a few seconds before putting a blank expression back onto my face. Turning to face her once again, I nod at her shirt.

"Whose blood is it?"

"His."

"How bad?"

"Real bad."

Knowing where this is going, I have to ask just to confirm, "Is there a chance he will come looking for you?"

"No..."

I glance down at the suitcase at her feet, cock a brow as I look at her once again, and then cross my arms while I stare at her. "So, what's your plan, Saraya? Why did you come to me?"

Her eyes fall to the ground as she says, "I didn't know who else to go to."

"Eyes on me, Saraya," I order and wait until we are gazing at each other. "Now, let's try that again. Why did you come to me?"

She sucks her bottom lip in between her teeth; I can tell she's slightly embarrassed, but I don't give a fuck. If she wants my help, she best get over her embarrassment quickly because there will be no room for being shy with what I will have in store for her if she stays.

"I didn't know who else I could go to. You and your friends have power in this town. I could have gone to one of them, but I knew you wouldn't like that."

"Smart girl." My voice is flat with just a trace of sarcasm. "So, what exactly are you needing from me, Lil' Sis?"

"Can you please not call me that." Her face screws up in distaste.

"Why not? Are you no longer my sister? Have you also disowned me in that aspect?"

"I never disowned you, Phoenyx..."

I quirk my brow at her before glancing at her bag again. "I take it you need somewhere to lie low?"

She nods. "If you don't mind. I know we haven't really..."

I cut her off, "You can stay, but there will be conditions."

"Okay. Thank you..."

My taunting chuckle cuts her off yet again, and I say, "I wouldn't be thanking me just yet, *Lil' Sis.*" Stepping back up to her, I bring my hand up and run my knuckles over her soft cheek in a light caress. "My terms may be a little steep for you."

She straightens at my words; the defiant spark that I used to love twinkles in her brown eyes. "Will you beat me like Kenneth did on a daily basis?"

My jaw tightens, but I don't let her see how her question affects me. Instead, I smirk and give her body a once-over before responding with, "Only if you beg for it."

Acting the gentleman for Saraya doesn't occur to me as I turn toward the door, calling over my shoulder, "Grab your bag. You can take your old room." Holding the door open is the extent of my duties as a gentleman. "Get some rest, and we'll talk in the morning. I'll send someone over to clean up your mess."

"Did someone say clean up?" Amara comes waltzing into the foyer but stops in her tracks as soon as she lays eyes on Saraya. "Everything okay, Nyx?"

"Yeah. Seems my little sister has gotten herself into a bit of a jam." I inform Amara as she saunters up to me and wraps her arms around my waist.

I know what she's doing, and I allow it. Amara and the guys all know about my past with Saraya, and now my little friend here wants to fuck with my sister's head. I'll allow it because it's the lesser of the evils that Saraya will encounter while staying under this roof.

"Has she now." Amara licks her lips. "That's unfortunate for her." She then turns her body into mine and asks, "Need a bed warmer tonight, Nyx?"

I grin at the feisty little devil. "That sounds pretty inviting." Reaching down, I take a handful of her ass and squeeze. "Be in my bed, completely naked, in twenty minutes. I'll see if the guys want to join us."

"Yes, Sir..." Amara winks and steps away before looking at Saraya. "Nice seeing you, Raya."

"Yeah, it was a pleasure, Mara," Saraya states dryly, trying to smile, but she can't quite muster one up.

I watch Amara's ass as she walks away and then grin when I look back at Saraya as I say, "It's hard to believe you remember her since you haven't thought twice about calling her. Weren't the two of you close once?"

"We were. It looks like she's changed quite a bit." Saraya's jaw is slightly clenched, and I have to stop myself from grinning even more.

"She definitely has..." It's all I say as I walk away, leaving my stepsister standing in the middle of the foyer.

"I don't care what the fuck you do with him at the moment! Just make sure the motherfucker doesn't die yet and be sure there is nothing that will lead them back to Saraya!" I slam the phone down and start pacing the office when a knock sounds on my door. "Yeah?"

Adrik pops his head in and looks around before coming in and closing the door. "Where is she?"

I don't need to ask him who he's talking about before I reply, "I told her to go to her room and get some sleep. She really fucked that piece of shit up. Cale said that the prick has at least twenty stab wounds, but he isn't dead."

"Damn—go Raya!" Adrik grins, but I only glare at my friend. "How are you taking her being here?" he asks once he gets serious again.

I shrug. "She's my sister. She has a right to be here, too."

"You know what I mean, asshole." Adrik walks over to my minibar and helps himself.

"There will be conditions. Saraya wants my help, and I'm already cleaning up her mess, so she will owe me big time. She thinks her ex-husband is dead, and I don't see any reason to have to tell her otherwise," I tell my friend, leaning my ass against my desk.

"You know, Nyx, you're thirty years old, and the timer has started..." my friend states.

"Yeah. What are you getting at?" I narrow my eyes at him.

"I don't know. I mean, we both know that you have never gotten over *her.* You could use that as a stipulation..."

I scoff at my friend. "What makes you think I want the lying slut after what she did to me?"

"Oh, please! You know why she did it. It's not like your father wasn't intimidating," Adrik argues. "But hey, you do you, bro. Either way, I've got your back."

"Yeah, I know you do." Looking at my watch, I push away from the desk. "Speaking of *doing* things, I've got a five-foot, deadly, little ninja waiting for me in my bed. Care to join us?"

"Mm, you know I like me a nice Mara sandwich," Adrik says, grinning, but then stops. "I thought you were done fucking her."

I shrug. "It was too tempting to pass her offer up when it was made right in front of sister dearest."

"Ouch, man. I bet that hurt," Adrik states as we head up to my wing of the Hall.

"Yeah, well, too fucking bad. Saraya chose a different life, so now she gets to witness how I live my life."

"What if this is your chance at a *second chance* with her? I mean, your parents are dead, Nyx. Nothing is stopping you from being with her now."

"She fucking stopped it the moment she gave away what she had promised to me," I sneer, digging my finger into my chest as I do.

"Okay, buddy. I was only asking." Adrik slaps the back of my shoulder as we enter my room.

I don't bother shutting my door. I know how loud Amara can get and how her screams will bounce off the walls, echoing down the hallway. Amara is ready and waiting for us to claim her as she lays on her stomach, her knees bent, and kicking her feet in the air. I run my hand down her spine, over her perfect ass, and right between her legs.

"Ah, someone is wet already."

"Of course, Sir. I'm always ready for my favorite men," Amara says over her shoulder while licking her lips.

"Good. Adrik, you get her cunt; I know how much you love destroying it on her. I want to fuck up this perfect ass of hers. You're going to take it like a good little slut, aren't you, Mara?"

Amara nods excitedly.

"Don't mind if I do!" Adrik jumps on my bed and positions himself underneath our playmate.

"Please, go easy on me," Amara pleads playfully.

"Yeah, sure, whatever you say," I tell her when I hear the snicker that slips out of her mouth.

I take my time undressing before I stroke my cock a few times. A certain brunette comes to mind and I try thinking of Emily's mouth being on me, or how I'm about to be inside Amara, but neither works. She's already getting inside my head.

Reaching for the lube in the nightstand drawer, I coat myself generously before squeezing some out and watching it roll down her crack. I position myself and press into the tightness, not stopping until she's gripping my entire length. *Fuck.* It feels too fucking good.

Lacing my hand through the hair on the back of her head, I drag her up until her back arches and ask, "Are you ready, Mara?"

"Fuck yes!"

"Good girl."

I pull out to the tip and slam into her, pounding her tight little ring and getting in sync with Adrik as he gives Amara what she loves. As if she knows what I'm up to, Amara's moans, cries, and screams are louder than usual. Yeah, my stepsister will see that I'm no longer pining away for her. She no longer matters, at least not at the moment.

Amara is fun. She isn't for any of us guys, though, and she'll be the first to tell you this. We've been friends with benefits for as long as I can remember. In fact, Amara is the one to whom Cray, Zilas, Adrik, and I lost our virginity. Her family has served our families for a few generations, so it was only natural that she also served us in this aspect.

However, unlike our fathers, who never gave a choice to those they used, we give Amara a choice. She *is* one of us even though she isn't an Heir. In fact, she's the one who came to us, offering herself to the Heirs of Nyte's Hall. Amara is essential to this hall in many ways, and tonight, Adrik and I are going to take advantage of having her hot little ass under this roof.

"Oh, God...yes!" she cries out as I grip her hip with one hand while the other is still entangled in her short black hair, slamming into her repeatedly.

Movement in my peripheral view catches my attention, and I look up to see Saraya stopped just outside her bedroom door, staring down the hall and into mine. Our eyes meet, and a slow grin grows on my face as I ask Amara, "Whose cock do you love pounding into this sweet ass of yours, Mara?" I thrust into her over and over, all while holding my stepsister's stare as I wait for Amara's response.

"Yours Nyx—I love your cock in my ass!"

I bring my hand up and then let it fall, slapping her tender flesh. "That's a good little slut."

Saraya jerks back at my vulgar praise and then disappears down the hall. Suddenly, a picture of my stepsister taking Amara's place sweeps through my thoughts, and my grin widens. *Oh yes. I do believe I know just how I will make Lil' Sis pay for my help.* Turning my attention back to the ass I'm in at the moment, I slam into it one last time and release my load with a ferocious roar.

TWO

Saraya

I shouldn't have come here. I knew it would be a mistake to seek help from *him*. He hates me, and I don't blame him. What I did to Phoenyx all those years ago was unforgivable, but I was a girl of seventeen. I thought he hung the moon, and I would have done anything for him—and that's why I did what I did. I did it for him.

I didn't want to be the reason why Phoenyx lost everything, and maybe it was also me being a pussy. I don't think I would have been able to handle what my stepfather was threatening me with. I still had one more year of high school, and Phoenyx was getting ready to leave for his first year at college. I would have been left alone...

Rinsing my hair in the shower, I push away the past and think about the most recent events. Phoenyx agreeing to help me is a huge relief. I honestly thought he would slam the door in my face. I haven't talked to him in twelve years, so his agreeing is a godsend...no pun intended. He may be a God of Nyte's Hall, but he's far from being one.

Now, the conditions that he mentioned may have me slightly nervous. Phoenyx is so much scarier in person than he is in the newspapers and magazines. Yes, I've watched from afar because, come on, do you ever really get over your first true love? He may have more tattoos and a hardness about him, but when I look into those gray eyes, I see the boy that I grew up with since the fifth grade. The boy who always protected me and the boy I eventually fell in love with.

I'm willing to do whatever it takes to ensure I don't go down for Ken's murder. It doesn't matter what I must do. I refuse to go to jail because I was protecting myself, but Ken's a cop. The *only* ones who can protect me are the Gods of Nyte's Hall. That said, they can also crucify me for killing a cop, so yes, I will do what is asked of me.

There is one little issue I'm afraid to look too much into—Amara. Are she and Phoenyx now together? Aside from Phoenyx, Amara was my best friend growing up; we told each other everything, but I never told her why I did what I did. I was sworn to secrecy. I really fucked a lot of things up the day I gave up love in order to protect not only him but also myself.

My stomach growls, so once I'm dressed, I decide to go to the kitchen and see if I can find anything in the fridge. I'm just leaving my room when I hear moans coming from down the hall. When I look in that direction, I freeze.

Cold gray eyes meet mine as Phoenyx stares at me from his room. It takes me a moment to realize he's thrusting into Amara, who is also straddling another male. It must be one of the Gods of the Hall, but that's not what has me stuck to where I stand. It's the male with inked arms almost the size of tree trunks, his pectorals, and the washboard abs that are working overtime with each thrust he takes. He looks hotter than hell when he fucks, and suddenly, an image of him thrusting into me that way, has my heart racing.

Phoenyx grins as he asks Amara, "Whose cock do you love pounding into this sweet ass of yours, Mara?"

"Yours Nyx—I love your cock in my ass!"

I jump at the sound of the slap to Mara's ass before Phoenyx praises, "That's a good little slut."

A ringing sounds through my ears, and I feel light-headed. Instead of returning to my room, I flee down the hall, not paying any attention to where I'm going. I can't breathe, and when I get to a darkened hallway, I drop to my hands and knees and try to take in some deep breaths.

I haven't had one of these attacks in years. It always came just after I saw a photo of Phoenyx with another woman or whenever he looked happy. That is until Ken caught on to what was causing the attacks and started beating me for it. The mere fact that both Phoenyx and Mara would do this to me tears me apart. I don't care what I did; I would never rub anything like this in their face.

"Well, well, well, what do we have here?" A masculine voice sounds from behind me. "Which one of the guys sent you to me?"

I look up, my long brown hair falling over my face, but I can see clearly enough that it's Zilas. Who can miss the rich, creamy chocolate color of his skin tone, paired with light green eyes? Growing up, he always had girls surrounding him, and he's only gotten better looking over the years.

"Zilas..." I whisper.

"You've found me, pretty thing. Are you hurt?" Zilas asks as he reaches out his hand to help me.

"No, just trying to catch my breath after having an attack," I tell him, pushing the hair from my face once I'm back on my feet.

It takes him a minute, but then his eyes widen. "Saraya?"

I snicker. "In the flesh."

"Does...Nyx know..."

Holding my hand up, I stop him from saying more. "Yes, he knows. Go ask him, but he may be a little busy at the moment."

Zilas studies me, and I don't miss the smirk he tries to hide. "So, what are you doing in my wing? Are you wanting to finally see what the women love about me?" He starts to back me against the wall.

"Ha, ha, Zilas. You're not funny." My hands come up and flatten against his chest just as my back hits the wall.

"Oh, I'm dead serious, Raya. Nyx always shares his women with us. Although I'm sure he's over you after that little stunt you pulled, you're nothing to him but the stepsister you wanted him to think of you as. He won't care who fucks his sister."

Ouch, that hurts.

"That's not necessarily true," says an amused voice.

My head snaps to the right, and I see Phoenyx leaning against the wall, about ten feet away, in just a pair of black sweatpants. "Phoenyx, I'm not...he..."

"I what, Raya?" Zilas cages me in with his arms and leans in enough that I feel his hot breath fan over my skin.

"If you want to fuck him, Saraya, then fuck him." Phoenyx chuckles. "I want to watch, though—it's only fair." The look in my stepbrother's eyes is pure lust-driven which has me wanting to squeeze my thighs together. "I would love to see all three of my friends take you. I bet you would love every minute of it. "

What in the actual fuck?

"Is that all you do around here—is have sex?" I shove at Zilas's chest, and this time, he moves back. "I'm not fucking anyone in this Hall!"

Their laughter follows me down the hallway until I reach the back stairs leading to the kitchen. Although I find myself still attracted to Phoenyx,

I'm not here to be anyone's whore. They seem to have enough women to go around, especially with that gentlemen's club they have recently opened. Club Unholy is a very popular club that is talked about all over the world. How they pulled that off is beyond me. I should be proud of them all, but a nagging feeling tells me there's something more to it.

"You lazy, ungrateful bitch! All I ask is that you have dinner on the table by the time I get home at six, and you can't even do that! What the fuck have you been doing all day?"

Ken's hand swings, and he backhands me, making me spin and slam into the China cabinet. I feel the blood rushing from the wound on my head instantly.

"I'm sorry. I got called back into work because of a coding error that had to be fixed immediately. I can have dinner on the table in thirty minutes."

Ken rushes me and grabs my neck. "How about I tell you that you have to wait because someone else was more important, and I couldn't fulfill one little fucking thing asked of me?"

"Ken..." I claw at his hands as I call out his name. "You're strangling me!"

"Good! Maybe I'll toss your body over the balcony and say you committed suicide."

"Please, let me go!"

"I'll never let you go. I'll kill you before I ever give you up." Ken flings me to the side, slamming me into the kitchen island. "Forget the food, I want to fuck now."

Bending me over the island, I hear him unzipping his pants, and I cannot let him stick his dick in me one more time. So, when he's busy trying to get his pants down, I make a decision and reach over and grab the butcher knife from the block.

I don't wait for the right time to do it. Swinging my hand downward, I dig the knife right into a meaty thigh, and a howl of pain ensues. "You fucking bitch! You're going to pay for that!"

I twirl and plunge the knife into his shoulder next, then his arm, then his hand. It continues as I scream and let all my anger out as I swing the knife down time and time again. "Fuck you, you son of a bitch! Burn in hell, you fat fuck!"

Dropping the knife on the floor, I back away from his still form. I don't know when we fell to the floor, but as I climb to my feet, the situation I just got myself into becomes clear. Fuck. I'm so screwed.

Just as I go to walk away, his hand wraps around my ankle, and I fall to the floor. Grabbing hold of the knife once again, I stab it into his stomach, and he finally lets go of me. A gurgling comes from his lips, and he stares at me as he rattles out, "You will pay for this..."

I sit up in the big king-size bed, panting and sweating. I almost forget where I am, but then the familiar objects start to take shape, and I begin to feel safe again. I lie against my pillow and close my eyes, but a thought runs through my head.

Am I really safe being back in Nyte's Hall again?

I know my stepfather is gone, but Phoenyx has changed. Will he be like his father now that I'm back and after our history together? Will he allow me to finally be free, or have I just moved from one prison to another?

Looking at the clock, I see that it's almost five in the morning. I'll never get back to sleep now, so I fling the covers off and go to my suitcase, where I packed one set of workout clothes. After changing into them, I leave my room and head to the gym.

It was the day my world fell apart that I started getting into working out. It helped relieve the pent-up anger and frustrations that I had on a daily basis. I hid it all well. I had to. Working out has become my solace and has stayed with me all these years. There were times I wasn't physically able to because of Kenneth's treatment of me.

To this day, I don't understand why my stepfather gave me to such a vile man after everything that happened *that* day of all days. I also gave him my promise and stuck to it. I never knew how much he hated me until then. I'm worried that Phoenyx will do the same thing. I know I said I would do anything for his protection, but there is one thing I won't do: marry again without love as the foundation.

THREE

"Is he still alive?" I ask Cale as we walk down the long corridor to the unused warehouse in the packing district.

We usually take care of this kind of business at the club, but this is a special occasion I will be happy to dirty my hands with. Amara won't be working alone this time around. Nobody fucking touches my property. I may not be fucking her, but she is still a Beckam by marriage, hence my fucking property.

"Yeah, but unless you want him to die quickly, I suggest not draining any blood from him this time. Let him heal a few more days, then you can have your fun," my guy says.

"Oh, he's going to wish for a quick death," I mutter as I look over at my partner in crime. "Isn't that right, little devil?"

Amara is strapped as always, never leaving the Hall without her knives and Glock. She carries a bag draped over her shoulder tonight, making me wonder what kind of toys she's brought with her this time. For a short little shit, Amara Nichols packs a mighty punch; no one ever sees her coming, and that's what makes her our deadliest weapon.

Her smirk says it all. "Ain't that the fucking truth."

Cale opens the last set of doors to the room where Officer Kenneth McNally lies cuffed and chained to a bed with an IV bag attached and a nurse sitting at his bedside. Okay, so the nurse works for us. She does what we need her to do, and she and her family live a very comfortable life with the protection of the Gods of Nyte's Hall.

"Good morning, Mr. Beckam, Ms. Nichols..." Sasha greets.

"Morning..." I reply while examining the patient.

"Morning, pretty thing," Amara responds. "Are you ready to try out greener pastures yet?"

Amara is what you call a pansexual; it doesn't matter the sex of the person, but whether she is attracted to them. Amara has been panting over Nurse Sasha since she started working for us. The nurse takes it all in stride.

Chuckling, she pats the little devil on the shoulder. "Sorry, but I'm enjoying the pasture I'm in now. If I ever decide to try something new, you will be the first to know."

I hide my grin at their banter and then get serious when Amara joins me at Ken's bedside, sighing. "So, what's the plan if we aren't drawing blood?" She sounds slightly disappointed with this news, but there are other ways to have fun. She's very creative when she needs to be.

"Well, I guess we find out what he can withstand in his current condition. We may only be able to create fear in him..."

"What the fuck..."

I stop her rant by holding up my hand. "Let's find out before getting pissy." I smirk down at her.

Taking hold of the fucker's pointer finger, I bring it all the way back, nice and slowly, until he wakes up screaming. I don't stop until I hear the snap, and then let go, leaving it at the odd angle. His scream is music to my ears; I miss getting my hands dirty.

"ARGH!"

"Oh, shut the fuck up already, will you?" I say, bored. "Did you care when my sister cried out whenever you hurt her?"

Recognition of my words clicks with him, and he blinks rapidly until his dark, beady eyes focus on me. They widen once he realizes who it is that he's dealing with.

"Phoenyx..." he rasps in a weak voice.

"It's Mr. fucking Beckam to you motherfucker!" I snarl.

He has the gall to dismiss my anger and proceeds to try and place blame on Saraya by saying, "I want to press attempted murder charges on *my* wife," he enunciates.

I find his words amusing—cute, really—and I snicker. "Wow, so are you saying that she choked herself? Is she the one that threw herself against the China cabinet and put that gash in her head?"

"Yes! That bitch is crazy, and I want her locked up!"

I crack my knuckles as I glare at the little pussy. He isn't the brightest crayon in the box if he's telling me to lock my own family up. I'm going to have to remind him just who the fuck I am. Amara is biting at the bit, so I give her a subtle nod, and she claps her hands excitedly before opening her little black bag.

Holding something up to Sasha for approval, the nurse shrugs and then nods before our little devil swings back around and shows me her favorite portable machine. I can't help but laugh at the glint in her eyes as she rips the blanket away from my brother-in-law's body.

"What the fuck? What is she doing?" Ken tries moving away but soon realizes he can't.

"Well, you see, Kenneth. You've lost quite a bit of blood due to my sister's self-defense methods, so we can't torture you the way we want—yet."

"Self-defense my ass!" he cries out. "That whore—"

My hand snakes out and wraps itself around his neck. "I suggest you watch your fucking mouth where Saraya is concerned," I sneer.

"S-she's my w-wife. I can call her a w-whore if I want."

"No, Ken, you can't."

"What's it to you? She's only your lousy stepsister; she came from nothing..."

I grin cynically. "You're right, Ken." I bring my face closer to his. "But she still isn't your whore. Do you want to know why?"

He says nothing as he tries swallowing past my grip on his throat. His face is only a tinge red, but that's more from anger than anything. I move my mouth just a hair's breadth from his ear as I say, "Because Saraya is my whore now. I have a lot of time to make up for and I'm going to do things to her that will make even the devil himself blush."

"She's your sister, you sick fuck!" Ken squeaks as I put a little more pressure on his throat.

"*Stepsister*," I correct him. "And she was mine long before she was ever yours."

"I did you a favor by fucking that tight little cunt. You would have been the laughingstock of the town..."

I see red at his words. "This is *my* fucking town! Nobody would dare laugh at anything I do, but they *would* frown at what you have done. Lucky for you, they'll never find out because you'll never see another soul again."

I nod at Amara, and Ken finally remembers that she's there. The fright in his eyes when they land on her makes me laugh. It's the norm whenever one of us Heirs brings our little devil along. Anyone on the wrong side of the law knows what it means when Amara joins us, even law enforcement.

"Please, whatever you're thinking, don't do it! I'll divorce the bitch—hell, I'll give her to you. You have my permission to do whatever you want with her!" Ken pleads.

I look at Amara and lift my brow as I ask, "Does that sound like someone who's in the skin trade to you?"

"It sure does, Nyx."

"What? No! You took that wrong..."

"Did I? It sounded to me that you were willing to give my sister to me to use and abuse. You know, like what you've been doing all these years."

"I just want to keep my life, that's all. I'll give you whatever you want, Phoenyx...Mr. Beckam!"

"Well, I can certainly say, without a doubt, that will not happen." I tell him, "You see, you've wronged my family by abusing one of its members, and now you'll pay the price." I glance at the prongs my little helper has in her hands and give her the go-ahead. "Mara..."

Keeping my eyes on my brother-in-law, I watch him try to buck, forgetting that he's been stabbed over twenty times and crying out from the pain. His cries cut off, and his body seizes as Amara turns on her little machine, sending electrical charges pulsing through his body. Knowing Mara, she went straight to the highest setting and now just sits there watching the results.

"Mara...we aren't killing him yet, remember that."

"Oh shit—my bad." She turns the nob back the other way, and Ken lies there, momentarily incapacitated.

"Please stop," he whispers.

"Did Saraya say those same words, or were your hands too tight around her throat?" I ask him, and when he remains quiet, I nod at Amara again.

The same results happen, but Amara remembers to shut it down this time. She's had her fun with this little toy, and now removes it, but she's far from done torturing him. Once she has her little machine put away, she pulls out a rolled-up cloth and, in the nicest voice possible, asks, "Have you ever been sounded, Mr. McNally?"

I choke on my laughter when I see the surgical steel and silicone rods all lined up once the cloth is unrolled. I also wince when the thought of what that means for my brother-in-law hits me, not that I feel sorry for him, I just don't want to be in his shoes. However, Ken's outburst over the next torture session has me bending yet another finger back until it snaps.

"You will treat Ms. Nichols with respect and like a fucking lady while in her presence. Do you understand me?"

"That psycho isn't coming near my dick with those rods!"

I snicker. "I don't think you have much choice, Ken."

Grabbing another finger, I break it quickly, then step away and address Amara, "As much as I would love to watch your little play session, I have a few things to do." I approach her and grab the back of her head, pressing my lips to her forehead. "Have fun and make it hurt. I'll see you back at the Hall later, little devil."

Giving me her sultry smile, she winks and says, "See you later, Nyx." I walk toward the door when she turns to Ken and says, "Finally, some alone time. Let's have some fun."

"Nyx, what are you doing here so early?" Zilas asks as I walk into the Club Unholy office.

"I stopped and paid a visit to my lovely brother-in-law and figured I'd stop in here to check out the schedule for the next two nights." I had a nice chat with my friend last night after Saraya took off in a hurry. We discussed my sister's little *issue,* and I gave him an update on my plans.

The plan is a simple one, Saraya will come work at the club until I figure shit out. We all pull our weight here, and she will be no different. If she wants my protection, she will do as I tell her. I wasn't lying when I told Ken that she was now my whore. Although she won't fuck anybody without my permission, and I won't touch her until I'm ready...if I'm ever ready.

I have a lot of animosity toward Saraya, and no matter how badly my cock wants inside her, I will hold off until I'm ready to have her. Thoughts of the past creep into my head, and I have to shake them off. I don't have time to dwell on that shit now.

"Why the next two nights?" Zilas asks.

"Well, I want to give my little sister my full attention while training her to wait on the club's customers." I grin.

Zilas coughs out a laugh. "She will never wear the mandatory uniform."

I shrug. "It's either that or house submissive, and I rather doubt she will go for the latter."

"You're cruel, you know that?" My friend chuckles.

"You haven't seen cruel yet. Saraya will learn her place quickly here at the club and at Nyte's Hall," I tell him.

"What about in your bed?" Zilas sits back and watches me carefully with a smug look.

I shrug again. "That depends on whether she can redeem herself."

I lie right to one of my best friends. I already know that my stepsister *will* end up in my bed, and my cock *will* be so deep inside of her that she won't be able to walk for days afterward. Thankfully, I don't have to tell Zilas to drop the subject because he does it all on his own as he gives me a heads-up on another issue.

"We need to have a little meeting before Friday," he states.

"What's Friday?" I ask, trying to think back to see if I need to remember anything.

"Jarod and Jax want to meet with all four of us. They say they have a proposal that we won't want to miss."

"Unless it has to do with them moving their drugs out of our town for good, I don't want to hear it." I look in the books at the schedule and then turn toward the door, but Zilas's next words stop me.

"They say they have hard proof that your parents were murdered." My friend sighs, knowing that this will change my former response.

"Fine," I grind out through clenched teeth. "Tell them four o'clock on the dot tomorrow, and not to be late." I then storm out of the office and out of Club Unholy, pissed off.

FOUR

Saraya

I'm not ready to see everyone just yet, not until I've had my first cup of coffee. So, instead of going down to the main rooms, I head to the kitchen in our family wing. I doubt I will run into Phoenyx in the kitchen. That man never stepped foot in the kitchen while we were growing up unless it was to steal cookies or brownies.

The memories of those days put a smile on my face. What I would give to go back and live them again. However, I've made my bed, and it seems as though I will never be forgiven. That's okay because Phoenyx is now where he deserves to be and wouldn't be had I not done what I had. I'm content watching him from afar, as long as I don't have to keep watching him with another like I did last night.

As I walk into the bright room, there is no lingering scent of eggs or bacon, not even toast. All I smell are cleaning products. The worst part is that there's no fresh-brewed coffee scent wafting through the air, which means I'll have to make some myself. I'm not opposed to doing it, but I guess being back home kind of brought me a bit of familiarity, or so I thought.

Aside from a skeleton crew, my stepbrother must have gotten rid of most of the help because there isn't a person in sight. It may be a good thing because I wasn't thinking when I came down here still in my pajamas, consisting of a cami and some very short shorts. It's almost noon, but it doesn't matter to me. I can't remember the last time I slept in like this.

Moving around the kitchen, trying to get accustomed to where everything is, I finally find the coffee and squeal in excitement. While waiting for the coffee pot to finish, I turn on some tunes and start making up a little snack tray to take to my room. God knows when I'll see Phoenyx again, so I'm unsure what to do with myself.

I'm just pouring my first cup of coffee into my cup when I almost spill it all over the place because a hand runs over my ass. I set the pot down and try to turn, but a hand grabs my neck and keeps me looking forward. My heart thunders in my chest as a picture of Phoenyx enters my head and suddenly a tingle starts in my nether region.

However, the scent that hits me is not masculine cologne, but a more feminine fragrance. The hand on my ass squeezes it just before I hear her voice. "You've grown up real nice, Raya. It's no wonder Nyx is pissed."

Amara's voice is seductively low near my ear as she continues to grope me. For someone who stands four inches shorter than me, she sure has a good grip and can keep me in place even as I struggle to turn around. Her little chuckle grates on my nerves.

"Let me go, Mara!"

"Mm, why would I do that when I'm enjoying my view now?" Amara asks, pressing her body against mine.

"I don't swing that way, Mara. You're wasting your time. Besides, by what I saw, it looks like you enjoy your men." I don't want her to know how much her being with Phoenyx has affected me, but it came out, and I won't take it back now.

"You're right. I do enjoy *my* men. They are my family, and I protect what's *mine.* I will not allow anyone to hurt any of the Heirs ever again. Keep that in mind, whatever your intentions are. Me, however, I love getting burned," she states and spins me around to face her. With her hand now on my throat, I'm still stuck in her grip.

"Please stop," I plead as her hand runs up my side. Her touch is doing something to me for some reason, and I don't like it.

"Awe, what's the matter, Raya? Are you afraid that you may like being touched by the female persuasion?" Her hand dips low, and she smirks. "Will I find a wee little wet spot if I go digging down under?"

"Mara, please...stop," I pant.

I can't see, but I'll put money on her wearing a pair of stilettos. Wearing them puts her at my height, and she leans in close, her hot breath fanning my ear as she says, "Anytime you feel the need to get off, come find me and I will happily oblige."

Before I can tell her it will never happen, she grips my jaw and crashes her lips on mine. I fight her, trying to shove her away, but it isn't until a booming voice growls out, "Get the fuck away from her, little devil!" that she relents.

Amara is slow to pull back; when she does, she grins, licking her bright red lips. Her eyes peruse me as she steps away, and she winks just before she turns and walks toward Phoenyx. I watch her stop and pat him on the chest as she goes to walk by on her way out.

"No worries, big guy," she says, looking over her shoulder at me. "She's all yours. Do with her what you like, but I want to watch." Amara goes up on her tippy toes and pecks him on the cheek. "Thanks for last night; my ass is deliciously sore."

Phoenyx doesn't smile, nor does he respond to her statement. In fact, he's glaring daggers at his little bed buddy at the moment. It only amuses Amara, though. She throws her head back and laughs as she exits the room.

When my stepbrother finally looks my way, he eyes me up and down before screwing up his face and sneering, "Go put some fucking clothes on. No wonder my friends are hitting on you; look at what you're wearing!"

"I should be able to wear whatever I want in my own house," I huff, placing my hands on my hips.

He raises his brow. "*Your* house? I'm pretty sure the last time I checked, *your* house is across town and has just had a dead husband removed from it."

"This is still my home, Phoenyx..."

"NYX!" He cuts me off as he growls out, "Phoenyx died long ago. Nyx is all that's left of that naïve young man." He then walks away, leaving me bewildered once again.

My heart literally breaks when I hear this. Gone is the shy, innocent boy who would share his lunch with me when we were in school. Gone is the boy who had a severe crush on me but had accepted being friend-zoned just so he could still be in my life in some way or form until I finally accepted that I also wanted more with him.

In that boy's place is a hard and unforgiving man, one who has had it hard in life and doesn't seem to care what anybody else thinks. He takes what he wants and owns it. Deep down I wish he would still want me.

The man before me scares the living daylights out of me, though. He produces fear in everyone and anyone who comes into his vicinity if he doesn't know or like them. I almost didn't recognize him among the tattoos. However, what's changed the most are his eyes. They used to be pretty, silvery eyes, always gazing lovingly at me, but they're now hard, gray, and empty. They almost look black and soulless at times. He looks like the devil himself, Lucifer in all his glory.

"You have got to be fucking kidding me right now!" I say in disbelief as I turn myself one way and then the other in the full-length mirror.

When I returned to my room earlier, I found a paper sack on my bed and a note telling me that I would start my shift at Club Unholy this evening and that I had better be ready by seven o'clock. Let's just say that it didn't go over too well with me.

I stormed out of my room and down the hall to my stepbrother's room, pounding on the door until he opened it. I wasn't sure if he was inside, but luckily, he was. He swung the door open angrily and glared down at me.

"What the fuck is your issue?" Phoenyx growled.

I was stunned momentarily at being that close to him without a shirt on. His pants were also undone, and the deep V leading downward was very prominent. I opened my mouth and then shut it again, forgetting what I was going to say.

"Well? I don't have all fucking day, Raya. So, either tell me what your problem is or go the fuck away." He looked me up and down, cocking his brow. "Unless, of course, you wanted something else altogether."

The heat was instant between my legs, but I came to my senses quickly and curled my lip in disgust. "You wish, Nyx!" I held the bag up to him. "If you think I'm going to wear lingerie and fuck people at your disgusting club, then you can think again."

He was quick; I never even saw him move. His hand gripped my throat, and I was against his door in a heartbeat. "I don't think I ever mentioned that you would be fucking anybody. But let's say, for the sake of the argument that I had—you would fuck whoever I tell you to fuck. You owe me, remember that."

"Nyx..." I reached up to try and pry his hand away from my throat, but I couldn't remove it, so I begged, "Please, Nyx."

He smirked at me and said, "No worries, Lil' Sis, I wouldn't do that to good-paying clients. The subs at my club undergo extensive testing to ensure they have a clean bill of health." He then moved me, so I stood outside his room. He reminded me one last time, "Be ready by seven. I'll come and get you." The door then closed in my face.

Standing here in a very tight maroon crop top that says *UNHOLY in black glitter* across my chest, a pair of black booty shorts, and fishnet stockings has me sighing with relief and still burning with anger. My ass cheeks still hang out, and I feel so exposed. On the other hand, I'm guessing I'll be waitressing since I have my own pen and menu pad with the name Raya on it.

I've never waitressed a day in my life, but if this is what keeps my stepbrother off my ass, so be it. I'll show him that I can be the best waitress he's ever seen. It can't be too hard, right?

FIVE

I don't know what the fuck I was thinking, having Saraya waitress out on the floor. Granted, she's pretty good at it—a little too good if you ask me. I don't know how many customers I've wanted to take to the back room and shove a fist right up their ass for looking at my stepsister wrong.

Tomorrow, I'll put her in the hostess spot. This way, I don't have to worry about her walking around with her ass cheeks hanging out. I'm sitting at the bar watching Saraya's every move. If anybody asks, I'm making sure she doesn't fuck up, but really, I'm making sure the customers keep their fucking hands to themselves.

"She's definitely grown into a beauty, hasn't she?" Adrik's deep voice comes from the stool behind me.

I don't bother turning to face him; there's no need, just like I don't need to answer him either. Adrik and I have a friendship that differs from what I have with the others. Being the two oldest Heirs, we've been through some shit together. Up until he served time a few counties over for some bullshit charge, we were inseparable. Now, he may or may not have a few secrets he isn't willing to share with me, and I'm okay with that.

"You two look like you're about to devour her." Amara's voice reaches me, and I turn to see that Adrik is, in fact, practically drooling over my stepsister.

His eyes meet mine, and I give him a subtle shake of my head. He responds with a nod, then turns away from the room, lifting his glass to his lips as a smirk dances across them. *Dickhead.*

I give our little devil my attention, only to see that she's standing very close to me, with her elbows on the bar, as she also watches Saraya. She's wearing another leather suit, only this time her tits are spilling from it, her nipples barely covered.

"Aren't you supposed to be working tonight?"

My attention returns to the floor, and I catch my little lamb looking toward us. Is that animosity on her face as she looks at our little devil standing close to me? I lift my hand and push some hair away from Mara's face, hooking it behind her ear.

She gifts me with her beautiful smile and says, "You're such an asshole." Her throaty laugh is loud enough for half the room to hear, and I grin as I shrug.

"Call me what you want, but I'll have you calling me your God if I want to later."

My comment only makes her laugh harder. "Don't mention it if you're not willing to deliver," she replies. "And to answer your question—I am—working, I mean. Randy is stewing in the Mechanic room. He's a bit tied up at the moment. Tell me, Nyx, aside from the chump stealing from us, did you know that he likes to rape little boys?"

I let the side of my mouth kick up. "I don't know what you're talking about, little devil."

"It's just as well that you don't answer," she says as she turns to walk away, only to stop again. "You haven't seen my favorite gag, have you? The one with the fat dick on it. His screams may become too much."

"Jesus, what are your plans for him?" Adrik asks from my other side. "I might have to come watch this one."

Amara claps her hands excitedly. "I'm going to perform my first circumcision and then clean it with the acid from one of the car batteries that we use for props."

"Oh fuck, never mind. I'll pass," Adrik states with discomfort. I, too, want to grab my boys and show them a little love after hearing about her little playdate.

"Will that end things, or just hurt like a son of a bitch?" I ask.

She leans into my ear and seductively says, "That is just the foreplay, baby. If you want to know what's in store for Randy the Rear Raper, then you're going to have to come watch."

Adrik and I both watch her as she walks away. I only watch because she puts some extra sway to her already fine ass. I won't stop how I live my life just to make Saraya feel more comfortable. She didn't give a damn about my feelings and what I was willing to give up for her, so why should I care now?

"You shouldn't have left so early last night," Adrik says. "I'm sorry for the mess on your bed. You know how little devil gets."

"You could have left out the blood play. It looked like a damn massacre on my bed sheets. Where the fuck are all the cuts, anyway?" I ask my friend.

He smirks and lifts his shirt to show his battle wounds from playing with Amara. "She may have gone a little deep with this one." He points to a small cut that looks to be glued together.

I shake my head and snicker. "When will you learn?"

"Hey, I find it hot when a woman takes charge for a bit. You should see her ass cheeks; I paid her back, no worries." Adrik downs the rest of the amber liquid in his glass and slaps my shoulder as he stands. I'm going to go play. You have fun getting blue balls."

"Fuck you. I'm training her; I'm not here for pleasure tonight."

Adrik looks to the end of the bar where Saraya now stands as she waits for her order to be filled. "Oh, but you could be, buddy." He nods towards my little lamb and then walks away.

I find Saraya sitting and rubbing her feet in the employee locker room. I frown because I don't know why her feet are hurting when I don't make my female wait staff wear heels. I know what that must feel like, and I'm sure it isn't pleasant to be on them all night, so I have them wear combat boots.

"What the fuck, Raya? You just had a break ninety minutes ago..."

"I know, I'm sorry, Nyx..."

"Mr. Beckam," I remind her.

"You told me to call you Nyx."

"When we are at work, you are my employee, not my *sister,* and you will respectfully call me by the same name as my other employees."

"Fine, *Mr. Beckam.* The boots you gave me are too small and squish my toes. The damn fishnets aren't helping either," she grumbles.

I frown. "Have your feet grown since you were seventeen? Are you not a size eight anymore?"

My little lamb sits up straight and studies me briefly before softening her features and nodding. "Yes, that is correct, but the boots are a size seven."

Anger rises within. *I asked her to do me one simple favor.*

"I'll speak with my assistant," I inform Raya. "Stay here, and I will go grab the correct size."

I search the inventory room for a size eight combat boot, and as soon as I find them, I head to the Mechanic room. You see, Club Unholy has a sectioned-off area where certain *activities* take place. It's where we take care of our business that has nothing to do with the kink world. It was Amara's idea to design rooms that she can work in but can also pass as scene rooms for the club.

I stop in front of the room I know she's in and look into the viewing window. Plastic lines the floor, and Randy, one of our informants, is spread eagle as he hangs from chains attached to the ceiling. His front is a bloody mess, but it doesn't look like she's used the acid on it yet.

Amara pops out from behind the guy and notices me in the window. Our little devil waves enthusiastically, only she's wearing one of those long gloves vets use for inseminating cattle. It's full of blood which tells me Mara is fisting the sicko. She's always said that if she ever gets the pleasure of torturing a pedophile, she would do just that. Looks like our little devil has hit the jackpot tonight.

I glare at her and lift the new pair of boots. As soon as her eyes land on them, she knows exactly what I'm talking about. Mara smirks and then pretends it's no big deal by shrugging, like it was just a prank. I'm not sure why it's bothering me so much that I'm actually getting mad at one of my eldest friends.

Amara has stayed by my side through that whole fiasco, and she helped me to pick up the pieces of a young man's broken heart and harden it so it will never go through that again. Saraya's entrance into my life once again is fucking with my head, and I don't like it. Still, I will have to discuss this with our little devil because by doing this, we are now down one person for the time it takes her feet to feel better.

"Tomorrow, you will learn the Hostess position, so I will have an appropriate dress delivered for you to wear. Be ready by three-thirty; I have a meeting at four, and I won't have time to come back to get you," I tell my little lamb on the drive home.

I keep referring to her as my little lamb, and I don't know why. I've been reserving that little nickname for the woman who will eventually sacrifice herself to me in marriage and produce the children necessary to continue my family's bloodline. Saraya is not that woman. Maybe once upon a time, but not now.

"What if this is your chance at a second chance with her?" Adrik's words from last night come back to haunt me.

No, it can't be my second chance. I'm too hard; she's made me into a monster who now takes what he wants. Saraya would never be able to handle me as I am now.

"I don't mind waitressing, Nyx."

My hands tighten on the steering wheel, and I glance at her, "I'm sure you don't, but as I said, you will train as a hostess tomorrow night, and for God's sake, wear comfy shoes."

"Well, maybe if I had been given the right size, my feet wouldn't have been hurting..." she mumbles under her breath like I can't hear. She's got gumption; I'll give her that.

I ignore her snide comment. Instead, my eyes drift down to her fishnet-covered legs. I don't remember her legs looking so long and toned. The uniform bottoms are so short it's almost like she's wearing swimsuit bottoms. I can see her legs all the way up to the apex of her thighs and that forbidden area that I was told could never be mine.

"Mm, Raya, I don't know how much longer I can go without having you." I kiss down her neck and across her collarbone as she lays on my bed.

We shouldn't be doing this in the house; it's too risky, but I had to taste her. Family has been around constantly; we haven't had time to ourselves in four days. Dad and Jessica are at a benefit, but I'm sure it's over by now. That doesn't stop me from making out with my stepsister. I just need a few stolen kisses and a touch here and there.

I palm her breast over her shirt and knead it. "Oh, God, Phoenyx..."

"Shh, baby. We can't let anybody hear us," I tell her and lift her shirt.

"Phoenyx, I want you..."

"You have me, baby."

"No, I mean—I want you."

"Not here, sweetie, but soon. Promise me that you are mine forever."

"I promise, Phoenyx..." she pants.

My mouth descends as I pull her breasts out of the cups. She moans and cradles my head to her chest. We are dry humping as I suck her nipple into a hardened peak.

Suddenly, my door opens, and I hear a giggle along with my father's booming voice before it abruptly stops. I jump up and stand in front of Saraya so she can fix her clothing.

"Sorry, son. I didn't know you had company..." his voice trails off when I feel Saraya move behind me. "What the fuck, Phoenyx? What is the meaning of this?"

"Oh, my God! Raya, what in the world?"

"Saraya, I think you had better go to your room right now," my father orders.

She says nothing as she runs from the room with Jessica on her tail. My father slams my bedroom door closed and faces me with rage in his eyes. When he stalks me, I stand tall and don't back down. However, I wasn't expecting the right hook that came my way.

The Hall comes into view, and I couldn't be happier. I need to put space between Saraya and I. It's been a long fucking night watching her in barely any clothing, but I only have myself to blame. I need a cold fucking shower. Maybe I should invite Emily over to help take care of this raging boner I'm now sporting. Oh, who am I kidding? That woman wouldn't do anything for me. Sighing, I groan inwardly...a cold shower it is, then.

SIX

Nyx

"Wake the fuck up asshole!" I kick the bed that Kenneth lies on, waking him from his slumber. "I want answers, and you're going to give them to me."

"What the hell, Nyx!" Ken dares to send me a glare.

Apparently, he hasn't learned his lesson yet. I take hold of his broken finger and twist, causing him to scream like a little bitch. Something isn't adding up where Raya and this fuckface are concerned, so I figured I had better come and try to get some answers.

"You're pretty fucking brave getting an attitude with me, Ken. Have you forgotten who I am? What? Did you think I'd go easy on you because I didn't bring our little devil with me?" I twist his finger the other way, pulling another scream from him. "News flash, if I come alone, it's because I am pissed the fuck off, and I want to get my hands dirty."

"W-what do you w-want to know?" he stutters as his face screws up in pain.

"I want to know why you married Saraya if all you were going to do was beat her?"

"I loved her...we l-loved each other..."

"Bullshit!" I yank on another finger, breaking that one, too.

"AGH!!!!"

I pull my gun out from the holster I wear under my suit jacket and cock it. Slowly, I press it to Ken's forehead, not giving a shit if he lives or dies at this point. Yeah, Mara will be butt hurt, but too fucking bad.

"Now, I will ask you one...more...time. Why did you marry Saraya?"

"I'm not supposed to speak of it to anyone—ever!" Ken stammers.

"Do I look like I give a shit about whether you are or are not supposed to say anything? The way I see it, you're not in the position to be able to say no to me, now are you?"

"Please, Nyx, if it was just your father, then I would tell you since he's dead, but there are more people at play here."

What the fuck?

I almost break character at what he says, but I remain as is, the tick in my jaw becoming more pronounced. I press the barrel harder against his forehead and say, "You're not leaving here alive regardless, so it's up to you how you want to die. I can make it quick and painless, or we can draw it out; the choice is yours, Ken."

Sweat beads around the barrel, and the fucker closes his eyes briefly before opening them back up and pinning his stare on me as he states, "You can find the answer to that yourself if you look hard enough, but I can't be the one to give it to you. Just know that your father was a sicker fuck than you realize. Just ask your sister."

"You're going to regret this, McNally," I tell him as I raise the gun and then slam it down on his head, knocking him out.

"So, what's the plan now, boss?" Cale asks as he looks over at Ken.

Tucking my gun back in its holster, I reply, "Find out who all my father associated himself with around the time Raya and I broke up. That fucker is scared of someone more than he's scared of me, and I want to know who the fuck it is. If someone is trying to run this town behind our backs, I want to know about it immediately."

"Yes, Sir. I'll get right on it and have answers for you as soon as I find them." Cale walks out of the warehouse with me, but he stays and makes a phone call while I get into my car and head back to the Hall.

I walk into the main living area of the Hall, and I hear music coming from the billiard room. *Fucking great. Loud music means Cray is entertaining.* Sure enough, as I near the room, I hear a female's laughter. Expecting to walk in on a naked woman, I stop in my tracks when the only woman I see in the room with Cray is Saraya.

"What the fuck is going on here?" The question comes out a bit rough.

Saraya is standing by the pool table, leaning on her pool stick while Cray is getting ready to take a shot. It all looks harmless, but I don't care;

I know Cray and trust him around Raya as much as I trust Mara. My entrance wipes the carefree smile off my stepsister's face.

"What's your problem?" Cray asks as he takes his shot. Making the ball into the pocket, he walks around the table, looking for his next shot.

"Oh, I don't have a problem. Just wondering what you're doing in here alone with my sister."

"*Stepsister...*" Saraya corrects.

Cray doesn't let my tone bother him as he shrugs. "I found her wandering around, bored, so I asked her to play a game of pool. What's the big deal?"

What is the big deal? Why does it bother me so much?

"It's not a big deal. I just don't want Raya to be late for work; we have to go in early today, remember?" I look at them pointedly because Cray must also be at the meeting.

"That's in like three hours." Saraya rolls her eyes, and I feel my anger rise.

"May I have a quick word with Raya, Cray?" I ask as I continue to stare at the woman that I can't seem to get out of my fucking head.

"Uh, yeah, of course. I'll go grab something to eat real quick." Cray, finding the situation amusing, whistles happily on his way out.

"So, what did I do now, oh mighty one?"

I smirk, because I find it cute that she thinks she can roll her eyes at me and get away with it. Now, on top of that offense, she's getting smart with me. Tucking my hands inside my dress pants, I stroll over to where she stands, trying to be less threatening.

I have to give her credit; she doesn't move a muscle. However, I do pick up on the slight hitch in her breathing, the only indication that my presence is affecting her in some sort of way. Her doe-like eyes stare unblinkingly at me as she waits for me to say something.

After an uncomfortable amount of time, I say, "For someone who should be acting grateful for the help I'm giving her, you're sure doing a lousy job at it."

"Oh?"

"Is that all you have to say?" I scoff.

"What would you like me to say, and I'll say it. I forget you like your women submissive..."

I reach out, grabbing the hair at the back of her head, not too rough, but enough to make a point. "You see, that's where you're wrong. I like the women I *fuck* to be submissive, but I love a woman with her own mind and who can think for herself." I notice her eyes soften, but I change that with my next words. "Regrettably, I don't look twice at those women anymore because they're also conniving little bitches." I release her hair roughly, causing her to catch herself on the edge of the pool table.

I almost don't hear what she says because she says it so softly. "You will thank me one day..." Saraya tries walking away but I grab her by the elbow.

"Why do you say that? What makes you think I will thank you? Do you think I'm going to thank you for giving away the one thing you promised me and ripping the heart out of a young man's chest? You think I can forgive such betrayal?"

Squaring her shoulders, Saraya glares at me. "Mark my words; you will thank me."

"What is it, Raya? What are you hiding?"

"I'm not hiding a damn thing."

"That's a fucking lie. You forget, *sweetie,* I know you better than you know your fucking self." I push a strand of her brown locks back away from her face, dragging my finger down her neck and over her collarbone. I stop in the center of her breastbone, staring at my finger as I continue to say, "I know you inside and out." My eyes jump to hers, and another smirk dances across my lips when I feel her heart speed up.

"Nyx..."

"I don't want to hear anything come out of that pretty little mouth unless it's the answer to my question."

"I'm not hiding..."

I slide my hand up, my fingers wrapping around her slim neck, and I lean in real close, our lips almost touching. "I *will* find out the truth, and if I find that you're lying, you better believe that I'll take you over my fucking knee, and you will feel my wrath."

My eyes dip to her lips, which look so soft and inviting, and for a minute, I remember what they felt like years ago. That was before they became stained with the filth of Kenneth McNally. Before that fucker stole what was mine.

"Let me go, Nyx."

I raise my brow at her demand, and instead of doing as I'm told, I squeeze just a little more and move my mouth to her ear, letting my lips graze her lobe briefly. She shivers at the contact, and I grin. She isn't unaffected by me. This will make the game so much sweeter.

"I take orders from no one, Lil' Sis, especially when they're coming from you. You, however, *will* take orders from me. You forget I know your little secret. This is the Heirs' town, and I can cuff you right here and call the authorities to come get you. Is that what you really want?"

She tries jerking away, but I still have her by the throat. I breathe in her scent for a moment longer before backing away. Staring at my hand around her throat, I suddenly have a picture of her lying under me with my hand on her throat and my cock nine inches deep inside of her as I plow her thoroughly. My cock stirs, and I inwardly curse, letting go of her neck and stepping back.

She thinks her order is what got me to let go. I'll let her believe that before letting her be aware of just how much I want to fuck the shit out of her. Maybe I should listen to Adrik and fuck her finally. Perhaps it will get her out of my system. It is only sex, after all, because I sure as hell can't trust her.

Stepping away, I remind her one last time before I leave her, "We will be leaving soon; your dress should be here any minute. If something doesn't fit, let me know immediately." Looking at her one last time, I leave the billiard room.

It's like I've been holding my breath since I breathed in the scent of Raya so I could savor it as long as possible. As soon as I step out into the hallway, I can breathe so much easier. I haven't the slightest idea why I let her get to me.

I jump when Cray speaks up from my right side. He's leaning against the wall by the door, munching on a turkey sandwich. The glare that I give him doesn't faze him at all.

"Just do it, Nyx."

"Do what?"

"Take her. She owes you." He shrugs.

"You know I don't sleep with unwilling women," I scoff.

"Who says she's unwilling? The way I see it, you both want each other." My friend shrugs again and then pushes his body away from the wall.

"Have you forgotten what she did to me?" I ask Cray incredulously.

"That's just it. Have you ever had revenge sex? *Fuck*—that shit is better than hate sex."

"Craydon..." I warn him, using his full name.

"Hey, all I'm saying is that it will eat at you until you get it out of your system." We study each other briefly before he continues, "Adrik and I were talking..."

"Oh, you were, were you?"

"Just hear me out, buddy. We all know that you still feel for Raya. You don't ever lose the kind of love you had, okay. I understand that she burned you, but even you can't deny that there is still something there. We've all seen it."

I sigh, the tick in my jaw becoming more pronounced the more pissed I get. "What are you getting at, Cray?"

"Your parents aren't here anymore, Nyx. Take her as your wife and fulfill your responsibilities. Marry her, breed her, and be done with it. Is there anyone else that comes close to her?"

That's neither here nor there. Why doesn't anyone get that?

Pinching the bridge of my nose, I respond in a tight voice, "You're one of my best friends, Cray, but I will cut your tongue out if you ever bring this up to me again."

I hear him chuckle and say, "Whatever, man."

When I look back up, he's moving toward the door to the billiard room. "Despite everything, Raya is still off limits." I don't wait for him to say anything, but I hear his laughter as I turn and walk away.

SEVEN

Saraya

I'm fuming. It seems no matter what I say or how hard I try, Phoenyx is not going to forgive my betrayal. Maybe I should just ask him to transfer money from my trust, and then I can leave the country. I'll get out of his hair, and he will never have to see my face again.

I hate that our parents thought it best to leave my inheritance in the hands of my stepbrother, like I wasn't responsible enough at the age of twenty-eight. It was only a year ago, for Christ's sake. They trusted Ken enough to hand me over but not my trust, I don't get it. Then again, Layton Beckam had always loved money and power, so I shouldn't be too surprised.

My mother was never the same after she married into the Beckam Dynasty. She told me that she was doing it for us, that we needed Layton Beckam, but I needed a mother who cared for me. I was already missing one parent, I couldn't afford to lose another, but that's precisely what happened as soon as my mother became Jessica Beckam.

I was the outcast in the family, the only one with a different last name. Sure, Layton was friendly enough for the most part—in the beginning—but he wasn't my father. I don't know who my father was; I don't even have his last name. My mother gave me her maiden name and told me it was a one-night stand gone wrong.

Luckily, my new stepbrother had taken a liking to me, and we became fast friends. He didn't have many friends, just the other Heirs and Amara, so we spent a lot of time together. Then, as we started getting older and moved to high school, feelings began to change, and things got complicated. We knew better than to get involved with each other, but for over a year, we were able to keep our relationship under wraps until that day when we threw caution to the wind and became careless.

That day changed everything. Not only did I lose the only boy I ever loved, but I lost my best friend, too. Instead of the fun-loving young man who promised me the stars, I now have a beast who would rather throw me to the stars than give them to me. It's always so uncomfortable around him. What makes it worse is that I'm still attracted to the asshole, more so now than I was over ten years ago.

The silence in the car on the way to Club Unholy is deafening, so I can't help but get excited when the club comes into view. I can't remove myself from the car fast enough once Phoenyx parks, and I'm relieved I didn't wear very high heels. I'd like to think I'm pretty graceful, but my stepbrother unnerves me to no end, and I'd probably end up falling on my ass.

"Saraya!" Nyx calls out to me, stopping me in my tracks instantly.

I turn around slowly and notice him sweeping the parking garage with his eyes before they land on me. As soon as he catches up to me, he doesn't stop but brushes right past.

"Don't ever take off like that without looking at your surroundings again." His gruff voice reverberates through the private garage as he heads for the elevator.

"Why would I have to look at my surroundings when I'm in a private garage? Do you not trust your security?" I rebuff.

Nyx swipes his key card in the slot that gains us access to the private elevator. Once the doors open, he holds his arm out, so the door doesn't close as he waits for me to enter first. I don't miss the second sweep he does, this time of my body as I walk past him. I hide my smirk as I turn and fix my gaze on the doors closing.

"Never trust anyone. You can never be too careful. Just because it hasn't reached my ears yet doesn't mean there aren't people out looking for you. I'm sure your pathetic husband has been reported as missing, and since you're nowhere around, you're a person of interest."

What Nyx says makes sense, but why does he have me out in public and working at the club if this is the case? I turn my head slightly and study him as he scrolls through his phone. He smells so fucking good that it makes my thighs squeeze together.

Wanting nothing more than to get under his skin, I retort, "It doesn't make a lot of sense—making me work in your club and having me come out in public if I'm a wanted criminal."

He scoffs, "You have to pay your debt somehow."

"I can pay you back by leaving the country. Just release my trust to me, and I'll be out of your hair. You'll never have to see me again," I tell him as I go back to staring at the doors.

It doesn't feel like the elevator has moved yet, and it's taking an awfully long time to get to the first floor. I glance at the buttons on the panel and see that none of them are lit up as of yet. I roll my eyes and step forward, ready to press the button, but Nyx stops me with one word.

"Don't."

"Are we just going to stand here all night? I thought you were in such a hurry to get to your meeting?" I cross my arms and lean against the wall.

Suddenly, he's in front of me, bracing himself with his hands on each side of my head as he glares down at me. My heart is going a mile a minute, wondering what the fuck is going through his head. All he does is stare coldly at me with those hard gray eyes.

"Nyx—"

"You will learn very quickly that when I do something, it's for a specific reason. Do not question me—*ever.*" He growls as his eyes dart to my parted lips.

"Please move," I say through gritted teeth, but it only brings a smirk to his lips.

"What's wrong, *Lil' Sis?* Am I making you uncomfortable?"

I try shoving him away, but he only captures my hands and slams them above my head. My chest heaves as my breathing quickens, and my stepbrother's gaze goes straight to my cleavage. The dress he purchased for me is beautiful. It's a deep burgundy, and it hugs all my curves, but at least my ass cheeks aren't hanging out. *No, but your tits are.*

Clearing my throat, I return his smirk as I say, "Not at all. I just didn't want you catching my cooties and holding it against me, as you do everything else."

"Make no mistake, Raya, your cooties would be the last thing I worry about." Nyx's eyes dip to my lips, then back to meet my eyes. I feel his hand slide over my leg before he lifts it up beside his hip. "Unless you're saying that you do have *something,* then maybe I shouldn't do this in case I catch it."

His hardness rubs against my core, and I try to keep a straight face. I hold my breath and wait when his head dips, but his lips never touch me. Instead, he breathes me in deeply. I need to do something before I break. I can't let Nyx see just how weak I am regarding him.

"You're going to be late for your meeting, *Mr. Beckam.*" The use of his surname causes Nyx to stiffen.

My stepbrother drops my leg and steps away without another glance at me. He presses the button on the panel and the car begins to move as he shoves his hands into his pockets. I feel the loss of his closeness, but this is how it has to be. Phoenyx will never forgive me, so I need to move on and try to start my life over all on my own.

"Monica, this is Saraya Abbott. I want her trained in the hostess position tonight," Nyx states as we stop in front of a gorgeous blonde standing at the hostess station.

The beautiful woman, who smiled brightly as soon as we walked up, now looks at me, and her smile falters before looking back at Nyx. I know this will cause a problem, so I quickly try to ease any concerns.

"I'm only here to help you, Monica. I'm not taking your job—"

"Yes, you are, Miss Abbott," Nyx corrects me quickly. "Since you can't waitress, I have to switch you out and put you elsewhere. This is the only other available position."

"Am I being fired, Mr. Beckam?" Monica is on the verge of tears.

My stepbrother places his hand on her shoulder and changes his tone from hard to understanding as he replies, "Of course not, Monica. This is only temporary. We will find you another position and keep you at hostess pay. In the meantime, I may need you to fill in as a house sub."

"Okay," the blonde seems to be appeased. "Will you be needing any services, Sir?"

I watch the grin grow on Nyx's face as he peruses Monica's body. "I may. I'll let you know." He winks at her, then turns to me and sternly says, "Listen to Monica's instruction; she's a great hostess."

He then turns and walks away, leaving me alone with this woman who obviously has a crush on her boss. The way he did me dirty just now will not be forgotten. He will hear my wrath privately, but for now, I will play the dutiful employee and do what I'm here to do.

"So, where did he find you?" The sneer from Monica is unexpected, especially if I may have just gotten her a ticket to ride Phoenyx Beckam.

I cross my arms and match the snooty tone she's giving me. "*He* found me at Nyte's Hall, where I *live*—with *him*," I say for added effect.

"You live with Nyx?" the blonde asks, unconvinced.

I straighten my back and respond, "Yeah, I do, and it's Mr. Beckam to you."

Monica snickers. "Who the fuck do you think you are? You can't come in here and just start bossing me around."

"I'm pretty sure your boss just told you who I was. He told you my name is Saraya Abbott, as in his *sister,* Saraya Abbott."

If I could capture the horrified look on Monica's face when she realizes my true identity, I'd display it for all to see; it's fucking priceless. She doesn't know that Nyx couldn't care less about me and that he would most likely get a kick out of seeing her treating me the way she was. I can already see that he will make it hard for me to make friends here. *Challenge accepted.*

❦

Just before the club opens, I make my way to Nyx's office. A high-priority client has a message for him, and since Monica didn't want to leave me by myself so soon, she's sending me to take it to him. I've never been upstairs yet, so I make sure to take in everything as I reach the top of the steps and turn left, just as Monica instructed.

As I near the door she described, I hear raised voices and pause momentarily. I don't want to intrude or disrupt an important meeting, so I stand just outside the door, contemplating what to do. I look at the envelope in my hand and read its name—*Mr. Tate.*

I remember Monica listing this man as one of the important clientele, but is he important enough to disrupt a meeting? Making the decision, I knock on the closed door. All the voices stop, and I hear Nyx call out angrily.

"What is it?"

Swallowing hard and straightening my back, I open the door and walk in. I don't say anything as I walk across the office; all eyes are on me. I notice the Heirs representing all four families of Nyte's Hall are here. Beckam, Sinclair, Carlson, and Donovan—the Gods of Nyte—are seated all around. They look menacing when gathered together like this. There are two other men in the room with the Heirs; identical twins with a much lighter disposition are sitting in front of Nyx's desk.

"I'm busy right now." My stepbrother scowls at me.

"I apologize, but you have a message from one of your important clients." Once I get to his side of the desk, I hand him the envelope.

"Thanks. You may go now," Nyx states with annoyance.

"Yes, Mr. Beckam."

As I walk past the twins, the nearest one reaches out and pulls me onto his lap. I try to catch myself, but my low heels slip on the floor, and I tumble into his lap. His arms go around me immediately, and he smiles.

"Well, what do we have here? Have you hired someone new and not told us, or are you hiding her for yourself?"

"Let. Her. Go."

The venomous sound coming from Nyx's mouth has me cowering, and he isn't even talking to me. However, the man who is still holding me only chuckles. He moves me so I'm situated between him and his twin.

They remind me of Roman guards with their strong jawlines, high, chiseled cheekbones, and straight Romanesque noses. These twins must turn a lot of heads. *I prefer tall, dark, and broody myself.* The twins don't quite do it for me; they're not my type. I steal a peek at my stepbrother for comparison. I guess I also prefer men that are tatted up and rock a hard body because Nyx Beckam definitely has the attributes that get my juices flowing, whether I want them to or not.

"Oh, come on, Nyx. You always share your toys with us," the one who captured me says to my stepbrother.

I don't dare look at Nyx, so I look at the others, and they're all wearing identical smirks. I try to break free of the twins' grip, but they only tighten it. I jerk when the quiet twin moves my hair from my face.

"You look really familiar. What's your name, beautiful?" quiet twin asks.

"None of your fucking business, Jax." Nyx glares at the guy before adding, "Now, if this meeting is over, I've got work to do." He looks at me and orders, "Get back to work."

Like it's my fault I'm even in this position to begin with. The twin who pulled me down gives me a sympathetic look and helps me to my feet. He never takes his eyes off me, and when I glance at the other brother, he's staring, too, only it's a different kind of look—like he's trying to make heads or tails of something.

I quickly take my leave as soon as I'm free of the guy's hands. I shut the door quietly, then lean against the wall, trying to steady my racing heart. I can hear Nyx's angry voice, but I pay no mind as to what he's saying because I'm still wrapping my head around what the fuck just happened in there. However, a loud bang draws my attention and I realize that Nyx must have slammed his fist down because his voice is even angrier.

"I think I've made myself clear, Jarod. I don't want to sound like a dick, but I want the drugs out of our town, so figure it out. Oh, and while you're at it, stay the fuck away from that employee of mine."

The scraping of chairs against the floor has me moving away from the door and down the hallway. The last thing I need is Nyx thinking I was eavesdropping. I can handle many things, but I'm finding that his accusations hurt me more than they should and being called his employee hurts just as much. Why do I care? *Because you still love the asshole, that's why.*

EiGHT

Nyx

"Well, what do you think?" Zilas asks, settling into one of the chairs the twins just occupied.

"What do you mean, what do I think? It's the same old shit. I'm beginning to believe their old man is wearing off on them. They keep stalling the removal of their drugs, and I'm not having it." I go to my minibar and pour me a few fingers of some Johnny Walker before taking my seat behind my desk again.

"That bit about your parents..." Adrik raises his brow.

"Is nothing that I didn't already know. That hotel fire was meant to kill my father and Jessica. I was also supposed to be at that fundraiser, or have you forgotten?" I don't mean to snap at my friends, but I'm tired of the runaround I keep getting from the twins. "Had I not been selfish and stayed behind to fuck your little French fling with you, I'd be six feet under, too."

Adrik chuckles. "Ah yes, sweet, sweet Claire."

Cray scoffs, "There was nothing sweet about that French whore."

A smile actually forms on my lips because Cray isn't wrong. That bitch acted all sweet and innocent, then had the audacity to steal from Adrik and then try playing the victim. Luckily, we have Amara, and she was all too happy to take care of her. I still don't know what happened to the woman; this is the first time she's been brought up since that night.

"Can we get back to what's important?" Zilas sobers us all up.

I feel guilty because I know how much this topic means to him. Hell, we had started trying to clean the streets of drugs long before the Feds came down on us, just before the fire that took my father and stepmother.

My friend had lost his younger brother to drugs a couple years ago, and we all vowed to get it off our streets and out of our town.

"The Kappels are dealing with the South Crew now. Did you know that?" Zilas asks as he looks at each of us.

"What the fuck? Do they have a death wish?" I ask incredulously. "Anybody who aligns themselves with the South Crew always winds up dead."

Zilas only shrugs. "Jax informed me of it before the meeting. He and Jarod aren't happy, but there isn't anything they can do about it now. Their father is in too deep already."

"Well, it looks like the twins may be taking over sooner than we thought," Cray adds his two cents into the mix. "Their father won't last long being mixed up with them. We should seriously think about taking care of the Crew ourselves."

"They're not in Nyte; we have no jurisdiction regarding the South Crew," I remind him.

"Maybe not, but the Kappels are in Nyte, one of the influential families in this town. Regardless of whether they're running drugs, we can't let the Heirs pay for their forefathers' mistakes. Like us, Jax and Jarod want a clean business—"

"There is nothing clean about the drug business," Adrik snickers as he cuts Cray off.

"That's not what I'm saying, dickhead!" Cray grins.

"Okay, okay, I don't have time to watch the two of you go at it." I smirk and continue, saying, "I want you both keeping your eyes on that crew, and we will deal with them if need be."

"What do we do about the twins?" Zilas asks. "This is why I don't like to mix business with pleasure. I hate that I like them because I really despise what they do for work."

"Aren't they into firearms? I may know of a few people that could help them out—IF they decide to switch professions and move away from their father's drug running." I tap my finger on my desk as I think.

The only problem with trying to think about anything at the moment is that I still have my fucking stepsister on my mind. The way she smelled in the elevator and looked in that sinful dress... I need to stop buying such seductive clothing for her.

Seeing Jarod pull her onto his lap made me see red. I know I was an ass and made it sound like she was at fault, but I won't allow her to know my true feelings. Never again will I let her have that power over me. If I have to make her hate me, so be it.

"So, you're saying you want to stop them from selling drugs and help them expand their gun trade? Either way, people die," Zilas states with disgust, making me roll my eyes.

"Do you honestly think that's what I would allow to happen? I'm talking about them being legit firearms dealers, and what are you talking about? You're packing as we speak!"

My friend thinks about this for a moment, then shrugs. "It could work, I guess, but only if it's legit—and my shit is."

"We're trying to clean this town up, not substitute one illegal business for another," I tell him. "Now, how about you all get the fuck out of my office. You all have your own offices to hang out in."

Adrik chuckles, "Oh, I'm leaving, but I'm heading down to look for my entertainment for the night."

He and Cray start for the door when I call out to them, "If you see Mara, tell her I want to see her."

"I'm sure that's not all you want," Cray winks at me.

"Fuck you, Cray."

"Nah, you're not my type, bro."

Flipping him off, I turn my attention back to Zilas, who still sits in front of my desk, staring at me. "What?"

"Are you ever going to talk about it?"

"Talk about what?"

He rolls his eyes at me before replying, "About you and Raya."

"What about us?" I frown as I look at my computer screen, so I don't have to look at my friend.

"I saw the feed to the private elevator..." he trails off.

"I was only trying to teach her a lesson."

"Bullshit! You forget there is audio in that bitch. I heard everything, and I saw your reaction. She turned you down again, and that upset you."

"You don't know what you saw. That's not what that was."

Sighing, Zilas stands up. "We were there for you when it first happened, and we're here for you now, but something tells me that there's more to the story than we know."

"So, what are you saying?" I lean back in my chair and glare at my friend.

"All I'm saying is that maybe you should try to find out *that* story before you do something you can't take back." He turns and heads for the door, but stops midway and turns back. "Otherwise, take your revenge and take her as your wife."

He's gone before I can give him a piece of my mind. *Take Saraya as my wife, my ass!* How is that revenge? I will be giving her everything—my name, power, and money—and what will I get?

You will be getting what you've always wanted—her.

Pulling up the security video, I rewind it back to when Saraya first left my office. I'm still pissed that the twins have taken an interest in her, but there's nothing I can do about it now. I will just have to watch her closely whenever they're around.

A grin appears when the footage pops up, and I see my little lamb standing just outside the door. I watch as her chest heaves up and down; what I wouldn't do to be able to shove my face between those beautiful globes. Continuing to watch her movements, I notice her jump and look at my closed door before she takes off down the hall.

I fast forward and watch her every move as she returns to the hostess station. *Damn, she looks hot in that dress.* Something stirs in my pants, and I say "fuck it" as I open them, reach in, and pull my throbbing cock out. I begin stroking it slowly as I watch my little lamb move around seductively without her realizing she's doing it.

Keeping my eyes on the screen, I let my mind go back to the elevator when I was two seconds from taking her. In my new memory, that's just what I do. I slip her panties to the side while holding her leg at my hip, and I thrust into her.

"Fuck yes...Raya..." I groan as I pump even faster.

In the video footage, she bends over to pick up a slip of paper that fell to the floor; her ass showcases itself as though it knows I'm watching it. As soon as she stands up again, my thoughts return to the elevator, where I snake my hand up and decorate her neck with it.

Holding her pinned to the wall, I fuck her hard and deep as she grips the railing behind her. I make her look at me as I finally take what should have been mine over ten years ago. In my head, I can hear her crying out my name, *"Nyx,"* and it only makes me more animalistic.

Suddenly, I feel my balls pulling up, and I know it's going to be a good release. I stroke my hand faster and look down, picturing my hand as Saraya's sweet cunt while I fucking own it. She comes for me—and I explode.

I let my head fall back and close my eyes, panting while my hand is still wrapped around my cock. My breathing is heavy as I try to control it enough to move. I'm too wiped at the moment.

A slow clap sounds through my office, making my eyes snap open. Amara grins from ear to ear, pushing away from the door and making her way to me leisurely. She doesn't say anything yet, but the wicked smile pasted on her lips tells me she has a lot to say.

Leaning forward to grab some tissue from the box on my desk, I scowl at my friend. "What the fuck do you want, Mara?"

Lifting her brow at me in amusement, she perches her ass on the corner of my desk and glances down as I finish cleaning up. "Cray informed me that you wanted me to come to your office. I came as fast as I could, but apparently—you came faster."

I scoff. "I didn't call you to my office so you could get me off..."

"No? Pray tell, if it wasn't the thought of you fucking my tight ass that got you off, then what was it?"

I'm just about ready to tell her to mind her own fucking business when I see her eyes land on the security footage. She glances back down as I tuck myself away, and then her eyes meet mine, and all amusement is gone.

"Are you fucking serious right now? She broke your fucking heart, Nyx!"

I slam my finger on the button that turns the footage off and then lean back in my chair to study Mara. She's always been protective of us but never stuck her nose into our business regarding women. She knows that women have only been a warm pussy for me to stick my dick in. This is a side that I'm not used to seeing.

"You're fucking jealous..."

"The fuck I am, Nyx."

"You are. The only question is—why?"

"I'm not fucking jealous, asshole, but do you really want to know what I am? I'm fucking livid. I'm livid at her, and now, I'm livid at you!"

Smirking, I swivel in my chair so I can face her completely and open my arms for her. When she doesn't come to me right away, I lift my eyebrow, and she rolls her eyes before huffing and coming over to curl up in my lap. I wrap my arms around her and kiss the top of her head.

"What's got your panties in such a bunch, little Mara?"

"I'm not wearing any panties..."

I chortle at her remark as she rests her head against my chest, as she usually does when we have our little heart-to-hearts. Amara takes on so much to prove herself to us that I make her take a few minutes every once in a while to stop acting like her badass self. This woman has seen and done a lot of fucked up shit in her life; she's earned her freedom from the chains our forefathers put around her family name.

Generations of Nichols have paid their dues to the Gods of Nyte's Hall and it's about time it ends. The others and I have tried to tell her she is free, but she's loyal to a fault and remains with us. We are family, and it seems we will stay together no matter what.

"The guys think I should take my revenge and marry *her*." I don't have to say anything else to Mara.

"You won't be happy."

"I won't be happy regardless."

Our little devil pushes away from my chest and stares at me, searching for something within the depths of my stone-cold eyes. Her demeanor changes, and she visibly relaxes.

"I will end her if she hurts you again."

"She won't. I won't allow it. Besides, I haven't said I will do it."

"You will."

"How do you know?"

Amara's petite shoulders rise as she shrugs and says, "Because you still love her."

NINE

Nyx

"Hey, boss," Cale greets as he takes the stool beside mine at the bar.

"Cale." I nod at Rigger, the head bartender, indicating that he's to get Cale his preferred beverage.

I don't allow my men to drink while on the job, but it's eleven-thirty at night, and I know Cale has been off duty since eight. If he's here at the club, it's because he has information for me. Cale keeps his sex life to himself. He has very dark tastes and prefers not to showcase them, even though we provide an outlet for people like him here at the club.

"I'm not sure if this means anything, but do you remember or know a Robert Stanton?"

I momentarily look to my right and stare at my right-hand man before I down the rest of the amber liquid in my glass. After taking a moment to suck the remnants of the whiskey from my teeth, I say, "Yeah, I knew him. He was Kappel's brother-in-law and a fucking slime. He came up missing about a month after I left."

Shrugging, I hold my glass up for Rigger to refill. Since I'm not here for entertainment, I'll allow myself one or two extra, depending on what Cale has to tell me. It probably won't be good if it has to do with Stanton. That guy was a piece of work. My father tolerated him because of the relationship between Stanton and Kappel. My father was the kind of person who kept his friends close and his enemies even closer. Both these men were in the latter category.

"Well," Cale goes on to say, "It seems that right before he disappeared, he had told a few people that he had fucked up and that if what he had done ever got out, he would be a dead man." Cale takes a sip of his bourbon, and I wait because I know there's more he has to say, and I'm correct as Cale states, "It was also said that whatever it was, your father was involved and had instigated it."

I scoff, "I wouldn't put it past him..."

"Another name was brought up also," Cale states.

I watch Rigger set my glass down in front of me before I say, "Go on."

"McNally was with Stanton when whatever it was had happened."

My brow furrows. "Ken would have been almost ten years Stanton's junior. What would he be doing hanging around with him?"

"That's a good question, and maybe one that you should ask our little warehouse guest next time you go see him." Cale throws back the rest of his drink and stands.

"Leaving so soon?"

"Yeah, I have an early day tomorrow. My boss is the biggest asshole you will ever meet," Cale jokes, and I grin.

"He sounds awesome to me."

Cale chuckles. "Don't stay out too late, Boss. You tend to be cranky when you haven't gotten your beauty sleep. Unless, of course, you have plans..."

I don't miss the slight glance towards Saraya.

Glancing in the same direction, I ponder his words. *Should I? Could I?* Amara's words come back to haunt me... *Because you still love her.* I don't love her, how could I? But anyone with eyes and a working dick would be lying if they said they didn't want her. Saraya is a natural beauty, but I've found that, like the Oleander garden plant, she's beautiful to look at, but is one of the most toxic plants out there.

Not everything that looks pleasing to the eye is safe. The slow loris has gentle eyes and looks nice and cuddly, but its saliva and fur can be very venomous when it feels threatened. The point is, I've already fallen for her beauty and thought she was different than others, but then she let out her poison and ruined me for all time. I'd be dumb to let it happen again.

As for marrying Saraya for revenge, that is a possibility as long as she signs a prenup. I could use a beautiful woman by my side, and she used to know the ins and outs of what being in this family is all about.

I let my eyes roam to her hips where the dress hugs each curve; they were made for childbearing. My cock stirs at the thought of fucking my seed into her sweet cunt and planting my spawn deep within. She has no say, really. All I have to do is tell her we will marry and be done with it.

Yeah, it's an asshole move, but it's not too different than her bitch move she pulled years ago, at least, not in my eyes. The question is, do I want to tie myself to a conniving bitch?

A chuckle from beside me brings me back to my current conversation. I turn back to my drink and toss it back. I have to get out of here. If I stay in the vicinity of my stepsister any longer, I'll end up dragging her to the nearest room, bending her over, and fucking the shit out of her. None of this can happen as long as her husband is still alive.

Pulling my phone out, I type out a message...

ME: Time to play, little devil.

A message comes through immediately, bringing a smile to my face.

LIL DEVIL: Can I get filthy?
ME: As filthy as you want...
LIL DEVIL: Be there in 5.

I tuck my phone away and grin at Cale as I ask, "Will you stay and keep watch over baby sister?"

He raises a brow. "I didn't realize I moonlighted as a babysitter."

"Hey, it's triple pay, and I just want you to make sure that none of these horny fuckers try anything with her. When her shift ends at two, I'll need you to drive her back to the Hall."

"Fine, it's not like I had any plans tonight anyway." Cale then taps his finger on the bar to catch Rigger's attention and orders, "Club soda."

I smirk at my right-hand man and glance over at Monica. I know that Cale has been wanting to get inside her, so I'm going to be a good friend and give him a bit of a heads-up.

"Monica will be a house sub while Saraya is hostess. You have your chance to have her. All I ask is that you don't break her. I would like to keep her as an employee; she's good at what she does."

Cale runs his tongue over his bottom lip, a hint of a smile forming as he considers what I'm telling him.

"I'll even make sure you're her first for the evening." I stand as I see Amara come around the corner.

"Deal. Tomorrow night, nine sharp," Cale states.

Grinning, I slap him on the back of his shoulder and say, "It's a deal. Thanks, buddy."

Mara laces her arm through mine, and we head to the hostess stand. Saraya is smiling at something one of the clients just said before they walked away, but when her eyes land on us, they falter. I almost let Amara go just to see that smile again, but I stay strong and squeeze Mara's arm instead as I address my stepsister.

"Cale will watch over you and take you back to the Hall after your shift. Don't give him any issues." I don't wait for Saraya's response, but I make sure I smile down at our little devil and hold the door open for her as we walk out together. The feel of Saraya's eyes burning a hole in my back has me grinning.

✦

"Tucker, why don't you see Sasha to her car. She will no longer be needed for this *patient*," I tell Cale's replacement as soon as we walk into the back room of the warehouse.

He and the nurse are playing cards while Ken sleeps soundly in the bed. They both eye me, then Amara with her handy black bag. I nod at Sasha's unasked question, and she returns it, knowing that my brother-in-law will be taking his last breath tonight.

"Once you're back, be sure to turn on the incinerator and wait for my orders," I remind my man, not that I really need to. They all know what happens once we have evidence to take care of.

"Wakey, wakey, while I make you all achy."

I hear Mara's singsong voice and look over to see her straddling Ken, rubbing herself over his crotch. I roll my eyes and cross my arms, waiting for her to stop toying with him.

"W-what the hell..." Ken says groggily and then tries to buck Mara off.

Throwing one arm in the air, Amara pinches his nipple with the other in order to hold on, pretending to ride a bull. "Yeehaw, motherfucker! Come on, baby, buck me harder..."

It takes everything I have not to laugh, especially when Ken gives up the fight and he starts sporting a boner. As soon as I see it rise, I know it won't bode well for him where our little devil is concerned.

"Aw, look at that, Nyx. His little friend wants to play, too!" The wicked grin Mara wears gives me cause to wince.

Playing with Mara is never a good thing. When the word play and our little devil are both involved, it means there will be lots of pain inflicted. The fact that she thinks Ken's dick wants to play already has my balls shriveling up with what those few words mean.

"Oh God, what are you doing? Get away from me—don't touch me!" Ken pleads with Mara as she pulls what looks to be a glove out.

"Oh fuck..." I curse and turn around, not able to witness this once I see her donning what's called a vampire glove.

"No, please! ARGH..."

I squeeze my eyes closed because it's too hard to keep them open when I know my brother-in-law's dick is getting grated like a block of fucking cheese. The little sharp teeth embedded in the gloves were not made for hand jobs, but our little devil likes using them.

"Oh, you like that, huh?" Mara asks, amused.

"Fuck! Stop...please!"

His pleading pisses me off, and I turn back around, marching right up to the bed to glare down at him. I ask him the same question as I've asked him before, "Did Saraya ever beg for you to stop when you were beating her? How about when you were choking her or raping her?"

"She's my wife, I can have sex with her whenever I want—it isn't rape..." Ken seriously thinks he did nothing wrong to my little lamb.

Without taking my eyes off Ken, I tell Mara, "I think he wants it faster. Jerk that cock until it's torn the fuck up."

"NO—ARGH!!"

I dig through Amara's bag and find what I'm looking for. Pulling out the open-mouth gag, I go to strap it to Ken's head, but he says something that gives me pause.

"Y-you wanted to k-know about the time Saraya and I h-hooked up. Well, I w-wasn't her f-first."

"That's bullshit! Saraya was a fucking virgin. That was supposed to be *mine*!"

Ken shakes his head vigorously back and forth. "No, she wasn't! S-Stanton had her first. I w-watched them fuck—I s-swear!"

That *fucking* name again! It can't be a coincidence that Cale found the information about Stanton, and now this fuckface is telling me that Raya fucked Stanton, too. All I see is red now as I strap the gag on, no longer caring to hear anything else Ken has to say. I then walk over to a cabinet where I know we keep some supplies for torture, and I grab what I need before going back to the bed.

"Well fuck, he passed out," I huff when I see Ken's head loll to the side.

"Oh, that's not a problem." Mara reaches into an inside pocket of her bag and pulls out a massive syringe.

"Of course, she would come prepared with adrenaline," I say out loud, but to no one in particular.

Her giggle sounds like a little girl's giggle when she plays. It's pretty fucking creepy if you ask me, but I let her do her thing. Watching her plunge the needle into Ken's chest is more amusing than I thought, but it's even funnier when the fucker wakes up, trying to take deep breaths with the gag on.

Before he can even recover, I start shoving the tube I collected down his throat. I'm not a professional, so don't ask me if I'm doing it right. I'm guessing by the way he's crying and trying to scream, it's not the correct way.

"Let's finish this, little devil."

"But I'm not filthy yet," she whines.

I look at Ken's dick which is shredded and bleeding out, and then I look back at her. "Really?"

Our little devil shrugs. "Whatever."

Amara grabs the container I brought over while I turn my attention back to Ken. Gripping his scruffy chin, I lean into him so I know he can see me. I want my face to be the last one he sees as Mara pours the acid into the tube.

"This could have been done quickly and painlessly for you, Kenneth. Now, you will feel my wrath as the hydrochloric acid takes effect." Watching the liquid enter the tube, I grin down at my brother-in-law. "First, you will feel a burn in your throat when it comes out of the tube. I'd add in drooling, but you're already doing that."

I observe the saliva dripping from around the gag, knowing it will soon be tinged with red. Moving back just a little before he starts the vomiting part, I meet his eyes once again.

"Be grateful for the tube, because your throat will be swelling soon, making it difficult for you to breathe. Next, you will start feeling the abdominal pain..."

His pull at the restraints tells me he's already feeling the former. Before I allow Mara to end him in her own way, I need him to know something.

So, making sure I won't get hit with any vomit if he decides to hurl, I move to his side and bring my lips close to his ear as I whisper the following words only meant for his ears.

"You can tell my father I win when you get to hell. I will have my stepsister; I will fuck her anytime I want. She will obey me in everything, and she will have my heirs. I won't beat her like you did, not unless it's with my cock, but make no mistake, I will reclaim Saraya Abbott McNally, and this time, I will keep her."

Ken grunts, and his body jerks, and when I glance up, I understand why. Amara has her favorite serrated knife plunged deep into Ken's gut, and she's slowly sliding it upwards, cutting him wide open.

I straighten myself, and fixing the cuff on my sleeve, I instruct our little devil, "I'm heading out, clean up your mess and take care of the body. Tucker can bring you home."

She waves me away as if I'm disrupting her work and says, "Yeah, yeah—go—I know what to do."

I lean in and kiss the top of her head. "You did good; a bit fucked up with the glove, but good. I'll see you in the morning." I then turn and leave our little devil to finish up the man who's already been dead for days. It's time I take control and do what should have been done years ago where Saraya is concerned—make her mine.

TEN

The audacity of that asshole! I'm not his to command; I will not roll over and submit to his demands! As soon as he walks out with Mara hanging all over him, I know they are going to go fuck, and I realize that he has that right. Just like I have every right to move on with my own life.

Trying to keep the animosity hidden, I remain the gracious hostess. Men have flirted with me and until now, I've laughed it off, but maybe it's time I flirt back. Monica keeps telling me that if I do, the tips would be double what I've made so far. Although the hostess position typically doesn't make tips, Monica says that the Heirs don't have an issue if we make them.

So, when the next client walks in the door, I paste on my biggest smile and introduce myself to him. It's not very hard to do when the man standing before me is very good-looking, with blonde hair and the brightest blue eyes.

"Ah, the Heirs know how to hire the most beautiful creatures to greet us, don't they?" The man lifts my hand and places a kiss on the back of it.

"Well, Mr. Beckam is family, so I thought I should probably help out around here," I tell him while giving him what I hope is a sultry smile.

"Oh? I didn't know Nyx had any more family around."

"I'm his stepsister and just getting out of a *relationship.*" I try to choose my words carefully, especially with strangers.

"How about you come to find me when your shift is over? I'd love to get to know you more."

Glancing over the man's shoulder, I notice the cocked brow on Nyx's lap dog and grin. Cale can wait until I'm ready to go home; I'm not a child. So, giving the man my attention again, I accept his invitation.

"I'd love to, Mister..."

"Mika. My name is Mika Tomlin."

"Well, Mika, Mika Tomlin, I will come find you once I'm free."

The handsome guy bites his lower lip as his eyes wander down my length before responding, "I'll be waiting."

I watch him walk off, and Monica squeals beside me, "Do you have any idea who that is?"

"Who, Mika?"

"Yes, Mika! His family owns the next town over. He is equivalent to your brother and the other Heirs. Mr. Tomlin *never* shows interest in anyone. He will pick a house sub, fuck her, and then go to the back room and play cards. He never pays attention to anyone!"

I break out in chills at hearing this, but I can't say whether it's a good or bad thing. What would Nyx say? *Who cares what he thinks? He's getting it from my ex-best friend, so why should any of it bother him?*

"Are Mika and my stepbrother friends? Mika almost made it sound as though he knew Nyx well." I question Monica, but she only shrugs.

"I've seen them have a drink together, but that's as much as I can tell you," she states. "If you ask me, I'd definitely tap that if he came on to me like he did you just now."

"I don't know. Things are—complicated right now. As I said, I'm just getting out of a relationship..."

"He's not asking you to marry him, Saraya, sheesh. Hell, he hasn't even asked you to fuck. He told you to come find him. As I said, he doesn't do that."

I peer over the clientele, and my eyes meet Mika's blue ones. The sparkle his oceanic-colored orbs have can be seen across the room, and I can't help but blush. Looking away, I notice Cale typing furiously on his cell phone. Knowing it's none of my business about who pissed in his cheerios, I go about my work as a couple comes waltzing through the doors.

I've only got an hour left of my shift, and I'm nervously excited about talking with Mika. I've never spoken to another guy like the way I'm going to with him. I always had Phoenyx as a teenager, and then everything happened, and the next thing I know, I'm walking down the aisle to marry Kenneth. *What do I say to him?* I busy myself, trying to take my mind off it by writing a list of things I must remember for my next shift, when suddenly *his* deep, stern voice is right there giving me commands once again.

"Get your things, Raya. Your shift is over." Nyx doesn't even look at me as he orders me around.

My anger rises at what he's trying to do. I now know what Cale was typing on his phone; he was ratting me out. Giving Nyx a stubborn look, I scoff and look him up and down as if to ask, *Who died and made you boss?*

"I'm not going anywhere. My shift ends at two, and then I have plans..."

"Cancel them." His jaw clenches as his tone turns menacing.

"Excuse me?"

"You heard me. I said cancel them. We are leaving now."

Putting my hands on my hips, I glare into his cold gray eyes and state, "I am not a child, and you will not treat me like one. I will be home when I come home."

Nyx isn't fazed by my little speech as he takes another step closer. Lowering his voice, so only Monica can hear because she's right beside me, Nyx's next words shock me. "You still have a reputation to uphold. As long as you are a part of this family, I will not allow you to whore around with every fucking client that walks through these doors."

Without even thinking, my hand comes up and slaps him across the face. Silence covers the room once the sound of my hand hitting his cheek is done echoing through the room. There are a few gasps that come from some of the club members, and even though my heart is racing because I know I'm in deep shit, I stand my ground.

Nyx grins and raises his hand, letting everyone know everything is fine. What others see is Nyx Beckam, a God of Nyte's Hall, amused by this situation as he smiles down at me. What I see when he looks at me is the promise of an unforgettable punishment.

"How about we discuss this privately—preferably—at home." He suggests.

"Yes, I think that's best." I agree, saying, "I'll be home shortly."

"I don't think you understand me, Raya." Nyx leans in close, so this time, my ears are the only ones to hear his next words as he says, "You are going to get your ass out that door, down the elevator, and into my *fucking* car, or so help me..."

"You wouldn't dare make a scene here, *Mr. Beckam.* Not with one of your *employees.*"

"Do you honestly think any one of these members would say anything? This is *my* town and *my* club, and you are *my fucking employee.* If anything, they would get a kick to see the great Nyx Beckam take his employee over his knee, bare her beautiful ass, and spank the shit out of it—even Mika fucking Tomlin."

That's what this is about. Nyx is pissed that I was making plans with another guy—*interesting.* Instead of arguing with him more, I collect my things and head for the door, but not before giving Nyx one last *fuck you* in front of everyone by winking at an amused Mika.

As soon as we're out the door, he grabs my elbow and pulls me toward the private elevator. He says nothing as we ride the car down to the private parking garage, where he again grabs me by the elbow and walks me to his car. He gives me an order only once I'm settled into the seat.

"Put your fucking seatbelt on, Saraya."

Oh, he's really pissed if he's using my whole name...

I wait for him to get into the car, so I can give him a piece of my mind, but nothing will come out. All I can do is stare at his profile as he starts the engine, but we don't move.

Nyx runs his hand through his hair before slowly turning to look at me. I can see the anger in his eyes, making them look stone-cold. "If you ever raise your hand to me like that again, I don't fucking care where we are; I will turn you over my knee. I am not fucking Kenneth, who deserves to be slapped. The only way I will raise my hand to you is when I'm reddening that ass of yours."

He's right; he isn't Ken. I shouldn't have done what I did, and I say as much. "I'm sorry. I never meant to slap you; it was automatic. However, I'm not a whore, and it was unfair of you to say what you did."

He chuckles cynically. "Aren't you, though, or was that just in the past? Tell me, dear *sister,* how many guys have you actually slept with?"

"That isn't any of your business, Nyx—"

"I'm making it my fucking business, because if you think you're going to sleep around with every Tom, Dick, and Harry, then we have a fucking problem! Now, I will ask you one...more...time. How many guys have you slept with?"

"Why does it matter? You seem to fuck whoever the hell you want! You had that woman at the Hall the first night I arrived, and you seem to like fucking Amara. You've fucked her at least twice now since I've been here—"

"Once. I've fucked Mara once since you have been at the Hall," he states as he cuts me off.

"Oh, please. Do you seriously think I'm that naïve about what the two of you were doing after you left here tonight?"

The wicked grin that forms on his lips unnerves me, but not as much as watching his hands go to the front of his pants and open them up. I'm not sure what he thinks will happen, but I look away immediately.

"Come here, Saraya."

"No..."

"Come...here."

"Fuck you, Nyx."

Suddenly, my seatbelt is unbuckled, and Nyx is grabbing the back of my head, bringing it down to his crotch. I catch myself, not letting him bring me any lower, but then he captures my wrists in his other hand and pushes my head down until my face is against his crotch.

"Take a deep whiff, Saraya. Does that smell like fucking pussy to you? Go on—smell my fucking dick!"

For a reason I can't even fathom, I do exactly that. I inhale the musky scent with a hint of—is that body wash or cologne? It definitely isn't pussy, and I doubt Mara smells like this. So, I was wrong. They didn't leave to go fuck, but that still doesn't mean I can't talk to other men.

As soon as he loosens his hold, I push up and away from him. I should be embarrassed but I'm learning really fast that if I don't start standing up to him, I'll find myself in the same situation as I did with Ken. Nyx would never hit me, I know this, but that doesn't mean he wouldn't fuck with me until I submit.

I glare at him. "Do you want a cookie? Oh, the great Nyx Beckam was able to keep his dick in his pants for five fucking minutes."

He throws his head back and laughs. It's sinister before he grinds his teeth and says, "At least I'll admit that I've fucked a lot of women. Then again, I didn't betray anyone while fucking any of them."

"Nyx, stop—"

"Oh, what's the matter? You don't like hearing the truth? Well, I love hearing the truth, so how about, for once in your life, you speak the truth to me. How many guys have you fucked?" His voice rises a few notches.

"It doesn't matter—"

He slams his fist down on the steering wheel and growls, "It does fucking matter!" His eyes are hard steel as he turns them on me and asks again, "How many?"

I look down at my lap and think back all those years ago when my stepfather barged into my room and forbade me to go near his son. He wasn't alone, but I paid the others no mind as my mind was trying to wrap itself around what Layton was saying. I was never to go near Phoenyx again.

"It isn't right, Saraya. Blood or not, you two are family, and we don't do that in this family. Listen to me well if you need another reason because that one isn't good enough. I have taken care of you like my own daughter, but when it comes down to it, you are still a bastard who doesn't know who her father is. Phoenyx will run this town one day and will need a queen by his side. You can never be that queen, Saraya."

"You can't stop us from being together. We love each other, and what others think doesn't matter," I try telling my stepfather.

"That's where you're wrong, little girl. I can stop you. I have already chosen your husband, Saraya. From this day forward, you will spend all your time with Kenneth." Layton points to the man who is a few years my senior.

Kenneth is decent-looking, but the way he smirks at me and looks me up and down as if I'm his next meal is creeping me out. When he moves toward me, I shrink back and start shaking my head.

"No, I won't do it. I love Phoenyx; we will be together," I argue, but it makes no difference in the end.

"You won't be together if he's dead, now will you? If the two of you disobey me, Phoenyx loses everything, and I will hunt him down like the traitor that he is. He will be dead to me, and I won't be having some imposter walking around in my dead son's body."

"You wouldn't!" I gasp at what I'm hearing.

"Fucking try me, little girl!"

I glance at Kenneth and back at my stepfather. Fear takes hold, and I lose all hope. I can't let Phoenyx lose his birthright because of me, but most of all, I can't have him lose his life.

"Okay. I'll stay away from him."

"Of course you will, because you will marry Kenneth."

"No, I won't, but I will stay away from Phoe—nyx..." my voice cracks.

"My son is stubborn. No, this will only work if you're married, so you and Ken will marry in three days."

"But that's my birthday!"

"Exactly," Layton smirks and then nods at Kenneth before he goes on to say, "As your future husband, Kenneth isn't impressed by virgins, so Stanton is here to help with that."

"W-what do you mean?" Dread fills me.

"Stanton will be ridding you of that nasty virginity per your fiancé's request."

"No! I'll marry Kenneth, but I won't do this!"

"You really have no say, Saraya." Nodding at the other man, Ken and Stanton come at me as my stepfather leans against the wall.

My future husband holds me in place with his hand over my mouth as another, much older man takes from me the very thing I promised to the love of my life. They don't care if they are gentle or not. They just take it, and my stepfather stands back and enjoys the show.

Once it's over and the man named Stanton leaves, I hear Layton talking to Ken, "Here, all the evidence is on this video if you ever need it to prove who it was that fucked the little slut. I've already sent it to my phone to alter it and make it look like she enjoyed it all. My son will never forgive her for this betrayal."

Before I pass out, my stepfather comes over to me and yanks me by the hair. He makes me look him in the eye while he threatens me with the one thing that has me swearing to secrecy.

"You will go along with my plan because one word of this to my son—not only will I end him, but I'll make you MY whore, and you will bear me a new Heir." He peruses my used, battered body and snickers before pushing me away from him and leaving my room.

I lost a lot of things that day. I lost all the love I had for my stepfather, I lost my dignity, and I lost my innocence. Most of all, and what hurt the most, is that I lost my best friend and the love of my life.

"Two," I whisper.

ELEVEN

Nyx

It's a little after eleven in the morning as I sit in my home office. I slept for shit last night after Raya and I returned home. After she admitted that she had slept with two people, confirming that she did sleep with Stanton, all I wanted to do was drag her to my room and fuck both of them out of her system.

At the same time, the stabbing pain I felt all those years ago when I learned of her first betrayal had come on full force. I wanted to punish her. I wanted to take her and humiliate her while degrading the fuck out of her for everything she had put me through.

Saraya made me into a heartless monster who will never again love another. As one of the Heirs and the head of the Beckam family, to which she belongs, I have full authority over her. The old me would let her live her life the way she wanted, but as I said, she made me this way, and now she will have to live with it.

She's testing my patience at the moment. Last night, once we got home, I told her to meet me in my office at eleven sharp. I told her we had things to discuss, and I didn't have all day. My little lamb is not here, and the longer she makes me wait, the more she will regret it.

After last night's stunt at the club and now her tardiness, my hand is itching to redden a particular body part of my dear stepsister. Saraya doesn't realize what it took for me not to do it in front of everyone at the club. For some odd reason, I didn't want anyone seeing her like that. I know; I'm fucked in the head. I want to humiliate her and degrade her, yet I don't want anyone seeing her like that.

A knock on my office door brings me back to the present, and I expect to find Raya standing there, but instead, it's Adrik. Smirking, he slowly wanders in with his hands in his pockets.

"Well, someone looks like they woke up on the wrong side of the bed."

"Don't."

"Don't what? I'm only calling it how I see it."

I lean back in my chair and scrub my hand down my face. "Sorry, Raya..."

"Ah, no need to explain." My friend chuckles. "You need to fuck her and get it over with."

"Oh, that's exactly what I will do, but not until I make sure she is chained to me. I'm taking your advice, and I'm going to marry the conniving bitch."

Adrik grins wickedly.

"What's with the grin?"

"Nothing. It's just that things will get very interesting around here."

"Yeah, well, stick around because it's going to get very interesting here as soon as she gets her little ass in my office. She's already late," I tell my friend with a scowl.

Adrik raises his brows. "Uh, you might be waiting for a while."

"Why is that?"

"Because your future wife left about twenty minutes ago with Mika Tomlin. I saw them walking out the door just as I was coming from my wing."

There are no words to describe the kind of rage that begins to burn through my veins. I swipe everything off the surface of my desk before leaning my knuckles on it and bowing my head. I need to get a hold of myself before I go off half-cocked. I have never felt so unhinged in all these years. Then, that *woman* shows up, and my control goes all to hell.

"Well, I was going to ask you if you know our little devil's whereabouts, but I think you may be better off handling this one." My friend sits on the corner of my desk as he crosses his arms.

"What is it? Please say it will allow me to use my fucking hands because I can use a solid punching bag at the moment," I grind out.

"My guys caught the perp who's been going around and killing those women," Adrik states. "Arlo and Charlie caught him red-handed early this morning. They decided to do a drive-by at the fucker's old burial ground.

Apparently, he thought that it's been a long enough time and figured he'd bury his newest victim."

"Motherfucker. I am so ready to deal with that fuckface," I tell him and push off my desk.

Adrik stops me from moving past him and hands me his phone. "You may want to see this before you go to him," he says.

I take it and hit play. Thankfully, Adrik's men have the infrared app on their phones to record at night. Then again, what I start watching isn't something anyone would want to see.

"Is he?"

"Yep," Adrik says, popping the *p.*

"That sick son of a bitch! How old was this one?"

"Arlo is checking on it, but she can't be older than nineteen if even that."

This fucker needs to die a slow, agonizing death. As much as I would love to be the one to do it, I know I'd be too quick. No, this is a job for Amara, but I'll definitely get it started as I take out my frustrations over Raya. Not only is this guy killing innocent women in our town, but we can also now add necrophilia to his list of crimes. Amara will be thrilled about this one.

✠

"I can do this all...day...long!" I say to the bastard.

On our way to the warehouse, Adrik's man, Arlo, got back to him about the victim. The poor girl had gone out with friends to celebrate her eighteenth birthday. She was just a fucking baby, and this piece of shit snuffed the life out of her and then violated her.

My fist pounds away at his face, ripping my knuckles open on his teeth, but I don't feel a thing. Between visions of what Saraya may be doing with Mika and then the memory of what I saw in the video of this fuckface, I'm relentless. I'm not trying to kill him; he doesn't get a quick death, but he will feel my wrath before Amara takes over.

Speaking of our little devil, her singsong voice rings out through the empty space of the warehouse. Adrik and I go to the door. Peering out of the back room, we see Mara walking toward the room with the incinerator.

"This way, boys—chop, chop!" She raises her hands above her head and claps.

Tucker, Arlo, and Charlie are dragging what I believe is a woodchipper across the warehouse. Tucker glares at me, and my mouth twitches.

"What does our girl have up her sleeve this time? Do we even want to know?" Adrik glances at me.

"I'm not sure, but I'm definitely intrigued."

Adrik and I start walking across the empty space when a commotion takes place just outside. I hear a familiar voice cursing like a sailor. The grin that appears on my face may be just a bit cynical.

I had Cale go after my little lamb and bring her back here as soon as he found her.

"Is it a good idea to have her see this?" My friend cocks a brow.

"It will be fine, trust me."

"Let me go, fucker!" Saraya swears as Cale drags her into the warehouse, and she tries to pry his hands off her. When she looks up and sees me, she starts in once more, "Did you send your lap dog to come and kidnap me?"

"Don't be ridiculous; you're not a kid anymore, so technically, it can't be kidnapping," I muse.

"What the fuck, Nyx? What is the meaning of this?"

"Well, since you so sneakily ditched our meeting this morning, I had no choice but to have my guy go and fetch you."

"Oh shit! I totally forgot about our meeting. I'm sorry—it was an honest mistake—you didn't have to go to this length. A simple phone call would have sufficed."

"Tell me, *Lil' Sis,* would you have come home had I called?"

"Well, I wouldn't have been rude and left the person I was out with—"

"You mean Mika. You were out with Mika Tomlin..."

"Well, yes. So what if I was? What difference does it make?"

I walk up to her slowly and caress my bloody fingers down her cheek, streaking her blemish-free skin with the blood of a necrophiliac killer. She tries jerking away, but I grip her chin. I glare hatefully into her doe-like eyes because I hate how my body reacts to her every time she's close to me.

"If you give a damn about his life, then I highly suggest you stay the fuck away from him."

"You can't tell me who I can spend time with, Nyx..."

"Can't I? I fucking own you, Saraya. *You* came to *me*, remember?"

"That doesn't mean you own me!"

Moving my lips to her ear, I lower my voice to a low-gravelly tone, and respond, "Fucking bet me."

Then, as gently as possible, I press my lips against her cheek. I release her chin and take a step back. I can see that I've shocked her; hell, I've shocked myself, but I don't have time to think about it.

"Follow me, Raya."

"I'm not going anywhere until you tell me what I'm doing here," she retorts.

I stop walking, but I don't turn around. Instead, I look to the side and then down, giving my stepsister one warning, "You can either follow me or Cale can bring you. It's your choice, but you will come with me either way."

I start for the room where the guys brought the machinery and see that Arlo and Charlie are now dragging our special guest to the same room. I hear Raya start cursing and know that she took the latter route, and Cale is now dragging her behind me. A slow grin creeps onto my face. *Oh, just wait until you see what I have in store for you, Lil' Sis.*

I step to the side as soon as I enter the room to see Saraya's reaction when she enters. She doesn't disappoint when she finally notices the scene before her. Her forehead wrinkles as she wonders what she's looking at. When her eyes land on the bloody man restrained by chains against the wall, they widen in shock, and then she snaps her head in my direction.

"W-what's going on, Nyx?"

"Well, you see, Saraya, you've been gone for a long time—years, as a matter of fact. Many things have changed, especially now that the Heirs have stepped up to run this town."

Her gaze flickers to Amara, who now stands beside Mr. Corpse Fucker, and her next question showcases a bit of jealousy. "What is *she* doing here? She isn't an Heir; she's just the *help.*"

I raise my brow, slightly surprised at the prejudiced comment. I, too, glance at Mara and then smile at how she just stands there, not taking offense to Raya's words. Although she isn't the *help* as Raya so graciously tries to remind us, Amara knows her place within our circle, and she's proud of it.

Walking over to her, I lift Raya's chin and smile as I say, "Green really isn't a good color on you, Saraya."

She scoffs and jerks her head out of my loose grip. "I am far from jealous. You're all worried about me sullying the family name, yet you keep Amara around who we all know can't keep her legs closed."

"That's because Big Brother loves it when I keep them open for him." Mara gives a throaty laugh, then winks at Raya. "Nyx, Adrik, Cray, and Zilas all love their Mara time. They have ever since they gave me their V-cards."

Saraya's head snaps back to me and I see the hurt in her eyes. I feel a slight ache, but I quickly push it away. I will not feel bad for giving myself to Mara after what she did to me. Raya not only hurt me, but she hurt Mara, her best friend, when she left the way she did.

"That's enough talk. I want to get this over with." I announce as I turn toward Mara, "I want Saraya to help you. She needs to learn how we clean up the town of Nyte from its filth."

"Wait, what do you want me to do?" The look on Raya's face is priceless as she begins to understand why she's here.

"You have the easy part, Lil' Sis. Amara will cut the prisoner up, piece by piece, and you will throw each part into the chipper, which will then spit out the remains into the incinerator."

A look of horror appears on her beautiful face as her head shakes vigorously back and forth. She can't take her eyes off the corpse fucker as she does so.

"Like fucking hell, I will!"

TWELVE

Saraya

"Mr. Tomlin. To what do I owe the pleasure?"

I had just finished eating and was passing through the front foyer when I happened to look out the window by the door. Mika Tomlin was walking up to the door. Thank God I had already showered and dressed, because I hurried to the door to open it before he could press the doorbell.

"Saraya," he said with a grin. "Just the person I came to see."

"Oh?"

"Yes, well, after the whole club scene with your brother, I wanted to make sure you were okay."

"Aw, that was sweet of you. Nyx is overwhelmed at the moment and is a bit overprotective of me. I'm sorry that I couldn't stay and chat," I tell him, slightly embarrassed by how Nyx acted the night before.

"Would you like to have lunch with me?" Mika's brow raises as he waits for my answer.

Although I had just eaten, I didn't want to pass this up, so I accepted his invitation. "I would love to, Mr. Tomlin."

"Please, call me Mika. My father is Mr. Tomlin..."

"Okay, Mika..."

When I step outside and turn to close the door, I spot Adrik heading our way, and I hope he didn't get a glance at Mika standing just outside. The last thing I need is him going straight to my stepbrother about me leaving with him. I had gotten a big enough lecture from Nyx on the way home from the club. Eventually, I tuned him out because I was beginning to get a headache.

Mika, on the other hand, was turning out to be a fun companion. He took me to a small bar and grille for a sandwich and fries and had me laughing the whole time. After he told me a little about his family, he asked about my last relationship.

As if right on cue, a familiar face appeared, and although he was saving me from having to lie about Ken, Cale's appearance pissed me off.

"Un-fucking-believable!" I murmur.

Mika turns and looks in the direction that I'm looking in, and he chuckles. "Well, at least I had you longer than I thought I would. Your brother must be pretty busy if it's taken him this long to send his man for you."

"I'm so sorry, Mika. I honestly don't know what Nyx is thinking..."

He held up his hand to stop me and said, "No worries, Saraya. I will talk to Nyx and ask him if I can take you out. Maybe he's old school, and with you being fresh out of a relationship, he just doesn't want to see you hurt again."

I highly doubt that is the case.

I don't say this out loud, of course. I smiled at Mika and tossed my napkin down before pushing my chair back. Mika stood like the gentleman he was.

"Thank you for lunch, Mika. I enjoyed our short time together."

"No, thank you for accepting my invitation," he said. "Hopefully, next time, it will be dinner without any interruption."

I nodded, but I knew that would never happen. Not if Nyx had a say in it. After Mika lifted my hand and kissed the top of it, I hurried over to the door where Cale stood staring at me. At least he had the mind not to make a scene by coming over to the table. I walked right past him with my nose in the air, so he knew I wasn't happy—not that he cared.

Now, I'm standing in a warehouse where the lapdog dragged me to, staring disbelievingly at my stepbrother. He's lost his fucking mind if he thinks I'm going to throw body parts into a damn woodchipper! *I think I'm going to be sick.*

"Oh, you will, Saraya. Do you want to know why?" Nyx asks after my resounding *"Like fucking hell, I will! "*

"I don't care what your reasoning is, Nyx. I will not take part in this man's murder!" I try backing up, but I bump into a hard chest.

Strong hands grab my arms, ensuring I don't fall, and I assume it's Cale. I'm surprised to see that it's Adrik and I mumble an apology, but he only smirks down at me.

"You may want to listen to his reasoning, Raya."

I scoff, "Nothing he says will make me participate in this, Adrik. I'm not a killer..."

I stop talking because the memory of stabbing my husband repeatedly is still fresh in my mind. Yes, it was in self-defense, but I still killed him, regardless. That's why I'm standing here now—in the presence of my stepbrother, who despises me.

"Maybe we should just let her watch the video," Adrik states as he looks at Nyx.

"She needs to learn to take my orders and obey them as expected. I shouldn't have to give her a reason why. It's the least she can do after all I've done for her recently. It's not like I'm asking her to be the one to cut the body part off. Although, I do hear that she's good with a knife."

Nyx smirks as he delivers his little spiel. Why my lady bits jump to attention as he does so, is beyond me. I'm past wanting my stepbrother at this point, or so I keep telling myself. He's been nothing but an ass since I arrived. Yeah, he's still hotter than fuck, but he's got the personality of a porcupine and a vicious disposition like a shrew.

"Come here, Raya," Amara calls out to me, but I only glare back at her, which makes her snicker.

As if in slow motion, the butcher knife the psychotic woman has in her hand comes down, taking the guy's hand clean off. He screams a second later and starts struggling against the restraints.

Mara picks up the hand and walks over to the woodchipper as she keeps her eyes on me and says, "I took this hand because it's the one he used to grab his eighteen-year-old victim while she was out celebrating her birthday."

My stomach churns as I watch her throw the hand into the chipper, thanking God that I can't see it come out the other end. Mara then returns to the guy and grabs his face.

"What else did you do to the girl?" Mara asks him as she holds the knife to his neck.

The guy sings like a bird, telling us precisely what he did to his victim.

"I took her when she stepped outside to make a phone call. I had been watching her and her friends all night. It was the perfect time to nab her.

So, I reached out through the shadows and placed my hand over her mouth, pulling her back into the alley.

I punched her, making her dazed so I could get her into my trunk. I then took her to my favorite spot. That's when I fucked her for the first time." He stammers through it all.

"Don't you mean that's when you raped her?" Mara sneers. "A young fucking girl who hasn't even begun living yet!"

"I know, I have a p-problem," he stutters.

"Go on. Finish telling everyone what you did to this poor innocent girl."

"A-after fucking her the f-first time, I held her down with my knee and I fisted her..."

"Where did you fist her?" Mara bares her teeth at him.

"H-her ass..."

Nyx walks over and hands Amara something and she grins up at him lovingly.

"Thank you, babe."

Nyx smirks and shakes his head before stepping back. I don't let the endearment get to me this time because I'm too jacked up on adrenaline at hearing this asshole. Instead, I keep my eyes on Mara as she puts a glove on and shoves her fist up the guy's ass. He howls in pain, and I smile for the first time.

"Talk while I fuck your ass, motherfucker."

"T-there isn't much more to t-tell. I then s-stabbed her in the side and fucked her a couple more times. I covered my cock in her blood and forced her to take me into her m-mouth...AGH! I-I then choked her as I fucked h-her again, and that's when s-she died!" He screams with the ending of his story, and I see Mara's arm, up to the elbow, buried inside his ass.

"Then what did you do?" Mara asks as she removes her arm and fist from his ass.

"Please... I'm sorry!" the man cries.

"TELL US WHAT YOU DID NEXT!"

"I-I then took her corpse to where I-I've buried other b-bodies and fucked her again."

When he gets to the part about fucking the corpse, I run to the wastebasket, and everything I ate today comes up. Anger rushes through me the moment my stomach settles.

"His dick," I snarl.

Mara quirks her brow and says, "Excuse me?"

"Cut off his fucking dick!" I grind out.

My ex-best friend grins and he pleads with her. He looks so fucking pathetic right now.

"He's been killing women in our town for months," Nyx's voice rumbles next to my ear. "I don't kill needlessly. We aren't the bad guys, Raya."

I try to even out my breathing but it's hard when Nyx is so close to me, and I can smell his intoxicating scent. Mix that with the sound of his raspy voice, and my body reacts, lubricating itself more than I'd like it to. I do the only thing I can do—step away.

Amara has the fucker's dick in her hand as she jerks him off. "It's easier to cut it off this way. It doesn't matter how scared they are, it always gets hard," she explains when I look at her questioningly.

As soon as it's hard, Mara grins at the man and his eyes widen in horror as she holds the butcher knife up for him to see. It comes down and slices through the phallus with no trouble, taking it clean off.

I remove the handkerchief from Nyx's breast pocket in his suit and go over to pick up the disgusting body part. When I go to toss it into the chipper, Mara stops me.

"No! I need that."

Not even wanting to know why, I hand it to her, and she shoves it into the guy's mouth, cutting off his screams. She then removes her overshirt and uses it to tie it around his head, keeping his dick in his mouth.

"Ah, so much better." Mara muses, "Now, where were we?"

"I believe the other hand is next," I tell her.

My stomach still feels sick, but I just think about that poor girl and her family, and then I see Ken's face in front of me. I see his fist swinging at me, and I see him holding me down every time he wanted to fuck me, not caring where we were at. He once fucked me while he played poker with his police buddies. He got a kick having them watching us, but he never once let anyone touch me. Stanton was the only one who ever had that permission the night my innocence was taken, but never again.

Snarling, I take the butcher knife from Amara's hand, and like the night I stabbed my husband, I let loose. I swing the massive knife at the man's side, hitting his hip. I never said my coordination was superb.

"How does it feel to be stabbed in the side, motherfucker?" I pull the knife out and swing at his kneecap next. "I don't think you will be holding anyone down with this knee again."

I can hear Amara squealing with laughter beside me while clapping her hands, but I don't bother looking at her. Instead, I swing the knife, like I'm swinging a baseball bat, and embed it right into his gut.

"Did you think it was okay to take the lives of so many innocent women? What are you thinking now—knowing that you are going to die at the hands of women?"

I start to swing again, but an arm grips me around the waist and tries pulling me back. I fight them but then *his* voice is in my ear.

"Don't make his death quick, little lamb. Let him suffer," Nyx pulls the butcher knife from my hand and hands it back to Mara. "Come on, let's get you back to the Hall. We have matters to discuss."

I let Nyx pull me from the warehouse, my chest heaving up and down as I try to catch my breath. I can't believe I did that! I was killing a man, and I was enjoying it.

"Look at me, Raya."

I look up at Nyx, who has me against the door of his car. A small smile curves his lips, and it isn't a sadistic or wicked one either. His next words are a huge surprise, though.

"I'm so proud of you, little lamb. You don't know how much that meant to me."

And then, he's opening the door and helping me into the car, not saying another word.

As soon as we returned to the Hall, I followed Nyx into his office. He had insisted that I ride with him, yet he refused to say two words to me. The tension was once again thick in the car, and although I wanted to shower as soon as we got home and wash away what we had just done, my stepbrother had other plans.

He told me to follow him, and there was no room for argument. It's best that I get this done and over with now. I don't have to work at Unholy tonight, so I want to just use the day to relax. Once I can get Nyx to give me my inheritance, I might look at places to travel to.

Nyx goes straight to his minibar and pours himself a drink and some in a second glass. When he tries handing it to me, I shake my head, refusing the liquor.

"No, thank you. I don't drink any hard stuff."

"Drink it, Raya. It's only a shot, and it will help relax you."

"Nyx, please don't—"

"Drink it."

Sighing, I take the glass from his hand and then toss it back. I wasn't expecting the smoothness of it. It was perfect. It slides down my throat easily enough, and the warmth that consumes me instantly calms my nerves.

A smirk plays on Nyx's lips. "See, I told you."

I hold the glass out to him and ask, "Can I have more, please?"

"No."

"What? Seriously?"

"If you're not used to drinking hard shit, then you have already had enough. I don't want you drunk for what we are to discuss." Nyx takes my glass and sets it down on the small bar.

"What exactly do you want to talk about, Nyx?"

"Your future," he simply states.

A sigh of relief escapes my lips at the thought of finally being able to talk to him about getting my money and getting out of his hair. I know I've mentioned it before, but he's ignored it. As much as I despise him now, I can't deny the deep attraction I still have for my stepbrother after all these years.

Some would say I need to tell him the truth about what happened that day, but would he really believe me? After all, I'm not sure what his father told him or *showed* him and how damning it truly was. No, unless he comes out and asks me for my side of the story, I will not give it to him. He seems to like assuming things, and it hurts if I'm being honest.

We knew each other inside and out; we were the best of friends, and for him not to talk to me first to find out what really happened? Well, that was the deepest cut I've ever felt. What he does now doesn't matter; nothing will ever compare to that.

"Okay..." The word trails out of my mouth as I slowly lower myself into one of the two chairs in front of his desk.

Have I mentioned how much it hurts sometimes to look at Phoenyx Beckam? To know what those lips of his feel like and how much I used to yearn for his touch? I still do, but I know our time has passed, which is another reason I must leave.

His hard gray eyes scrutinize me from across his desk once he sits. I don't dare be the first to look away; I will not show weakness in front of him. Had I looked away, I may have missed the softening of those eyes for the briefest of moments, or maybe it was just a trick of the lighting because, once again, they are as cold as ever.

"You have mentioned your trust before, and I haven't given you my answer to that..." His words trail off.

I hold my breath, concerned with what his answer may be. Contrary to what I say about leaving, if he releases my money, that will make the reality of me going all too real. I know it's for the best, but that won't make it hurt any less. I may despise who he's turned into, but I haven't stopped loving the boy he once was.

"I will release your trust to you on two conditions," Nyx informs me, and my hope begins to sink.

I should have known there would be conditions; always conditions with him. Although, he really hasn't asked for much since taking care of Ken's body for me, so maybe it won't be so bad. So, I sit here and wait for him to continue.

"First, you must agree to sign a prenup."

I stare at my stepbrother, trying to figure out what a prenup has to do with my inheritance. Ken is dead, and even if he wasn't, it would be too late to sign one since we are already married.

"I-I don't understand. Ken is dead—"

"Fuck Ken. This has nothing to do with him, and you're right; he is dead, and he will never be found..."

"So, what prenup are you talking about then?"

Suddenly, something clicks, and I straighten up in the chair, my head shaking back and forth. A grin so deviously placed on his lips greets me as Nyx nods. *No—he can't mean...*

"Oh, yes, *Lil' Sis*—you and I will finally say *I do*."

THIRTEEN

Nyx

Fuck, when Saraya started going to town with the butcher knife on that piece of shit, it was the hottest thing I'd ever seen. I wanted nothing more than to take her right there, drenched in his blood and all. Instead, I dragged her away and now I sit here in my office, telling her we will marry.

"No."

"Excuse me?" I ask, thinking I heard her wrong.

"I said no. I'm not marrying you, Nyx." She wears a straight face as she looks me dead in the eye.

"I don't remember asking, Saraya. You and I *will* marry. I need a wife who can handle this life and knows the ins and outs of this family. That wife *will* be you. You will stand by my side and bear my heirs. This will be beneficial to you as well. You will have the protection of my name."

Saraya stands and turns like she's going to walk away. "You cannot make me marry you, Nyx."

"STOP!" I growl out.

She obeys and turns to face me. Her beautiful face is full of rage, making her even more gorgeous. I crook my finger at her, commanding her to come to me.

"I'm fine right where I stand, thank you very much."

Oh, does she have a fucking mouth on her. Where is the timid woman I found on my doorstep not long ago? I'm not complaining much; I love a woman with a backbone.

"I will count to three, Raya. I will turn you over my knee if you're not standing before me. One..." I trail off and wait three seconds.

She dares to cross her arms and lift her perfectly sculpted brow at me.

"Two..." I count out; my fingers are already itching to redden her sweet ass.

Just when I'm about to say *three*, she rolls her eyes and comes forward, planting herself beside me. I push my chair back, grab her tiny wrist, and place her before me. Her ass now leans against the edge of my desk.

"Much better. Now, as I was saying—"

"I don't care to hear what you were saying, Nyx. I will not marry you. Besides, as long as Ken is missing, I can't marry another for at least two years."

I smirk.

"It's cute that you forget who the fuck I am. We are the law here in Nyte. When are you going to remember that?" I slowly drag a finger up the side of her thigh and gaze up at her. "I'll give you one week to decide whether you will accept my offer. After that, the offer is off the table, and you're on your own without my protection. You will not show your face on my doorstep again, and I will release your funds as I see fit."

Raya narrows her eyes at me.

"That sounds like blackmail to me."

I shrug and say, "I don't think of it that way. I see it as a win-win for us both. I get a wife who's fit to stand by my side..." I trace the edge of her pants across her midsection, feeling her jerky reaction when her shirt rises. My finger touches the soft patch of skin as I continue saying, "And you get the protection of my name and being the wife of one of the Gods of Nyte's Hall."

She slaps my hand away, and I catch her wrist, giving it a slight tug so she falls into my lap. I grab her around the waist to hold her back to me, knowing she can feel the hardening of my cock.

"There is no denying that your beauty still affects my body, Raya. You can't deny it, either. Just think about it, but know that you will have way more freedom as Mrs. Nyx Beckam than if you continue being Mrs. Kenneth McNally. Especially when they come looking for answers about his disappearance."

Her quick breath intake tells me she's forgotten about that part. Without my protection, she will be free game to anyone wanting to avenge Ken.

Letting my hand slide lower, I cup the apex of her thighs, and I can feel the heat radiating through the material covering her sweet cunt. I shouldn't rub or press my fingers into her because I want her begging for it. I should be strong and show her that I'm not easy to break like I was when I was younger, but fuck, I can't do it.

Sliding my hand up and then slowly moving it into her pants, she never once tries to stop me. Her breathing quickens, and as soon as my fingers find her wetness, I chuckle. I allow just the tip of one finger to enter her and then I stop, letting her feel me inside of her but not giving her what I know she wants so badly.

I let my nose run up and down her neck as I inform her of one major rule, "As long as you're thinking about being mine, Saraya, you will not engage in any kind of conversation or outing with another man. Do you understand?"

"Nyx, I—"

"Do you understand?" I cut off whatever she was about to say and then pull my finger free as I drag my hand away, ensuring it glides over that sensitive bundle of nerves.

"Yes..." she replies breathlessly.

"Yes, what?"

"Yes, I understand. I will not talk to or go anywhere with any other guy until I decide what to do."

I bring my lips to her ear, and in a low, raspy voice, I say those two little words that women seem to love, "Good girl."

Reluctantly, I help Raya off my lap, not without feeling her up and smacking her ass as I do. Without saying another word, my stepsister hurries out of my office, and I can't help but grin. I know I affect her the same way she affects me, which only makes me wonder why she did what she did all those years ago. I stick my finger into my mouth and taste her for the first time after years of going without. My cock only hardens more, and I stare at the empty doorway. *I will fucking have her, no matter the cost.*

Unfortunately, my thoughts turn to when my father made me watch the video over and over for two fucking hours. The moans of pleasure coming from the lips of the girl I loved destroyed me over and over. I never saw the face of the guy she was fucking, just his back as he hammered into her from the top. Now, I wonder whether that was Stanton or Ken at the time. I always thought it was Ken, but now I know it could have been either.

I curse my father for showing me that video and for allowing that to take place. She was still his daughter by marriage, and yet he allowed her to whore herself to two men. The disgust comes back in full force, and I go to my minibar for another drink.

Tossing the whiskey back immediately, I return to my desk and get to work drawing up the prenup. Saraya Abbott-McNally will commit herself to me whether she believes it or not. It's only a matter of time.

There's a small party going on at the Hall. It's what we do about twice a month. We invite a few friends and an abundance of women because, come on, most of the women we know like their fun with multiple men. You could say it usually turns into one big orgy, but the Heirs tend to not fuck in front of outsiders unless it's in one of the voyeur rooms at the club.

Tonight is no different; unlike past parties, I don't have any females hanging on me. I've already warned them all not to touch. Now that I've decided to marry my devious little stepsister, I will stay away from others because that's how it should be when one is devoted to someone.

I can't say that the women are staying entirely away. Four of them remain close in hopes that I change my mind. They can hope all they want; only one woman will get my attention *if* she comes down to the party. Something tells me Raya is trying to avoid me as much as possible.

I saw it in her eyes and felt it when I touched her earlier; Saraya wants me. She hates the ultimatum that I've given her, just as much as I hate how she had deceived me all those years ago, but even I cannot deny any longer that I still want her, nor can she deny wanting me. I've thought about just fucking her to get it out of my system, but something tells me that I won't be satisfied with just one time.

I don't fuck women more than once. Amara is the only woman who has ever had Nyx Beckam multiple times, and now her time has ended. It's been fun, but I started pulling away in that department before Raya returned. I felt it was time that Mara began looking around for her own man instead of fucking around with the Heirs.

Eventually, we all have to marry, and Amara wouldn't have been any of our chosen wives. She's one of our best friends; she's one of us, except the only thing she inherited was her family's debt. Although we're ending that with our generation, she's still here, serving us, because this is her home—*we* are her home. I had only fucked Mara that night to show Raya that her presence didn't matter to me. At least, it didn't at that time.

Speaking of our little devil, her laughter drifts through the room as she plants herself on the other side of a female that Zilas is deep-throating with his tongue. Amara, not being an Heir, will fuck anywhere and is not ashamed of it. She yanks the woman's dress up to her hips and finger bangs her right there.

"Gotta get you ready for my boy to fuck. His cock is so fat, it will tear you in two if you aren't ready," Mara warns the woman with amusement. "You should see the damage he does when he takes my ass, but it's oh so fucking good." She bites the woman's earlobe and must shove more fingers into her because the woman moans really loudly.

Zilas lifts her leg so Mara has better access, and now the whole room can witness it all. I find it amusing that these women come here knowing they will be used in humiliating and depraved ways, but still—they come. No pun intended. We respect them unless they give us a reason not to, like attaching themselves to us.

I get that all women want to be *the one* to catch our eye; they all know of the five-year time frame for us to find a wife. They all want us, but what they don't understand is that is precisely why we don't allow them to get attached to us. Our future wives will not be found at any of our parties. We cannot marry a woman willing to give herself to multiple men like they do and who we know are only out for our money.

Glancing around the room, I see that Cray is playing strip pool with a female, who appears to be losing since she's down to just her panties. Her small tits are perky as she stands there waiting for Cray to make his next shot. They all know he's a pool shark, so I can't feel sorry for them one bit.

Adrik is carrying a passed out woman who allowed him to give her sleeping pills just so he could rail her unconscious body. He will record it and make her watch it once she wakes up and he will fuck her again as she does. It's his kink and as long as the women are aware of it, I don't say a word, none of us do.

I return to watching Mara and Zilas prepping the woman. I like being a voyeur; sex is an art and I appreciate a good piece of art. My phone buzzes with an incoming message and I reach into my pocket to retrieve my phone. I'm smirking at Mara as she shoves her fourth finger inside the woman after she begs Mara for more.

One of the women sitting at my feet must get bored because she gets up and heads over to Cray. *It's no skin off my back.* I glance at the other three women, and they smile at me, but I don't return it. Instead, I bring up the message on my phone, and alarm bells start to go off.

UNKNOWN: I know what baby sister did.

Before I can respond back, not that I will, another message comes through. This time, it's a video message—one that has me filling with rage. In the video, I see Saraya walking into the kitchen. There is no sound on the video, but I don't really need audio when the actions alone have me boiling to a point where I feel like I may explode.

When Ken backhands Raya the way he did, I almost break my phone as my fist tightens around it. I make myself loosen my hold, only to tighten it again as he bends her over the counter and tries raping her. It's not until the next image that I loosen my grip again, and a grin spreads across my face. Raya is stabbing the fuck out of her husband, making me proud as fuck.

The video goes black, and I sober up. Pushing myself out of the chair, the women at my feet frown at my departure, but I don't give a fuck. Only one woman matters at the moment, and she's not here.

Without a word to anyone, I walk out of the billiard room and head toward my wing of the house. If my little lamb is still indecisive about marrying me, this may help convince her. She needs me now more than ever.

FOURTEEN

Saraya

"The fucking nerve of him!" I say out loud once I'm in the confines of my room. "Where does he get off touching me the way he did?"

You never tried to stop him.

Arguing with myself isn't helping. I'm pissed that Nyx would just take what he wants because he's Nyx fucking Beckam and thinks that he can do whatever he wants. At least, that's what I'm trying to convince myself is the case. However, deep down, I'm pissed that he hadn't finished what he had started.

What I should be more pissed over is the fact that he thinks we will marry. I will not marry without love ever again. He cannot make me go through with it. I'll sell whatever I can find at my house and leave. I just have to figure out how to get into the house without being seen.

Stripping out of my blood-soiled clothes, I turn the shower on and step under the hot spray. The water turns pink, and my thoughts return to my stepbrother's office. How could he touch me while I'm covered in someone else's blood? Does he get off on killing?

The more important question is, what changed his mind about me? Granted, I've seen the lust in his eyes a time or two, but the way he talks to me and treats me as if he genuinely hates my guts gives me pause as to what his motives are now. Why does he think it's a good idea for us to marry?

I miss the boy he was, and my best friend, but Nyx isn't that person anymore. So, I may still have our good memories of him, but I cannot see myself with him now, no matter what my treacherous body says. I'm sure he is still good deep inside, but my *betrayal* did too much damage.

It wouldn't hurt trying to explain to him what happened.

It's far too late for that. Nyx didn't want to trust in my loyalty to him back then, so what's the point? The damage has been done. I'll just bide my time and figure out where to go from here once this week is up. I have some savings of my own, but I'm not sure it would be safe to pull it out.

By now, my employer has undoubtedly gone to the police since I haven't been in to work, and I haven't called them. In all this chaos, I'd forgotten about it, truth be told. I think about my outing with Mika, and I curse.

"Shit! That was so careless of me. I can't be out in public like that until this shit with Ken is cleared up." Mumbling to myself, I quickly finish drying off and step out of the shower.

There isn't anything I can do about it now. I'm just lucky that none of Ken's police buddies spotted me while I was out and about. Then again, what I participated in this afternoon is just as bad. *I seem to be turning into a serial killer.*

I laid down after my shower, exhaustion finally taking over after the eventful afternoon I had and then the lovely little *chat* with Nyx. It's dark out when I open my eyes, and my stomach rumbles. Yawning, I stretch, and suddenly, a feeling comes over me, which makes me think I'm not alone.

As soon as I make a move for the lamp beside my bed and light floods the room, *his* deep, masculine voice saying, "Good evening, little lamb," scares the shit out of me. I almost fall off the bed, needing to grab the nightstand to catch myself before I did just that.

"Jesus, Nyx!"

"My bad."

"What the fuck are you doing in my room?" I growl as I run my fingers through my hair.

He only shrugs. "I knocked; you didn't answer."

"So, what? You figured you could just come in and make yourself at home?" I ask in disbelief, "How long have you been here?"

"Long enough to make me want to ram my cock into your ass as it stuck out from under the covers, but not long enough that I ran out of the willpower holding me from doing just that."

The smirk on his face can be taken two ways; either he's fucking with me, or he's enjoying making me blush. Knowing his sadistic tendencies, it's most likely the latter.

"What is it you want? Why are you here?"

Nyx just stares at me. His hard gray eyes assess me longer than I'd like before he finally speaks. "I got a message, and I thought you needed to be aware of it."

"Okay..."

"Will you put some fucking clothes on, for fuck's sake?" Nyx scowls at my attire.

"I'm in sleep shorts and a cami because I was sleeping! *You* are in *my* space, uninvited, so you can deal with it. If you can fuck with your door open, then I can wear my pajamas any time I want."

"Has anyone ever told you that you're mouthy as fuck?" He's amused by my rising temper.

"I never used to be. It seems like you're bringing out the worst in me."

"I never said that it was a bad thing." He grins, then says, "I'm just saying you're mouthy."

Rolling my eyes, I cross my arms and glare at my stepbrother sitting in the chair facing my side of the bed. How he can look so devilishly handsome and yet have such a shitty attitude is beyond me. He's cocky and thinks he's God's gift to women.

You like his cocky attitude; it makes you wet.

I want to slap my inner self for reminding me of these small bad habits of mine. I can't deny the truth of my thoughts, though. I just can't shake Phoenyx Beckam.

"Are you going to tell me why you're here, or am I just to believe that you're a creeper who loves watching women sleep?"

"My name isn't Adrik," he states.

My brows dip low. "Adrik likes watching women sleep?"

Nyx gives me a wicked grin. "Actually, he prefers to fuck them while they sleep, but enough about Adrik," he says, then taps on his phone before tossing it to me. "Let's talk about how the fuck someone has video footage of you stabbing your husband."

"Huh?" I look down at his phone and watch the scene from the last night I was in my home. "I don't understand?"

"My men checked the camera footage while doing clean-up, but there was nothing to erase." Nyx sits back and crosses his right leg over his left knee.

"Of course, there wasn't. I was sensible enough to erase it..."

"Smart girl. Now then, who the fuck could have gotten it in that short of time?"

"I-I honestly don't know," I stammer softly, unable to take my eyes off the video.

"You do know what this means, don't you?"

I look at my stepbrother and don't have to ask what he means. I can see it in his eyes. The bastard will try and use this to get me to agree with the marriage.

Narrowing my eyes, I shake my head. "This means nothing. I still have a week to decide."

"Somebody knows that you stabbed your husband numerous times!" Nyx sneers, but it doesn't scare me.

I shrug. "That video also shows what Ken did to me first. It was self-defense—"

"They can doctor it, Saraya!"

It's on the tip of my tongue to say, *like the one your father doctored when he had his friend rape me,* but I stop myself from doing so. Instead, I flip the covers off me and climb from the bed.

"I'm not going to let another asshole dictate my life! I've had enough of that to last a lifetime," I say pointedly at Nyx.

Of course, he would think I'm only talking about Ken. If he only knew that the first one to ever dictate it was his own flesh and blood. I see a flash of hurt cross Nyx's features for a second before his face hardens again.

"Call me what you will—"

"I meant whoever it was that sent you the video." I correct what he thought I meant. Although, he's an asshole, too.

"Where the fuck are you going?" Nyx is out of the chair and approaching me as I head for the door.

"I'm hungry and don't want to fight with you right now. I don't have the strength."

He grabs my arm and spins me around until my back is against the dresser. "We need to talk about this, Saraya!"

"No. *You* feel the need to talk about this. I want to eat and fuel up before going toe-to-toe with you. Now, please let me go."

"Make me..." He's toying with me now.

The fucker is going to play with me until I give in. Well, newsflash, he's never been around me when I'm hungry. I'll do whatever it takes to get me to the food faster, but talking isn't one.

"*Now,* you're being an asshole."

"Mm, how about I get in your asshole?" His voice lowers to a dangerously sexy tone.

"In your dreams..." I try to shove him away, but it's no use. I glare at him and order, "Move," through clenched teeth."

He steps closer, smirking when our chests touch.

Tingles shoot through me, and I try to move away, but it's useless because I'm stuck between two hard objects, a dresser, and a big oaf. I try searching my brain for ways to escape this, but I can only see one way—shock him into moving. So, smiling inwardly, I wait until he leans in close enough.

When he starts to say something, I go up onto my toes and crash my mouth against his, hoping to shock him into backing up. Only—it doesn't. It has the opposite effect on him as he grabs the back of my head and pushes his tongue into my mouth.

The kiss takes me back to another time. A time when we couldn't get enough of one another. I've missed his kiss, among other things, and I find myself fisting his shirt in my hand, trying to keep him close.

A moment later, I feel Nyx's hand slip into my shorts, and I'm brought back to the present. Panic takes hold, and I try to come up with an excuse for him to stop, but there isn't any, and to be honest, I don't need one; my denial should be enough.

"No!"

I shove him back with all my might, and he must not have expected it because he stumbles back, dazed. I use this time to move past him and to the door, flinging it open and rushing from the room.

"Saraya!" Nyx calls out.

"I'm hungry, Nyx..."

I'm just getting to the top of the landing, where the four wings meet when I'm shoved against another hard surface. Nyx's rugged body is unrelenting, and he rubs himself against me while my back is to the wall.

"You think I should give this to you, little lamb?" His cock is large and pulsating under his pants as he presses harder.

"Oh, please, I know you, Nyx. You wouldn't want to get any diseases. Remember, I'm damaged goods..."

"That's not what I said—"

I cut him off, "Stop trying to fucking edge me. If you don't want me, then just fucking stop because I'm getting bored with your antics." I try pushing at his chest, but he's ready this time. "Nyx, stop..."

My plea is a pathetic one as it comes out a bit breathless. His bulge is rubbing right on that sensitive bundle, and I can't stop the slight moan that escapes me.

"Admit it, Raya. You want me..."

"Fuck you..."

"Do you really want me to? Do you want me to slide these shorts to the side and thrust my cock into your wet cunt?" he continues to tease.

"Nyx—Jesus. If you're going to do it, then just do it and get it over with; otherwise, stop fucking around and leave me alone..."

I try to sound condescending, but I'm unsure if I pull it off.

He moves so we are cheek to cheek, his day's growth scratching me as he bites out, "What if I told you that I will never give you what once belonged to you, what you could have had any time you wanted until you decided to throw it away?"

His words reach deep into my soul, but all they do is anger me when I think of what I did, of what I gave up for *him!* So, gritting my teeth, I respond in a manner that I don't even recognize myself—a response that comes from over ten years of built-up anger and hurt.

"Either fuck me if you're going to fuck me, Nyx, or leave me the hell alone, because I'm so fucking tired of your bullshit—"

I'm not sure when he pulls himself out, but suddenly, my leg is lifted, and my shorts are moved to the side as he thrusts himself into me. He's huge and lengthy, and when he buries himself deep inside, I can't help the cry that breaks free from my lips at feeling so full.

It's left me in a daze, trying to get my thoughts together. *Nyx is inside of me. He did it; he actually did it!* By the time the shock wears off, he already has both my wrists gathered in one hand and is holding them above my head as his other hand holds my leg at his hip. Pulling out, he slams back into me.

"This is what you wanted, isn't it, little lamb—my cock inside you?" His hot gaze burns into me, and I can't even form any thoughts.

Nyx is right. This is what I wanted, whether I believed it or not. This just feels—right. I don't respond to him, though. I will never admit that he's right. However, what I do instead is almost equivalent to admitting it. My moan is loud and long as he takes from me what he wants.

His lips come to mine, but he doesn't kiss me. Instead, he asks, "Does it feel as you imagined all those years ago, Raya?"

"God, yes!" My willpower leaves me as I answer him, not caring anymore as I chase the climax that I feel is just beyond my reach.

Nyx chuckles. "I knew it. I knew you would be a slut for my cock. After all, you're letting me fuck you right here in the hallway. My friends will see us, but I think you like that notion, don't you?"

His words sink in, and that's when I hear the voices coming up the stairs. Laughter followed by a female squealing echoes through the hall. I try pulling my hands from his grip, but he only tightens it.

"Nyx..."

"No, not until you come, little lamb." He plunges in even deeper, hitting that perfect spot, and I'm a goner.

I don't care if anyone else is in the vicinity. I'm there; all I have to do is reach a little further...

"Oh fuck, that's hot!" Cray's voice is full of lust.

When I open my eyes, I see the Heir standing at the top of the steps with a woman over his shoulder. She can't see, but Cray's taking in the whole scene. For some reason, the sight turns me on even more, and I thrust my hips more, fucking Nyx the best I can in the position I'm in as I stare at one of his best friends.

"See, you like being watched. It seems my little lamb is an exhibitionist," he grunts out as he continues to thrust.

"How about we take it to a room and have fun together?" Cray grins.

"Nobody...fucking...touches...her...but...me," Nyx says with each thrust. "Watch all you want, but I'll be the only one fucking...this...cunt from here on out," he enunciates some of his words with deep thrusts.

As he states this, I can feel the spittle landing on my cheek when it shoots out from between his clenched teeth. I'm done for. I come hard against the wall in the hallway as his friend watches Nyx drive his cock into me over and over.

"OH GOD...FUCK YES!" I cry out.

In the next instant, Nyx thrusts deeply once more and holds himself as he spills inside of me. He didn't wear a condom. *Fuck. I left my birth control behind at my house in my haste to leave.* His groan as he continues to unload makes me forget about everything else, as yet another climax takes hold of me.

FIFTEEN

Nyx

Well, fuck.

This is *not* what I had planned when I came to her room. Although her ass was looking very tempting when she was asleep, I was proud of myself for not doing what I wanted to do. I wanted to wake her as I slid my cock deep inside her. Sex with Saraya was never supposed to happen unless we were married. Now, I don't know if I can stay away from her.

I press my forehead against hers as I catch my breath. I haven't come that hard in a very long time. Raya's cunt fits me like a fucking glove, wrapping around my girth like it was made just for me.

"Let me go, Nyx."

Her voice brings me back, and I stare at her, trying to get my bearings. My cock is still deep inside her while my hand continues to hold her knee against my hip. I can feel our mixed fluids seeping out around me. Her face doesn't hold that blissful look like most women have after I've fucked them. If anything, she looks panicked—almost scared.

Saraya's eyes bounce back and forth between me and somewhere behind me, and I'm now reminded that we have an audience. I want to know what Raya is thinking. Is she pissed? She egged me on—practically dared me to do it.

"Leave us, Cray," I order my friend without taking my eyes off Raya.

"Man, that was hot as hell. Fucking your stepsister like a starved man..." His voice trails off as he heads toward his wing.

"Let me go, Nyx—please," Raya chokes out.

I notice her eyes glisten, and instead of being the caring man I should be, I harden my resolve because I don't want my little lamb to weaken. I want to see the fight inside her. It's the only way she will survive Nyx Beckam.

Letting go of her wrist, I grip her neck while keeping her knee at my hip. I smirk wickedly, licking my lips before biting the bottom one. I push deeper into her sweet cunt as I dip my head and take in the scent of her.

"I didn't say I was through with you."

She pushes at my chest with little effort while my name dances on her lips, "Nyx..."

"I've fucked this cunt, so it's mine now, Raya. You should know that I never fuck a woman more than once, but you, my little lamb—you will be the first."

"This was a mistake..." she says with a moan.

I squeeze her throat more, reminding her, "You came to me; remember that."

I bite her earlobe and start fucking her hard once more. Releasing her throat, I grab her other leg and lift her until she locks her feet together at my lower back.

"Say it, Raya. Say this cunt is mine now."

"No..."

I growl and then turn us around. Without pulling out, I take us back to her room, not bothering to shut the door. When we get to her bed, I reluctantly pull out and rip her shorts off her before thrusting back into her.

"You will see that you need me, Raya—make no mistake."

"You don't even like me," she says as she meets me thrust for thrust.

"Who says we have to like each other?" I ask, then spread her legs wider so I can watch my cock own her gorgeous cunt.

"Oh fuck—you're so deep!" Raya grunts.

I chuckle. "And you're taking it like a good little slut, aren't you? You fucking love it—admit it."

"Fuck you..."

"You already are honey."

I pull out, flip her over, and yank her hips up before plunging into her heat once again. With one hand on her hip and the other on her shoulder, I hold her in place and just fuck her hard. I'm going to come again, and I'm taking her with me.

My little lamb fists the bedding as she cries out each time I sink into her. My hand squeezes her hip even harder as I get closer, and just knowing that I'm going to leave my mark upon her body sends me over.

"Fucking come with me, Raya!" I order through a clenched jaw.

Like a good fucking girl, her cunt constricts around my cock and gives me what I want. We come together once more, and I'm left leaning over her with my forehead pressed against her back as I catch my breath.

I need to get the fuck out of here.

I hiss when I pull out of her, already missing the warmth that her cunt provides, but this isn't a fucking Hallmark movie. I'm not going to turn into a sap and cuddle with her. Instead, I tuck myself back into my pants while I watch her still positioned with her ass in the air.

I see the marks I've left already and smirk before I slap her ass. "Thanks, Raya, it's been fun, but I've got a party to return to. I'll be expecting your answer by the end of the week."

Yeah, it's a dick move, but I figured it'd be best if I keep it this way. I don't need her catching feelings for me. Even if we marry, it will be one of convenience; there can never be any love between us.

My little lamb has been hiding from me all weekend. Aside from the surveillance footage not showing her leaving, the only telltale sign that she's still here is that coffee is made every morning. I had got rid of my personal staff a few months back. It was ridiculous to have a staff when it was only me living in this wing. I suppose I should bring them back.

Raya is pissed at me, and I don't blame her one bit, but it's how it needs to be, for me anyway. I can't let her sink her claws into me again; I don't think I would survive it a second time, no matter how tough I am. I shouldn't say I wouldn't survive, but anybody within ten feet of me probably wouldn't survive. I would lose the rest of my humanity for sure.

Lil' Sis has grown up to be a gorgeous dark-haired beauty, and now that I've been inside of her, I need to possess her in every way. The other night, I said I didn't want her catching feelings, but that's a lie. I want every little piece of her, including her heart, but it will not be returned.

I received two more messages over the weekend, threatening they would make Raya pay if she didn't turn herself in. My men are working around the clock trying to figure out who this fucker is. Whoever it is, they are fucking with the wrong woman. Conniving bitch or not, Raya is mine, and no one will threaten her.

"Hey, do you happen to have the files on that project for the new housing units?" Zilas comes strolling into my office.

"Yeah," I reply and get up to grab them from the filing cabinet. "You know, I looked these over, and it really isn't a bad deal."

My friend sighs, "I know, but it's too close to the east side where we have yet to clean up the drug houses. I'm not sure anyone will want to live in that area. I have a different location in mind, but we may have to try and buy a portion of the land from the Kappels."

I scoff, "Do you honestly think they will sell to us when we're trying to run their drugs out of town?"

Shrugging, Zilas says, "It's a piece of land that they aren't using, and it's useless to them. They wouldn't be very smart to deny us the sale."

"Well, good luck with that."

Zilas scrutinizes me, then crosses his arms before saying, "Cray told us what happened the night of the party. You've been pretty quiet since that night. Do you want to talk about it?"

"There's nothing to talk about. I fucked her, claimed her, and will marry her as soon as she gets her head out of her ass."

My friend chuckles and shakes his head. "I hope that isn't how you explained it to Raya."

"Not in so many words..."

"Jesus, Nyx."

"What? I'm not going to forget her betrayal just because I finally fucked her. This marriage is one of convenience and that's all. I don't know why my father was so hard-headed over us being together. Saraya has always proven to be a good partner in this life."

"Your father was an asshole, Nyx. That doesn't mean you have to follow in his footsteps."

I glare at my friend.

Another knock on my doorframe draws our attention from the topic at hand. Amara stands just outside the door, smirking.

"I don't mean to interrupt your lover's spat..."

I roll my eyes. "What do you want, Mara?"

Zilas and I watch as she sashays into my office in one of her skintight suits. She drags her finger across my friend's midsection and winks at him before coming over and placing her palms on my desk.

"Little birdie told me you got your dick wet in Lil' Sis. Is that true? Did I miss it? I heard it was a fun time—right in the hallway for all to see." Mara licks her lips as her eyes go to my crotch before dragging them back up to meet my eyes with a cocked brow.

"Cray needs to mind his own fucking business. I fuck where I want, and I fuck who I want, and he knows this. He's just pissed because he wanted to join, and I wouldn't let him," I explain, bored of having to do so.

"Will you ever let us join? It could be fun. It's been a while since the five of us have been together, and having a new toy to play with, well..."

I glare at Amara but try to keep the anger out of my tone when I reply, "Raya is not a new toy. She *will be* my wife, and all of you will respect her as that. I will not share her with anyone."

Zilas's grin annoys me, and Mara's stunned look makes me feel bad. After all, she was there to help pick up the pieces of my broken heart, along with the guys. Pinching the bridge of my nose, I take a deep breath and exhale.

"I'm sorry, Mara. I know what she did to me, and I won't forget it, but I need a wife and even you can't deny that she would fit the description best." I stare at her, hoping she sees the struggle I'm going through with all this myself.

This is a struggle for me. I keep telling myself that I hate the bitch, but at the same time, I'm drawn to her, and now—I'm addicted. I've been cursing myself out for taking Saraya like I did. I should have waited, but she was like a siren calling to me. I just hope she doesn't steal my soul because she's already taken my heart.

"No, it's fine. I get it. Just remember that I'm not afraid to gut her now that we are older. I hope she knows that." Mara examines her nails like she's bored with the conversation, and I smile.

"I know this, and I'm sure she does, too. But honestly, she's refusing at the moment."

"Wait. What?" my feisty little friend gasps.

I shrug as I relay to them what Raya told me, "She says that she doesn't want anyone telling her how to live her life anymore. It doesn't matter if I'm trying to keep her safe."

I don't know why I even care. If Raya doesn't want my protection, why am I even pushing it? *Because she's back in your grasp, and your father is not in your way this time.* I keep telling myself this, but I honestly don't know if it was just my father who kept us apart. Would she have given herself to another had we stayed together? After we were caught, it hadn't taken her long to jump into bed with someone.

Something nags at me, but I can't figure out what it is. Amara clearing her throat reminds me that I'm not alone, and I give her and Zilas my attention once again. I hadn't realized that Mara had come around and now stood between me and the desk. I was too far into my thoughts to notice her move.

"So, does this mean there will be no more Mara sandwiches with Nyx?" she asks, but before I can answer, Zilas steps up to her.

"You don't need him, little devil. Adrik and I have got you. We will get you taken care of like we always do."

Amara smirks and turns toward Zilas, lifting her knee and letting him hold it. "But it's so much fun when all four of my guys fuck me into a coma."

"Okay, you two can go fuck somewhere else. I've got work to do." I shove them to the side and out of my way, grinning.

"Come on Zi... I've got a new toy that I want to try out, and since Nyx is being a pansy ass, I guess you're the lucky one who gets to try it out with me."

"Mm, count me in, as long as it's you that it's going inside—not me." My friend licks his lips and carries Mara out the door, grabbing the folder he came for as he walks away.

"Don't forget to look into that land, Zilas," I call out to him. "You're supposed to break ground in a month!"

I chuckle as I hear them snickering, and then Mara squeal. That's how it's always been between us. We always had fun, but now that Raya is here, it's time to get serious and think about the future. I always knew I was meant to have a future with her, only now, it's going to be much different than the two of us dreamt up all those years ago.

SIXTEEN

Saraya

"Thanks, Raya, it's been fun..."

Nyx's words have been running repeatedly in my head all weekend. That egotistical son of a bitch had the nerve to say that to me! How did I ever love him? I don't care what happened in the past; how he acts towards me now is uncalled for.

Then why can I not seem to stay away from him, and why do his actions turn me on so much?

I've been hiding in my room all weekend because I know he's watching my every move. If I'm going to leave, it's got to be once we're at the club. I'm hostess tonight, and I will be on my own. I'll use my break to slip away, and it'll be too late by the time they realize I'm gone; that's my plan anyway.

I thought about finding my own way to the club tonight, but I don't want to get on his bad side just before I leave. I can't let anything get in the way of me leaving. I know that if I stay, I will become trapped, with no say in how I live my life. Nyx has given me a week to decide whether to marry him, but I know he's only pretending to give me a choice. In the end, my stepbrother will get his way.

If it was Phoenyx, I'd marry him in a heartbeat. I still love *that* guy, but Nyx is my monster. The one your parents warn you about, and maybe that's why my lady bits fire up whenever he's around. Something about the way bad boys turn up the heat in every way, even when they don't realize they're doing it, gets me fired up and my lady juices flowing. However, in my stepbrother's case, he does know, and he uses it against me.

A knock sounds on my door, and I roll my eyes, thinking it's Nyx. To my surprise, Adrik stands on the other side when I open the door, prepared to tell Nyx to leave me alone. In his hand, Adrik holds out a clothing bag on a hanger with a boutique bag in his other hand.

"For you, Raya."

"What is this?" I ask after taking in his devastatingly good looks.

All the Heirs are drop-dead gorgeous, but the issue is they all know it, so you can only imagine how big their egos are. However, Adrik and Zilas are the two who are the most down-to-earth and tolerable to talk to.

"This would be your evening's attire. A message was also passed along. The rest of your wardrobe will be delivered tomorrow afternoon." He winks at me and gives me his signature smile.

I sigh. "If Nyx would let me go to my house, he wouldn't have to buy me new clothes."

Adrik's smile falters a little before he clears his throat and says, "He's only trying to protect you. You came here for just that, did you not?"

I hate that he's right, but I nod and reply, "Yeah, I guess so."

"Listen." Adrik brushes past me and lays the items down on my bed. "Nyx may seem a little rough around the edges, but you must understand why." He lowers his voice and glances toward the door before he says, "You didn't see the state he was in when all that shit went down. I think there's more to it, and I'll only say this once. You can take my advice or not, but I think that if there *is* something that needs to be said about the past, it needs to come out. That's the only way things will become easier for you."

I cross my arms and look down at the floor. "A lot happened back then, and some things are better left in the past. Some things should have been brought up when it happened, but they weren't, and I'm afraid it may be a little too late to fix it."

Adrik squeezes my arm and says, "It's never too late—"

"What the fuck is going on in here?"

I jump at Nyx's angry voice, but Adrik only chuckles. "Down, boy. I was delivering your gift and just giving your girl here a few words of advice."

"I'm not his girl!" I say vehemently.

"Yeah, okay..." Adrik grins and heads for the door but stops and places his hand on his friend's shoulder. "You never have to worry about any of us Heirs trying to take your girl. We know she's off limits."

I roll my eyes at Adrik's words but then turn when I see Nyx's glare on me. As they exchange a few more words, I walk to the items on the bed and open the clothing bag. A gasp escapes my lips when I see the black, sequined evening gown. It's beautiful but different from what the hostess would wear. Although it is sexy, it's more on the elegant side.

"Is something wrong with the dress?"

I jump again, only this time, Nyx is standing right behind me, his hand slipping around my waist. He pulls me against him and nuzzles my neck. I try to pull away, only succeeding in having him tighten his hold on me.

"Nyx, please let me go."

"What's wrong, little lamb?"

"Stop calling me that. I have a name..."

He chuckles. "I like my name for you better. Now, why don't you go get ready? We'll leave in an hour."

When he lets go and steps back, I quickly move away as I reassure him, "I'll be ready."

Smirking, Nyx turns and walks to the door. "Oh, one more thing," he says, turning back to look at me. "Wear your hair up tonight. I want to see that pretty neck of yours."

My mouth is agape as I watch him leave my room. *Did he just compliment me?* With his hands in his pockets, he begins to whistle. Nyx Beckam—whistling! Does he seriously think he's *that* amusing?

I stand staring at the empty doorway momentarily before snapping out of it. I'm irritated that I let him get to me this way. Thank God he mostly kept his hands to himself; otherwise, he would have figured out that his little show did not leave me unaffected. My treacherous body can go eat a dick—preferably not Nyx's.

❧✠❧

The slit up the left side of my dress shows off more leg than I would like, but apparently, it's just what Nyx likes. As I sit in his car, the fabric keeps parting, but when I try holding it closed, my stepbrother growls and shoves my hand away.

"Leave it. I bought the dress for a reason."

"Why do I not have a say in what I wear? My body, my choice—you know?"

He gives me a genuine smile, or at least I think it is, until he opens his mouth and ruins it.

"When you're with me in my club, you wear what I buy you. I will never buy you anything inappropriate—well, at least not for others to see."

He rests his hand on my bare thigh, where my dress keeps opening. When I try pushing his hand away, his grip tightens, and he gives me a warning look. It's not that it repulses me—it's actually the opposite. So, with a racing heart, I sit here, trying to keep my breathing even so he doesn't become aware of what he's doing to me.

I'm so lost in thought that I don't realize we have arrived at the club until we pull into his parking spot. A chill comes over me as soon as he lifts his hand from my thigh, but again, I don't let it be known. I need to get out of here tonight. I don't think I can handle this treatment—I'll give in too easily.

"Stay here until I've checked the area."

I swear, I've never rolled my eyes as much as I have since living back at the Hall. He grips my chin and turns hard gray eyes on me.

"You wanted my protection; now deal with it."

He exits the car without waiting to see if I'll respond. I don't bother watching him until his frame shows up in the side mirror on my door. He's wearing a black suit with a crisp white shirt. The collar is open at the top, showing off some of his tattoos. I lick my lips; I remember the way he looked when I saw him fucking Mara. Broad with rippling muscles throughout his chest and torso.

When he opens my door, he holds his hand out for me to take. He stares at my legs until I cover them up, then he goes back to watching our surroundings. It's more than usual, and suddenly, I get a prickling feeling that we are being watched. I know it's his actions that are making me this paranoid, so I try to push the feeling aside.

Nyx refuses to let go of my hand until we're tucked away inside the elevator. Unlike last time, he pushes the button for the floor we're going to and I'm not sure if I'm happy or sad about it. The memory of our first time in the elevator flashes through my mind, and my pulse quickens again.

The car stops just before we get to our floor, and I see it's Nyx's doing. He turns to face me, looking me over as though he's ensuring I'm put together properly. When his eyes meet mine, it becomes difficult to swallow. I try so hard to remain held together in front of him, but then he looks at me the way he's doing right now, and I almost fall apart.

"Thank you for wearing your hair up."

"It's not like I had much choice when the *Boss* gives an order," I state sarcastically.

His smirk is sexy as fuck.

"I have you dressed this way and wearing your hair a certain way because you will be with me tonight."

Alarm bells start going off in my head. "What do you mean I'm going to be with you? I'm hostess tonight; it's on the schedule."

"Yes, well, the schedule has changed. I want you at my side tonight. Some important clients are coming in and I want you on your best behavior. In fact, I will be introducing you as my girlfriend."

"What?" I choke out.

"These men are sharks, and they love fresh meat. I don't want you working up front while they are here. I want you by my side."

"Who are they?"

"You've already met two of them," he states, and a look of annoyance comes over him.

"The twins..."

"Yeah, the Kappel twins. Their father and his brother are coming in, along with Jarod and Jax. We've been trying to get them to move their drug business out of Nyte, and I'm hoping we can do just that after tonight."

"You saw what the one twin did the last time he saw me. What makes you think he will keep his hands to himself now?" I ask.

"Simple. This time, you're mine. Which is why you will play the doting girlfriend."

"Oh? Would you like to put a collar around my neck and have me kneel at your feet while I'm at it?" Sarcasm always helps when I'm feeling unnerved, and I definitely feel it now.

"That would be a pleasant sight, but something tells me you will never be happy kneeling at my feet."

I scoff, "Like you care about what makes me happy—"

"Hey!" Nyx grabs my chin. "Whether you believe it or not, I don't want to see you unhappy, even after everything."

We stare at one another briefly, and the weirdest thing happens. I believe what Nyx says, and I nod slightly. He lets go of my chin and caresses the backs of his fingers down my cheek.

"Now, be a good girl and take my arm."

I narrow my eyes at him.

"The moment these doors open, I want you in girlfriend mode, which includes smiling and staring adoringly at me," he states as he smirks.

"You're pushing your luck, Beckam."

He tsks at me, "That's *baby* to you." He presses the button, and the elevator doors open before I can give him more of my mind.

Instead, I paste a smile on my face. He wants a doting girlfriend, then he will get one, but I doubt he will like it very much. A smirk replaces my smile as I walk beside Nyx, holding onto his arm.

SEVENTEEN

Nyx

I'm walking around with a constant hard-on of my own making. I knew Raya would look killer in that fucking dress, but I wasn't counting on just how fucking sexy it would be. I'm second-guessing having her in the room while we talk shop with the Kappels.

I was more concerned with Raya being out on the floor when they arrived that I hadn't thought about what they would be ogling while she was in the room with us. She's an intelligent girl, and hopefully, she will heed my warning and stay by my side. Otherwise, Cale will be right outside the door, and I will have him take her to my private room here at the club if need be. She may not like that so much. Bad things happen to naughty girls who get taken to my private room here.

I'm not going to lie; walking through the club with Raya on my arm feels right. I can feel the anger I have toward her slowly dissipating, but my lack of trust in her is still holding on strong. I'm still determining how this will work without the trust, but I have to at least try. I'll still make her pay to an extent; after all, she did me so dirty and needs to answer for her actions, but I'll make sure she gets pleasure from doing so.

I won't be a complete dick, but she will be mine to do with as I please. Call me what you will, but even though Raya will make up for her betrayal, I will make it worth her while at the same time. After all, I am a lover when it comes to women. I may want to conquer them, but it's always in a good way. I'm just not sure if my little lamb is ready for what I have in store for her.

Passing the bar, I nod at Rigger, indicating that he should send my usual to my booth. He looks at Raya, smiling, as he holds up a bottle of the bubbly, but I shake my head. My little lamb will drink what I drink. I have a feeling that she would prefer it over the girlie shit.

"Are we not going to your office?" Raya looks around nervously.

"We will, but for now, I want to enjoy the Shibari performance that will be on stage soon," I tell her. Then I lean close to her ear and ask, "Have you ever been tied up, little lamb?"

I hear her little intake of breath, but she gives me the cutest little glare. "Does being handcuffed while your ex-husband takes what he wants from you count?"

The grin that I'm wearing at making her uncomfortable drops. Suddenly, I want to bring that fucker back to life so I can kill him all over again. Placing my hand around her waist as we walk, I pull her into me more.

"Nothing that motherfucker ever did to you will ever be anything like what I have planned for you. I promise you will love *every fucking thing* I do to you even while you're hating me."

She gives me a big fake smile, remembering to play her role, as she asks, "Who says I hate you, *baby*?"

I bite back my grin. "The looks you give me can cut through bulletproof glass. You would rather murder me in my sleep than be here with me right now."

"Hm, that does sound tempting, but fortunately for you, I'm really trying not to turn into a serial killer. I mean—I've already killed two people."

I know I'm an ass for making her believe she killed Ken, but I'm not ready to give up my fun with her just yet. It's all I've got, keeping her under my roof at the moment. Until I'm ready to forgive her enough for what she did to me, I'll let her keep believing what she does. Besides, someone out there wants to see her pay for Ken's disappearance. I'll be damned if I let them get to her.

We reach our booth, or alcove, as some would call it, and I pull a chair out for her to sit before I take the one closest to the entrance. Hillary, one of the waitresses, brings us a bottle of Johnny Walker and pours a few fingers into a glass for me before doing the same for Raya.

"In the future, please serve Saraya first." I'm not an ass about it; it's just a little reminder.

"Yes, Mr. Beckam. I'm sorry."

Hillary scuttles away, and I feel my little lamb's heated stare.

"What?"

"Why would you say that to her?"

I lift my glass to my lips and savor the smoothness of the liquid as it slides down my throat before answering Raya. "Because they should always pour the woman's drink first. It's what they are taught, or have you forgotten that tidbit from the one day you waitressed?"

Rolling her eyes, she doesn't answer me but brings her glass to her lips. I watch her take a sip, and it's just as I thought; her eyes light up as soon as the whiskey hits her throat. She's my little whiskey girl—I knew it.

When I said I wanted her to play the doting girlfriend, I didn't think she would follow through with it. Since we've been sitting here, in my semi-hidden alcove, she's done just that, even when nobody has their eyes on us. Her body is pressed into my side while her right elbow rests on the back of my chair. Her fingers twirl in the hair that has grown just a little too long down the back of my neck.

I've placed my hand on her bared left knee thanks to the slit, and it's remained there this whole time. I can feel every time the performers do something that turns Raya on because her thighs squeeze together. I finally allow my hand to slide up her silky thigh until my thumb grazes her panties. Her intake of breath tells me that she's fully aware of my hand being so close to her heat. I turn my head, so I can see her reaction, and find her eyes closed as she bites her lower lip.

I slip my thumb into her panties and caress the bare skin underneath. I want nothing more than to thrust my digit into her and finger fuck her right here until she comes all over it. I'm salivating just thinking about tasting her arousal. When I circle her clit with the pad of my thumb, she reaches up with her other hand and fists the lapel on my suit jacket as her forehead presses against my shoulder.

To anybody who would walk up to our table, they'd think that we really do like each other. I'm curious what Saraya's game is. I know what mine is, but for Raya to be acting this way, she's got to be cooking something up. I'll figure it out, but in the meantime, I have other pressing matters. The four men coming our way, led by Hillary, have reminded me of just that. Reluctantly, I pull my thumb from her panties.

"Showtime, little lamb."

"Oh? I thought I was playing my part this whole time." She tries to hide the slight lift to her lips, but I catch a glimpse of it before it disappears.

Just to be an asshole, I pretend to scoff, then say, "Try harder."

The little siren pulls on the hair at my nape. "Oops, my bad."

Knowing the Kappels have a clear visual of us, I smirk at Raya. "Paybacks are a bitch," I say in a low gravelly voice before I grip the back of her neck and pull her in for a brutal kiss.

I only stop once I feel her melt into it, and when I look at her, her lips are swollen, and she's got a slight glaze in her eyes. If I were to feel between her legs, I bet she'd be soaked. She can lie all she wants, but I affect her just as much as she affects me.

"Well, well, well, what do we have here?" Jarod's amused voice reaches us.

"Fuck you, Jar." I keep my tone tight but still a bit playful.

I do like the guy; I just don't like them running their business in our town. The twins have told us before that they would take care of it if they were in charge. Unfortunately, Kappel senior has an issue with retiring. My father, along with the other Heirs' fathers, really didn't have a choice. It was either step down or go to prison for the rest of their lives.

"Nyx..."

"Clyde..." I respond to the elder Kappel.

"Had I known we would be entertained by a beautiful woman; we would have been here sooner." Clyde Kappel, head of the Kappel drug family, lifts Raya's hand and kisses the top of it.

A growl-like sound erupts from my mouth, "Watch yourself, Kappel. I don't share this one."

The older man smirks before sitting while his brother and two sons remain standing. I reclaim Raya's hand and rest it on my thigh, surprised she doesn't try to move it. I can tell my little lamb is a bit nervous; Kappel is a big and intimidating man, so I keep my hand over hers as I pour another few fingers of whiskey into her glass.

"You don't have to worry about us with Saraya," Clyde states, shocking me that he knew her name when I haven't mentioned it.

I don't think I mentioned it the first time the twins met her, either. A strange feeling comes over me, and I look past the twins, making eye contact with Cale. This one little gesture tells him to stay alert.

"You're early," I say when I meet Clyde's dark eyes. "I wasn't expecting you for at least another thirty minutes."

The man shrugs. "I thought I'd come early and have my pick for the night. Something tells me I will need to relieve some stress by the time we are done talking."

"I don't mean for that to be the case, but we have a lot to talk about, and I've heard disturbing rumors that I would like to clear up. So, if you're ready, we can head to my office now." I tell him, not giving a fuck about his stress level.

"Sounds like a plan," the older Kappel states and stands up again. "It was a pleasure to meet you, *Mrs. McNally.*"

"It's Ms. Abbott, and she's coming with us," I sneer at how he calls her by her married name.

"You mean to tell me that the great Nyx Beckam is going to allow a female in one of his meetings?" Clyde's laugh is boisterous but stops short when he hears my next statement.

"Not just any female—my fiancée and future *Mrs. Beckam.*"

I feel sharp nails sink into my hard thigh, but I don't pay them much attention. I wouldn't have said what I said, but something isn't sitting right with me. Clyde Kappel knows exactly who Raya is.

"I am not my fucking father. I want these streets cleared of drugs. I can't stop people from doing them, but I'll be damned if I allow them to buy them in our fucking town!"

Raya stands behind my chair, her hand on my shoulder, squeezing and rubbing the tension from them whenever they tighten. I doubt she realizes she's doing it, but it's helped keep me more grounded.

"Not one, not two, but three fucking underage teenagers overdosed last month alone, Kappel! They were *your* drugs mixed with some other kind of shit. Who do you have selling your product on our streets?"

Clyde makes a face.

"Impossible, my product is clean—"

"No fucking drug is clean!" I interrupt him, slamming my fist on my desk.

Zilas sits in a chair not too far away with a pissed-off look. He is most likely thinking about his younger brother's life, which was taken too soon as well. I don't blame him one bit. I remember Zeke being a carefree kid who always had a smile on his face; everyone loved him.

"I will talk to Pike and make sure he isn't adding anything to it." Clyde sighs, rubbing the bridge of his nose.

"I don't think you understand what I'm saying, Kappel. There is no need to talk to whatever the fuck his name is because you're getting your shit out of this town. Go sell it in Vayle—I don't give a fuck. As long as it doesn't cross our border again."

I'm two seconds from getting up and strangling Kappel senior when my office door opens, and in strolls Amara, grinning from ear to ear. She's got blood splatters on her face and dried blood stains her hands. She blows Clyde's brother a kiss, making his eyes widen at the sight of our little assassin walking through the door.

Amara's been busy working on getting some asshole to talk about the topic at hand. We've been investigating the deaths of the three young teenagers, and the guy who is currently in the *Hospital Ward* room at the moment has been seen selling to high schoolers. He's not the one who sold the bad shit, but he knows who did.

"Have I missed the good stuff?" Our little devil asks, stopping beside Clyde's chair.

The twins are sitting on the couch, amusement dancing on their face as they enjoy the little show. They've both had Mara multiple times and are far from scared of her, but what they don't know is that she would slice their necks wide open right after she makes them come and then laugh about it. Our girl is completely unhinged.

"There is no need to bring *her* into it," the older Kappel states.

I smirk.

"Awe, do you not want to play?" Mara runs her blood-encrusted finger across his shoulder, messing with him.

"Mara, play nice. We are only talking at the moment," I say to her, keeping my eyes on Clyde.

Our little devil sticks her bottom lip out and walks around my desk to stand beside me. I hear movement on my other side, where Raya stands, and when Amara tries caressing my cheek, a delicate hand snakes out and grips Mara's wrist.

I snap my head toward Raya, and the look I see her giving her ex-best friend makes me grin. My cock stirs at the profound jealousy I see etched in her features.

"Touch him and see what happens."

Those words coming from my little lamb's mouth have me shouting at everyone to leave my office. "Get the fuck out—now!"

"We aren't finished—" Clyde's brother gets cut off when I glare at him.

I bring my eyes back to Raya and order, "Let her go."

My voice is calm but has an edge to it. After hesitating briefly, Raya flings Mara's hand away. The reaction only makes our little devil snicker, but she backs away before turning and skipping from the room.

"Nyx..."

"Go," I tell Zilas when he stops in front of my desk.

Everyone else is heading for the door, but he looks at Raya with concern in his eyes. I don't understand what it is with my friends coming to her aid when they think I may do something to her.

"Let's just calm—"

Cutting him off as I take Raya's wrist in my hand, I snarl at my friend, "I'm about to do just that, but you need to get the fuck out of my office now!"

Zilas looks between Raya and me, and he grins. "Aye, aye, Captain."

As soon as the door closes, shutting the two of us inside my office, my little lamb tries pulling away from me. "Why did you send them away? Just because I don't want your whore touching you when we are supposed to be playing at being engaged?"

I grin. "Jealousy looks fucking gorgeous on you."

"Fuck you, Nyx..."

"Oh, you're about to." I grin wickedly. "I just didn't think you wanted an audience again when I fuck you bent over my desk this time."

EIGHTEEN

Saraya

I stare blankly at Nyx as if watching a second head sprout from his neck. I cannot have heard him right, but he stands there like he's waiting for something. Crossing my arms in front of my chest, I cock my brow at him.

"Excuse me? Can you repeat what you just said?"

"No, Raya. I didn't stutter, and you heard me the first time." He stands and steps closer to me.

"I don't think—"

"What, little lamb? You don't think what? That you heard me or that this is a good idea?"

My legs tremble, but it's not from being scared. It's from me trying to keep my arousal from dripping out even more than it already has. *How the hell does he do this? Why can't my brain and my body get on the same page?* I try straightening my back and showing him that he doesn't intimidate me, but this action only seems to amuse him.

"I'm not going to play your little games, Nyx!" I turn to remove myself from his space, but suddenly, I'm spun around, and I can feel heat against my back.

"Do you honestly believe that you don't want this?"

Nyx's hot breath is in my ear, his arm around my waist, and his hand—well, let's just say I now know why he bought me this dress.

"You can't fight it, little lamb. Believe me, I've tried."

What's he saying? Does Nyx really want me the way I want him? I know he likes to fuck with me, and what man doesn't want to get fucked?

The other day, I was weak and didn't care, but now? Do I dare give in because we really want each other deep down, or do I walk away?

Trying to hold off until I know for sure what I want to do, I scoff and say, "Oh please, you fucked me just to prove that you have power over me. Don't try feeding me all this bullshit about not being able to fight it."

He presses himself into my backside and grinds out, "Does this feel like me just fucking with you, Raya? I wish that's all it was, but you keep doing shit that turns me on, and I'm having a hard time holding myself back. I'm tired of doing it, so I will take it from now on because I know you want it just as much."

"You don't know shit..." My words come out in a whisper as I try to calm my racing heart and throbbing pussy.

"Oh yeah?" Nyx questions just before shoving his hand inside my panties. "What is this then, Raya? Why do my fingers slide back and forth so easily? Tell me..." he growls when I don't answer.

Not wanting to give him what he wants, I say the first thing that comes to me, "There were seven other men in this room, Nyx. Who says you're the one that made me wet?"

I should have known that was the wrong thing to say. Nyx's reaction is instant. The hand around my waist moves upward and grips my neck, not entirely cutting off my air but enough for me not to be able to struggle.

"You think you're funny? How about we talk about these *other* men so we can figure out just which one of us is going to make you our little slut for the night."

My hands come up to grab his wrist, but that's the extent of it. I don't try to remove his hand because I know I won't be able to. Truth be known, I really don't want to.

"You may not like the results," I tease.

"I'll be the judge of that. Now, shall we start eliminating the other players?" His teeth sink into my earlobe with impatience when I remain quiet.

"Damn it, Nyx..."

"Ah, there's that voice. Now tell me, little lamb, was it old man Kappel, who most likely can't get it up unless he takes that little blue pill he carries in his pocket every time he visits our club? Maybe it was the brother. He usually gets his brother's sloppy seconds, though."

"You're fucking disgusting! Do you know that?!"

Nyx chuckles. "I'm not the one getting wet thinking about old ball sacks, Raya."

That's it. I'm not going to stand here and listen to this! I yank on his wrist, but it's as I thought; it's no use. However, Nyx spins me around, so we're now facing each other. With his hand still on my throat, he pushes me back until my ass is leaning on the edge of his desk.

"It seems we've gotten two of the seven out of the way. We can also dismiss the other Heirs. We both know none of them turn you on like I do." He smirks.

"There are still the twins. You know what they say about double the pleasure..." I lick my lips before biting down on the bottom one.

Yeah, I'm egging him on, and I'm enjoying every fucking minute of it. I want to see how far I can push him. I know he won't hurt me—at least not in a bad way. I should be ending this asinine conversation, but I don't have the willpower to walk away from something I know will bring me immense pleasure—so I don't.

His grip tightens around my neck. "No more talking; your mouth can be used for more pleasurable things. However, since we've yet to determine the person responsible for your sopping-wet cunt, you will answer me in other ways. Can you be truthful for once, little lamb?"

His last words hurt. I've always been truthful with him, but this is something that we will never be able to agree on, so I must accept it for now. I don't nod my response, but I do narrow my eyes at him since speech is now hard with his vise-like grip.

My stepbrother snickers and lets his eyes wander down my body. He moves the fabric of my dress aside and, using his legs, spreads mine open as he stands between them.

"Damn, Raya, you really are soaked, aren't you?" He looks around the room before turning his hard gray eyes back on me. They've got a slight gleam to them as he states, "They weren't this wet a moment ago. Only the two of us are here now, and you're dripping like a leaky faucet, Lil' Sis."

I slap at his wrist, but it only amuses him.

"Tell you what. I won't make you admit out loud that it's me you want deep inside this sweet cunt, but you *will* admit it to me. You can show me that you can be truthful by undoing my belt, opening my pants, and pulling my throbbing cock out. Prepare it to take what will be his real fucking soon."

Jesus. What the fuck is wrong with me? The way Nyx talks to me should be a red flag for every sensible female out there. I must be colorblind because all I see is green, and as if I'm in some sort of trance, I do exactly what he told me to do—be completely truthful.

I keep my eyes on his the entire time I open his pants and pull him out, even when I have his cock in my hand and feel just how girthy he is. I don't dare look at it because I know I will give away just how greedy I am for it.

Nyx's jaw is clenched as I hold him in my hand. Apparently, my being *truthful* isn't enough because he then says, "This is the crucial part, Raya. Tell me that it's me that makes you wet and nobody else. Let's eliminate the rest of those fuckers by you doing one simple thing. Do you want to know what that one thing is?"

I don't know, do I? Nodding without realizing I'm doing so, the smirk on Nyx's face grows. I know I won't like what he's about to say, but I'm too far gone to care. I want him inside me, and I want his thick cock doing very bad things to me.

"I don't think I even need you to do anything. The look in your eyes tells me exactly what I need to know," Nyx states amusedly. "What I'm going to do next is I'm going to rip these panties from you, and then you're going to line me up, so I can push my dick deep inside you. Are you okay with that?"

I've run out of patience. In a whispery but menacing voice, due to the grip on my neck, I sneer, "Stop fucking around, Nyx. You know very well why I'm wet. Now either fuck me or let me go so I can find someone else to do what you can't."

I don't feel the fabric of my panties being torn, only the stretch of his cock as it pushes into me. "Oh, fuck..."

"You wanted it, little lamb, and now—you're going to get it." Pulling out, he thrusts back into me with a vengeance. "Pull your tits out. I want them in my mouth."

Well, shit, if this isn't the hottest thing I've ever experienced. That's not entirely true—our first time was equally as hot as this. Why is it that I never found my ex-husband's dominance as hot as I find my stepbrother's? The way he takes control has me feeling—powerful, if that makes sense. He does it in such a way that it comes off almost desperate—like he needs to have me, or he will just die.

That's the difference between Ken and Nyx. Ken needed the power over me because he was an asshole, whereas, with Nyx, it seems that he needs the power to keep himself from succumbing to a lonely life without the love of a particular woman—me.

Regardless of what we both say and our actions, our feelings for each other are as strong as they were in the past. We just need to find a way to break free of the chains holding us back and embrace this second chance we have been given. However, we are stubborn. One of us must give in first and take that step if we are ever going to rectify all the wrongs done to us. The question is which one of us will do it.

I let that question drift to the back of my head as I come back to the present and what is happening to my body as Nyx fucks it like a starved man. I guess we've both been starved for far too long. So, forgetting all my grievances against him for the time being, I give in to the pleasures Nyx is forcing upon my body.

I hadn't realized he had let go of my throat and was now latched on to my bared breast. Gripping his hair, I force his head back and his mouth off, wincing as his teeth scrape against the sensitive skin.

"Fucking kiss me, Nyx."

The wicked grin he gives me has my walls clenching around his cock as it plunges into me. Nyx's mouth crashes against mine, and we kiss with such passion that it feels like we've been doing it for years. We are so in sync with the other, and that's how I know we are meant to be, whether we believe it or not.

I moan when my climax hits, and he fucks me harder. He pulls away from my lips just far enough to say, "I'm going to come, Raya. I *will* claim you, and it will settle the talk about marriage. If I come inside you again, we *will* marry."

I'm too out of it to care what he's saying. "Please..." I beg, for what... I'm not sure.

"Fuck!" Nyx jerks into me three times, thrusting in as deep as he can on the last one, and that's when I feel it—he's coming inside me again.

"I need to get Plan B."

Nyx casually looks sideways at me as he tucks himself back into his pants. I watch his eyes move to my stomach and then meet my eyes again. I can't tell what he's thinking, which makes me nervous.

"No."

I blink.

"Excuse me?"

He stands in front of me, his hand going to the back of my neck, and I automatically tilt my head back without him pulling it back on his own. Nyx brushes a few strands away from my eyes and tilts his own head to the side.

"Did you not agree to marry me when I was nine to ten inches deep inside you?"

I scoff, "Do you not know how big you are?"

He just shrugs. "I've never needed to measure. As long as I pleasure you with it, that's all that matters."

Shoving at his chest, I try to move him, but he's like a brick wall. "Stop being such a fucking asshole, Nyx. I never said I would marry you, and I definitely never said you could knock me up."

"I specifically remember hearing you say *please* when I told you I was going to come inside you. I also told you that we *will* marry if I did just that. I gave you the choice and," he leans in, brushing his lips across my ear, and says, "You made it."

"That's not fair..." I stammer.

"No, what's unfair is you trying to change your choice when it's already been made. What's not fair," he continues, "Is that you want to make sure my seed doesn't take after I so generously gave you so much of it."

"You can't be fucking serious! We haven't spoken in over ten years, and now that we are, you treat me like shit on the bottom of your shoe. Now, you want me to have your spawn?"

He irritates the hell out of me! How dare he just assume I would be okay with getting pregnant. It's just another way to trap me, and I won't let him do it!

Nyx grins at me as if I've said something funny. He then briefly presses his lips to mine before saying, "At least that spawn will be the cutest spawn ever made." Backing up, he points to a door in his office, instructing, "Go use the restroom to freshen up. We have rounds to make on the main floor."

I stare at him in disbelief, but he's already dismissed me as he starts flipping through papers on his desk. Before I say something I can't take back, I hurry into the restroom and close myself in. Leaning my hands on the vanity, I look at myself in the mirror, and all I see is a woman who has just been thoroughly fucked.

Then, straightening myself back up, I give my reflection a little pep talk. "I can't do this. I need to get out of here

NINETEEN

Nyx

It's been a long fucking night, and all I want to do is get out of here and take Raya home. I know we still have shit that must be hashed out, but I'm beginning to feel like we may actually be able to get past everything. I'm not sure if it's just a gut feeling or if it's because being inside her makes me lose myself completely, and I have a sense of belonging. Either way, I am making Saraya Abbott mine once and for all. I'm reclaiming what should have been mine all these years.

Speaking of my future wife, I frown. She excused herself—I look at my watch—twenty minutes ago to use the restroom. Glancing around the room as I sit in the VIP section, the Kappel twins are rattling on about their latest tag team conquest from the night before. My friends and Heirs are scattered throughout our section, indulging in the evening's offerings.

"Nyx, did you even hear a word I said?" Jarod captures my attention.

"Hm? I'm sorry; what were you mumbling about? I lost interest when you started discussing sword crossing with your twin while sharing the woman." My lips twitch, knowing that the twin doesn't like it when I point out the *particular* parts of his stories.

"Fuck off, Nyx. I swear you only pay attention to the parts when I talk about my dick. Do you have a hard-on for my cock, Mr. Beckam?" Jarod asks in an amusing tone, but regardless, I don't like it.

"If you ever ask me that question again, I will personally cut the fucking thing from your body and shove it down your throat," I threaten in an unamused tone of my own.

"See! There you go again, talking about my dick..."

His twin chuckles but cuts it off the moment I raise a brow at him.

Jax is more respectful of my position than his brother; he's quieter, but it's because he takes everything in. Jax is brilliant, graduating at the top of our class, and from what I hear, he did the same at the University he went to. This twin is very cautious of every situation that he encounters, unlike Jarod.

"You know," I say as my attention returns to Jarod. "They say those who talk themselves up tend to be doing so in order to make themselves feel better since they actually *lack* in that department."

Snickers can be heard from around our alcove, which causes Jarod to blush a little. Lucky for him, the woman now sitting on Cray's lap speaks up for him.

"Although I've had bigger, Mr. Kappel is far from inadequate. He's definitely got the length that I love." The brunette smiles and winks over at the twin.

Unbeknownst to the woman, in sticking up for Jarod, she's now turned Cray off from wanting her tonight. He taps her leg and tells her to get up as he helps her to stand.

"We're done here," my friend says, then calls another woman over, who quickly takes the other woman's place.

The brunette pouts, but when Jarod grins and motions her over, she recovers and happily goes to sit between the twins. They both descend upon her the instant she settles herself.

"Fucking whore," Cray states under his breath, and I smirk.

I look at my watch again, and my frown is back, along with a dreadful feeling. I leave the others while I go in search of my little lamb. Not caring if anyone is inside, I walk into the women's restroom and find only two women inside, who smile flirtatiously at me, but I pay them no mind.

I then find Monica at the hostess stand and ask if she has seen Raya. She informs me that my little lamb had stopped to talk to her for a moment but then told her she needed to grab something from my car and has yet to return. Alarm bells begin going off in my head, and all I can think of is that whoever was sending me the messages had gotten to her.

I rush out the door and down to the parking garage, knowing I won't find her there. Just as I thought, the elevator doors open, and I find an empty garage. My car is still parked where I'd left it, with no sign of Raya anywhere.

"Son of a bitch!" I curse out loud as I reach into my pocket and pull out my cell phone.

I hit one number and wait for the other end to pick up.

"What the fuck, Nyx? Where'd you go?" Adrik asks.

"Never mind about that—Raya is gone. We need to watch the video footage to see who took her."

"How do you know someone took her?" he asks, but I already know Adrik is on his way to the surveillance office.

"What do you mean? Where else would she be?"

"Well, maybe she was tired and returned to the Hall," Adrik states.

"No, she wouldn't have left like that without telling me." *Would she?*

"Okay, if you're sure."

I hear the security guys greeting Adrik as I step off the elevator and head toward him. I hang up without saying another word. Hurrying to the security office, I can't stop the different scenarios that could have happened from popping into my head.

"Go back to when she left my side. I want to see everyone she interacted with," I tell Adrik as I pull my phone back out and try calling Raya's phone.

It goes straight to voice mail. I try going to the app to trace the tracker in her phone, and my brows furrow. The tracker says she's in the bathroom, which I had already checked.

"Are you seeing this?" Adrik asks.

I glance at the screen and freeze. I see red as I watch my little lamb getting into the back seat of an unknown car. She looks back, over her shoulder at the entrance, and then at the camera. Raya gives a look of regret to the camera but still gets into the car.

I punch the nearest wall as I leave the security office and head for the restroom. I end up tearing the room apart until I dump out the garbage can and find the small tracking device I had put inside her phone under the battery. Fuck! I knew I should have used the app instead of an actual device, but I never thought she would ever find it. It's a bitch nowadays to get the backs off phones to get to the battery, but she did it.

I'm unsure whether to be angry or worried. On the one hand, I'm fuming that Raya would leave by herself, but at the same time, I'm afraid that her little stalker friend will find her before I do. I hope Adrik is right and she went back to the Hall, so with this in mind, I head back to the parking garage and to my car.

I swipe everything off Raya's dresser in anger. Anger that she left without telling me, but most of all, anger because she left *me*. How dare she leave after everything I've done for her, after everything we had done together? I thought we were on the same page. This just goes to show that she can't be trusted. Did she leave because I told her no when she asked about Plan B?

At this point, it doesn't matter. Raya is mine. I know she feels like I do; she can't fight it. She ran because she was scared. This thought gave me pause to smile. Seems my little lamb wants to play, but I don't think she realizes just how determined this lion is. Nothing—and I mean nothing—will stop me from finding her and bringing her back.

A notification on my phone draws my attention. It's the notification telling me that someone is in Raya and Ken's house, and I now know where the object of my current obsession is at this very moment. A wicked grin grows on my lips, and I head out of Raya's room.

My phone rings just as I'm climbing into my car once again and I see Cale's name pop up. "Yeah," I answer.

"I've got a Lieutenant Austin Giles here at the warehouse," he states, "He's the one that has been sending you messages about Saraya."

"Hold him there. I've got something to do at the moment."

This is a good thing. This means I can take my time in chasing my little lamb, now that the threat to her has been eliminated. I know she still needs to lie low until I can make it all go away, but I no longer have to worry that someone will take her from me.

It takes me only a short time to get to the other side of town, arriving at the house where Raya had lived with Kenneth. I still cringe at that bastard having what should have been mine, but we are past that. Raya is mine now, and nobody else will ever have her.

Shutting my headlights off as I pull into the driveway, I frown. The house looks dark and empty. She's probably making sure not to draw attention to herself. *Good girl.* At least that's what I think until I unlock the front door with the spare key I had made and find the space completely empty.

I pull my phone out to use the flashlight as I walk through the dark house. It's not a big house, but it isn't tiny either. It's a modest size for a cop's salary and an accountant who only worked part-time. Yeah, I did my homework after Raya showed up on my doorstep. It seems Raya got demoted to only working so many hours after she went through a string of absences. They only kept her on because she was good at what she did.

I find the master bedroom and see the closet and dresser have been rummaged through. The black dress I had her wear tonight lays across her bed. Fisting it in my hand, I bring it to my nose and take in the floral scent of her perfume, and my dick hardens. Not wanting to leave the dress behind because she looks stunning in it, I bring it with me as I finish checking the house.

Ken's office is the last room I come to and the only other room that looks like Raya had entered. A wall safe is wide open, and I'm willing to bet that there was money inside that is no longer there. I know my little lamb wanted her trust so she could leave and start a new life for herself, and although I wouldn't have had an issue with giving her the money that is rightfully hers, deep down, I didn't want her to leave.

I look inside the safe, knowing that it's been cleaned out but needing to make sure. I find a few pieces of legal papers and a few watches. By the looks of it, Raya was in a hurry. A couple of hundred-dollar bills still lay towards the back, but that's not what has me examining the inside as closely as I am.

I find a hidden compartment in the back of the safe, so I run my hand around until I find the small button to open it. I find only a couple of flash drives, but they're enough to pique my interest. I pull them from the safe and go to the computer, firing it up immediately. They are important if these were kept in a secret part of the safe. Let's see what good ole Ken was hiding.

Grunting and moaning fills the room as the sound comes over the speakers. It's a familiar sound—one that I will never forget. The sound is embedded into my memory, every moan, cry, and grunt. The slapping of skin sickens me. I don't need to finish watching this because it's the same video my father showed me.

Inserting the next one, now that my mood has soured tremendously, I no longer want to watch anymore, but I need to see what is on these other drives. For a while, all I see is a view from a camera that Ken wears. I only know this because he showed himself in the mirror.

Fast-forwarding the video, I stop the moment I see Stanton and my father as Ken walks into my father's office. There is a bit of static with the audio, but I can make out my father's voice as he scolds Ken.

"It's about fucking time you get here. Are you sure this is what you want? It's not every day you get to fuck a virgin."

I jerk at my father's words and turn the volume up.

"I don't want a virgin bride. Do what you must if you want me to marry her," Ken's voice comes over the video.

I watch as all three men walk through Nyte's Hall, only stopping once they get to Raya's bedroom door. What I witness next is *not* what my father showed me or the video on the first drive. Raya was fighting for us the whole time. I try to turn my head away the moment Ken grabs her and holds her down, but I don't. This is my punishment for believing my father over my best friend. I should have known better; I should have known that Saraya would never betray me like that. I never once gave her the benefit of the doubt.

The possibility of rape was never in question when I was shown the video of the love of my life betraying me. I drop to my knees as my eyes remain glued to the screen. The video was altered; it had to have been. Nothing about this is consensual. Now, I will punish myself by watching the truth. Pain slashes through my chest as Stanton tears at Raya's bottoms, and without a care for her condition, drives himself into her while Ken covers her screams with his hand.

I notice my father recording the whole thing in the background, but I still don't understand how I could have thought it was consensual. I have to watch the other video again because I'm missing something.

I'm lost in the tears streaming down Raya's face in the video. Even her nails digging into Stanton's arms don't seem to deter him. Eventually she goes silent and just lays there as Stanton finishes himself off.

She protected me. My little lamb went through hell in order to keep me safe from my own father. I hang my head in shame, and for the first time in I'm not sure how long, I let tears trickle down my cheeks.

"Here, all the evidence is on this video if you ever need it to prove who it was that fucked the little slut. I've already sent it to my phone to alter it and make it look like she enjoyed it all. My son will never forgive her for this betrayal."

My father's voice has me wiping my face and concentrating on what's being said. Rage fills me when Ken's camera catches my father going to

Raya. At first, I thought he was going to do more of the unthinkable, but thank God all he did was threaten her with it. I now understand why she didn't come to me, but I still wish she had.

I can no longer blame her. I need to find her, and tell her that I know the truth. I pull the flash drive out and hurry from the house, not caring if I leave the computer on or the place unlocked. My only concern is finding Raya before I lose her for good.

TWENTY

"Thank you for waiting for me. I hope I didn't keep you waiting too long." I settle into the back seat of the Uber I called to pick me up from the club.

I hated leaving *him,* but he left me no choice. I scoff to myself, thinking how ironic it is that Nyx did just that. He's been making all my choices, not letting me choose for myself, and this one was no different. The moment he told me that I couldn't take any Plan B, he took my choice to stay with him away.

It's for the best; now, he can get on with his life. He can continue fucking Amara and whomever else he wants to dip his stick into. That appendage of his is the only thing I will truly miss. *Boy can that man fuck.*

My thoughts return to earlier, in his office, before he fucked it all up. After Ken, I never thought I would like to have my body dominated, but the way Nyx did it was different, and my body responded to it. We fit perfectly, and that scares the shit out of me. Nyx will never forgive me for the past, and until I'm ready to come clean about it, I can't really blame him, even if I think he should have come to me.

Closing my eyes, I recollect how he felt inside me. How he held me in place by the neck as he took what he wanted from my very willing body. A tingle erupts in my center, and I snap my eyes open. No, I can't think about it, not yet anyway.

I run my hand through my long dark tresses. *God, Nyx is going to be so pissed when he learns I found the tracker in my phone and left.* I can't believe he thought he could hide it from me. After knowing I lived with someone who kept track of me for over ten years, one would think Nyx would know better. Maybe he didn't know the extent of Ken's depravity, but what he's learned since I came to live at Nyte's Hall should have given him some clue.

He must think I'm some naïve girl unaware of this world's big, bad wolves. The way I came to his doorstep, a shaken and scared woman he hadn't seen in over ten years—I don't really blame him. After tonight, Nyx will know not to underestimate that woman.

I've spent my whole adult life protecting the one man I've ever loved. Once my mother and stepfather died, I started to plan my escape. I wasn't quite ready to leave that night, but Ken left me no choice. I knew we had cameras that would capture what happened, proving it was self-defense, but there were so many corrupt cops on the force that I wasn't taking my chances, so I got rid of all the footage.

I was running on adrenaline at that time and never thought to go into the wall safe and grab the money I knew Ken had stashed there. It's corrupt money, but it's what's going to help me in my time of need. I'm desperate, and that's one of the reasons I took the chance and went back to the house.

I had the Uber driver park on the street, and I slipped through the shadows until I came to the basement window in the backyard. I knew the latch was broken; it was one of the many things I tried getting Ken to fix, but he never did. I was in and out in less than ten minutes. I only grabbed enough clothes for a couple of days, planning on buying new ones once I got to where I was going.

I had memorized the numbers on the safe thanks to Ken as he opened it numerous times while having me sit there in his office. There were too many times to count when he had wanted me unclothed and just sitting there, waiting for when he was ready to use me. I close my eyes and swallow the bile wanting to rise from just thinking about it.

"Um, Miss, I'm not sure what's going on, but I think we're being followed." The driver's voice causes my eyes to snap open, and I turn in my seat.

Just as the bright beams of light hit my eyes, the car is jerked forward as the vehicle behind us rams into us. A scream bursts from my mouth as I'm thrown forward. I catch myself before flying through the two front seats.

"What the fuck?" the driver curses.

"Step on it!" I order.

"What have you gotten me into, lady?"

"Why are you blaming me for this? I don't know who that is. It's probably a jealous ex of yours!" I scowl.

The thought of Nyx being the one that's behind us flashes through my head briefly, but I quickly squash that idea. No matter how mad my stepbrother may be at me, he would never intentionally hurt me physically. Can this be one of Ken's friends who sent Nyx the messages?

"I am happily married, thank you very much!"

"Are you sure?" I ask sarcastically.

I know this is about me, but I'm so tired of people just assuming things about me that I feel the need to retaliate. Another hit to the back bumper has the car jarring forward, but not as bad as the first time.

"If we can make it to town, they'll probably back off..."

"What do you think I'm trying to do? You asked me to go the back way, and now we're stuck on these windy roads where I have to slow down around every curve! I'm not a racecar driver, you know!"

"Well, I'd say now is a good time to practice," I growl.

We're just coming around a curve when we are hit again. This time, they hit us just right, sending the car onto two wheels before it topples. The small car rolls, tossing me around inside. I see the lights of the other car just before my head hits something hard, and darkness takes me.

Grunting hits my ears as I come to. A throbbing in my head makes me want to throw up, but I can't do that while I feel myself being jerked this way and that. Something has hold of my ankle, and as my eyes blink open and I fight the vomit that wants to come up from the pain, everything starts coming back to me.

The car is upside down, and my upper body is in the front, with the passenger seat just above my head. I glance over at the driver, and I wish I hadn't. Although he was wearing his seat belt, it didn't stop the metal chunk from embedding itself into his side.

I'm not sure if he's dead or just passed out, but I don't have time to find out as I'm slowly pulled out by my ankle. The moment I get a glimpse of the person pulling on me, I begin thrashing. I don't care how much my head hurts; I can't let this fucker get me out.

"Son of a fucking bitch! You will pay for that, Saraya!" the person snarls.

The voice sounds familiar, but with the ski mask over their head, I have no way of knowing who this asshole is. It's got to be one of Ken's cop friends. Why else would they be hiding their identity? They all know better than to go against the Heirs, but this group of cops takes their orders from someone else. I'm not sure who—I only know this from bits and pieces of conversations I've heard over the years.

"Don't fucking touch me!" I claw at the seat while trying to keep myself inside the car.

Hearing a groan, relief floods me, knowing that the innocent driver is still alive. Taking note of the metal still in his side, I glance around for something sharp that I can use myself to help fend off this motherfucker. I'd pull the sharp metal from the Uber driver, but I don't want him to bleed out.

Thankfully, I find a large piece of glass and grab it. When the perpetrator's hand grabs my calf and starts dragging me out, my hand comes down, swiping the sharp piece at him. I make contact, and he curses.

"You bitch!"

"Leave me the fuck alone then!"

"That's it..." He lets go of my limb, but then I gasp and glower as he pulls a gun out from behind him and holds it at the driver's head. "Get the fuck out of the car now!"

"Jesus, okay! There is no need to hurt him—you've done enough..."

I scoot my ass out, intending to somehow get the gun away from him. After all, if he's one of Ken's friends, I know he's not one of the brightest crayons in the box. I've met Ken's friends. *But what if it's not one of his friends?*

I push that thought out of my head as I exit the car. My head throbs and I get dizzy from all the movement, but the stranger doesn't seem to care as he grabs my arm and yanks me to my feet.

"Ouch!" I cry out. "I'm pretty sure I have a concussion..." I feel a massive bump on the back of my head.

"I don't give a fuck," the guy states. "Had you turned yourself in, this wouldn't be happening!"

"What are you talking about?"

I'm pretty sure he's talking about Ken, but I'm not admitting to jack shit. He can do and say what he wants. I will bide my time because I know Nyx will be searching for me. I almost smirk at the thought of my stepbrother finding me in the condition I'm in because of this asshole. I may be hating on Nyx now, but I know him. He doesn't take kindly to people touching, never mind hurting, what is his. If I've learned anything in the short time I've been living back at the Hall, it's that I am Nyx Beckam's property.

"You know perfectly well what I'm talking about. You're a cop killer, and you're going to own up to what you did."

"I don't know what you're talking about."

"Where the fuck is your husband, Saraya?"

I shrug and say, "Probably holed up with his whore. Why don't you tell me since you all fuck the same woman," I taunt. I've known about Ken's affairs for years.

I find myself on the ground once more with a throbbing cheek that now matches the pain in my head. I'm guessing he didn't like that very much, but fuck that. I'm not going down without a fight. I've spent too many years tiptoeing around because of my stepfather and Ken. I refuse to be used like that again.

"Fucking coward..." I spit at his feet.

He yanks my head back by my hair and gets in my face as he sneers, "What the fuck did you call me?"

"I didn't stutter. I said that you're a fucking coward!" My glare burns with rage.

He stares at me momentarily before throwing his head back, laughing. His hand tugs on my hair as his body shakes with amusement before saying, "Man, if only Ken could see you now. I bet he'd whip that attitude right out of you."

"Well, he's not here now, is he?" I remind him, which only turns him into an asshole again.

"You're right, he's not, and now you're going to pay..."

The last thing I see is his hand coming down, and then darkness envelopes me.

When I wake up again, I'm on the ground and not alone. Two other males in masks stand with the fucker that caused the accident. It's not long before I realize that my wrists and ankles are secured, but the part that I'm most worried about is the fact that I'm in a deserted junkyard.

"Ah, Sleeping Beauty finally wakes," Asshole number one states. "Stand her up, boys, so she can get a better view of what will happen."

"Don't fucking touch me!" I struggle as asshole number two and three grab me by each arm and haul me to my bound feet. "You do realize that as soon as Nyx finds out that you took me, shit's going to hit the fan, mainly your shit, when he comes after your asses."

Assholes two and three glance worriedly at each other.

"Don't fucking listen to the bitch. He will never find her..." asshole one says to his buddies before turning toward me.

"You do know who Nyx Beckam is, don't you?" I ask.

"You think I'm worried about the fucking Heirs?"

"You should be..."

I'm trying to make small talk to stall. I need to think of a way out of this predicament, but I'm afraid that won't happen. It's only a matter of time before this asshole gets tired of my snarky attitude. He wants information, mainly about where his friend is, and once he realizes that I won't tell him, I'll be useless to him.

"Now, let's stop this nonsense and get down to business," he says and nods in a specific direction before continuing. "You're going to tell me what I want to know, or else you're going to be next."

I follow his line of sight, and that's when I see it. There is a man tied to the top of a car. He seems to have passed out, which is good because he won't feel it when they put the car through the crusher.

"I don't know what you're talking about..." I whisper as I watch in horror while the crusher gets closer and closer to the guy. "Stop it! Why is he up there? What has he done?"

"He's a traitor. The moment I told him what the job was, he quit. We can't have that in our line of work."

"You are fucking cops!"

Unfortunately, the guy chooses this time to wake up, and his screams are heard for a few brief seconds. I shouldn't have turned my attention toward him because, at that moment, the crusher comes down, and red squirts out from the sides.

"Now, are you going to tell me where Ken is?"

"Fuck—you!"

Asshole one sighs and then nods at his two buddies, who begin dragging me toward the crusher. I can't walk even if I want to; all I can do is allow them to pull me.

"I don't know where he's at, I swear!" I call back because it's God's honest truth. I don't know what Nyx has done with his body.

"Admit it, you killed Kenneth McNally!"

"I—"

Shots ring out, and the next thing I know, I'm falling to the ground as my two guards drop like flies. I don't understand what's going on until I hear the familiar baritone of the one person that I was running from.

"She can't admit it because it isn't true. *I* killed that piece of shit husband of hers; I finished him off days after he attacked her."

My jaw drops as I see Nyx standing there, still holding the smoking gun that took out assholes two and three. I want to jump for joy and kiss him all over the face—until his words sink in—he what?

TWENTY-ONE

Nyx

When I leave, I take the back road because it's closer to the warehouse where I'm meeting Cale. I have Tucker trying to track down Raya; he's good at finding people, just like Cale is. That's why I keep the two well-compensated; they are the best.

Something up ahead has me pressing down on the accelerator until I'm upon the scene, and I slam on the brakes. It's the same car that my little lamb left in only now it's smashed and toppled over. My heart drops into my gut, as I jump from my car.

"RAYA!" I call out as I run over to the twisted scene.

A few more feet and the vehicle would have hit the guardrail and gone over the side, which has a massive drop-off. I'm trying to figure out how this could have happened as I continue to call out her name.

"Help!" A weak voice reaches my ears, but it's male.

I skid to a halt, falling to my knees, looking inside the smashed car. There is no sign of Raya, only the driver hanging upside down by his seatbelt with a piece of metal going through him. I jump back to my feet and run to the other side to see if she crawled out, but she's nowhere.

I look over at the guardrail and start tugging at my hair. *What if she was thrown from the car and went over the side? No, that can't be! There is no way I can lose her like this!*

I rush back to the driver and question him. "Where is the woman you were driving for?"

"W-what? Please, help me..."

As much as I want information, I can't just leave him hanging there, so I help him out of the seatbelt and drag him out and away from the car. There is no evidence of a gas leak, but I don't want to take any chances.

Once I have him at a safe distance, I ask again, "Tell me where the woman is who you were transporting."

"Please, call for help..."

"I will, but if you don't answer my fucking question, the only help you will need is the coroner!" I'm losing my patience.

"I d-don't know where she w-went. He t-took her..."

"He? Who the fuck is he?"

"I don't k-know. H-he ran us off t-the road then took her," the driver states.

"What was he driving?"

"I don't know, i-it's too dark..."

"FUCK!" I yell out, frustrated, before pulling my phone out and calling for help.

I start walking back to my car when the driver calls out, "Where are you g-going?"

"I'm going to go kill some motherfuckers..."

Walking through the warehouse, I don't stop when Cale starts trying to talk to me. I keep going until I come to the room where we hold the fuckers we need to question, or torture, however you want to look at it.

Lieutenant Giles is hanging by his wrists, his feet barely touching the floor. Evidence of Cale's questioning covers the fuckers face, but I don't let that stop me from walking right up to the guy and giving him a right hook to his jaw.

You can hear the crack of his jaw echo through the room. I swing again, this time landing my fist in his ribcage. I then grab his shirt and glower at him when I growl out my only question for him, "Where the fuck is she?"

When he doesn't answer me, I start using him as a punching bag, letting out all my anger. I can feel Cale's presence as he stands there, leaning against the door, taking in the show before him. Only when I need a little break to catch my breath do I glance over at my right-hand man.

"Why the fuck isn't he talking?" I run my hand through my hair to get it out of my face.

"Probably because he can't without this..." Cale holds up a severed tongue between his fingers.

"What the fuck? I hope you got answers before you decided to cut it out!" I glare at him.

"Of course I did."

"Then why didn't you not stop me just now?"

Cale grins. "Because you looked like you needed to let off some steam—and it was fun to watch."

I scoff but then look back at the bloody asshole just dangling there, now unconscious. I wipe my bloody hands off on the only clean area of the guy's shirt before joining Cale, where he leans by the door.

"So? I don't have time, Cale. Someone took Raya, and I need to fucking find her!"

"Well, had you stopped when you arrived, I would have told you. You have been wasting time on this fucker, so I just let you get it out of the way. Now, I suggest you head to the junkyard because that's where you'll find her."

"Junkyard?" I question, but don't stay to hear an explanation.

Cale calls out behind me, "I've already sent Tucker a text. He'll meet you there!"

I can't remember the last time I ran. My men run, I don't, but you better believe I will for *her.* The video flashes through my head, and pain slices through me again. *Fuck, I'll be spending the rest of my days making it up to her. That is, if she lets me.*

Getting to my car, I start the engine and take off before my door is even closed. Leaning over to the passenger side, I open the glovebox and pull out my Glock, checking it to ensure it's loaded. I still have no idea who these fuckers are, but I'm about to find out. I assume it's another corrupt cop if Lieutenant Giles was involved.

Looks like I'll be cleaning up the PD as soon as all this shit is over with. They fucked with the wrong person this time. You know what they say when someone fucks around—*fuck around and find out.* That's precisely what's going to happen—they're going to find out what happens when you fuck around with what's *mine.*

I turn the headlights off as I pull off to the side of the road, where I see Tucker climbing out of the cab of his truck. He's dressed in all black, whereas I'm still in my suit, but I don't give a shit. I'd go in there, guns blazing, if I knew it wouldn't hurt Saraya.

"Do *not* let Raya get hurt," I warn Tucker. "Let's assess the situation, and then we will move in. No one leaves here alive. Do you understand me?"

"Yes, Sir."

We hurry through the entrance and keep to the shadows until we hear angry voices. It makes no difference to me what they're saying, the fact they're speaking to my little lamb with such disrespect has their death warrant already filled out.

"You do know who Nyx Beckam is, don't you?" I hear my little lamb's snarky voice, which brings a grin to my lips, and I thank the big guy for keeping her safe.

"You think I'm worried about the fucking Heirs?" A snicker comes from a male. I don't have eyes on them yet, but I already know he's in charge.

"You should be..." Raya warns, and she's right; they would do well to listen to my girl.

More chatting ensues as we make our way closer, trying to find a good position. When I finally lay eyes on my little lamb, I... see... red. Her clothing being torn is bad enough, but when I see the swelling around her cheek and eye, it takes Tucker everything he has to hold me back.

Screams grab my attention just before blood sprays out from the car crusher. *Jesus, is that what they plan on doing to my little lamb?* Wanting to ready my gun, I shrug Tucker off, letting him know that I'm good before I find a position where I can take out everyone who needs to be taken out.

I point up at the guy working the machinery, indicating that Tucker is to secure that position. He nods and falls back into the shadows as I turn my attention back to Raya and the dead men walking. I grin when I hear her curse at the fucker, but it doesn't last long. The moment the two goons start dragging my girl toward the crusher, and she starts calling out, I raise my gun, take aim, and pop off two rounds—hitting each of my targets.

"She can't admit it because it isn't true. *I* killed that piece of shit husband of hers; I finished him off days after he attacked her."

I don't dare look at Raya because I can already feel her stare burning through me. She's pissed, but I'll deal with that later. I walk out of the shadows, my gun now pointed at the last asshole standing. *Fucking Captain Frank Denver. I always knew he was a corrupt cop.*

"Untie your ankles, Raya, and come to me," I instruct, but Frank is fast and has his own gun pointed at my little lamb in a matter of seconds.

"Not so fast, Beckam. She still has to own up to stabbing her husband," the fucker growls out.

"The fuck she does. If you saw the video, then you know it was self-defense!"

"Not as many times as she stabbed him. Besides, she made sure the evidence was taken care of."

"Hey, dumbass, did you forget that you sent me the video?"

The captain blinks before realizing the mistake he made. He makes another one when he cocks his gun and says, "No whore deserves to live when a good man is dead because of her!"

"I suggest taking that fucking gun off her right now and step away from her." I stop about ten feet away from them.

Frank gives me a wicked grin and says, "Go ahead and shoot me, and I'll make sure I take her with me."

A noise from above catches Frank's attention, and he looks up. I take this time to lunge forward just as Raya frees her ankles and rushes toward me. Frank swings his head back in our direction, and a shot rings out just before I unload my gun into him.

Everything happens in slow motion. I can almost see every bullet fly through the air, embedding itself into the captain. His body jerks every which way as blood seeps through his clothing instantly. I drop to the ground, my breathing heavy. It isn't until all goes quiet that I feel the sting at the same time Raya cries out.

"Nyx!"

She rushes toward me, her wrists still bound, and drops to her knees beside me. I reach out to take hold of the rope, but pain slices through my chest, stopping me from moving any further. Looking down, I see the red stain growing bigger and bigger on my chest.

"Stay with me, Nyx! Don't you dare fucking die!"

I hear Tucker rush over and tell me that our men are on their way, but I don't pay him any attention as I stare at my little lamb. She's pissed, but I can see her eyes beginning to water.

"You're safe, little lamb. Don't cry."

Tucker uses this time to pull his knife out and cut through the rope on Raya's wrists.

"Yeah, well, you're not! You are in so much shit with me, so don't you dare die on me!" She tries glaring, but it doesn't come off that way; she's scared.

"Do you honestly think I would allow myself to get killed when I have a hot little woman to turn over my knee and spank the shit out of for running away from me?" I try to chuckle, but the pain is too much, and it turns into a loud groan.

Raya pulls her shirt off, not caring that she's left in just a sports bra, and presses her shirt against my chest. Putting pressure on it, the action causes her to get really close to me, and I can't help putting in a special request.

"Kiss me, little lamb."

"What? No, you're bleeding out, Nyx!!"

"Well, if I'm going to die, then I want to feel your lips against mine one last time," I tell her, more as a joke than anything, but it would be the truth if I were dying.

"No, because you're not dying. I won't let you—"

"Get that fucking mouth over here right now, Raya. Don't make me tell you again." I cut her off with my demanding voice.

I notice the lust enter her beautiful brown eyes just before she lowers her head and brushes her lips against mine. However, it's very short-lived because she's pulling away a few seconds later. She hovers over my mouth as she stares into my eyes.

"Talk to me that way again, and I'll let you bleed to death." Raya cocks her brow as I grin.

"You love it, don't deny it. That cunt is dripping for me right now, isn't it?"

"You're an asshole—"

"Nyx!" Another female voice interrupts Raya's, and then Amara stares down at me with concern written all over her face. "We've got you. You're going to be fine."

I'm being lifted and try to reach out to Raya, but she's no longer beside me. I can't see her. "Raya," I try calling out, but there's no response. An oxygen mask gets placed over my face, and that's the last thing I remember.

TWENTY-TWO

Saraya

Why? Why did Nyx do it? He threw himself in front of a bullet for me even though he hates me, or at least that's how I perceive it to be. Let's not forget about what he said, either. *He* killed Ken days after I had stabbed him? Was he just saying that, or was that the truth?

I want to stay with him, but when the Heirs arrive, I get shoved back by no other than Mara. I should fight harder to stay by his side, but I'm unsure what to do. I'm still confused by everything that has transpired, and I highly doubt I have the right to fight with Amara to be the one to stand by his side.

Adrik walks by me as Zilas and Cray load Nyx up into the van they brought, and I reach out, stopping him. "Can I get a ride back to the Hall before you go with them?"

The Heir looks me over and sighs, "We are taking him back to the Hall. Our doctor is already there waiting for us, but you should know my answer would have been no."

"Oh, I see. Well, I'll go to my room and stay out of the way..."

"No, you won't. You will be by our side while we wait for the doctor to tell us about his condition," Adrik says, crossing his arms in front of his chest.

"I don't think—"

"I don't care what you think, Raya. What I do care about is that my best friend got shot because of you—"

"I didn't ask him to!" I state angrily.

"Let me finish, Raya," Adrik says, annoyed. "Nyx got shot because of you—the woman he loves, and he will be hurt if you aren't with us as we wait. *You* are the one he wants there waiting for him to wake up."

I scoff.

"Don't do that, Saraya."

"Don't do what, Adrik? I won't get my hopes up that Nyx loves me and wants me here. He's shown me time and time again that it's the exact opposite."

Adrik runs his hand through his hair, sighing. "You and Nyx are stubborn as fuck. Do you know that? Trust me when I say that my best friend has *never* fallen out of love with you. What you did fucked him up big time, but he could never really be free of you."

"You don't know what happened... none of you do." Try as I might, I can't keep the tears from stinging my eyes, so I look away.

"We know what Nyx told us—"

"I know what Nyx thinks, but he doesn't know what happened either!" I don't mean to have those words come out, and the frustration in my voice is evident.

I'm so tired of hearing how I did my stepbrother dirty. Maybe it is time for the truth to come out; it's not like Stepdaddy can make good on his threat anymore. At the end of the day, I'm the one who has to relive it all, and maybe that's what's stopping me.

"I think we should get going. I brought the spare keys to Nyx's car, so we will drive that back. You're not going to run off again, are you?" I can hear the irritation in his voice; the accusation is there. *Had I not run, Nyx wouldn't have been shot.*

Guilt does take hold, and I hope to God that he pulls through this. I do love the asshole, I can't deny that, even if we can't be together. However, even if my feelings were different, I still wouldn't want him dead. This isn't how it's supposed to end.

"What is she doing here?" Amara sneers, glowering at me when Adrik and I walk up.

She's standing outside a door at Nyte's Hall with Cray and Zilas but moves to block it when she sees me. With her arms crossed in front of her chest, Mara glares at me. I get it. I got her fuck buddy shot, but that doesn't mean I'm going to cower away from her. Assassin or not, Amara Nichols doesn't scare me.

"You know Nyx would want her here. Stop being a bitch, Mara." Zilas is the one to speak up this time.

She scoffs, then asks, "Would he?"

"Mara..." Adrik says in a warning tone.

"You can't be fucking serious! Have you all lost your mind? A hot little pussy moves in, and you all forget about what she did to our friend?"

My ex-best friend is fuming over this. She takes a few steps toward me, and I do the same, not backing down.

"Correct me if I'm wrong, but didn't you corner me in the kitchen, propositioning me? In fact, *you're* the only one who has come on to me or has taken liberties. I think maybe you're jealous because I've fucked Nyx a few times now and won't give you the pleasure."

"You bitch!" She moves to come at me, but Cray grabs her around the waist.

"Calm down, little devil. Now is not the time, and Zilas is right; Nyx would want her here. If anything, he'd want to ensure she doesn't take off again. Raya being here lets us keep an eye on her."

"I'm not going anywhere." I cock my brow at the two of them.

"Stop egging her on, Raya. Mara isn't someone you want to mess with..." Adrik steps between me and where Cray still holds Mara as he stares down at me.

"She wouldn't dare hurt me because then she would be hurting her precious Heir." I tilt my head back to look Adrik in the eye.

"We don't call her our little devil for nothing, Raya," he states. "She'd rather ask for forgiveness than permission."

"Ha! Like I would even ask for that!" Comes Mara's snarky response.

Rolling my eyes, I turn and cross the hallway, leaning against the wall to watch the door to Nyx's temporary room. Amara can bitch and moan as much as she wants to, but I'm not leaving this spot until I know Nyx is in the clear.

No sooner do these thoughts cross my mind than the door across from me opens, and a middle-aged doctor—I believe Adrik called him Mahony—steps out. He's got some salt-and-pepper hair, but otherwise, he's a good-looking guy. We all straighten ourselves and give our full attention to him.

"Mr. Beckam is a fortunate man. The bullet didn't hit anything vital. I do want to watch him for internal bleeding, so Sasha will be staying until morning when I come to check on him." He digs into his pocket and pulls out what looks to be flash drives before walking to Adrik. "He asked me to make sure I gave you these. He said they are to be kept in a safe place."

"Can we see him?" Amara rushes out.

Dr. Mahony holds his hand up to stop Mara from going to Nyx's room before relaying, "Um, Mr. Beckam requested that nobody go in the room until he wakes up, except for Raya. He instructed me that I'm to bring her in as soon as I'm done, and there isn't anything more I can do at the moment, so..."

"Why the fuck does she get to go in?" Mara glares at me once again.

"I don't know Miss Nichols, but it was requested by my patient, so I will do as he says."

I want to grin and stick my tongue out at Mara in a childish way, but I keep my composure and hurry to the room. I'm not prepared to see Nyx in this state, though. He looks too vulnerable. I push some of his hair off his forehead and gaze down at him.

At this moment, he reminds me of his old self, Phoenyx Beckam, the boy I was madly in love with. The blankets come up to just above his stomach, and his chest is bare except for the white bandage covering the area that was covered in red just a short time ago.

I take his hand, making sure that I don't disturb the IV lodged inside of it. I would never dare do this if he was conscious. He would probably pull away from me with disgust. At least this way, I can calm my heart for a bit as I feel the warmth of his hand in mine.

"It's late, Mrs. McNally. You should get some sleep. Mr. Beckam will probably sleep for the next few hours." The doctor begins packing up his things. "The nurse will be near in case she is needed."

"Please don't call me by that name. I'm Saraya Abbott..."

"My apologies."

"I can't leave him. I need to make sure he's okay." I never take my eyes off Nyx as I carry on the conversation with the doctor.

"I didn't mean for you to leave. In fact," Dr. Mahony chuckles, "Mr. Beckam demanded that I order you to sleep on his left side."

My eyes widen, and I snap my head toward the doctor. "You can't be serious!"

Snickering, he nods towards our sleeping patient and says, "I'm always serious about one of the Heirs. They mean what they say, so if Mr. Beckam says you are to sleep on his left side, you will sleep on his left side. Unless, of course, I need to have one of the others come in and chain you to the bed."

Why does it not surprise me that my stepbrother still tells me what to do even in this state? I feel my lips twitch as I try to hold back my grin. I glance at his left side and ponder what to do.

Something tickles my cheek, and I try swiping it away with my hand, but I feel nothing there. Snuggling deeper into the warmth beside me, I feel it once more and swipe at it again. A deep chuckle pops my eyes open, and I see Nyx grinning at me.

I'm snuggled into his left side, and his elbow is bent, so his finger grazes my cheek. "Good morning, little lamb."

Trying not to jar him too much, I sit up quickly and apologize. "I'm sorry. I hope I didn't hurt you."

I glance at the spot where I initially fell asleep, and my brow furrows. We're in a king-size bed, and I was on the other side, by the edge. How did I move all the way over to where Nyx is lying?

"No need to apologize. You didn't hurt me at all. Doc has me on some strong pain meds." His smile is a bit goofy, and I have to suppress a smile of my own.

Climbing from the bed, I ask, "Are you hungry?"

His gray eyes darken, and he replies, "Ravenous."

I notice the blanket tent and gasp. "I'm not talking about that, Nyx! You're injured! You almost died!"

He scoffs, "It's only a flesh wound. I am perfectly fine if you come over here and ride me. You can have full reign of my body." He wiggles his brows, and now I really do smile as I shake my head.

"Absolutely not."

"I can order you..."

I cock my brow and tilt my head. "Oh, can you?"

He nods.

"Pray tell, what will you do when I don't heed your commands? It's not like you can come after me." I peruse his body, grinning.

"Maybe not, but I have friends that will restrain you and impale you onto my cock if I ask them to."

I snicker, mainly to hide the fact that his words actually turn me on, but I'll never admit it. "You're too possessive of me. You will never let them be part of anything like that."

He chuckles before saying, "That may be, but I have no qualms with them seeing you naked or being fucked by me. I think I've already proved that to you. You know what? I think you loved every minute of Cray watching you get fucked. You came so hard for me, little lamb."

Clearing my throat after his words start a fire deep in my core, I ignore them and instead tell him, "Your little bed buddy has been dying to see you, so I'll go get you something to eat—"

"Which bed buddy are you talking about?" he cuts me off.

I gape at him. "Amara. Jesus, how many do you have?"

"That depends on what you consider bed buddies. The guys and I have shared a bed many times with Mara..."

I can't stop the anger rising, but then Nyx finishes his sentence.

"In the past. All of it is in the past, little lamb. I will only share my bed with one person from here on out."

The way his eyes burn into me only turns up the heat within, and I find myself squeezing my thighs together. "I'll tell them you're awake, and I'll be back with your food." I reach for the door handle.

"Raya?"

I pause and turn my head to look back at him. "Yeah?"

"Hurry back..."

Swallowing hard, I nod and slip from the room.

TWENTY-THREE

Nyx

All four of my friends are sitting in my room, speechless. They don't want to believe what I'm telling them; hell, I don't want to believe it either. I've been a dick, and now I'm hoping that Raya will forgive me.

"I knew there was more to it; we," Zilas says as he points between himself and Adrik, "knew there had to be more to it."

"We all knew Raya growing up, and that was so out of character of her to do that..." Adrik states.

"And yet none of us questioned it further because Layton had the video." Cray hangs his head.

"Are you sure this video is legit?" Amara asks, a bit snarky.

I stare at her, my anger growing the more I see the indifference in her eyes. She's been my rock—*our* rock—all these years, so I understand why she is hesitant to believe it. *Is Amara afraid that I won't need her anymore?*

"I didn't get a chance to compare them back-to-back fully, but I do believe the video that came from Ken's camera," I state. "I'm not sure what all is on the other flash drives, but I want to keep them in a safe place until I can find out.

"I've got you, Nyx," Adrik assures me.

"So, what now?" Mara asks.

"You stop being a bitch to her. Do you think you can do that?" Cray grins as he pulls Mara onto his lap. "Or am I going to have to take you to my room and fuck the bitch out of you?"

Our little devil smirks and says, "It may take more than a fuck to get that out of me."

Cray reaches up and grabs her throat. "I think that can definitely be arranged. You don't have anybody to torture in the next few days, do you?"

"Not as of right now..." Mara grabs his crotch through his pants.

"Okay, you two—take it to your own room. I can't fuck just yet, and watching the two of you go at it in front of me will be torturous," I tell them, grinning.

"Awe, my poor baby. Do you need a sucky, sucky?" Mara licks her lips.

I scoff, "You know damn well that if I did, it would be Raya doing it all."

Amara pouts, but then Zilas pulls her from Cray's lap, telling her, "I have something you can suck on. How about you go to my room and the three of us will come take care of you in a minute."

Amara glances at me, something wistful passing through her eyes before it disappears. "Okay," she states, turning back to Zilas. "But don't take too long, or else I may start the party without you."

"Mm, I hope you do, little devil." Zilas yanks her head back by her hair and kisses her brutally.

Slapping Amara's ass, Zilas, along with the rest of us, watch as she sashays out the door. I will never regret losing my virginity to one of my best friends, but I wish it had been Raya. What's done is done. All we can do is try to make things right and move on.

"So—" Adrik asks the same question Amara did a little while ago, "What now?"

"Now, I'm going to do what I never thought I'd do and beg for Saraya's forgiveness."

"You can't blame yourself, bro. Your father is the one to blame..." Cray states the obvious, but I beg to differ.

"Is he? Raya was one of my best friends back then; she was one of us, and we were quick to believe the worst of her because my father, who didn't want us together, showed me a video. I should have known better..."

"The great Nyx Beckam is going to get on his knees and beg a woman for forgiveness?" Cray grins wickedly, then asks, "Will you record it?"

"Fuck you, Cray. Don't you have a pussy to be plowing right now?" I throw one of the pillows at him, then wince when it pulls at my wound.

A throat clears, and we all gaze at the doorway where Raya stands with a tray. "Sasha says that you have to take your pain pills. She'll come in and check on you as soon as you finish eating."

"Look at this, guys. Our boy here has a hot little helper taking good care of him. Maybe we should leave them alone; he may need a sponge bath." Adrik winks at Raya, and I grin at her blush.

"I'm sure the nurse is the one that gets paid to do that." Raya's sharp tongue is quick to address Adrik's little comment.

"Oh, but you're much prettier to look at." I lick my lips as I rake my eyes up and down her body.

I think I've made her speechless because her lips clamp shut, and she comes forward, placing the tray on the nightstand without saying anything else. When she turns to leave, Cray, Zilas, and Adrik jump up and head for the door.

"We have somewhere to be," Zilas informs Raya. "You're going to have to help Nyx eat."

"But..." The door closes, leaving just the two of us in the room.

"Come here, little lamb."

"Nyx, I don't think—"

"Then don't. Just come here." I pat the spot on the edge of the bed beside me. "You and I need to have a little talk."

Just because I know I've been wrong all these years doesn't mean I will change into a simp. I'm Nyx fucking Beckam, and although I'll do what needs to be done to make sure I keep Raya by my side, she *will* learn that what I say still goes. That doesn't mean she can't *persuade* me to change my mind. She may be the only one capable of doing just that.

Instead of sitting on the bed, she pulls a chair closer and sits. Smirking, I cock an eyebrow but let her have her way—for now. Once I'm healed a little more, I'll have to remind her where her place is.

"Well? What is it we need to talk about?" she asks, crossing one leg over the other as she leans back into the chair.

She's in brown leggings and a cream-colored, oversized shirt that's hanging off one shoulder. The minx isn't even wearing a bra, and I can see the peaks to her perfect breasts jut out every time she moves.

"You."

"What about me, Nyx? I thought you knew everything." My response annoys her, but I don't let it bother me.

"I did, too, but maybe I don't."

Her body tenses, and as I stare at her, she fidgets. "I don't understand what you mean. Can you please stop being so cryptic and just tell me what it is that you might not know?"

I shake my head. "How about you tell me instead. Start with the day that I was told of your betrayal."

She clears her throat, uncrosses her legs, and stands up. "I'm leaving..."

"Tell me," I call out to her before she reaches the door. "Tell me *your* side of the story, Raya."

❖

Saraya stares out the window, arms crossed in front of her chest and lost in thought. I use this time to gaze at her profile. Her features are just as beautiful as they were when we were kids.

I remember when we met for the first time. Saraya was in the fifth grade, and I was in the sixth grade, but even then, I thought she was the prettiest girl I had ever seen. We became fast friends and were inseparable. It was the six of us against the world. Of course, Raya and Mara formed a different kind of friendship, gossiping about boys and whatever else females gossip about.

I always tried not to let their *boy talk* bother me because I knew Raya would be all mine one day. That day came during her freshman year. I gave Raya her first kiss, and eventually, I gave my little lamb her first orgasm. I was supposed to be her first in everything, but the last was stolen from me.

"Raya...talk to me."

"What do you want me to say, Nyx? It was a long time ago. There's no need to dredge up the past..."

"There is if we are even thinking about being in each other's future," I tell her, a bit surly.

She turns and meets my stare. "Who says we will be? If you release my trust, I can be out of your hair."

"Who says I want that?"

"Oh please, Nyx. You can't stand that I've entered your life again; I've disrupted the mighty Beckam Heir's play time—"

"Stop it!" I say sternly. "Don't be putting fucking words in my mouth, Raya. You have no idea what I'm thinking."

She rolls her eyes and resumes staring out the window.

"Tell me about that day, Saraya." I make it sound like an order, not a request.

She exhales, and when she does, I see her transformation go from annoyance to detached as her spine straightens. I can only see her profile, but I don't miss the cynical smile on her lips.

"What do you want to hear first? How I begged for us to be able to be together before promising to stay away from you in order to save your life, or how your father shut me up by having his friend rape me? Oh, maybe I should start by telling you how Layton fucking Beckam threatened me that if I were to say anything to you, he'd kill you then make me his whore to give him a new Heir!"

Raya looks at me now, but it's with indifference, and although I heard all of it on the video, hearing it come from her is so much worse. Honestly, I don't know how I will ever make all of this up to her, but you better believe I will try. I hold my hand out to her, but she only stares at it as if it will hurt her.

"Come here," I say softly, and she scoffs before looking out the window again. "I said, come here!" I put more authority behind it and finally, she pulls away from the window and stands beside me.

"Well, I'm here..."

Her attitude makes my cock jerk, and I give her another order as I hand her a pillow, "On your knees."

Narrowing her eyes at me, she does as she's told. The bed sits high enough that only her head and shoulders are visible, but it's enough for me to grab her hair and keep my little lamb's attention on me.

"You wanted the fucking truth, *Phoenyx*! I didn't betray you—I *saved* you! Believe me or not, I really don't give a fuck anymore."

I stare into her brown doe-like eyes, a grin slowly appearing on my lips before I ask, "Have I ever told you how fucking sexy you are when you get your panties in a bunch?"

"Nyx..." Raya says in warning.

"Don't use that tone with me, little lamb. I have something to say, and I want to make sure you hear it loud and clear because I'm only going to say it once."

"Well, spit it out then. I don't have all day..."

I cock a brow. "Hot date?"

"Ha! I wish. I know better than to try dating at the moment. Your little twat blocker, Cale, ruins that."

Grinning, I stare at her. She never knows when to give up—I love it!

"If it's your twat that's needing attention, I'll be more than happy to keep it company, and Cale will be nowhere in sight."

"Nyx..."

"I'm sorry," I say flat out, all joking aside.

"W-what?"

"I said I wasn't going to repeat it. I was a dick, and I should have come to you. Fuck, I should have known better than to think you would betray me like I thought you had, and for that I will have to live with that guilt."

"Oh, so you are just going to believe what I'm telling you now?" Raya asks sarcastically.

I tug on her hair more and pull her toward me, ignoring the pain in my chest. She pushes herself up to relieve some pressure as she glares at me.

"I already knew the truth. It killed me to watch the *real* video of what happened. I needed to hear it come from your pretty little lips, though. It fucking guts me even more to hear you say it, to have you relive it, but I deserve this pain and so much more because nothing will ever compare to what you went through, Raya. I owe you my fucking life!"

I take her mouth before she can say anything and kiss her with everything I've got. I need her to know that I *am* that same boy from all those years ago; I've just grown up and learned how to not take shit from anyone. For her, I will be Phoenyx Beckam. For the rest of the world, I am Nyx, Heir to Nyte's Hall, and I will burn this motherfucking world down for her, trying to make up for her loss of innocence and all her years of captivity.

TWENTY-FOUR

Saraya

I've been keeping my distance from Nyx for the past week. I don't know what to think of his attitude toward me now; it's like constant whiplash being around him. I'm not sure if his injury is factoring into his mood swings, but one minute, he's sweet and playful, and the next, he is angry and domineering. Okay, maybe more frustrated than angry, but it comes off the same where Nyx is concerned.

He's pissed that I still haven't given him my answer about marrying him. He thinks that I should just fall at his feet and worship him just because he's apologized for what happened and his role in it all these years.

Don't get me wrong, my stepbrother is hot as hell and can fuck, but I will *not* worship at his feet. We still have a lot to discuss about where to go from here, and quite frankly, I'm not ready to forgive him just yet. I'd like to see the lengths he will go to redeem himself.

I'm supposed to be trying to pick an outfit for work tonight. I refuse to keep wearing the clothing Nyx keeps having made for me, because I don't want to lead him on. For some odd reason, Amara decided to go back to my house and grab all my clothes. Unfortunately, I don't really have the type of clothing that is suitable for Club Unholy.

Between being lost in thought, thinking about Nyx, and trying to find something salvageable that I can throw together to wear, I don't hear anyone come into my room.

"Boo!"

I jump, grabbing my chest as I spin away from my closet. My heart is now racing from this little scare, and I glare at the petite woman before me with a wicked smirk on her face.

"Goddamn it, Mara! What the hell?"

"Oops, my bad." She chuckles. "I didn't mean to scare you."

I give her a skeptical look before turning back to my closet. "What do you want?"

"Is that any way to talk to your BFF?"

I turn around and cross my arms, scoffing, "BFF? Really?"

I'm trying to figure out what she's about, why she's been nice, when it hits me—*she knows*. If she knows, then they all know, but since she's the only one who's been a bitch to me, unlike the others; I never caught on. Now, it's starting to make sense.

Amara shrugs. "The past is the past, right? Every day is a fresh start..."

"You're sounding like a church-going, goody two shoes, Mara. It's very off-putting and doesn't suit you at all."

"Oh, thank fuck! I didn't know how long I could act like that for." She steps up to me and slips her hand around my waist.

All I do is lift my brow.

"So, we can let bygones be bygones, right?" Mara asks before biting her lip.

"You're still not getting any from me, Mara. I don't swing that way." I step back and out of her reach, and she lets me.

"Well, you're no fun. I can always make you let me; you know." Her threats go in one ear and out the other.

I know she would never intentionally hurt me because then it would piss Nyx off, and I'm still trying to figure out whether she truly loves him as just a friend or romantically as well. Of course, Nyx says they're only friends, but I've seen some of the looks she gives him when she thinks nobody is looking.

"You should try joining me and Nyx sometime, Raya. I bet you would enjoy it." Amara just never stops; it's amusing sometimes.

"I think that may be a bit difficult when Nyx has already said the two of you were done."

Trying to keep my reaction at a certain level so she doesn't see just how disturbed I am that they have fucked in the past is hard, but I think I do a decent job of it. Mara and I can never get our friendship back, even if she were to beg for forgiveness on her knees. Her fucking the love of my life is why our friendship can never be the same.

I'm still not sure I can get back with Nyx because of this little issue, either. However, I know that with Nyx, there were no other feelings but friendship, and just the need for a good fuck is why he did it. I feel that Amara, on the other hand, has deeper feelings on the matter.

She's quick as she rushes me, slamming me against the wall. With her hand on my throat, holding me in place, her other hand cups my sex through the jeans I'm wearing, and she gives me another one of her wicked smiles.

"Forget Nyx, Raya. I'll make you feel everything you've felt with him and then some. I know what makes women tick, and I promise you that you will have the best fucking orgasm. If a cock is what you need, I have a variety of strap-ons."

Her touch does nothing for me; it never will. I stand here, smirking as I listen to her little speech. The second she leans in and tries to kiss my lips, I turn my head, catching her bright red lips on my cheek.

"Mm, playing hard to get?" She snickers.

"I'm not playing, Mara. I've told you you're not my type, but hey, I'm honored that you want me so much..."

She scoffs, "You have no idea what you are turning down, Raya."

I lift my hand and lightly brush some of her hair from her face. "Oh, I think I do. You see, I can still remember Nyx's cum running down my thighs the night I ran. I can still feel that magnificent stretch his cock gave my pussy every time he plunged inside me." I lower my voice and say, "My cunt is fitted to take Nyx's cock and his cock only. Can you say the same when you fuck all the other Heirs?"

When all she does is grin at my words, I continue and ask, "Has Nyx ever stopped you from taking birth control or Plan B because he *wants* his seed to take? Why do you think I ran that night, Mara? Nyx was taking away another choice, and I couldn't do it anymore."

Mara lets go of my throat and steps back. "You're lying. Nyx doesn't want kids yet."

I lift my brow at her and cross my arms at my chest.

"Did you take any?" she asks. "After you left?"

"Do you honestly think I've had time?" My tone is smug, but deep down, I'm worried about this very thing.

Amara glances down at my stomach, then meets my eyes once more as she says, "I'll go get you some..."

"It's too late. It's been more than a week. We're just playing the waiting game now, but it's not like it would matter anyway because we've had unprotected sex twice now."

"Stupid, stupid woman! How could you be so careless?" Mara begins to pace in front of me.

"Oh, I'm sorry that the man I fell in love with years ago decided to have unprotected sex with me. I'm sorry that he's told me we *will* be marrying, and I'm *really* sorry that you can no longer have sex with him!"

"Fuck! You don't get it..." Mara's voice trails off, and she goes over to shut my bedroom door.

"What are you doing? I need to get ready for work..."

"No. First, you'll sit down and listen to what I have to say."

Amara is very demanding, and whatever she wants to talk about seems important. So, I move and sit on the edge of my bed and wait for her to start. When a minute passes, and she's done nothing but pace and chew on her thumbnail, I get fed up and stand.

"Well, that's been a nice conversation, but if you don't mind—"

"Fucking sit down and let me figure out how to say what I need to say!" Mara glowers at me, and I roll my eyes before sitting again.

"Amara—"

"There is something on one of the flash drives that Nyx brought back that is very disturbing, and it concerns you. Nyx hasn't seen it yet, but the rest of us have. Once he does watch it, shit is going to hit the fan, and an all-out turf war is going to break out unless we can figure out how to keep it under the rug."

"O—kay, what is it?"

Mara sighs as she pinches the bridge of her nose. "I shouldn't say anything, but after everything that has happened and what you went through, you deserve to know."

I sit here with bated breath, waiting to hear what's putting Mara so on edge. The fact that they're keeping it from Nyx tells me it can't be good. However, Amara's next words have me gasping in utter disbelief.

"The flash drive has the answer you've been looking for your whole life. Saraya, I know who your father is."

I can't concentrate on work tonight, but I have no other choice because if I were to skip out, then Nyx would know something is up. His little guard dog, Cale, is here watching out for me while he's still recovering. He fought with the doctor because he wanted to return to work, but it was useless. The Heirs threatened to restrain him to the bed if he tried.

I'm coming from the break room when I walk past one of the back rooms that only gets used by the Heirs—mainly Amara. There's giggling coming from the room labeled Chem Lab, and my curiosity gets the best of me. I push the button that opens the blinds, hoping that Mara doesn't have them closed from the inside, and I smile when she comes into view. However, my smile falters when I realize the scene she's doing with the male on the other side of the window.

The male is stripped bare and cuffed to a metal table. Amara is also naked as she straddles the man, fucking him hard, but that's not what's disturbing. In Mara's hand is a beaker with some kind of greenish-yellow liquid in it, and it's fucking smoking out of the top.

My mouth drops as she tips the beaker and pours some of the contents onto the man's face. He screams from behind the ball gag he's wearing as his face begins to melt. Mara, being a sadistic little bitch laughs and keeps bouncing away on the guy's cock as she tortures him.

Unable to watch anymore, I close the blinds and head back to the front, trying hard to keep my stomach contents from coming up. I know they only hurt bad people, but damn, shoot them or something. Why she feels the need to go to those lengths—while fucking them, at that—is beyond me.

Over an hour and a half later, I'm still thinking about that horrific scene. It's not until about an hour before I'm scheduled to leave when thoughts of Mara's torture disappear because the Kappel twins walk in. They're all smiles as soon as they see me standing at the hostess stand. As always, Jarod flirts with me, but his brother pushes him forward, preventing him from getting his ass kicked when Cale comes over and stands beside me.

Any other time, I would curse Cale out, but I'm not in the mood to deal with that shit show at the moment, so I mutter a "thanks," and he goes back to the bar area to keep watch. I do have to shake my head at him when Mika comes waltzing through the door and Cale is once again ready to come over.

"Good evening, beautiful. How has your night been?" He's respectful and doesn't try to overstep when he sees Cale watching us.

After a few pleasantries, he moves on, and I return to standing here bored until Cray approaches me. I haven't talked much with the Heir since he watched Nyx fuck me. It's a little embarrassing to think about, but at the same time, a tingle starts between my legs at the memory.

"I'm heading back to the Hall, and Nyx wants me to bring you home. He says you've worked enough tonight." He smirks.

"My shift isn't over..."

Cray snaps his fingers, and Amee, a house sub, comes over. "You will finish as hostess tonight."

"As you wish, Master D," the woman says, grinning.

I quirk my brow at him as we walk out the door. "Master D?"

"What?"

"Is that really what you go by here at the club?"

"No." He grins. "It's what all women call me."

I roll my eyes and ask, "Why D for your last name and not C for your first."

He shrugs. "Tell me, Raya. Do you prefer to say dick or cock?"

I choke out a laugh, then reply, "Definitely cock. Dick makes you sound like an asshole."

"Exactly, hence why I prefer D, as in dick and asshole." His white teeth gleam in the elevator lighting.

All I can do is shake my head, amused. Why he wants to be known as an asshole is beyond me, but hey, whatever trips his trigger.

Stepping into the private garage, I follow Cray to a sleek black motorcycle. I believe people call it a crotch rocket. I stop and stare at him like he's crazy.

Rolling his eyes, he hands me his helmet and states, "You will be safe. Nyx would not allow me to bring you home on it if he thought it was a danger to you."

"I don't give a fuck what Nyx thinks. These things are death traps! I've seen way too many accidents online."

Cray's smile stretches across his face. "I won't repeat what you just said about not giving a fuck to Nyx. I do take offense, though. I will not put you in harm's way; you're one of us. Now, get that tight little ass on the back."

I yank the helmet from his grasp and smirk. Once the helmet is secure and I watch Cray get on, I lift my leg over the back and settle in behind the Heir. Leaning into him, I speak louder than usual so he can hear me when I say, "And I won't tell him that you think I have a tight little ass."

Cray throws his head back, laughing.

I'm not sure how he did it, but Craydon Donovan has taken my mind off the news hidden within that flash drive Mara told me about. I haven't seen the video, but I could tell that what she was saying was true, and it's been eating at me ever since. Cray has chased those demons away for the time being with his cocky attitude and playfulness.

"Hold on, little Raya, wouldn't want you falling off..."

I no sooner wrap my arms around his waist than he's doing a small wheelie as he takes off like a bat out of hell. My screams echo through the garage before turning into laughter as we break free into the warm night air, leaving Unholy behind us.

TWENTY-FIVE

Nyx

Two whole fucking weeks, my little lamb has hidden from me. I know she's still at Nyte's Hall because Adrik has told me so. Raya's getting along with the other Heirs, but she's kept her distance from me, and I know why.

She owes me an answer.

I thought we would talk about everything during my recovery time, but I guess she has other plans. I let a grin spread across my face because Raya has no idea what kind of position she has put herself in.

I've been recuperating for fourteen days, and although I'm far from healed, Doc has permitted me to move around the Hall freely. I still can't go to the club, but at least I won't have Mahony or Sasha, my special guard dogs, watching my every move. I now know why my little lamb dislikes Cale.

It's late afternoon when I finish my shower, dress in sweatpants and a black T-shirt, and leave my room. Having the nurse tend to me was nice, but she wasn't Raya. Now, I need to go find the object of my obsession because I have needs that nobody else has been able to help with, and I've had an itch for a really long time.

"Take it easy, Mr. Beckam." Dr. Mahony instructed me this morning, "No straining yourself and no heavy lifting."

My only response was, "Well, I guess I'll need someone to help me every time I take a piss, now, won't I?"

He wasn't too impressed by my words, but do you really think I gave a fuck? Nobody is going to tell me that I can't fuck my girl, and that's precisely what I'm going to do once I find her. She can deny it all she wants, but we both know that she's addicted to me, as I am her.

Once again there is no answer when I knock on her bedroom door. My hands ball up into fists as I try and keep the irritation at bay. Typically, I would walk away, not knowing whether Raya was in her room, but not this time. This time, I twist the doorknob and push the door wide open.

Empty.

"Looking for little Raya, are you?"

I swing around and find Cray leaning against the wall across the hallway with a big ole smirk on his face. Rolling my eyes, I shut her door and head for the stairs, ignoring Cray altogether. I don't need to catch shit from my friends. They've been up my ass ever since they watched the video themselves. They're finding the situation way too amusing for my liking.

They're all waiting to see me grovel, but that won't happen in front of them. I don't owe them shit, and I refuse to be their entertainment. I get that I fucked up, we both did. It seems we were young and easily influenced, but now that we are older and know better, we need to figure this shit out because I refuse to go another day without calling her mine.

When all is said and done, Saraya Abbott *is* mine, but apparently, I need to give her time to get used to the idea. Time is up now. I'm going to find her and reclaim her, and she's going to accept it because Nyx Beckam *doesn't* take no for an answer.

I pass a still smirking Cray but slow down when I hear him say, "I saw her heading to your kitchen. You may want to make her change. I may not make a move on your woman without your permission, but that doesn't mean my dick won't get hard at seeing her in *certain* attire."

I don't look at him when I warn him, "That permission will never come. Raya is off limits to all of you..."

Cray's laughter is all I hear as I continue downstairs, heading in the direction that my friend directed me in. I prepare myself for what I presume will be a delightful picture of my little lamb working in the kitchen wearing clothing that makes my best friend hard and knowing that I will have to punish her for it.

I hear her as I approach the swinging door, humming a tune I'm unfamiliar with. Pushing the door open a crack, I find my little lamb standing at the stove, adding some hamburger to a pan. I find it a bit amusing and cute.

Saraya has been cooking all my meals, and I really need to thank her personally. So, slipping through the door silently, I walk up behind her, admiring her *very* short skirt. Cray wasn't lying; my dick is instantly hard as I peruse her slender legs, from her bare feet all the way up to where they disappear right before her beautiful ass.

I take hold of her hips and grip them tight, knowing she's going to jump. Feeling her in my grasp again sends a jolt through me, and suddenly, my irritation from her avoiding me again takes hold.

"Jesus, Nyx!"

I ignore her as I dip my head and nuzzle her neck while I grind myself against her ass. She tries to move away, but I won't allow it. Without saying a word, I lift her skirt, push her panties aside, and run my fingers through her folds. The moisture pools instantly, and I chuckle.

"Nyx..."

I yank the front of my sweatpants down and push into her, not stopping until I'm balls deep inside her. She's trying to stir the hamburger but pauses when she gasps with my intrusion.

"Nyx, you need to stop. I'm trying to make dinner since *someone* decided to let the help go..."

"And?" I ask, "Did I tell you to fucking stop?"

I pull out to the tip, then thrust back into her, letting her gorgeous cunt swallow me whole. My little lamb hisses with the intrusion, but it only makes me want to fuck her harder.

I chuckle when she pauses her cooking and instruct her, "Don't forget the seasoning, little lamb."

"Nyx, you shouldn't be exerting yourself..."

"Salt, pepper, garlic powder, and chopped onion, Raya." I lift her leg and plunge deeper into her depths, groaning at the way her walls grip my fucking cock.

"Phoenyx—I can't!"

"Does it look like I give a fuck if you're cooking? I'll take you... anywhere... and anytime... I want." I thrust hard and deep in between my words. "We both know this greedy girl will welcome me whenever I want it." I reach around and pinch her clit, making her cry out.

Raya pants and moves her hips to meet mine, but I'm not sure whether she is aware of herself doing so. I bite her neck, and she moans as her head rests against my shoulder. With her eyes closed and mouth hanging open, Saraya, in the throes of passion, is so fucking hot. The fact that it's my cock making her feel this good only adds to my ego.

"Don't burn the meat, baby." I give a slight chuckle.

"Oh fuck—I'm going to come, Nyx..."

I thrust in a few more times just to fuel her climax, and then I pull out just as she's about to explode. My own cock aches, but it will wait. I'm not ready to give her what I know her body wants.

"What the..." Raya complains.

"That was just the appetizer," I say, turning as I tuck my throbbing cock back into my sweats, "You'll get the main dish soon enough."

"Fucking asshole..." comes from her pouty lips, and I snicker.

"Yeah, but you want this fucking asshole." Those are the last words out of my mouth before I walk out of the kitchen.

ME: Eat with me in my room.
LIL LAMB: No.
ME: That wasn't a request, Raya.
LIL LAMB: It's still no.
ME: Don't test me, baby.

She leaves my last message *open,* making me wonder if she will defy my orders. I know she doesn't like being told what to do, but I love riling her up. I love doling out punishments more, and she will be adding to her long list of punishments if she doesn't eat with me.

Lucky for her, when she brings me my food, there are two plates on the tray. I smirk at her, earning me a glare from those beautiful brown eyes. She says nothing as she sets the tray down on the bedside table.

"No, bring it to the table in the corner so we can eat together," I tell her, earning yet another glare.

I tilt my head and watch her ass as she walks to the corner where said table is at. Damn, that skirt really is super short. I frown with displeasure as I walk up behind her and lean over her back.

With both my hands on each side of her, braced on the table, I bring my mouth to her ear and say, "I'm going to burn that skirt if I ever catch you wearing it outside of our wing of the Hall."

"What? Why?"

"Because you don't need to be flaunting that beautiful ass in front of my friends. They can only take so much and are already annoyed that I won't share you."

I watch as she swallows hard before responding with, "I don't flaunt—"

I grip the hem of her skirt and hold it to her body, cutting off her words with my own, "This is how high your skirt is in the back," showing her how it sits just above the bottom of her ass cheeks when she's bent over. I may have accidentally let a finger or two slip between her thighs as I do so. She's still wet from earlier.

"Don't..."

"Don't what?"

Raya pushes herself back, taking me by surprise and making me step back. "Don't start something that you're not going to finish."

My cock jerks, and the next thing I know, I'm spinning Raya around to face me. Slipping my hand around her throat, I push her back until her ass is against the edge of the table.

"Pull it out, little lamb."

"What?"

"You heard me. I said pull... it... out. I told you the main dish was coming, and now, I'm ready to serve it, so pull it out."

Raya's eyes flash with need before she glances down at my package. "You're hurt; you shouldn't be doing this..."

"I didn't ask for your opinion. I gave you an order, little lamb. Now, will you follow it, or will I have to take it once again?"

Raya glowers at me, but her hands swiftly push my sweatpants down past my hips, letting my hardness spring free. I want to flip her over and redden her ass so badly, but I won't. I want to see just how far she will let me push her before she gives me hell.

"What do you want to do with it, little lamb? Tell me..."

She gazes into my eyes, and I cock my brow. She then looks down, and I have to grind my teeth when she wraps her hand around it. The hand around her throat moves up to grip her jaw, but it's all I do.

"Take my panties off," she murmurs.

My eyes light up, and instead of taking them off properly, I rip them off. "There—done."

Reaching behind her, Raya shoves the tray over and sits on the edge of the table. I wince as she pulls me with her by my cock. When I growl at her for doing so, she gives me a beautifully wicked smile.

"What are you waiting for, Nyx? Are you going to fuck me?"

"No."

Confusion crosses her delicate features, and I hold back a grin, waiting for her to say what she wants. I can see the irritation in her eyes—she's frustrated. Good.

"If you want my cock inside you, then make it happen," I tell her.

"Fuck you."

She lets go of my length and then moves away. Maybe she's not used to asking for it. I have no doubt that sex with Ken was anything but consensual, and she had no choice. Instead of asking her what she wants, which can wait until another time, I sit and hold my hand out.

"Nyx, I think it's best—"

"—that you get that ass of yours over here and ride my cock," I cut her off.

The little minx stands there, biting her bottom lip, contemplating what she wants to do. I want to give her the choice as long as she makes the right choice. I'm not trying to be a dick, but I know she wants it. She's getting inside her head, and we all know what happens when he does that.

"Be a good girl and come here."

She crosses her arms.

"This *is* going to happen, Raya. I'm just giving you the chance to take control." I begin stroking my cock for her. "It's no secret that I want inside that glorious cunt of yours, so why is it so hard to admit that you want me there, too?"

"It's not that, Nyx. I'll happily admit to wanting you, but sex won't fix the underlying problems we have."

I stop stroking to say, "I know, Raya. We will talk about it, but right now, I need to be inside of you—it's been too long."

I hold my hand out once more, and after staring at it briefly, Raya takes it and lets me pull her to me. For the first time in God knows how long, I ask instead of demand, "Will you please sit on my cock and ride it?"

Laughter bubbles out of my little lamb, but she swings her leg over and hovers over my shaft until I'm lined up to her wet slit. We both moan as she descends, and our foreheads press together as she adjusts to my size again.

"My God, Nyx..."

"No shit. You feel fucking amazing, but I'm sorry, this can't be slow. I need you to fuck me hard, baby. Can you do that for me?"

"Are you sure you're up for it?" She cocks her brow at me.
"Oh, you better believe it..."

TWENTY-SIX

Saraya

Nyx is incorrigible!

How am I supposed to stay mad at him when he flaunts that delicious piece of meat in front of me like that? I'm worried that we will never work through our issues if we keep pushing them aside in order to have hot sex. This will be the last time—I swear.

"Don't fucking move," I hiss when he tries thrusting upward.

When he doesn't listen, I stop moving altogether. Nyx holds my hips in place and takes over, but like hell if I'm going to allow him to injure himself because he's too stubborn.

I try climbing off, but he only smirks and thrusts harder. I truly begin to worry, so I do the only thing I can think of—I slap him across the face. It's not a light slap, either. His head snaps to the right, his hair flying into his face as it does. All movement stops except for the thunderous beating of my heart.

When he turns to look at me, my eyes widen, and I curse, "Oh fuck!"

Grabbing his face, I check his mouth only to see a small gash in his lip from where his tooth punctured it. He'll survive. Nyx stares at me in amusement, but I don't return it. Instead, he gets my glare once again.

"Oh, little lamb, what have you done?"

"You said I was in control; you were going to hurt yourself, Nyx! I'm not sorry. Maybe next time you will listen..."

If I'm being totally honest, I do feel bad. Why am I raising my hand to another person when I hated it when it was done to me?

"Stop that."

"Stop what?" I ask Nyx.

"You're not sorry. Stick with that. Don't get in your head and start feeling bad about hitting me when I deserved it. It's not like you did it out of spite, Raya."

"How do you always know what I'm thinking? It's fucking creepy."

Nyx sighs. "I know you better than you know yourself. I always have."

I know he's right, but it doesn't make it any less creepy. I cup his cheek and examine his bloody lip. Before I know what I'm doing, I lean in, and my tongue darts out, slowly licking the blood away. I feel him jerk inside of me. My hips—having a mind of their own—gently move back and forth as I taste the very essence of my stepbrother.

When I feel him start to move, I let out a little snarl of my own, and with my mouth still pressed against his, I say, "Don't fucking move. Let me do it."

He stops instantly, a slight chuckle escaping his lips. "You are so fucking hot like this, Raya, but you're so going to get punished for it later."

"You'll have to catch me first..."

Nyx's hand grips the back of my neck and holds me in place, so his other hand can come down on my ass. Thankfully, my skirt is in the way, so it hampers the sting a little. Either way, it still turns me on, and I take Nyx's lips, opening mine to let him in. I continue to rock and grind, making sure to rub my clit against him.

When his hand grips my hip, and I feel him start to swell, I stop entirely and pull back. "Don't fucking come yet, Nyx."

"I'm not making any promises, little lamb. Now, get back to it before I throw you over the table and fuck you like a common whore."

"There's nothing common about me, *brother*. As for the whore part, well, you only get that if you're a good boy for me."

I don't know where the sassiness is coming from. She's been dormant for so long that I thought she'd be gone for good. I see now that it only took the right person to bring it out in me. Nyx can be a cocky ass all he wants, but I'll be damned if I let him walk all over me. Knowing I don't have a life hanging over my head, true freedom is just a hop, skip, and jump away. The only question is, will I find it again with Nyx, or is it too late for us?

Nyx's growl should have been warning enough, but when I don't pay attention to it, I find myself being lifted and thrown over the table just like he said. My first reaction is the worry that he may have hurt himself, but then, when he holds my head down against the table and thrusts back into me, anger mixed with excitement crashes through my body, and I find myself both fighting and fucking against him.

"Look at you, little lamb. The lion's got you in his clutches now, and he's going to eat you up."

"Damn it, Nyx...please!"

I don't know if I'm begging him for more or for him to stop; either way, all he does is laugh as he slams into me from behind. My eyes roll to the back of my head as he hits that sweet spot repeatedly. My muscles tighten with the oncoming orgasm.

"Am I being a good boy now, little lamb? Come for me, baby—come now!" His command ends on a growl as he plunges into me one last time and stills.

I feel his release, and it sets mine off. My walls grip him, and he curses before pulling out a little and thrusting back in. He loosens his hold on my head but tangles his fingers into my hair.

"Fuck, Raya...what are you doing to me?" He thrusts a few more times as I'm still coming.

"Oh God...yes...f—uck!" I lay spent underneath him as his forehead rests against my shoulder blades.

His phone ringing brings us both back to reality. When he straightens up, I think he's going to pull out, but he pushes me back down and tells me to stay before answering his phone.

"Beckam..."

He traces his fingers up and down my back as he listens to whoever is on the other end of the call. The caress feels good, but I don't want to overthink it. I can't afford to fall harder for Nyx when I'm unsure what our future holds.

"What the fuck do you mean Pike wants to talk to me? Why would I want to discuss anything with the leader of South Crew?"

Nyx's voice is angry. I've heard of the South Crew; they're bad news, and Nyx would do well to avoid them.

"Fine. Tomorrow afternoon at the old train station. Tell him to be there at two sharp; I won't wait for him." There's a pause, and then Nyx explodes, "The hell I will bring her! What the fuck does he want with Raya?"

My head whips around, and I meet Nyx's cold gray stare. I would think he's pissed at me, but his hand caressing my spine says otherwise. He finally pulls out slowly, helping me to stand as he continues listening to the other person. Before I can move away, though, he pulls me in and kisses my lips. He then points to the chair, indicating I am to sit and eat.

I appease him for the time being until he hangs the phone up and says, "Eat."

"Who was that, and why the fuck does the South Crew want to see me?" I question him.

"I don't know why, but don't worry because you're not going with me."

"Nyx, you can't be going out with your injury!"

"I'm fine, Raya," he says, but it looks like something is bothering him and he's wanting to ask me something.

"What is it?"

"You don't know why Pike would want me to bring you, do you?"

"What? No! I've never met the guy before. I've heard of the Crew when Ken talked about them, but that's the extent."

He nods.

Wow, he actually believes me!

"Who was on the phone?" I ask again since he didn't answer me the first time.

He waves his hand and states, "It was just Jarod passing along a message for his father."

My spine stiffens.

"What's wrong?"

I'm not sure if I'm allowed to say anything because I remember what Mara said, but I think it's best to tell Nyx. He should know. I don't want to keep anything from him anymore.

"Nyx, you should know something."

I slide one of the plates over to him, and he takes it, waiting for me to go on. I'm just not sure how to say it. How pissed will Mara be?

"Well, what is it?" he asks.

"Um, well," I reply before pausing, but then I just blurt out, "I found out who my father was—or is."

⁂

Maybe it wasn't the best idea to relay the information that Mara gave me to Nyx. One minute, he was sitting across from me eating the spaghetti I brought to the room—which has now turned cold—as I talked, and then he was gone. Dropping his fork, he stood, threw his napkin down, and stalked from the room. I've been sitting here trying to make sense of what just took place.

After about five minutes, I finally stand and start clearing the plates, piling them back onto the tray to return to the kitchen. Mara comes flying into Nyx's room like the Tasmanian Devil and grips my wrist, stopping me from lifting the tray.

"What the fuck, Saraya?! I told you we needed to tread lightly when we told Nyx about the other video!"

I yank my wrist away from her and step closer to the little devil as I glare at her. "I'm really getting tired of your animosity, Mara! I've never done shit to you, so stop acting as though I have. What I tell Nyx is none of your concern, especially when it involves *me*!"

I know I should probably watch my step with this little assassin, but seriously, I can't help but lose my shit when it comes to her. Maybe I shouldn't have said anything, but that isn't the case. I'm done keeping secrets from Nyx. If we have any chance of making it, we have to be open and honest with each other. I'll still make him work for my forgiveness if only to see him grovel, but I know I will forgive him in the end. There is no doubt after what just happened between us.

"Well, I hope you're happy because Nyx is on a rampage now!" Mara states, crossing her arms at her chest.

"Why? I don't understand. Jarod called him to relay a message about Pike wanting to meet up, and he wants Nyx to bring me. I then told him what you told me about my real father."

"You don't fucking get it, do you?" Mara scoffs, shaking her head.

"Get what? Nobody tells me anything, so how am I supposed to *get* anything?!" I grab her arm and demand, "Tell me what the fuck is going on!"

Amara takes in the sight of my hand on her arm, then returns her eyes to mine. "You've got some balls; I'll give you that." She yanks her arm away before saying, "Word on the street is that South Crew will be joining alliances with one of the wealthy families in Nyte, making that family the wealthiest in town."

"What am I missing?" I ask, a bit confused.

Mara rolls her eyes and sighs, "They will take over running the town. South Crew has others in their pockets, making them very wealthy, but they are nobody unless they align themselves with a *somebody*."

"How would they do that?" Dread fills me as the answer to my own question dawns on me.

Mara must see it on my face because she says, "Ding, ding, ding, you've got it."

"You mean to tell me that he would give me—"

"YES! Your sperm donor plans on giving his only daughter to the mighty drug lord, Pike."

The air seems to vanish from my lungs as I drop into one of the chairs. "Do they know?" I ask her, "Do the twins know about this...about any of this?"

Mara sighs. "We haven't found any evidence to say they do, so no—I don't think your brothers know what your father is up to or why."

TWENTY-SEVEN

Nyx

I stand here panting, with my hand over my chest wound. Fuck! I exerted myself too much. Fucking Raya isn't the cause of the pain, though. No, it was the destruction of the billiard room where I found three of my four friends fucking around, and I went ape shit on them. Thinking back, I know I could have handled it better, but fuck—I was livid.

"What the fuck do you think you were doing by keeping this information from me?" I had roared as soon as I walked into the room and saw Cray, Zilas, and Amara fucking around.

"Calm down and tell us what has your panties in a bunch." Zilas stepped away from Mara, fixing his clothing.

I glared at our little devil and sneered, *"Why don't you tell me everything you told Raya about her fucking father."*

The surprise at hearing this crossed her features briefly, but she also came forward. Her top was long gone, her breasts spilled out over the cups of her bra. The tight leather skirt she'd been wearing was bunched over her hips, and she didn't move to straighten any of it. The smirk on her face was the only indication that she was trying to entice me, but to her dismay, it didn't work.

"I think someone needs a good fucking, or his dick sucked at the very least." Mara had licked her lips.

My cock hadn't stirred at all like it had in the past whenever she had mentioned or offered sexual favors. I have my little lamb back, and she will be the only one relieving any tension I may have in the future.

"I'd take you up on the offer, but I don't want you to know what Raya tastes like." I had said it to hurt her at the time, and it worked, but now I kind of feel like shit for doing it.

She had straightened her spine and clothes before turning her back on me and going to the bar to get herself a drink. Zilas's voice drew my attention to him.

"This is why we hadn't told you yet. We knew you would fly off the handle had you discovered that Kappel was Raya's father."

"How can I protect her if I'm left in the fucking dark about shit?"

"You needed to heal first, Nyx! You were shot in the chest, for fucks sake!" Zilas exploded on me, but I didn't back down.

I got into his face and snarled, *"And I would do it all over again if it meant protecting her! How dare any of you think playing with Raya's safety is okay!"*

"Dude, we didn't see any harm in holding off telling you until we could do it in a way that you wouldn't go off—"

I had cut Cray's words off by picking up the nearest armchair and throwing it over the bar, shattering the long mirror behind it. With my chest heaving, I hadn't stopped there. Next came the table beside the chair and then one of the lamps. The fear that gripped me at the thought of what would have happened had I not known about Kappel's motives only fueled me more.

It had taken all three of them to calm me down and stop me from completely destroying the room. Once I had calmed down enough, I pushed them all away and fled. Now I'm standing here, pain slicing through my chest and thoughts of what I'm going to do to Kappel once I get my hands on him.

As soon as Raya informed me of her father's identity, I knew, without a doubt, that Kappel had used her as a pawn in his little game. Kappel has wanted God status for as long as I can remember; that's why our fathers kept him close. If you ask me, he should have been taken out long ago.

Where does Clyde Kappel get off ignoring his daughter for all these years and then think it's okay to use her when it suits him? You can't tell me he didn't know she was his daughter. It now makes sense how he treated her when he met her at Unholy. It was unusual for him not to flirt or make passes at any female, and Raya is fucking gorgeous.

If Kappel thinks for one minute that he has any legal rights to my little lamb, he will find out quickly just how wrong he is. Raya is fucking mine.

Mine to keep, mine to use, mine to fuck, mine to protect, and the most important one—mine to fucking love. Saraya Abbott is my queen and will give the town of Nyte their next heir, and I will be damned if anyone tries taking her away from me again.

I sit in the blacked-out Sedan's back seat with Adrik while Cale drives. Zilas and Cray are in the SUV behind us, and Tucker, along with Arlo, Charlie, and Kato, one of Cray's men, are in a third vehicle. We aren't ignorant of the fact that we are coming to meet a drug lord. I left Mara back at the Hall to protect Raya in case this was some kind of a setup. I'm not too worried, though. Nyte's Hall is a fortress, and we have plenty of security.

The fact that Pike wants to meet with me, and knowing what I now know, there is a good chance that he's going to want to get rid of me as soon as I tell him that he's not getting Raya. He probably assumes that I will just hand her over to him. Clyde would have been better off taking care of her ex and giving her to him sooner. He should know that I protect what's mine.

As we sit here and wait for these assholes to show up, I glance over at Adrik. I'm still not too happy with any of them for keeping shit from me. It doesn't matter the reason. Regarding Raya, I need to know *everything*, and Adrik, of all people, should know this.

"I won't apologize, Nyx. Had you not just been shot a little over two weeks ago, we would have told you, but you're fucking injured; you shouldn't be here now." My friend stares at me like I should agree and forgive him.

"What the fuck would you do if it was the woman you loved?" I ask him.

A smirk grows on my friend's lips. "Women love me, but I don't love them back. I only love what they can do for me, and don't pretend you weren't like me. Before Raya showed back up, you went through women like crazy."

"I'm not denying it at all," I reply and shrug. "All of that has changed now that Raya is back. The need to consume her—to own her, is back in full force, and no other woman will ever come close to what that fucking woman does to me."

"I get it, I do, but what good are you to her if you hurt yourself because you're not healed entirely? Nobody can protect her as good as you because you love her—she *needs* you."

I scoff as I think of my little lamb's attitude and sassiness. Wondering if what my friend says is true. She's survived this long on her own, but I understand what he's saying. That doesn't mean I have to like it.

Pulling my phone out, I type out a message to my little lamb.

ME: Are you being a good girl for our little devil?

Grinning, I set the phone on my thigh, knowing that she was going to be pissed at my question. When my phone buzzes with an incoming message, I read it and throw my head back, laughing.

LIL LAMB: If by good girl you mean have I not throat punched her yet or stabbed her with a spoon, then yes...I have been a good girl.
ME: A spoon?
LIL LAMB: Yes, a spoon. It's dull and will hurt a hell of a lot more...duh.
ME: Don't sass me...
LIL LAMB: Then don't say shit that will make me sass you.
ME: Keep it up, little lamb...

When nothing more comes through, I pocket my phone and sigh. That woman's mouth gets my dick hard every fucking time, but I never want her to change. A frown quickly replaces my grin when I think about Raya and Mara being together. Mara is dangerous. I hope Raya doesn't push her too far.

I pull my phone out once again.

ME: Don't do anything to harm her, even if she pisses you off.
LIL DEVIL: Oh, I will do something, but no harm will be involved.
ME: Mara....
LIL DEVIL: What? Then you better hope your little lamb is a good little lamb because this wolf has been hungering for a taste.
ME: You won't...
LIL DEVIL: Won't I?

I growl and toss my phone on the center console.

"What's the matter? Having a little tiff with your little lamb?" Adrik chuckles.

"No, *our* little devil will be in a heap of trouble if I come back and find out she's touched what is mine!"

"Oh, I doubt Mara will hurt Raya—"

"I'm not talking about her hurting her..."

"Ahh, I see," he says, then turns his head so I don't see his grin, but it's too late.

I'm about to lecture him when two SUVs similar to the one Cray and Zilas are in pull up. Adrik and I check our pieces, just in case. I put mine back in its holster under my suit jacket while Adrik tucks his in the back of his pants. When we exit the Sedan, a strapped Cale also joins us.

Laughter comes our way from the approaching drug lord. "You look as if you're ready for a war, Phoenyx Beckam."

I glare at his use of my name. "It's Nyx, but you can call me *Mr. Beckam.*"

"Aw, are we not friends, *Phoenyx?*"

Pike's attitude tells me that he's here to rile me up. I need to keep my head straight, not let him get to me. Shoving my hands in my pockets, allowing my jacket to open enough to show just a peek of my piece, I look the guy dead in the eye.

"What is it that you want, Pike. I'm a busy man these days." I act bored as I ask.

"You were told to bring the girl." Pike's smile turns into an annoyed grin as he looks around and says, "Yet I don't see her among your little gang."

We have three more bodies than he does, so I'm not too worried about whether he tries starting anything. He'd be stupid if he tried. Deciding to play with him just a bit, I grin at Adrik, who returns his own before my eyes land on Pike again.

"Our little devil is at home, so no worries, you're safe from her."

The drug lord runs his fingers through his goatee and snickers. "Ah, yes. Your little assassin is a spitfire who I would love to tussle with—some other time—but I think you know who it is I'm referring to."

I shrug. "The only other *woman* that I can think of is *my* fiancée, who is still in *my* bed, where I left her."

He doesn't need to know the truth. If I had my way, she would be in my bed, too crippled to walk after the hard fucking I want so badly to give her. The smirk that grows across my face only adds fuel to the flames I've ignited.

"Kappel, her father, has promised his daughter to me. It's part of our alliance." Pike tries to keep his cool, but I can tell he doesn't like being tested. *Too bad this isn't a test!*

I look to Adrik and to the other two Heirs before my attention goes back to the asshole. "I'm sorry. I'm a bit confused as to what you are talking about. I've never known Kappel to have a daughter, so for him to promise you one, isn't this something you should take up with him?"

"Don't try to be funny, Beckam. You know damn well who I'm talking about. Saraya McNally is my future bride."

"I think you mean Saraya *Abbott,* daughter of the *late* Layton and Jessica Beckam. Saraya Abbott, who is also *my* stepsister and responsibility—oh, and the future *Mrs. Beckam.*"

The drug lord sneers in disgust. "You would fuck your own sister?"

I shrug. "Why not? It's legal, she's hot, and her cunt fits me like a fucking glove."

Cray and Zilas chuckle behind me, but I don't dare take my eyes off the fucker in front of me. I can see it in his eyes that he's about two point five seconds from drawing his weapon on me.

"If that's all you came here for, then this meeting is over..." I turn to walk back to the car, but he stops me.

"I only want to be able to handle my business in the town of Nyte. It's got so much potential. I'll forget doing business with Kappel if you and I can come to an agreement."

"You don't get it, asshole, do you?" Zilas is the one to speak up this time and I stop to ensure Pike doesn't draw on him. "We are cleaning the filth from the streets of Nyte, and that includes drugs. Why the fuck would we make any kind of deal with you?"

"Watch yourself, boy," Pike sneers. "You better know your place and let your boss handle the business."

Oh shit! He did NOT just go there...

Before any of us can get to him, Zilas has his Glock out and shoved against Pike's forehead. The drug lord's men all draw on my friend, so we do the same. With twelve gunmen pointing their guns, I'm worried that someone may not come out of this alive. Well, worried that one of *our* men won't come out of this alive.

"I highly suggest you do your homework before coming into our fucking town and making demands or insulting us." He leans his face closer to Pike's and says, "Zilas fucking Carlson—at your motherfucking service, bitch."

Pike grins and then uses his hands to order his men to lower their guns. "My apologies, Mr. Carlson. I hadn't realized that *all* the Heirs would be in attendance."

"Yeah, well, when someone is trying to bring trash into our town and take what doesn't belong to them, you better believe that you will deal with all of us."

Cray and Adrik step forward to stand beside me, and Pike's eyes land on us. "I see. Well, my mistake. I will have to meet with the Kappels about *other* arrangements."

Zilas steps back, lowering his gun, and responds, "You do that. While you're at it, make your arrangements for another town and keep your fucking shit out of ours."

Pike nods and steps back before returning to the SUV he arrived in. I don't miss the glare he sends us as they pass by on their way out of the old train station parking lot.

"We haven't heard the last of him. You know that, right?" Cray's voice breaks through as I stare at the departing vehicles.

"Oh, I know," I reply. "He will be back, and we will be ready."

TWENTY-EIGHT

I set my cell phone down and look at Mara. She's smirking as she stands there waiting for me. She irritates the hell out of me, but I need her help, so I have to be nice for the time being.

"What?" I ask.

"Is Daddy checking in on you?"

I shrug. "He just wanted to make sure I hadn't killed you yet."

Mara scoffs. "As if you could."

Rolling my eyes, I stand before her. "Are you going to show me how to do this or not?"

"I don't know why you want to learn this when it's easier to teach you how to stab or shoot someone."

I've been having Amara teach me basic defensive moves, and we've now moved on to the chokehold. Nyx isn't always around me, and I don't want to depend on a man to defend me every time.

"Have you forgotten that I already know how to stab someone?"

"Ha! Yes, but can you actually kill them?" she muses.

I glare at her. "I suppose you had a hand in helping with Ken's death, too, didn't you?"

"Well, Nyx did ask me to assist. I still can't believe you fucked that pansy ass..."

"Yeah, well, you will do anything if a life is hanging over your head," I say, then tilt my head and stare at her. "Well, maybe you wouldn't, but any other decent human would. Anyway, I'm learning defense, and I won't always want to kill my opponent right away, so it's good to have other options."

"Whatever. I—" Mara's phone vibrates, and she looks at it before grinning at me.

"What?"

"Nothing. Seems Nyx needs an itch scratched."

"Oh?" I cock my hip and place my hand on it as I ask, "What itch exactly is he needing to be scratched?"

"Well, I did offer him a few services yesterday, but he still had your stench on him, so he turned them down—at that time."

The fuck?

Is he really trying to hook up with Mara? No, I don't believe it, but I think it's best to teach *little devil* a lesson about staying away from men who don't belong to her. I know I haven't officially accepted him, but it's only a matter of time and a lot of groveling on his end before I make the call.

"You can have him back when I'm done with him. Now, can we please get back to this?" My tone has a slight edge, but I don't care. It only amuses Mara, anyway.

Smirking, Mara tosses her phone onto the chair in the billiard room where she's been showing me moves. She moves in behind me, and with her wearing her stiletto boots, she can reach around my neck.

"You want to wrap your dominant arm around the fucker's neck and bring your other one up to grab behind their head like this." I feel her hand at the back of my head as she tilts my head forward, putting pressure on my neck. "This will help you maintain control of them as you apply pressure to the neck. Never put pressure on the throat. You want to cut the blood flow to the brain and make them pass out, and it won't work if you're putting all the pressure on their throat."

I can feel myself getting lightheaded. Spots are dancing before my eyes, so I tap her arm. Mara snickers, then she steps back. Gasping for air, I glower at her.

"Did you have to put so much pressure on my neck?"

Mara shrugs. "You needed the full effect."

"My turn."

I blink a few more times to make sure I'm okay and not going to pass out. Mara scoffs but turns, giving me her back. She may have been my best friend back in the day, but as long as she keeps trying to fuck Nyx with me around, she will always be an enemy that I keep close tabs on. So, what I'm about to do won't weigh on my conscience at all.

"Don't cry if you don't get it on the first try. Not everyone is perfect..."

I glare at her back, my hands curling into fists. What was Nyx thinking, leaving me here with her? Trying to breathe deeply so I don't actually hurt her, I take in her slender form. It doesn't matter how small she is; Amara is a force, so I need to make sure I have hold of her well.

I have a plan.

Stepping close behind her so her back is against my front, the bitch rubs her ass against me, chuckling. I ignore the movement, wrap my arm around her neck, and then bring my other hand to the back of her head.

Leaning in, I make sure my hot breath grazes her ear, and softly, I ask, "Like this?"

I hear her breath hitch, and she nods. "Now add a little pressure, and as long as I don't tap you, you're not doing it correctly."

Smirking, I do as I'm told, and soon, I feel her tap, but I don't let go. Mara starts to struggle, and I push us both down, pressing her into the hardwood with my body so she can't get up. She's strong for sure, but I'm able to keep her down and keep her in the chokehold until her body goes limp.

When I finally let go, I feel for her pulse, and once I find it, I breathe a sigh of relief. She may not be my most favorite person, but I don't want to kill her. I actually expect her to be faking and jump up any minute, but when she remains lying there, I stand slowly and stare down at her still form.

I'm unsure how much time I have left, so I rush through the Hall and retrieve my burner phone from my room, along with a set of car keys to one of Nyx's many cars. He's going to be pissed, but I've always wondered what it was like to drive an Aston Martin. Not just any Aston Martin, but the new DBS 770 Ultimate. He usually drives his older black '69 Camaro that is in mint condition, but he also has a 550 Spyder—all black. The guy is broody for sure, and you can see it in the way he dresses and now, his cars.

Pressing the button on the key fob, the alarm beeps as the doors unlock, and I slide into the seat covered with sleek black and deep red leather. The car smells like *him*, and I take a moment to savor the scent. The engine purrs to life, and I'm heading down the driveway in no time, pressing the button for the front gates to open before any security can stop me.

No doubt they'll be on the phone to Nyx within seconds, which is why I grabbed my burner phone. I'm sure he put another tracker in my phone when he replaced it after the accident. I make a mental note to check in on the Uber driver from that night, and then I get my head in the game once again.

I need answers. Answers that my mother refused to give me, and new ones that I now have. Only one person can answer them—my father. Where has he been my whole life? Has he always known about me, and the most important one that has my blood boiling is, what gives him the fucking right to think he can give me away to some dope-slinging drug lord?

I pull up to a set of iron gates. A mansion is set back past a rolling, green, well-manicured lawn. It's nowhere near as big as Nyte's Hall, but it's still massive. The guard at the gate looks me up and down, smiling.

"Well, what can I do for you, beautiful?" He shows me his pearly whites, and I turn on my own charm.

"I'm here to see your boss. Mr. Kappel isn't expecting me, but I can guarantee he will want to see me. My name is Saraya Abbott."

I don't acknowledge my married name anymore, and I'm pretty sure Kappel will know me by this name. When the guard steps into the little shack and picks up the phone, I watch as he keeps his eyes on me, a grin appearing just before he hangs the phone up.

"You are more than welcome to drive up to the main house. Mr. Kappel will meet you at the front door personally." The guard winks at me, then presses a button, opening the wrought iron gates for me.

I wiggle my fingers at him and smile. "Thank you so much. It's so nice to meet such nice people these days."

My smile drops the second I pass him, and I'm out of his view. Another moment of that shit, and I might have thrown up. The poor sap is probably going to go into his little shack and jack off to the memory of me. Although he's a decent-looking guy, a quiver runs through me at the thought of him doing just that.

Regardless, I follow his instructions and drive up to the front of the mansion, only to see Clyde Kappel, a.k.a. Daddy Dearest, standing at the top of the steps with his hands in his pockets, grinning. Again, I feel like vomiting, this time at just the mere sight of the man who provided the little fuckers that invaded my mother's egg. I guess I should be grateful to the asshole for helping give me life, but in all honestly, there has only ever been one thing that was good in the life he gave me, and that something is going to be *pissed* when he learns of what I'm doing.

Taking a deep breath in, then exhaling, I exit the car and head straight up the steps. Unlike with the guard, I don't put on airs for the man before me. He, on the other hand, is grinning from ear to ear.

"The meeting over already? I didn't think you would come see me after your—"

I cut him off with a glare. "I don't know if the meeting is over because I didn't go. Now, unless you want everyone and their dog to hear what I have to say, then I suggest we go to your office."

Anger replaces his grin, but he keeps his mouth shut, turns, and walks back into the house. I'm trembling inside, but on the outside, I'm as calm as can be. Seeing this man face to face after his audacity to try and *exchange* me for a part in bringing down the only real home I've ever known, let alone the only man I've ever loved, has me wanting to strangle him with my bare hands.

As soon as we're closed in his office and he takes a seat behind his desk, I walk up to the opposite side of it, lean on my hands, and glower at him. We stare off until, finally, I feel like I'm going to explode. In a very low and menacing voice, I ask him the one question I need him to answer right now.

"What gave you the fucking right?"

Kappel sits back in his chair and steeples his hands in front of his face. He scrutinizes me briefly before he begins, saying, "Your mother was smart to keep her mouth shut about your parentage. She thought I was stupid and didn't know, but what she didn't think about was how faithful I knew she was to me even though she was my mistress.

I never made Jessica promises. She was a good fuck, and she knew her place. She knew I wouldn't leave my wife for her—or for any of my mistresses for that matter—just like my wife knows that her place at my side is safe, so she turns a blind eye and allows me my *playthings*."

His words are only making me angrier. My mother may have pushed me aside when she married Layton, but she's still my mother, and I know how much she struggled until she met Beckam.

"I'm not here for a fucking back story. I don't give a damn about the past, but what makes you think that you can come into my life now and trade me to get what you want? I am *nothing* to you. I'm not a Kappel. If anything, I'm more Beckam than Kappel."

Clyde scoffs, "You would rather accept Layton Beckam as your father over me? A man who would go out of his way to have your real father's brother-in-law come in and rape you of your virginity just to prove to me that *he* owned you? You were nothing but a pawn in a game he was playing against me!"

His words make my chest tighten. I knew nothing of this, but I can't let him see how much it affects me. He can't know that I'm holding on by a very thin thread at the moment. When will all these surprises stop coming at me like this?

"Yeah, and what did you do to stop him or get back at him for doing so, Daddy Dearest? You still allowed him to marry me off to a monster who did nothing but abuse and rape me every fucking day I was with him!"

Kappel slams his fist down onto the desk. "I had Stanton killed for what he did to you! You were supposed to marry Phoenyx and join our families, but Layton wouldn't have it! He took that away from me. Yes, I allowed him to marry you off to Kenneth because your husband was one of my men."

I jerk back at this, no longer able to hold in my surprise. The cynical smile that appears on his face actually scares me a little. I watch as he slowly stands and walks around his desk, causing me to take a few steps back.

"Ken took orders from me, not Beckam. I told him that as long as he kept you in line until I knew what I would do with you, he could have you any way he wanted." Kappel shrugs. "He was married to you, after all, and a wife should always do her wifely duties, just like a daughter must always do her daughterly duties."

"You're fucking sick!" I sneer at him. "Fuck you and whatever plans you have. I'm not your daughter, so forget all about me."

As soon as I try to flee his office, two men, built like powerhouses, snatch me up and hold me in place. Kappel walks over to us and grabs my

jaw tightly.

"I don't think that will work for me, *baby girl.* Now, you'll be a good girl and stay in the room my men put you in until I can hand you over to your future husband."

Fear grips me now. How could I have been so stupid? Why did I think that this man would be reasonable? I kick out, demanding that I be released, but he only laughs harder.

"All in good time. Now be good while I go call your fiancé." He turns but stops when a familiar voice calls out from down the hall.

"I'm right fucking here, Kappel!"

TWENTY-NINE

Nyx

The moment Nial called to tell me that Raya left the Hall, I hauled ass out of the old train station lot. Little does my little lamb know that all my cars and motorcycles have trackers on them. Although I'm livid she left the safety of the Hall, I can't stop the grin from appearing on my face. My girl has good taste in cars, I see.

My Aston Martin is the newest addition to my collection, and she's earned herself a good spanking for taking it. But first, I must retrieve my little lamb from wherever she may be.

"Call Mara and find out what the fuck happened," I order Adrik. "I'm going to bring up the tracker."

Tapping my phone, the app pops up, and instantly, the red blinking light homes in on her location, and the blinking dot isn't the only red I see. My fist meets the door panel, causing Adrik to jump.

"What the fuck?"

"Go to Kappel's!" I growl out to Cale, and he nods.

"Are you fucking serious?"

"As a fucking heart attack..."

Suddenly, Adrik bursts out in boisterous laughter, and I send him a glare. "Sorry, buddy. It's just that I do not envy you at all; you've got your hands full with her."

As livid as I am, a smile reappears, and I mumble, "Don't I know it."

I feel Cale accelerate the sedan as we zoom through the city. The cops know better than to stop us. We trump the local police in most things, but there are still areas that we don't cross due to the federal government getting in the way, so we have to be creative—torture and homicide being a few.

When the mansion gates come into view, the sedan slows to a stop, and a guard steps up to the window. As soon as he notices Adrik and me, he nods and says, "I'll let the boss know you're coming up."

Cale, knowing precisely what needs to be done, already has the dart gun prepared and shoots the tranquilizer into the guard's neck. In one swift move, Cale is out of the car and grabbing the stumbling guard, dragging him into the little shack before resuming his place behind the wheel. He smirks at me through the rearview mirror, and I nod my approval.

"Stay outside and watch for more guards. If I'm not back out in five minutes, storm the place," I instruct Adrik and Cale. "Let the others know, too."

"Mara finally texted me back after not answering my call," Adrik states and holds his phone up for me to read.

MARA: That little hellion choked me out! I'm going to strangle her for real next time I see her!

After reading it, I grunt not only to hide the chuckle that wants to burst free but also to express my displeasure at seeing Mara's threat. I will not allow my friend to lay a hand on my little lamb. I exit the car as Adrik returns a text to our little devil.

So, Raya likes choking people, huh? I can't wait to wrap my hand around that slender neck of hers again, making her come hard as I choke her. I'm sure it will be much more pleasurable than what she did to Mara.

Walking up the front steps, I don't stop when I get to the door. I walk right in and through the front foyer. Hearing Raya's angry voice is the only thing that stops me in my tracks.

"Release me, now!"

"All in good time. Now be good while I go call your fiancé." Kappel's voice grates on my nerves, and I round the next corner as I reach for my gun.

"I'm right fucking here, Kappel!" I point my piece right at the fucker's head. "If you know what's good for you, you will have your men take their filthy paws off my girl."

I can see the tick in his jaw from where I stand. Something tells me that my appearance is not what he had anticipated. I don't dare take my eyes off the older man as I direct my next words to Raya.

"Come to me, baby."

I hear her struggle and curse at the men holding her, and I raise my brow at Kappel. Finally, he looks at his men and nods. Raya is at my side the next minute, and I pull her into me, needing to feel her and reassure me that she's okay.

"That was a stupid move on your part, Kappel. Why the fuck you made a deal with that piece of shit, using a pawn that was *never* yours, is beyond me," I sneer.

The man dares to grin wickedly. "Eh, you win some, and you lose some. In my case, I feel like I'm winning."

I'm hit in the back of my head, and darkness dances all around but doesn't take hold. However, I do drop to my knees as Raya is yanked from my side.

"You bastard!" my little lamb growls at her father.

"I've been called worse. You will do well to curb that tongue of yours, Saraya. I don't think Pike will stand for the sass."

"Raya, stay calm, baby. Breathe..."

There was a time when we were kids when Saraya would get upset over something, and I'd have to calm her down. It's no different now. I say the same words I used back then, and I'm rewarded when I hear her inhale and then exhale.

"Aw, look at the two of you," Kappel says mockingly. "Get the fuck over it. Saraya has Kappel blood running through her veins, and she will do her duty as a Kappel."

"What did you just say?" Jarod and Jax join their father.

Grabbing the back of my head, I'm trying to get my equilibrium in check, but I still laugh cynically, then say, "Don't tell me that dear ole Dad didn't tell you about you two having a baby sister."

"What's this about, Father?" Jarod asks.

I notice how Jax stares at Raya, and I know when he realizes he knew all along. I remember the first time they met Raya in my office. Jax gazed at her with a look of familiarity. Subconsciously, he knew.

"Jarod, Jaxon, meet your sister, Saraya." Kappel grins smugly.

"What the fuck? You didn't think to tell us that we had a sister?" Jax sneers this at his father, which makes Clyde glare at his son.

"I didn't have to tell you shit. She's a bastard, a nobody, a whore's—"

"Don't fucking finish your sentence, Kappel!" I growl, cutting him off.

His words hit Raya hard, and the next thing I know, she moves fast, elbowing the guard holding her in the gut, then turns and knees him in the nuts. I use this time to reach for the knife I keep hidden in my ankle holster and swing around, jabbing it through the neck of the guard standing behind me.

He stumbles back, and I spring forward, taking hold of Raya's wrist, putting her behind me, and order, "Grab my gun from his pants, baby."

"Can we calm the fuck down?" Jarod calls out angrily.

"Your father fucked up, Jarod, and now, he will pay the price," I inform the twin.

Just then, there's a commotion behind us, and the rest of the Heirs and our men, including Amara, come rushing around the corner. Mara got here fast, and although she sends a glare Raya's way, it's only for a split second before her attention is back on the four men in front of us.

"Having to save your ass once again, Raya..." Mara looks at me briefly and cocks her brow at my glare. "What? It's the fucking truth."

"Head in the fucking game, Mara."

"Guards!" Kappel calls out.

Cray laughs, then says, "Your guards are fucking pansy-ass pussies. They ran at the sight of us, Kappel."

I look at the one guard still standing by his boss's side. "Decide now. Your boss is coming with us, and you can either die while defending him or turn around and join the others. The twins will be in touch."

The guard looks at Clyde, and then the twins, where he sees the subtle nod of Jax's head. He turns and walks away.

"Get back here right now!" Kappel's face is red with fury.

I look over my shoulder and nod at Arlo and Charlie, who move forward and take hold of each of Kappel's arms. He struggles, but it's useless. When he realizes this, he begins to beg.

"Please, we can discuss this. You can have her Nyx; I'm fine with that!"

I get up in his face and say, "I will have her only if *she* says I can have her. But make no mistake, Raya loves me, so she will be mine."

I don't care if Raya thinks I'm jumping the gun. I know her, and even though I have a lot to make up for, at the end of the day, she will accept me. If I have to wait until she's satisfied that I've groveled enough, so be it; I'll have fun helping her make up her mind.

"Take him," I tell Arlo and Charlie.

I stare at the twins, waiting to see if they'll interfere. When they say nothing, I nod and state, "Your reign in the Kappel family starts now. I hope you make better choices than your father did."

I turn and take Raya's hand, but Jax's question stops me. "Can we visit Saraya sometime? I'd like to get to know our sister better."

I glance at him and Jarod, then look at my little lamb as I reply, "That's up to her, but I think it's best if you give her some time."

Raya's warm brown eyes soften at my words, and I glimpse a tilt to her lips before I turn back to the twins. "Be sure your mother doesn't cause a fuss over this. I'm not one to hurt a woman, but—"

"I don't mind at all," Mara chimes in, smirking.

"I can promise you that our mother won't say a word. Hell, she'll probably be celebrating by the end of the night," Jarod drawls.

"And you?"

I have to question them because, at the end of the day, he's their father. I don't know what he was like behind closed doors with his family. Jax's next sentence, however, tells me all I need to know.

"Just let us bury him. You know, make it look good."

I nod, then follow the rest of my crew out of the Kappel mansion. A tinge of regret takes hold of what we need to do to the father of friends, but Clyde's been making his bed for years, and I'm not about to make the same mistake our fathers made. We vowed to clean up the town of Nyte, and we will do just that.

Wanting to question him about Pike because I feel there is more to their little alliance than what we know, I instruct the men to take Kappel to the warehouse while I take Raya back to the Hall. The ride is quiet, almost somber because neither of us says a word. It's only when we're almost home that my little lamb speaks up.

"Nyx, I'm—"

"Don't. I can't hear it right now, Raya."

"But—"

"I said—don't! I don't know if I can control my temper if we talk about how royally you fucked up, so just—don't."

She tries pulling her hand away, which is still in mine, but I tighten my grip and keep it on my thigh. I give her a warning look before returning my eyes to the road. She just doesn't get it—the danger she puts herself in time and again. One of these times, I'm not going to be able to get to her, and that scares the shit out of me.

Raya wants to take charge of her life, and I get that; believe me, I do, but to go off half-cocked isn't the way to go about it. I will get injured for her as many times as it takes, but it would be nice if, for once, she would just listen and think before she reacts.

As if on cue, a pain starts to throb in my chest where my gunshot wound is. I absently bring my hand up and rub it.

"Are you okay?" Raya asks with concern.

"I'm fine. It's nothing a pain pill won't take care of as soon as we get back."

"Nyx, you need to be careful and stop exerting yourself. You're not healed all the way yet."

I scoff. "When you stop running away and landing yourself in trouble, I'll rest." My words slap her in the face, but it wasn't my intention, not really.

"Don't blame me for your injuries, Nyx! It's not like you didn't make the decision to come after me..."

"You're right. I did make the decision to come after you because I'm fucking stupid. Here I am, trying to protect you—which, by the way, you asked for—and in return, I get shot and knocked in the back of the head. You're welcome, by the way."

Raya is quiet for a moment, and then I hear her soft voice as she says the two little words she probably hates to say.

"I'm sorry..."

I don't respond to her. Instead, I step on the gas because the sooner I get us home, the sooner I can take a pain pill. I'm going to have to feel better than I do if I'm going to fuck the ever-loving shit out of the woman beside me—and fuck her, I definitely will.

"Go to your room, little lamb. I'll come talk to you in just a bit, but first, I want you to wash the filth of the day off your body," I order as soon as we pull up to the Hall.

"I'm fine, Nyx. I don't need a shower."

I cock my brow at her, and she rolls her eyes. Grabbing the back of her head before she can exit the car, I pull her to me until our faces are inches apart. Her breath is sweet as it hits my face, and I lick my lips.

"You will shower, and you will remain undressed, because you have earned a punishment, and I plan on delivering it right before I fuck that delectable cunt of yours," I tell her. "I will kill for you, and I will destroy anyone or anything that tries to hurt you, but know that there will always be one person who will hurt you in the most pleasurable way, and that is me. I may defend you, but I will also punish you, so make sure you factor that in when you're deciding to stay or go. Oh, and know that I will make it extremely hard for you to decide on the latter."

"Okay," she replies breathlessly.

"Good girl. Now go, I'll be there soon."

THIRTY

Nyx

I stand silently in the doorway to Raya's bathroom, watching her shower through the glass wall like a pervert about to pounce. The pain pills are kicking in, and I slowly begin to undress, not wanting to wait another minute. I need inside my little lamb, if for no other reason than to remind her who she fucking belongs to and where her place is.

I kick off my shoes and quietly remove my belt, tossing it behind me and onto the bed. I'll be needing that later. Stripping off the rest of my clothes, I pad over to the shower and step in behind her, not caring that she's startled by my appearance. My hand covers her mouth, not because I don't want anyone to hear, but because I don't want her talking when I'm about to give her my instruction.

"You are going to be a good fucking girl and place your hands on the glass. Then, you will spread these luscious thighs," I say as my hand glides up one of them. "And you'll stick your ass out to receive my punishment."

"Can't we do this after I shower?" my little lamb rushes out as soon as I remove my hand.

"Not a chance. I need to fuck my cunt, but I can't do it until you've been punished, so do as I say and turn, little lamb."

When she goes to say something else, I hold my finger to my lips, and hers clamp tightly together. My eyes roam over her nudeness as Raya places her palms on the glass and spreads her legs. However, her ass never juts out.

Smack!

My hand comes down on her wet ass, making it sound a lot harder than it actually was.

"Ass out, little lamb. You know you'll like it, so why are you being so disobedient?"

"I'm not your fucking submissive, Nyx."

I chuckle. "Oh, don't I know it. The funny thing is, I don't want you as my submissive, Raya. I want you just as you are. Do you know why?"

"Why?" She turns her head to the side, trying to see me, as she asks.

I step forward, letting my length slip between her thighs, and I lean into her ear. Nipping her earlobe, I then say, "Because it's so much more of a turn on this way. Making you submit to me, knowing there isn't a submissive bone in your body when it comes to me, turns my dick purple, and it throbs with the need to be inside you."

My little lamb lets out a soft whimper, and her ass begins to gyrate against me. I step back and smack her ass again. She presses her forehead against the glass.

"Nyx..." My name is a breathless plea on her lips.

When I hear the way Raya says my name this time, all thoughts of punishment escape me, and I drop to my knees behind her. Spreading her legs wider, I shove my face between them and drag my tongue from her clit to the pucker surrounding her tight little hole that my cock will take at some point in the near future.

"Oh fuck!" she cries out, but I don't stop.

Pushing a finger into her ass, I return to her clit and work it with my tongue, flicking it back and forth before sucking it into my mouth and scraping my teeth against it. When she tries to move away, I slap her ass again.

"Don't fucking move. You are disturbing my supper."

I then plunge two fingers into her dripping cunt and fuck her hard with both hands. Having my finger in her ass and two in her puss, my cock is jealous as fuck and leaking like a sieve.

"Come for me, little lamb."

"Fuck, Nyx..."

"You will be really soon, now fucking come!" I slip a third finger into her cunt and a second in her ass, and she takes it like a champ.

"Uh...yes...don't stop...fuck!" Her walls squeeze my fingers, and she comes hard.

"That's it, just like that, baby." I work her over until she's spent, then stand up. I turn her to face me and push her wet hair from her face before taking her lips in a brutal kiss. Gripping her hair and holding her to me, I take what I want and then yank my mouth away. "I'm not done with you yet. On your knees, Raya."

"What?" she asks, still partially dazed.

I tilt her head back, so her eyes meet mine. "Be my beautiful little whore and get on those pretty little knees."

I then put pressure on her shoulder, and she drops to the floor. When she only stares at my cock, I swing my hips, slapping her in the face with it.

"Seriously?" she snarls.

"It's not going to blow itself, little lamb."

"Well, no shit, but can I at least admire the beauty of the pain it's causing you first?"

I grin at her sass and then the truth of everything hits me. I fucking love this woman even more than when we were kids. I knew deep down I still had feelings for her. Hell, I knew it may have been love, but this, this is so much more.

I entangle my fingers into the hair at the top of her head and tilt it back again. "Stop talking and start sucking. Show me who owns this fucking cock."

The sparkle that lights up her eyes at my words is the only thing I need to tell me that she feels the same way. She could have run far away, but instead, she came to me, and I don't believe for one minute that it's because I was in charge of her trust. No, she came to me because she knew it was time to reclaim what we were denied—a life together.

When her lips wrap around me, my breath hitches. I've never felt anything like it, or maybe I never wanted to. Biting my bottom lip, I watch as my stepsister sucks my length like a porn star. She has me ready to blow within minutes until I pull out to get control of myself.

"Jesus, Raya..." I close my eyes and take deep breaths.

"Aw, what's the matter? Can't hang with the big dogs?" She fucking smirks at me.

I ignore her question and ask one of my own, "How much dick have you sucked in your lifetime, little lamb?"

The glint in her eyes dulls as she replies, "Just one, and I made sure I did it so badly that he never made me do it again. He had his whores do it for him."

My jaw clenches, and I bite out, "Good, then I'll be the first one to coat that pretty little throat with cum."

She nods.

I thrust back into her mouth and fuck her throat viciously as she grips my thighs. Water cascades onto her face, and still, I fuck her. I've never felt anything like it.

"I'm going to come, be ready, and swallow it all."

I roar out my release, and even though I know her throat will be sore, I slam into it a few more times before burying myself all the way down it. When she begins to struggle from lack of air, I pull out and jerk myself until I'm empty. Ropes of cum decorate her chin and breasts by the time I'm done, and before the water can wash it away, I swipe it up.

"Open..."

She grins and sticks out her tongue, wrapping her lips around my finger to clean it off. My dick stirs all over again, regardless of the release it just had.

"Tell me you're mine, little lamb." I help her to her feet and pull her into my chest. "Tell me..."

Shaking her head, she pushes away from me and says, "I belong to nobody at the moment."

I'm so stunned that those words came out of her mouth that I just let her go. Did I imagine it all? Was it just wishful thinking on my part? My eyes return to her retreating form, and that's when I see my little lamb's extra sway to her hips. *No, fuck that. I didn't imagine shit. Raya is mine, and I'm going to fucking prove it.*

Bent over the side of the bed, her wrists wrapped in my belt at her lower back, I'm on the twelfth smack of her punishment. I have her face turned toward the open door so she can see if anyone comes to our wing and sees her paying for her behavior. I doubt they will, but there is always a chance.

Smack!

"Tell me again why you're receiving this punishment."

"Because you're a brute..."

Smack!

I grin. "Wrong answer, baby. How about we try it again?"

Smack!

"Because I love the pain..."

Smack!
Smack!
Smack!
"Let's see how truthful that is, shall we?"

I shove my hand between her thighs and find her soaking wet. I groan inwardly, feeling my cock grow harder under the towel I have wrapped around my waist. Fuck me...

Saraya wiggles her fucking ass and chuckles. "Come on, *Master Nyx.* I've been a very bad girl; you can't be done with my spankings already."

Growling, I glance at her reddened ass cheeks and decide she's had enough. I turn her to her side and angle her just right before ripping off my towel, lifting her leg, and thrusting into her sweet heat.

"You want to run that smart mouth, little lamb? I'm going to show you what punishment really is."

I fuck her hard, stopping only to slap her clit every once in a while. I'll then rub it violently as I fuck her and bring her to the brink before taking my cock away.

"Asshole!" she pants, and I grin wickedly.

"Yeah, but I'm your asshole—admit it."

"No."

I plunge back into her, this time rolling her more onto her back, so her arms are stuck underneath her, and I press down on her lower belly. I watch as she throws her head back, and she tries meeting me thrust for thrust, but the moment I feel her start to tighten, I pull out yet again.

"Argh!" She glares at me.

"Tell. Me. You're. Mine."

"Fuck. You. Nyx."

My eyes widen with amusement when an idea comes my way. I leave her wide open as I walk over to where I dropped my pants before the shower and retrieve my phone from them.

"What the fuck? You're not recording this!"

"Nah, not this time anyway." I type in a few words and toss it onto the bed beside her head so she can read it.

ME: Come to my wing. I have something for you to watch.
ADRIK: On our way.

"No, you didn't!"

I shrug. "Tell me the truth, and I'll shut the door. Otherwise, my best friends are going to watch me fuck the ever-loving shit out of you."

"That's blackmail!"

"You seemed to like Cray watching you get fucked. Four isn't any different."

Her brow furrows. "Four?"

"Well, yeah. You don't think Mara would want to miss it, do you?"

"Why is it so important that I admit anything to you, Nyx? Can't we just fuck and enjoy it?"

I shake my head back and forth slowly.

When the faint sounds of footsteps are heard coming up the stairs, annoyance crosses over her face. Raya remains stubborn for as long as she can before blowing up.

"Fine! I'm yours, Nyx. There, are you happy now?"

I shake my head no.

She looks adorable as she curls her lip up. "Yes, Nyx, I belong to you. I will marry you and carry your heirs."

Even though it's said with a bit of attitude, my cock jumps, and I move to the door just in time to see my friends round the corner. I grin and say, "Sorry, boys...Amara, there is nothing to watch."

Shutting the door, I move to the bed and stare at the woman before me. With her brown hair ratted from all my ministrations and fanned out, Raya looks like the perfect mess.

"The lion is going to devour his little lamb now, Raya. Are you ready?"

"Goddamn it, Nyx. Can you just fuck me already?"

Yanking her thighs apart, I say, "Anything for you, Raya." I spit down, letting my saliva mark her pretty little cunt, before I claim her in an entirely different way.

THIRTY-ONE

Saraya

I caved. All it took was my stepbrother exerting his dominance in that sexy as fuck way he has about him, and...I...caved. I thought he would end up using it against me had I let him have his friends watch, so I gave in. I had a weak moment.

Who am I kidding? Phoenyx is my weakness.

His length stretches me as he thrusts in slowly and then pulls himself out. He watches his cock penetrate me, and I watch him as he does so. It's so erotic. I never thought sex could be like this. My first time was taken from me and Kenneth—well, let's just say that even if he had a better tool, he didn't know how to work it, unlike Nyx.

My fucking God!

He uses me for his pleasure, and I'm here for it. However, just because I gave in and told him what he wanted to hear doesn't mean I won't give him hell. I may have agreed, but I never gave a time frame.

"Uh...Nyx...yes!" I throw my head back when he plunges in deep.

A sting on my breast as he slaps me has me moaning even more. Who knew I would honestly like this kind of pain.

"Look at me when I'm fucking you, and you call out my name, little lamb. I want you to see the man with the only cock that this cunt will ever know for the rest of her life."

"Stop giving me orders..." I pant out.

Nyx stops thrusting and slowly pulls out. "Our girl is dripping, baby. She's needy. Are you sure you want to continue arguing with me?"

"What the fuck?" Is he seriously just going to stop?

"Only good girls get Nyx Beckam's cock..."

Fuck this. I'm calling his bluff—there is no way he's going to just walk away. *Would he?* I'm trying so hard to match his cockiness with my sass, but it's getting harder every day. I need to step up my game.

Shrugging, I shove him away with my feet and sit up. With my hands still behind my back, I walk toward the door and say, "Fine. I'm sure someone in this house will finish the job that the mighty Nyx Beckam couldn't finish—even Amara will do."

Turning my back to the door so I can grab the knob with my hands still bound, I twist and open it, but before I can open it too far, it's slammed closed again. A big, masculine hand rests on the door above my head, and I smirk. I drop it before I turn back around so Nyx doesn't see it.

His hand comes up to grip my jaw, and he squeezes just enough for it to be uncomfortable, and then he warns me in a tight voice, "If you ever go seeking sexual gratification from anyone other than me, you will *not* like the consequences, little lamb."

"Oh? You share others with them, but I'm not good enough?" My words have the desired effect, and Nyx jerks back a little.

Of course, I know it's a good thing that he doesn't want to share me, but I've given him too much already; the least I can do is fuck with him. I want him pissed. I want my stepbrother filled with so much irritation that he takes it out on me. Yeah, I want Nyx to fuck my brains out because I *need* it.

"Let me tell you something, Raya. All those other women whom I have fucked, meant nothing to me, so why would I care if my friends had them too?"

"What about Mara?"

"What about her?" He finally loosens his hand on my jaw so I can speak more coherently.

"You all are friends, and yet you share her. I'm sure you care for her to an extent."

"Mara is my friend... she's like a sister to me—"

"I *am* your sister, Nyx." I remind him of our relationship.

He grins wickedly, bringing his head down and teasing my lips with his. "Mm, that's what makes it so hot, Saraya. You are the forbidden fruit, and you know me. Never tell me that I can't have something because I will take it and make it mine." He lifts my leg and thrusts into me as he continues to say, "In...every...single...way...possible." Thrusting between each word.

He then releases my face and cups my breast, so he can devour it as his mouth latches onto my nipple. Nyx is thick, and when he gets in deep and hard, I feel it in my very soul. My wrists being bound only heightens the pleasure as he pulls out and then slams back into me.

"You are *mine*, Saraya. Now that I have you back, I'm never letting you go." His mouth is back on me, nipping and biting at my chest and neck.

His words sound amazing, but his actions are what speak volumes. I once had a husband who would say sweet words to me, trying to trick me into thinking he was truly sorry for all the wrongs he had done to me. In the end, he only wanted me to be a willing vessel for him. His *vile* words would start back up, the moment he pulled his pathetic little cock from me.

"I knew you were a needy whore. You can't even stick to your guns and hold your ground. You give in way too easily because you're nothing but a little cock slut." He would say anything he could think of to degrade me; my all-time favorite being, *"Too bad Stanton wasn't still around, huh? You probably want another go at him. You just loved letting him fuck that virginity out of you. I did Nyx a favor by taking you for my own. He would have been so disappointed with that cunt of yours. You wonder why I fuck other whores. Take a good look in the mirror, Saraya! You're a used up whore!"*

Ken would then proceed to beat me. Those were his actions after using loving words to get what he wanted. I know Nyx is nothing like Ken, but it's now ingrained in me and so hard to just let go.

"What if I want to go? Will you hold me against my will?" I dare ask.

A growl rumbles against my flesh.

"It's tempting, but no. I will, however, fuck you every chance I get to remind you why you want to stay. You will have everything you need as long as you're by my side."

How about love, Nyx? Will I have your love, too?

His words sound pretty in the moment, but is it really how it will be? I may have said we would marry, but I can't do it until he loves me again. Is he willing to open up to me like that again, now knowing the truth?

I moan as he hits my G-spot repeatedly, and I feel my climax build. I try thrusting with him, but it's hard with the predicament I'm in.

"Release me, Nyx. Let me fuck you right."

His grin goes straight to my pussy every time.

"I love seeing you at my mercy, little lamb."

"Nyx."

"Hm?"

"Release me, now."

"Come for me, and I'll release you."

Without warning, Nyx grabs me by both thighs and lifts me so he can take us to the bed. He then pulls out long enough to position me on my knees, pushing my head down and pulling my ass up.

"Now *that* is a fucking gorgeous view." He slaps my ass and impales me once again, fucking me until I'm crying out his name and coming like a freight train all over his cock. "That's my girl—such a good little whore for me."

Something warms in my chest at hearing his words. It's fucked up, because Ken used to call me a slut and a whore all the time, but it's different coming from Nyx's mouth. It makes me feel—proud.

As soon as he empties himself inside me, he removes his belt and repositions me on the bed, so my head is now on the pillow. He cares for me like he would one of his subs, and I want to argue with him about it, but I'm too drained to say anything. Instead, I close my eyes, and I'm fast asleep soon after.

❖

When I open my eyes, I rub the sleep from them and swing my feet over the side of the bed, only there is no edge of the bed, just more mattress. That's when I realize I'm in the center of Nyx's king-size bed. However, my being in Nyx's bed isn't my only surprise.

On a table beside the bed, a tray covers a heated dish loaded with eggs, bacon, pancakes, and sausage. A single red rose is placed in a slim vase with a folded card at its base. I smell the rose first before picking up the card and reading.

Little Lamb

I made the foods I knew you liked when we were kids; I hope you still like them. I'll be sure to hire the help back by this afternoon.

As for the rose, it's the first to be plucked from your mother's prized rose bush. I chose the most beautiful bloom for you because you deserve all the beautiful things life offers.

Now that the mushy stuff is out of the way, hurry up and eat, so you can get that cute butt to my office. I need to go to the warehouse, but I will wait for you.

XXX

The Lion

I giggle at the note. It sounds like the little lamb may be taming the lion. Can I be so lucky as to have that happen? Do I really want to tame him? My brows furrow at that last thought. I miss Phoenyx, the boy, but Nyx as the man—well, he's definitely dug his way into my heart.

I love how protective and possessive he is—to an extent, but I know it's only because he cares. His dominant nature is a huge turn-on where my body is concerned, and although I don't want to be submissive to him, I can't deny that he has a way of controlling me as though I am.

Finishing breakfast, I pull one of Nyx's t-shirts over my head and hurry to my room for a quick shower. I don't want to keep him waiting if he wants to go to the warehouse, and I want to go with him. I need answers, too, so I hope he doesn't plan on making me stay here again.

Snatching my phone off its charger, I head to Nyx's home office, just down the hallway from my room. The door is cracked open, and I hear his voice before entering.

"I'm not going to make her do anything she doesn't want, Jarod. I understand you want to meet her officially, but just give her some time. Somehow, I think that she'll be ready a lot sooner than you think she will be. You don't know Raya like I do. She's got a backbone and can handle herself for the most part."

My heart swells hearing his words, and just when I'm about to go in and throw myself at him, his next words cause me to pause.

"Her only downfall is that she acts before she thinks. She keeps putting herself into situations that she shouldn't be." He must be talking on the phone because I don't hear Jarod in the room.

I lean against the wall outside his office and think about what he just said. He's right, of course. I've done it twice now, and he's been injured both times. If he would just let me be a part of whatever he does, I wouldn't have felt the need to take things upon myself. I'm not blaming him, but we must work as a team if Nyx wants us to work.

I push myself away from the wall, straighten my shoulders, and knock on the door. For some reason, I feel nervous and have no reason to be. When I hear Nyx's voice telling me to enter, I push the door open and stroll in confidently.

I walk to one of the chairs in front of his desk, but Nyx shakes his head no and holds his arm out, indicating he wants me to come to him. I stand my ground, knowing it's going to piss him off, and I shake my head before taking a seat.

"Let me call you back, Jarod. There is something I need to see to at the moment." Nyx stares at me the whole time he talks to the twin.

As soon as he sets his phone down, he sits back and rests his chin in his hand. His eyes never leave mine. I clear my throat to break the silence and say, "Thank you for breakfast—and the rose. It was beautiful."

"Was? Please tell me you didn't crush it in a fit because I gave it to you."

A chuckle erupts and I give him a sincere response, with just a little bit of sass in my reply. "No. It's still safe in the vase you put it in. Whether you believe it or not, not *everything* you do irritates me. It does show that you have a little bit of a heart inside your chest."

"Shh, don't say that too loud."

I grant him a smile before asking, "So, what's on the agenda?"

"Come sit on my lap, and I'll tell you," Nyx teases.

"I think it's safer if I stay right here."

He shrugs. "Suit yourself..."

I watch him stand and head for the door.

"Wait! Where are you going? I thought you wanted to talk to me."

"I did, but since it's evident that you don't trust my intentions, then I'll leave you be and go about my day." Nyx buttons his suit jacket.

"You're wearing that to the warehouse?"

"Of course. I always dress appropriately when doing business," he states before raking his eyes down my attire.

After my shower, I threw his shirt back on because it's soft and comfy, and then pulled on a pair of biker shorts, tying the shirt at the waist. I jump from the chair.

"I can be ready in five minutes!"

"Ready for what?" Nyx questions with a raised brow.

"To go with you. You're not going to make me stay here again, are you?"

"You said that you would rather stay here." He reminds me of the words I spoke just minutes before.

I narrow my eyes at him. "You know perfectly well that isn't what I meant."

Nyx grins, but it turns into a sigh. "I know, and I had all intentions of taking you, but do you really want to see your father be tortured and killed?"

"Clyde Kappel is just a donor; he is *not* my father..."

Nyx smirks, strolls to me slowly, and cups my face. "Are you sure?"

I nod. "Yes, I'm sure."

He gazes into my eyes, and I can't help but fall for him a little more when he says, "There's the queen I need by my side. You're the only one that could ever be beside me, little lamb."

His lips brush against mine, then he deepens the kiss for a few seconds before stepping back. He takes my hand and pulls me with him.

"Wait, I need to change."

"Nah, I like seeing you in my shit."

"Nyx..."

"Besides, it will be so much easier to strip you later when I'm ready to fuck you again."

I scoff. "You'll be lucky if you get another kiss from me," I say dryly.

Nyx side-eyes me with a grin and responds, "Hm, we shall see."

THIRTY-TWO

Nyx

"Here, have some water, Clyde. You look parched." I slide the glass over to the older Kappel; he has just enough chain length to pick it up and bring it to his lips.

He pauses when the glass is about to reach his lips, questioning, "How do I know you didn't poison it?"

Rolling my eyes, I take a sip, then hand it back. "Satisfied?"

Arlo and Charlie ensured our little prisoner was kept in a room with the heat turned up and nothing to quench his thirst. So, once he's seen that I've drunk the water, he guzzles it until the glass is empty.

"Now start talking," I demand, taking the glass from him.

"What do you want to know?"

"How about why you thought it was okay to give me to a fucking drug lord when you have never reached out or acknowledged me a day in my life?"

My little lamb stands beside me, arms crossed and sneering down at the man who gave her life. I couldn't deny her coming after she assured me that she would be fine with disposing of her sperm donor. If she can hack it, I want her by my side in all business dealings. Well, maybe not the dangerous ones, but those will have to be discussed.

Clyde titters, then states, "That's precisely why I did it. You're just a bastard and mean shit to me, but apparently, you're pretty enough to be wanted for a good fuck. So, why not use you to get what I wanted?"

My hands curl into fists, wanting to hit him so badly, but my little lamb steps up and swings her fist instead. Kappel's head whips to the side, and blood drips from a cut on his lip. I glance down and see that she has a pair of metal knuckles on her fingers. *The sneaky little vixen!* I hadn't seen her lift them from the implement table when we walked in.

I look behind me, and Charlie stands in the doorway, smirking. He apparently witnessed my little lamb's sticky fingers. I guess I'll just stand back and let her ask her questions first.

"Layton is dead. Why didn't you go to Nyx about an alliance?" Raya's question startles me momentarily.

She's always wanted to know who her father was, and even though he's a piece of shit, I'd have thought she would still like to know why he didn't want her. Hell, I want to know the answer to that question.

Walking over to her, I slip my hand around her from behind and pull her into me so her back is flush against my front. Dipping my head, I speak loud enough for Kappel to hear.

"It makes no difference had he come to me or not because you have always been mine, little lamb. He wouldn't have gotten anything from me had he tried. You are not for sale; you never have been, baby."

"Jesus Christ, get a fucking room!" Clyde states and then coughs a little.

I watch sweat bead on his forehead, and I smirk, saying, "Why, when I was already balls deep inside her until the wee hours of the morning?"

Clyde ignores me and stares at his daughter. "He's right. I wouldn't have gotten anywhere with him. Even if I did go to him and we had an alliance, the other three Heirs are still in my way. Of course, you could have just entered a union with all four of them, and it may have worked—"

I'm the one to move fast this time as I carefully shove Raya out of the way and rain blow upon blow down on Kappel's face.

No one talks about my girl being with any other man—not ever!

"Nyx! Stop, you're going to kill him, and we don't have our answers yet." Raya's voice breaks through the red haze, and I pull back from the bloody asshole. Running my hand through my hair to get it out of my face, I then spit down on the pathetic fucker.

"Watch what you fucking say about her!"

"You act as though I didn't care at all." Clyde spits some blood onto the floor. "I had my brother-in-law killed for touching you, didn't I?"

I scoff. "Tell us why you did that, Clyde, because I *know* it's not because you really cared."

The sinister smile that appears on his face tells me everything, and I step aside, making room for my little lamb to get to him the moment the words are out of his fucking mouth. He doesn't disappoint, either.

"Why else would I be pissed? Do you know how much a Kappel virgin would have fetched?"

Kappel's eyes were on me, thinking that the danger would come from my direction, so he was completely unaware when Raya practically flew through the air, attaching herself like a spider monkey as she took a page from my book and hit him continuously. Only she still has the knuckles on her hand.

"You son of a bitch! I was just a girl..." she screams.

I finally grab her from around the waist and pull her off him. "Hey, baby, all in good time. We have plenty here to entertain ourselves as we end him."

I turn Raya to face me and brush some of her hair back. A streak of Clyde's blood soils her face, but instead of disgusting me, it stirs my cock awake, and I have to talk it back down. I press my lips to her forehead, letting them linger for just a few seconds.

"Charlie, how about we get our guest here some more water? I'm sure he wants to wash out his mouth," I instruct, without taking my eyes off Raya.

"Yes, Sir."

"How do you want to do this, little lamb. We'll do it however you want."

Raya bites her bottom lip and glances at Clyde. My hands drop as she moves away from me, circling the older man. I can see the disgust on her face, but I can also see the resemblance now that they are together. She has his eyes, especially how they are glowering at each other.

"What is Pike up to? Why did he want an alliance with you, Daddio?" Raya squats in front of him and waits for his response.

"I must say, you have more balls than your brothers do—"

"Quit the bullshit! We want answers. Have you forgotten that you are *beneath* the Gods of Nyte, and you answer to *them*?"

I cover my mouth with my hand, trying to contain the proud grin I bear behind it. I always knew that she belonged by my side. She's fucking magnificent.

Kappel glares at his daughter for reminding him of his place, but still answers her question. "All I know is that Pike wanted to distribute his new product here but knew it would never happen as long as the Heirs were still in control. That's why he needed me; we needed each other."

"So, you would marry me off just so you could have this town?" Raya asks a bit sulkily as she creeps closer to Kappel.

I eye her warily. My little lamb has switched tactics and I'm not sure if I like the change of events. It almost like she's trying to seduce him—her own father. I know that's not the case, but it doesn't stop my stomach from churning.

"You don't mean shit to me, Saraya. I told your mother never to get pregnant by me, and she didn't listen. All you're good for is making alliances."

I'm watching Raya closely, so I notice her body tense slightly before she continues. "So, if I'm nothing to you," she says, then pauses and places her hand on his knee. "Then you won't mind if I impale you..."

I'm circling to the side to get a better view, and I see her lick her lips. I'm just about to end this little scene when she catches me off guard again. She reaches into the side pocket of her leggings and pulls something out as she finally finishes her sentence.

"With my little friend!" Raya's hand snakes out, and she's digging a knife into Kappel's groin. "This should have been done to you years ago, you bastard!"

"AGH!!!"

She's forgotten that his hands have some slack, and he brings them up and begins choking her. I rush to them and pry Clyde's hands from around Raya's neck. She's fucking laughing at his attempt to kill her.

"Move!" I order her, but she ignores me and twists the knife in further. "Raya, I said fucking move!"

When she meets my eyes, she realizes that I'm pissed, and she backs away. When she is far enough back, I pick up the glass that Charlie brought back and shove it at Clyde.

"Fucking drink it because I don't know when you will get more or if you will get more."

Kappel swipes the glass from my hand and guzzles it down. I look over my shoulder at Charlie, and he nods, signaling that the job is done. Good. Now, we wait.

⁂

First sweating, then coughing, and now it seems Clyde is having difficulty breathing. His eyes widen, and he shakes his head. "I've lost too much blood," he states.

"I'm sure you have, but that's not why you're having all these other difficulties, Mr. Kappel."

"Nyx?"

I push aside my irritation at Raya's earlier behavior and smile at her. "Yes, little lamb?"

"What did you do?"

I simply shrug. "I haven't done anything, not really." I snap my fingers, remembering earlier, and say, "Aside from hitting him just a bit ago. You're the one that went ape shit on him and then stabbed him in the dick."

Charlie chuckles from over by the door.

"Stop being a smartass, Nyx. What did you do?" She comes to stand before me and crosses her arms. "Enough with the secrets already."

I sigh.

"Do you know what tetrahydrozoline is?"

"Do I look like a damn pharmacist?"

She never sees my hand coming as it grips her jaw, and I pull her close. "Keep going with your little smartass comments, and you will find a big ole cock in this pretty little mouth, shutting it up."

"Is that supposed to be a punishment?"

I snicker, crush her lips with mine, then pull away, letting go of her jaw. "I swear, that mouth..."

"May never take your cock again if you keep being an asshole."

She's got me all fucking flustered.

"Do you want to know, or do you want to keep running your mouth?" I ask her.

I need to distract myself before I decide to take her right here and now; fuck her damn father. He'll be dead within minutes, anyway. Yanking her into me, I turn us to face Clyde as he's starting to turn a little bluish. My hands wander, making Raya's breath hitch as one hand slides up and under my shirt she's still wearing and the other slithers inside her bottoms.

"Tetrahydrozoline is found in eye drops. It's clear, odorless, and mostly tasteless. It can be very deadly if consumed, and you don't seek medical attention." I tweak her nipple and she gasps.

"Y-you b-bast-ard!" Clyde barely gets out.

"You drank it, though," Saraya states breathlessly.

Shrugging, I further explain, "I took a sip, so I'm fine—unlike Daddio over there." I dip my head and nibble on her neck.

"Death by eye drops—that's a first for me," Raya says, amused.

I bring my lips to her ear and whisper, "If he doesn't die soon, I may have to put a bullet in him because I have an insatiable need to fuck you right here."

Raya gasps and glances at Charlie, pretending he doesn't know what we're discussing. Fuck, I don't care who's around; I'll throw her on this floor, blood splattered and all, and fuck that sassy behavior right out of her—well, for at least a few hours.

Clyde begins to jerk as his body seizes, and we watch as if he's going to do tricks or some shit. My hand cups Raya's sex—which is soaked, by the way—and I plunge two fingers into her tight cunt as we witness Kappel begins to take his last few breaths of life. I'm enraptured by the way Raya is responding to me in this situation and it turns me on even more.

"Come for me, little lamb. Let that fucker see who it is that owns your every orgasm before he takes his last breath."

"Oh fuck...Nyx."

"Yes, baby. Look at him. See what we did to the asshole who tried to give you away. I'm right here fighting with you, Raya. We're going to rule this town with the others, and it all starts this moment. Now, fucking come!"

The sweet sound of my little lamb coming all over my fingers the moment Clyde's head lolls to the side and his eyes stare back at us blankly, echoes through the room. She jerks on my hand as her walls tighten around me. I remember that we aren't alone, and I growl out to Charlie.

"Leave, now!"

"Yes, Sir." Adrik's man replies with a knowing smile.

"You can't be serious!" My little lamb shakes her head as she starts coming back to her senses.

"Oh, I'm dead serious."

She moves away, and I let her, sucking her essence off my fingers as she does.

"Nyx, we can't—"

"Who fucking says I can't fuck my woman whenever I want?" I bite down on my lower lip as I peruse her body. "Strip, Raya."

She glances at the body, still chained to the chair.

"He's dead, Raya. He isn't going to see a thing. Besides, you just let me finger bang you right in front of him as he was dying."

"It's so—wrong."

"Do you want to know what's wrong? The fact that I've told you to strip, and you are still wearing your fucking clothes."

I stalk her as she continues to back away. My hands quickly work my belt buckle, and I slide it out of the hoops. Holding it up, I grin.

"What do you plan to do with that?" Raya eyes the belt suspiciously, as she should.

Snapping the black leather between my hands, I stop walking as soon as her ass hits the table beside her dead sperm donor. Reaching out with one hand, I caress her cheek, rubbing my thumb over her bottom lip before pulling it down and baring her lower teeth.

"That's for you to decide, little lamb. You've earned a punishment, so you can either A, get the belt on that cute little ass of yours, or B," I reply, "wear it as a necklace."

THIRTY-THREE

Saraya

A necklace? Why does that sound so fucking hot?

I stare at the leather folded in half; in hands I know can do the most delicious things to a woman. Slowly, my eyes roam over his chest, then up to his face, where I meet smoldering gray eyes. What comes out of my mouth next surprises even me.

"How about option C—both A and B?"

My heart races as I see the stormy look that comes over Nyx's face. He's right, I just orgasmed in front of my dying sperm donor, and to be perfectly honest, I'm not going to make it back to the house. I want Nyx now. I want to feel his cock stretching me wide as he fucks me in the only way he knows how—deep and hard.

Grabbing the hem of my shirt, I try not to think about the dead body only two feet away as I lift it over my head. My bra goes next, and then my bottoms, taking my panties with them. Stepping out of my flats, then clothing, I turn and bend myself over the table that I bumped into, and look over my shoulder at Nyx.

His jaw is clenched, and he fists the belt in his hands as he stares at me with a hunger I've never seen before. When he doesn't move, I say three little words that have my stepbrother rushing to me.

"I'm ready, Sir."

"Grr," he growls and presses into me from behind. "Do you see what you fucking do to me, little lamb?"

"Well, do something about it then."

I feel my ass cheeks spread just before Nyx rubs his hardness up and down.

"I'm going to fuck your ass soon, little lamb, but I want to do it at the club, where I can have you restrained and watched. I'm going to take it in the voyeur room, so everyone knows who fucking owns this perfect peach you've got."

Jesus. How can he make the filthiest talk sound sexy as hell? This is all new to me, yet I'm comfortable with it all. Is this what it means to have that one person you were always meant for? Is my stepbrother my soulmate?

"Oh God..." I pant, gripping the edge of the table as he continues to dry hump me.

Suddenly, I feel the belt go around my neck, and he makes quick work of tightening it until it's nice and snug. My back arches when he pulls back on it, and his hand comes to my front to pinch my already-hardened nipples.

"Look at you, little lamb. You're about to get fucked right in front of the corpse of the man who gave you life. You're my good little whore, aren't you?"

"Yes," I whimper. "Now shut up and just fuck me already."

"Mm, I love it when you try being demanding."

I feel him fumble with his pants, and then he's thrusting into me without a care as to my comfort—and I welcome it. He holds the belt, so it remains snug as he pounds into me, grunting and groaning.

"I'm going to fill you with my little spawns, Raya. I hope you're ready for a Hall full of our kids."

Nyx's words spear me because he doesn't know what I did. He's going to be beyond pissed if he finds out that I had Dr. Mahony give me the shot. It was after the whole Plan B debacle. I don't want to have a child if the father isn't going to be in their life, and at that time, I wasn't sure if I was going to stick around.

The more events that took place, keeping me from leaving, the more I realized that they must have been God-sent because I do not want to leave Nyx again. This is our second chance, and I want to see what happens. However, keeping this little secret from him won't go over too well when he finds out.

"Fuck, Raya. I need you to come because I'm about to fill you full," Nyx growls from behind me.

I'm just about there, but when he yanks the belt, making me stand with my back to him, his hand goes to my clit, and it's all it takes to be able to give my stepbrother what he wants—I come for him.

"Good fucking girl..." he snarls in my ear before giving me his release.

"We should probably make sure you're not carrying a little something extra before you continue going on these little warehouse calls with me." Nyx comes up, wraps his arms around me from behind, and splays his hand against my stomach. "I wouldn't want anything happening to them."

I bite my lip and say, "I should get my period in the next week or so..."

"And if you don't?"

"Nyx," I sigh his name as I pull away. "Can we *not* talk about kids just yet? We aren't even married. We've only just come together again..." I pause and hold my hand up, knowing where his mind would go. "No pun intended, perv."

Giving me his most wicked smile, he shrugs. "Well, I won't wear a condom with you, Raya. I want to feel all of you when we fuck, and we've already discussed how I feel about Plan B—"

"I got the birth control shot."

I cut his sentence off when I come clean with him, saying it so fast that I wonder if he even understood what I said. However, the look that appears on his face tells me what I need to know—he heard me, and he isn't happy.

"When?"

"Not that long ago—before the whole kitchen event. I had gotten my period, so I knew I wasn't pregnant. I won't lie; I'm not sure it was in full effect when we had sex that day because I hadn't had it in my system that long."

"You didn't think to discuss it with me first?" I can hear the hurt in his voice, but his expression is one of fury.

His words piss me off.

Straightening my spine, I lift my chin and state, "I don't need permission to get on contraception, Nyx. I'm almost thirty years old—and I wasn't sure I was even staying. Had I gotten pregnant, the choice to stay or go would have been taken from me. I'm sorry if you don't understand that, but you can go fuck yourself if you think I will ever allow another man to dictate my life again."

I slip my feet into my flats and storm from the room. I hear him curse before he calls out my name, but I ignore him and keep going. I don't stop until I get to his car and get in. Unfortunately, I must ride home with him, but it's not like we've never ridden together without talking.

Nyx has other plans as he gets into the driver's seat. Instead of starting the car, he sits back in his seat and stares out his window.

"I'm not used to this shit, Raya."

He pauses as if wanting me to say something, but I remain silent, so he continues.

"For over ten years, I've lived for myself, taking whatever I wanted because I knew I could—because of who I was. I no longer had the one person I loved most, so what was the point in being that person anymore?"

I swallow hard, tears threatening to fall at any moment as I listen to what Nyx is saying. I can't say anything even if I want to because there is a lump in my throat. Relaxing in my seat, I let him take my hand when he reaches for it, but I don't dare look at him. I'm not ready to be that vulnerable in front of him yet, and if I gaze into those gray eyes, I know I will break.

"I don't mean to be a dick—not to you, anyway. I have a lot to make up for already without having to add more to it. The thought of you carrying my child means something to me, Raya. Yes, I have four more years to produce an heir or lose my place, but that's not why I want you to have my child."

"Nyx, I..."

I can't seem to utter a goddamn sentence.

"No, Raya, it's okay. I get why you don't want to get pregnant yet. I also understand that we weren't in a good place back then—not like we are now. I'm upset that you felt you couldn't tell me you went back on it once we settled the topic about you leaving."

Clearing my throat, I'm finally able to speak. "It's not something that I thought about twenty-four seven, so I'm sorry if I didn't just blurt it out each time we were together; I had other things on my mind."

"You should know that you are the only one that I want carrying my child. I would have waited until the last possible moment to find a wife if need be, but now that I know you are back in the running, I won't settle for anyone else."

Damn it! Why does he have to say these things? I need him to be the brute I know him to be so I can keep my emotions in check, but I don't think I can for much longer. We just killed somebody, then fucked right beside the body, and now we're talking about sappy shit. Who would have thought that Nyx Beckam had a sentimental side to him?

I burst out in laughter, surprising us both.

"I don't think this is a laughing matter, Raya."

"I'm sorry. It's not, and that's not what I'm laughing at," I tell him as I wipe my eyes.

"Then what is it?" The scowl he wears only makes me start laughing again.

"We just fucked beside my sperm donor's body, and now we're talking about kids. You're showing me a side of you that I've been wanting to see ever since I came to you, and yet, I'm sitting here wanting nothing more than to have you acting like the brute you've been."

He stares at me as if I've lost my mind.

"I know, it's crazy," I state, laughing even harder.

"I fucking love you."

All laughter stops when I hear Nyx's confession. I stare back at him.

"What did you just say?" I breathe softly.

"I said, I fucking love you. I've never stopped loving you. It's why I never gave another woman the time of day outside of being a sub and never took on a permanent sub. Nobody could ever compare to you."

The vulnerability I now see in Nyx's eyes does me in, and I feel the first tear fall. Once again, I'm speechless. His hand squeezes mine, but other than that and our breathing, there is no movement or sound as we gaze at each other.

Suddenly, I'm across the center console, straddling his lap and kissing the shit out of him. I'm unsure whether I came over here or if he pulled me over, but it doesn't matter because I *need* to be in his arms right now.

My hands hold each side of his head as I open my mouth and let him in. I'm unsure how long we sit here and make out, but my lips are numb when I pull away.

"I love you too, Nyx."

"Phoenyx..."

"Huh?"

"Call me by my real name like you used to. I only ever want it to come out of your mouth."

I lean back, my eyes darting back and forth as I study him. "Can I have both?"

Nyx furrows his brow. "What do you mean?"

"I mean, I want Phoenyx, but it has to be *all* Nyx in the bedroom."

His grin grows slowly before he says, "Maybe I should take you home and show you what *Phoenyx* can do for you in the bedroom, too."

I lick my lips, then suck my bottom one into my mouth. "Mm, now *that* sounds like a good plan.

Nyx and I are laughing over a story he just told me. A story about a time when he and Cray had gone skinny dipping with some females their first summer back from college. Apparently, nobody had warned them that the fish liked to nibble in the river they were in. Nyx and Cray had their first experience being molested by fish, and they've never gone skinny dipping again.

There's music coming from the billiard room, so I head that way, but Nyx stops me. "Hey, where are you going?"

"Calm down, big guy. I just want to pop in and say hi. Not all of us have to be assholes all the time."

I don't see his hand fly through the air, but I do feel the burn on my ass when it makes contact. We're close enough to a wall that he guides us over to it with his hand gripping my ass cheek and pushes me against it. I gasp, then giggle like a schoolgirl.

"If you ever tell me to calm down again when I'm anxious to fuck your gorgeous cunt, you will be sorry." His voice is husky, and his hot breath tickles my neck just before he bites my earlobe.

"You need to stop being so greedy, or I'll put you on a no-sex diet." I take him by surprise by spinning around and grabbing his hardness as I say, "Now, how about you be a good boy for me like I was a good girl for you earlier? We will say hi to everyone, and then I'm all yours."

His hand wraps around my throat, getting me excited, and he states, "Saraya Abbott, you are fucking trouble. You're stubborn, willful, and that mouth is very talented in many things, one of them being too fucking sassy."

"I already know this, and we are one and the same, babe, so why are you wasting time telling me what we both know?" I stare at his mouth, watching one side of it kick into a smirk before descending on mine, but only briefly.

Nyx steps away, and we head to where the others are. Upon entering the billiard room, we see only three people. Adrik, Amara, and a redhead that I've never seen before.

"Ah, look what the cat dragged in." Mara smirks. "You may want to take your little lamb somewhere else because we are about to have some fun with Red."

"Come on, Raya. I doubt you want to see this." Nyx's hand wraps around mine but I stand my ground.

"No. I want to watch."

I'm not sure what's about to happen, but if Mara is saying that I don't want to see it, then I most definitely do want to see it. I look over at Adrik, whose grin is wicked, as he picks up a bottle and a white cloth. When I raise my brow in askance, he happily explains.

"Cora doesn't take sleeping pills, so she brought her own party favor."

"I love it when Adrik puts me under chloroform. He knows just the right dosage to give me." The redhead giggles, and I glance back at the Heir. However, *Red* continues talking. "Mara promised me she would join this time, and I can't wait to watch the video afterward."

Only when the woman mentions the video do I see the camera set up, facing the pool table. Are they seriously going to knock her out and have sex with her? Mara must notice my questioning gaze because she once again mentions me not wanting to be here.

"Go if you can't hang. Not everyone is into what we're into," Mara muses before gripping the other woman's hair and crashing her mouth against hers.

Adrik, thinking he needs to reassure me, speaks up and states, "She brought it, and she asked for this. I'm only obliging."

My mouth runs for the second time today before I know what it will say. "I want to watch."

"What?" Nyx asks, turning me around.

"I want to see what it looks like when someone fucks a person who is passed out. As long as it's consensual, I don't see a problem with it," I tell him.

"Oh, it's consensual." Cora grins when Mara pulls away.

"You're sure?" Nyx confirms, and as soon as I nod, he drags me over to an armchair and sits me down on his lap.

I watch in anticipation as Adrik douses the cloth with the liquid and holds it to Cora's mouth. Mara turns the camera on as Adrik lays the now unconscious woman down on the pool table. They both make quick work of removing the woman's clothing, and then Mara goes down on the woman while Adrik shoves his cock in Cora's mouth.

They make a mess of the woman as Adrik releases himself on the woman's face and chest, and just when I think it's over. Mara straps a dildo on, and they reposition the passed-out woman. She looks like a ragdoll as they move her this way and that way.

"Does it turn you on to watch this, little lamb?" Nyx whispers in my ear.

"It's—fascinating. I've never seen this done before."

Adrik lowers Cora down, impaling her on the strap-on, before picking up the bottle of lube and smearing it on her ass. In no time at all, Mara and Adrik are DPing Cora, and for some fucked up reason, I find it hot as hell. Adrik brings Cora's body flush against his chest and plays with one breast while Mara plays with the other.

I've never thought I would enjoy watching this, but here I am, getting hot and bothered over it. Would I ever do it? Fuck no—but it's hot to watch, knowing that this is what she wanted.

THIRTY-FOUR

Nyx

I'm sitting in my office at Unholy, trying to catch up on some much-needed work since I was held hostage at the Hall for weeks after the shooting. I'd like to say that I'm getting shit done, but I can't. Too many thoughts are running through my head from earlier today.

The warehouse events were nothing compared to witnessing my little lamb watching two of my best friends fuck an unconscious woman. It being consensual with—Cora, I think her name was—didn't take from how fucking sexy the scene was or how deliciously hot Raya was. My dick was hard the whole fucking time.

When Mara and Adrik switched positions and started DPing the woman, I couldn't just sit there any longer. So what do you think I did? You better fucking believe it. I slid my hand into my little lamb's bottoms, and I finger fucked her right there. I didn't give a fuck if my friends kept looking over, and neither did my little lamb.

Raya thrust against my hand like she was riding my cock, rubbing up and down on me. When the time came, we all released together. Yeah—me included. My boxers were full of cum by the time we made it back to my room, and then my sexy as fuck stepsister dropped to her knees and cleaned me off.

We had spent the next two hours fucking. After all, I had to show Raya what *Phoenyx* was like in the sack. All in all, it was a full day of debauchery, and I definitely wouldn't mind doing it all again—minus killing Clyde. That fucker is right where he should have been years ago—in a wooden box.

I turn the monitors on to see what my little lamb is up to, and there she is, being the gracious hostess she is. Raya seems to have a permanent smile on her face. I think that's my doing. I hadn't realized just how much I was hurting her by being the dick I was. Oh, I'm still a dick, but for Raya, she will get the side that no one else will ever see.

As I'm staring at my queen, two men come walking into the front door and stop to talk to her. I've never seen them before, and I don't like their appearance in our club when I don't know who the fuck they are. I'm just about to call the hostess stand when I see Raya reach for the phone, and my office phone rings a second later.

"Talk to me, gorgeous."

"How did you know it was me?"

"Because I'm watching you." My tone carries the smirk I'm wearing.

Raya turns her back on the two men, which I'm not happy about, as she glares at the camera. She looks adorable when pretending to be angry.

"Don't you have better things to be doing than creeping on me?"

"Like fucking you—yes."

"Perv..."

I chuckle, then ask, "Tell me, little lamb, who are those men you seem to be entertaining down there?"

"Ha! Keep it up, and I'll take them to a back room and show you how I can *entertain* them."

My cock stirs with the sass coming from her mouth.

"You do that, and I'll have to show you just how much I own that cunt you're threatening to share with others. Now, be a good girl and tell me who the fuck they are."

I watch her bite her lip, my words affecting her more than she cares to admit. I also see the annoyed look the two men share with each other. I don't like it, and instead of waiting for Raya to tell me who they are, I tell her I'm on my way, and rush from my office.

"Where's the fire?" Zilas asks, smiling as I breeze past him.

"At the front door. Come with me—maybe you'll know who these fuckers are," I tell my friend, and he drops his smile, falling in step beside me.

I quickly tell him what I saw on the monitors, and he furrows his brows. "I was just coming to tell you that a couple were coming in to discuss the building complex that was discussed for that land on the East side of town, but it's a man and a woman."

"Yeah, well, I sincerely hope that these two fuckers weren't sent in their place because they're not the type I want to do business with."

We can't get to the front of the club fast enough. I hate that Raya is there with them, even if they are in sight of the bar. I'm sure Rigger is busy enough doing his own job.

When we round the last corner and the hostess stand comes into view, I sigh in relief seeing Cale leaning against the stand and making small talk with Raya. I'm sure it's all for show; Cale is good at recognizing situations immediately. He's supposed to be off the clock, so I'm grateful he's even here.

"Gentlemen, what can we do for you?" I ask as we walk up.

I go straight to Raya and slip my arm around her waist so they both know she is off-limits.

The taller of the two states, "We are here to discuss some business with the Heirs of Nyte's Hall."

Zilas and I glance at each other before I smile and reply, "Well, you're looking at two of them. Did you schedule an appointment?"

"Can we speak in private?" the same one asks while the other remains quiet.

"Tell us what this business is about, and we will decide whether it's worth our time."

"Oh, I think you will want to hear what we have to say," the quiet one finally says, glances at Raya, and then looks into my eyes.

Now I'm really on alert. Something isn't right, and if that look was any indication, Raya has something to do with it. Before I can agree with anything, a familiar voice joins in.

"Well, what do we have here? Do we have a problem?" Our little devil stands behind the two men, already cracking her fingers.

The taller one must know who Mara is because he's quick to calm the situation by saying, "No, Miss Nichols, no problem at all. We are just trying to gain an audience with your friends."

"Who the fuck are you?" the shorter one asks, earning an elbow from his partner.

"Shut up," the taller one orders the other through tight lips.

Maniacal female laughter starts and then suddenly stops. "Who's your *little* friend, Michael?"

Apparently, Mara knows one of them as well. I'm not a fan of not knowing what the fuck is going on. I step forward after giving Cale a knowing look and waiting for him to move closer to Raya.

"I think it's about time that someone starts fucking talking."

"Well, Nyx. You see, I met dear ole Michael last year when the Feds came into town because of your father." She shrugs and says, "We had a little fun, and then he left."

"I-I would have called, but you never gave me your number..." Michael states.

"Oh dear God, why the fuck would I want you to call me back? You're lucky I let you leave with your life. I was half tempted to put you out of your misery with what you have to live with." Mara's eyes drop to the guy's crotch.

I laugh inwardly, but my little lamb, on the other hand, couldn't do the same. I look back at her and grin when I see her hand covering her mouth. When I focus on the Michael guy, I can see the embarrassment on his reddened face.

"So, you're with the Feds?" I jump to the point.

"Yeah, you can say that," the small one responds.

"No, we're with the Bureau of Investigations, specifically," Michael corrects his partner before looking at Mara.

I glance at Mara, and she nods towards Michael saying, "He's okay, but asshat over here is another story. I don't know who the fuck he is, and he's already on my last nerve."

"That's good enough for me. Michael, you may come with us. Asshat, you be a good boy and wait here."

That must have been the wrong thing to say because a commotion takes place behind me when I turn around to walk away. I turn back to see Zilas holding the guy with his arm angled oddly behind his back.

"I highly suggest you keep your hands to your fucking self," Zilas barks out. "You're already walking a fine line coming up into the Gods' territory, demanding shit."

"Let me go! I'm Michael's boss! I should be the one to go—"

"We don't give a shit who the fuck you are! If little devil says she doesn't trust you, then *we* don't trust you."

"*She's* the little devil?" Asshat asks, stunned.

"Yeah, she is. Do you have a problem with that?" I ask him.

"N-no. I'm sorry. I'll wait here."

Michael isn't sure what to do as he looks back and forth between us and his boss. It's a bit irritating, and now *I'm* wishing that Mara had killed him a year ago.

"Stop wasting our time, Michael. We're busy men; either come with us or get the fuck out." I don't wait for his response.

Leaning over, I kiss my little lamb's lips and pull her into my body. "Call me if you have any issues with the other one. I'll be keeping an eye on him from the office, too."

"Just go. Don't worry about me, I'm covered." She moves the slit in her dress aside and showcases the knife tucked away in a holster around her thigh.

"Mm, I'm going to remove that with my teeth later; you know that, right?"

Raya gives me a sultry smile as she says, "Only if you're a good boy."

Growling lowly, I leave my little lamb standing there before I decide to take her to the coat room nearby and show her just how much of a good boy I can be. Her seductive chuckle has my cock twitching as I walk away. Paybacks are a bitch, and I'm going to have fun showing Raya just how much.

"What the fuck do you mean the Bureau wants you to bring Saraya in? What the hell has she done?" I stand behind my desk, ready to pounce on the motherfucker.

"I'm sorry, Mr. Beckam, but Mrs. McNally is the prime suspect in her husband's disappearance. Since he's a police officer, the Bureau of Investigations had to step in."

"I know what the fuck the Bureau does, but what I want to know is why Raya is a suspect? She came running to me after her husband beat her and tried choking her. How the fuck is she supposed to know what happened after that?"

"W-well, that alone gives motive, Sir," Michael stammers.

"Motive for what exactly?"

"Well, for murder, of course."

"Is he missing, or has he been murdered?"

"At the moment, he's missing, but we are pretty sure it's the latter."

"No, you're assuming, and that's not good enough. Even if my brother-in-law was murdered, and Raya had done it, she would have had every right to kill the fucker for laying his hands on her. This PD is so fucking corrupt that we have already started looking into cleaning house. We want real cops policing the town of Nyte, not shady fucks you all call police officers."

"I'm sorry, Mr. Beckam. I don't make the laws..."

"What about the other ones that have gone missing recently?" Amara asks. "Are you trying to tell us that you think Saraya is involved in their disappearances, too? From what I hear, they were all friends."

"I heard the same thing," Zilas states. "They were all on Clyde Kappel's payroll. Have you asked him?"

Michael pulls out a notepad and writes Kappel's name down. "This is the first I've heard of Kappel being involved with the three officers."

"So, you knew about the others and still came after Saraya?" I ask, anger evident in my tone.

"It's protocol, Sir, being she is the wife."

"*Was* the wife. He decided to beat her, and now he's disappeared. Recent information has also surfaced, proving that she was forced to marry him by my father, so that makes their marriage null and void in my eyes. I have already sent in a petition on that alone."

"I'm sorry, Mr. Beckam. That doesn't change the fact that she needs to come in and—"

I cut him off by handing him a card and saying, "Contact my lawyer about it. Now, get the fuck out of our club before I have you removed."

Michael rushes from my office, and I slam my hand down on the desk. "Why the fuck does this have to happen now? It's all bullshit! They know better than to come at the Gods of Nyte!"

"Chill, Nyx. They have nothing..." Zilas tries calming me.

I inhale and then exhale.

"They're testing us," I state. "They know better than to come at us. The Bureau never stepped in when our fathers were in charge. It's time we show them we're worse than our fathers."

I don't care if what they're assuming is true or not. They will never find any of the bodies. What I do care about is that they are trying to pin it on my little lamb. They are going to fucking regret trying to come for what's mine.

THIRTY-FIVE

Saraya

"What did you do with the body?"

I look over at the man still sitting by the door waiting for his partner, and then I look at my surroundings. "Are you talking to me?"

"I don't see anybody else here, do you?"

"Well, I'm not quite sure what you're asking me."

"Your husband's body. What did you do with Kenneth McNally's body after you killed him?"

I had a feeling that's what he was talking about. My heart is racing. *What is Nyx telling this guy's partner? I don't want to fuck up whatever story he's come up with.*

"I'm sorry, mister?"

"You can just call me Wilson," he replies snidely.

"Okay, well, *Wilson,* I'm sorry I can't help you since I don't know where my husband is."

"You seem pretty cozy with your stepbrother, *Mrs. McNally.*"

Oh, I do not like this guy very much. I can't let him see that he's getting to me, so I do what I do best when backed into a corner. I pull my big girl pants up and turn on the sass.

"I go by *Abbott* now, and if I seemed cozy with my *stepbrother,* Wilson, it's probably because I spent all day fucking him. Is that a crime?" I step out from behind the hostess stand and hold out my wrists, saying, "Because if having my stepbrother fucking me and making me come multiple times in the course of five to six hours is illegal, then please, lock me up and throw away the key."

I've shocked him—good. I wait for him to say something, so when all he does is twist his face up in disgust and turn his head, I smirk and return to my place behind the hostess stand. Not long after, his partner comes back, and I hear him mention Kappel's name. Once again, my heart starts racing. I feel sweat bead on my forehead as I pretend to write things down. Finally, after what seems like forever, they take their leave, and I blow out a breath.

"What's wrong, *little lamb,* can't take the heat?" Mara smirks at me.

"Fuck off, Mara. I'm not in the mood."

The little psycho strolls over and rests her elbow on the stand before me. She studies me, earning her a glare, but then she states, "You're really not scared, are you?"

"Scared of what exactly?" I lift my brow.

"Of me. I can make grown men shit their pants, but you don't bat an eye. No, you try going toe to toe with me and even dared to choke me out."

I shrug. "We grew up together. I know you can kick my ass, but maybe my subconscious just doesn't realize how dangerous you are and thinks that you would never try killing me."

Mara scoffs and says, "I'd kill any one of the Heirs if it came down to it."

It's my turn to scrutinize her for a moment before leaning in and whispering, "I call bullshit. You would rather die than have to kill any of your *brothers.*"

I may have stunned her momentarily as her body stiffens, then relaxes. "Even if that were true, which it's not, that doesn't mean I wouldn't take you out."

"I beg to differ. You would never hurt Nyx like that, so it looks like you're stuck with me, sweet cheeks."

I don't hear what she says next because I see Nyx over her shoulder talking to that woman I saw leaving his house the first night I arrived. The woman smiles flirtatiously, but I can't see Nyx's face clearly due to his back being turned slightly. I'm not so worried about him, but I'll be damned if anyone flirts with him.

"Who the fuck is that?" I ask Mara, stopping her mid-sentence.

She follows my line of sight and then snickers. "That's Emily."

"Is she his ex or something?"

"God no!" she laughs. "Nyx has never dated, not since you, anyway."

I snap my head toward her. "Seriously?"

"Yep." She pops the *p* at the end. "You have always been the one that got away and took his heart with you."

I tighten my lips and turn back to look over her shoulder. I can feel my blood boil as the woman stands there, batting her eyes at my man.

"So, what's the story? She was at the Hall the night I arrived."

Mara waves her hand and says, "Oh, that was nothing. She had just started at the club, and Nyx was auditioning her."

I notice the smirk as she finishes her sentence, and I know I shouldn't, but I ask anyway. "Auditioning how?"

"She gave him a blow job in the billiard room. I then threatened her that if she spewed any of his cum onto the floor, I'd use her tongue to clean the whole floor."

"Are you fucking with me, Mara?"

"There is only one way I'd fuck with you, Raya, but you keep refusing the good time I'm offering," Mara says seductively.

I roll my eyes and shove past her, saying, "Excuse me, but I need to go educate someone."

I walk over to where little Miss Sunshine stands, a little too close to my man. Just before I approach them, her hand comes up, and she places it on his bicep and laughs. I don't say anything to the little hussy as I shove my way between the two and slide my hand up to the back of Nyx's neck.

"I've missed you, baby." I pull his head down just as he grins and kiss him.

Nyx slides his arm around my waist and pulls me in closer.

The woman must not have gotten the hint, because she has the audacity to clear her throat and state, "I'm sorry, but I was talking to him first and was just going to ask Mr. Beckam to scene with me. Maybe you will have better luck next time."

I pull back and grin at Nyx.

"Be good, little lamb," he warns me with a knowing smirk.

I spin around. "*Emily,* is it? You have two options, and I really hope you choose the right one. Option one, you can get your ass back to work and *never* put your hands on my fiancé again, or option number two, I can drag you out back and beat your ass for touching *Nyx.*"

The woman's eyes dart back and forth as if waiting for Nyx to chastise me.

"Don't look at him—look at me—he won't save you. He's most likely already planning on how he's going to fuck me tonight." I turn to look at him, and he shrugs.

"You ain't wrong."

When I return my attention to Emily, she's already hurrying away, and I snicker. Nyx spins me around and into his arms. "Jealous much?"

"Excuse me? I have not waited over a decade to be able to have you just for some floozy to come along and put her paws all over you. What were you discussing anyway that had her smiling like she was?"

He grins wickedly. "You."

I jerk back. "Huh?"

"She asked me who you were since she just returned from a medical leave, and I told her you were my stepsister."

"You knew how I would react when I saw her flirting, and you lied to her anyway. That is so wrong."

"I didn't lie. You are my stepsister. A stepsister that I love doing bad things to." He nibbles on my neck.

I'm just getting into the PDA when a couple walks through the door. "Shit! I have to go greet some guests."

Nyx looks over to the doors. "Ah, I think they are the couple Zilas has been waiting for."

"Oh, really?"

"Not like that," Nyx laughs. "I had better go greet them."

"Hey! We need to talk about tonight's visitors," I tell him.

"Yes, we will. Let me take care of this with Zilas, and I'm all yours."

"*All* mine?" I lick my lips.

Nyx winks at me, then turns to the couple, shaking both of their hands and leading them to the offices upstairs. I catch a glimpse of Cale, and I'm surprised to see him going to a back room with Monica, the woman I kind of took the hostess job from.

Good for him. Maybe now he can take that stick out of his ass and leave me the fuck alone.

Nyx and I never do get to talk. Business keeps him at the club for longer than I want to stay, so I ride back to the Hall with Amara. I don't mind riding bitch on the back of a bike, but I prefer a man being the one to drive it. Mara is a crazy bitch on two wheels!

Waking up this morning, I see that Nyx made it home. His body is entangled with mine, making it nearly impossible for me to get out of bed. Not wanting to wake him up in case he hasn't been sleeping long, I slowly move his arm one centimeter at a time. Just when I think I will get free, Nyx wraps me in his arms again.

Frustrated, I give up trying to be nice.

"Babe, if you don't let me go, your bed will be soaked."

"Hm?" he hums with his eyes still closed.

"I'm going to piss the bed if you don't let me up."

He finally lets me go, mumbling something about "golden showers" and "not being his kink." I chuckle as I head to the connecting bathroom. I go through my morning routine and head down to start the coffee, but when I get to the kitchen, there's already a pot made.

Now I really feel bad because Nyx must not have been home for too long before coming to bed. After pouring my coffee, I go straight to the fridge and pull stuff out to make breakfast. When I turn, I jump and scream, dropping everything in my arms, including the carton of eggs.

"Oh dear, I'm so sorry! I didn't mean to scare you." A woman in her fifties, maybe, holds her hand to her chest as she stares at me with concern.

"I'm sorry, who are you?" I ask.

"I'm Jessica Parker. Mr. Beckam hired me to help in the kitchen. You can call me Jessica."

"Oh yes, he said he would hire someone. It must have slipped his mind to tell me." I chuckle and then get to work cleaning up my mess.

"Let me do that for you since I startled you," Jessica offers, but I refuse.

"No, I insist, Jessica. I'll clean this up, and you can find something to whip up for breakfast."

"Okay, I can do that. Will Mr. Beckam be joining you this morning?"

"I'm not exactly sure—"

"Yes, Mr. Beckam will be joining his beautiful fiancée for breakfast," Nyx states as he waltzes into the kitchen. He bends down and kisses my head. "What happened here?"

"Someone forgot to tell me he hired someone, and she scared the shit out of me when she came in."

Nyx snickers apologetically. "Sorry about that, I meant to."

He pulls me up and into his arms. Before I know it, his mouth is on mine. I don't care if Jessica is in the room—I wrap my arms around his neck and literally climb up his body until my legs are wrapped around his waist. One of his hands goes to my ass to help support me, and the other goes to the back of my head.

I can feel his hardness through the basketball shorts he's wearing, and a feeling of accomplishment pours over me. I love that I do this to him. I never thought I would feel this way again, and even though we bicker, I wouldn't want it with anyone else.

I groan when Nyx pulls his mouth away.

"Behave, little lamb. I don't take Mrs. Parker as being a voyeur, so unless you want to lose the help so soon, I suggest you stop trying to get into my shorts right now." Nyx sits in the chair at the small nook but keeps me on his lap.

I slap his shoulder. "I was not trying to get into your shorts, but it is easier to have you hold me up than to hurt my toes by standing on them just to reach your lips."

"Hey, it's okay. I love the spider monkey in you."

"Do you even know what one of those creatures looks like?"

"Yes, and it's a good thing I'm not *that* shallow. It's your sassy disposition that captivates me." Nyx grins wickedly, but I push myself off his lap anyway, not caring if he's joking.

"Well, I guess I shouldn't feel too guilty that I'm only with you for what you have in your pants then." I throw back at him, keeping my smile hidden from him.

Jessica, acting motherly, breaks in and says, "Now, now, you two had better start getting along, or I will kick you out of this kitchen and not feed you."

"He started it," I whine jokingly.

"Nuh-uh!" Nyx replies childishly.

Jessica just chuckles and shakes her head as she finishes stirring the pancake batter. "Breakfast will be ready in about thirty minutes, so you two lovebirds can go hash out whatever needs hashing."

I finish cleaning my mess up, grab my mug of coffee from the counter, and walk out of the kitchen. I can feel Nyx's eyes on me the whole time. I poke my head back into the room and stare into his gray eyes.

"You and I need to have that little talk we were supposed to have last night. Now would be a good time to have it."

"Are you trying to tell me what to do, little lamb?" Nyx asks as he gets up and pours his coffee.

"Not at all, but I have something you want, and if you know what's good for you, then you will follow me." I give him a cheesy smile.

"First ordering me around, and then blackmailing me. Hm, sounds like a certain little lamb is looking to get punished," he says, following me out the door.

I don't deny or confirm his statement, but either way, the thought of Nyx spanking my ass, or better yet, my pussy, has my lady bits tingling.

THIRTY-SIX

Nyx

All four of us Heirs are here at Unholy meeting with Jarod and Jax. Raya is pissed because I got called away before we had our talk. I invited her, but she's not ready to see the twins yet, especially after what happened with Clyde.

"This better be good," I tell them. "I have a pissed-off woman at home because I got called away, and I hate it when my little lamb is angry."

"Sorry," Jarod states. "I just thought you should know that the Bureau of Investigations came by first thing this morning."

"I figured they would since I told them to talk to your father."

"Well, why the fuck would you do that when *you* have him?" Jarod's temper rises, and I raise a brow.

"Just because you're Saraya's blood doesn't mean I won't put you in your place. Blood means shit when they can't be trusted. To answer your question, they wanted to take Raya in for questioning. We had to lead them away from her."

"What did you tell them?" Adrik asks the twins, not taking his eyes off the stage with the girls practicing on the pole.

"We told them that he's out of town until tomorrow. We wanted a chance to talk to you."

"Okay, good," I reply. "This is what you will do then. Your father is coming home tonight because he's not feeling well. You're going to find him in the morning, and you're going to call the doctor. Dr. Mahony will make a house call and then call the coroner, which just so happens to be one of our own. We only use him for emergencies, such as this."

"So, our father is..." Jarod's sentence trails off.

"Dead—yes." My name isn't Willy Wonka. I'm not going to sugarcoat the shit.

Jax nods, but I can tell that Jarod isn't taking it as well. Everybody knows what happens when you fuck with the Gods of Nyte, and Clyde was no different. He just got comfortable because of our fathers.

"Before you say anything, you should know that he insulted Raya continuously; there was no saving him after that," I inform them.

"I understand," Jax states.

My attention returns to his brother, and he nods in agreement. I really hope we aren't going to have issues with this matter. The last thing I want to do is take the last of Raya's blood relatives from her, even if she doesn't really know them yet.

As if reading my mind, Jax asks, "How's Saraya taking it?"

"Raya is fine. He meant nothing to her, and all he wanted to do was use her for his own benefit," I say with disgust.

Jax nods and says, "I get it. I want her to know that we are nothing like our father. We would never..."

"Yeah, she knows it, but she still needs time."

"So, are we all on the same page about what needs to happen?" Zilas stands, buttoning his suit jacket as he does.

"Yes, we are." Jarod is the one to reply this time, and he no longer has that look about him as he did just a few moments ago.

"Good. Now I can get back and try *soothing* my little lamb." I smirk at the twins.

"Damn it, Nyx! Don't go there..." Jax groans.

"Then I suggest not coming to the club this weekend, because I have plans for my girl." I laugh as they hurry off, unable to get out fast enough.

"That was a dick move," Adrik states, shaking his head in mirth.

"Well, they will have to get used to it if they want into Raya's life," I tell my friend.

"Do you think they'll try anything once you marry her, like getting a piece of the pie, so to speak?" Cray finally speaks up after being silent throughout the whole meeting.

"I would like to think not, but who knows anymore." I sigh. "Honestly, if they can get their shit together and change the business, it wouldn't be all that bad. We've already discussed this."

"Yeah, I think they'll do good by us, but still, it wouldn't hurt to still be careful," Adrik states.

I nod as I stand. "Not to cut our little chat short, but I have a girl I'm going to need to smooth things over with, and I'm very much looking forward to it." Smirking, I button my own suit jacket and follow the guys out.

It's early, but there are always workers in and out, especially the performers. We nod at those who say hello and ignore workers who look at us with flirtatious eyes. None of us ever want to give hope to those who work at the club, because there will never be a relationship between an Heir and a club employee.

Raya working for the club isn't the same, because she's one of us. Hell, she doesn't need to work here any longer, but she's enjoying it, so I let her be. She doesn't work as a sub, either—no one will ever touch her—and it's apparent nobody will ever touch me if Raya's little show with Emily the day before says anything.

I grin at the memory. The way she shoved herself between me and Emily was amusing and had my dick stirring. That woman doesn't know what she does to me.

"Mr. Beckam..."

I turn and see Monica already here, so I stop and let her catch up to me before I ask, "What are you doing here so early?"

She blushes. "I'm sorry—"

"She was with me, Boss." Cale comes up behind her. "We fell asleep in one of the aftercare rooms."

I try to hide my smirk. "I see. What is it you need, Monica?" I return my attention to the woman whose face is bright pink with embarrassment.

"Um, I was wondering if you could remind Saraya that inventory needs to be ordered today, and since she's been keeping track of it..."

I nod. "I'll have her come in early and take care of it."

"Thank you," Monica says before bowing and muttering a quick goodbye.

"What did you do to her?" I ask Cale, grinning.

"Nothing she didn't beg me for." His grin is wicked, stopping me from asking any more questions.

"Well, try not to fall asleep here again. We aren't a fucking hotel..." I try saying this as sternly as possible, but my smirk gives me away.

"Yes, Boss." Cale slaps me on my shoulder and then walks out of the club fucking whistling.

My little lamb lies on my bed, unaware I've entered the room. She's on her stomach, her knees bent, and her feet moving around in the air. Her brown locks are thrown into a messy bun, and as I follow the slender column of her neck, I notice the earbuds in her ears.

She's flipping through a magazine as I slowly walk up behind her. When I get to the edge of the bed, I gaze down and take in the booty shorts she's wearing. Her ass peeks out, teasing me—daring me—to take a nice bite out of it. That will have to wait for now, because what I want is south of those cheeks.

In one swift move, I take hold of her legs, yank them open, and dive between said legs, pulling the shorts aside so I can get to the prize. I hear her screech, but I don't give a fuck as I lap at her center.

"Phoenyx!"

Again, I ignore her, and when she tries moving away, I grip the tops of her thighs and hold her tight so she can't get away. I'm feasting now; not even my little lamb can pull me away from this meal. It isn't until she gives in and begins moaning while trying to grind against my face that I loosen my hold.

I fuck Raya with my tongue from behind, the muscle thrusting in and out, then flicking it back and forth over her clit before thrusting into her again. When I think she's about to come, I smack her ass.

"Don't you dare come yet."

"Oh God, Phoenyx...I need to..."

My full name on her lips has something happening inside my chest. Something that I thought I would never feel again, not since it was torn from its cavity so many years ago.

I need inside her!

Tearing her shorts from her body, I make quick work, opening my dress pants before pulling her to the edge of the bed. Her earbuds slip from her ears in the process, and I lift her ass, thrusting inside of her cunt. It's so warm and welcoming as it squeezes the fuck out of me. The groan I allow to slip out is loud. I want her to know that she feels so fucking good.

Looking down at the curve of her back, I trace my finger down her spine, all the way to her crack. I lean into her, bringing my fingers to her mouth, and order, "Suck."

My girl sucks two of my fingers like it's my cock, twirling her tongue around and around before taking them deep. When I shove them in deeper, she doesn't gag—that alone has my cock jerking inside her.

"Fuck, baby. Is there anything you aren't good at?" I don't expect an answer; however, she responds when I remove my fingers.

"I don't do *good* around you. It's either naughty or nothing..."

I work my fingers back down to her ass crack and slowly push one into the tight little hole as I ask, "Oh? Why is that little lamb?"

"Oh, fuck," she exclaims softly at the invasion.

"Answer me, little lamb. Why can't you be a good girl for me?"

"Because good girls don't get punished."

If I thought my cock was hard already, I wince at how much harder it just got from Raya's little confession. Does she not know what she does to me, never mind when she says this sort of shit?

"Woman, I will punish you any fucking time you want me to. I will give you the pain right alongside the pleasure you crave so much; all you have to do is ask."

"How about I do the ordering, and you submit?" I can hear the slight snicker in her voice with her suggestion.

"Now, now, little lamb, you know that's not how it works."

She's about to give her retort when I insert a second finger into her ass and quicken my hips. As I fuck both her holes, I take hold of her messy bun and really start fucking her hard.

"Uh...oh God...just like that...don't stop..." she pants, as I take what I want from her willing body.

"Come for me, and I'll let you ride my cock however you want, baby."

"Yes... don't you dare fucking stop!"

As much as I want her to come, her words sound like a challenge to me, so I pull out of both orifices, grinning. Her mouth has earned her a punishment that she isn't going to like. She now has to wait for her release.

"What the fuck?" she whines.

I slap her ass and then shove two fingers back into her. "You want to come, and yet, you try telling me what to do. Tsk, tsk, little lamb. Now, you don't get to come. Maybe if you ride me real good, you can earn your orgasm back."

"Uh...stop being a dick," she moans while still running her mouth.

"You can be naughty all you want as long as you ride me good. Can you do that, baby?"

"Fuck you, Nyx!"

My smile is wicked as she continues to curse me, all while humping my hand. "You already are, little lamb, and it looks like you're enjoying it immensely."

Suddenly, her warmth is no longer surrounding my fingers. Instead, I feel the heat of her glare as she kneels before me on the bed, glowering at me. I wondered how long it would take for my little spitfire to realize what she was doing and come to her senses. She gets so lost when I'm inside her that she forgets she doesn't like submitting to me.

"How about you stop running your mouth and get on your back." She snaps, and I smirk. "You want me to ride you, yet you're still dressed *and* standing."

My grin grows as I begin to slowly pull off my clothing. I had already relieved myself of my jacket, and my pants are actually around my ankles now that I've stood up straight. I undo the buttons down my dress shirt before tackling the cuffs. My little lamb is getting impatient, which only amuses me more. She's so fucking sexy when she's annoyed with me.

Finally, as I stand before her in all my naked glory, Raya takes me in, licking her lips. She's so distracted that she hasn't noticed I've moved closer to the bed, so my legs are now pressed against the side. Like a snake, I strike out, my hand wrapping around her neck.

"Have you forgotten how I like my women in bed?" I ask huskily, feeling her pulse quicken beneath my fingers.

Raya doesn't miss a step, and not even two seconds later, her hand is wrapped around my ball sack as she replies, "Well, it's a good thing that I'm not *women*. I'm the *woman* who you want to fuck. You came to me, Mr. Beckam, so I think it's only fair that you ride bitch this time around."

My eyes widen with enjoyment. Finally, a woman who matches me in *everything*. I still won't be her bitch, but I'll play her game for a while; under one condition, that is.

"Let me plug that ass, and you can have your way with me."

"Excuse me?"

"I told you that I'm going to take that ass in the Voyeur room; we need to start preparing it."

"Like hell..."

"You almost got off with me fucking both holes; I guarantee you're going to love getting your ass fucked, and we already know that you like being watched."

I throw out the first olive branch and let go of her neck, caressing her cheek instead as I change tactics. I brush my lips against hers as I stare into her beautiful brown eyes. They are usually warm, but they almost seem black at the moment. Whether it's due to anger or lust, I'm not sure.

"Kiss me," I murmur against her mouth when she hasn't moved.

It takes a bit, but I can feel when she gives in. Her body begins to relax, and when I run my tongue over the seam of her lips, she opens for me, allowing me entrance. We both moan the moment our tongues touch, and I forget what I was trying to do to her.

The next thing I know, we're both lying on the bed, our mouths still fused together. Raya has a spell over me that envelopes my entire body, and I give in. I don't care who submits to who as long as I can feel her around me again.

"Fuck me, Raya," I break our kiss to whisper this. "Fuck me and take your pleasure. You can have it all."

THIRTY-SEVEN

Saraya

"You're not forgiven, you know? I need more than a good fucking to make up for leaving me this morning."

Nyx and I are still lying in bed after the amazing sex we just had. I still have to give him shit, though. I don't want him thinking that he can just leave in the middle of an important conversation with me and think he can make it up to me with great sex.

He's on his back, and I'm on my side, with my head on his shoulder and my left leg thrown over his. Nyx holds me to him, kissing my head and chuckling as I say this. I amuse him all the time, and I'm not sure if I should be insulted. Does he ever take me seriously?

"You must understand, this meeting was about *helping* you," he states.

"Yeah, well, our conversation was about helping me, too."

"I'm sorry, little lamb. I'll think twice before I leave you while in the middle of a conversation."

I can hear the smile in his voice.

"You think I'm a joke, don't you? I don't need you to pacify me, Nyx, but I don't want you brushing me off whenever you get a call like you did."

"I asked you to come. We could have finished the conversation in the car, but you didn't want to go," Nyx reminds me as his fingers graze back and forth on my arm draped over his chest.

"I'm not ready to see the twins yet."

"I know." He sighs.

We grow quiet for a little while, me thinking about how good it feels to be in Nyx's arms. Stepbrother or not, I love him and never want to lose him again. However, I don't think I'm ready to admit it to him just yet.

"Monica asked me to remind you about inventory due today. I told her you would be in early to work on it."

I nod. "Yeah, I was going to tell you this morning, but everything happened."

It grows quiet again, but it's a comfortable kind of quiet. The kind where you can just lay there and drift off to sleep, not having a care in the world. Nyx comes off as a tough guy to everyone, and he truly is, but Phoenyx is the exact opposite. I love both sides of him, but right now, Phoenyx is the man I need.

"Marry me, Raya."

I stiffen.

"What? I already told you I would."

"No, I mean, like soon. I need to know you are completely mine, and I don't want to chance anyone coming to take you from me again."

I tilt my head to look at his face. "I'm not going anywhere, Phoenyx."

He rolls us over so he's above me and says, "So what does it matter if we do it now?"

"We still have a lot to deal with. We haven't really talked about the past and everything that happened," I remind him.

Lifting my leg to his hip, he slides himself right into me, and I can't stop the moan that comes out from being filled by him. My heart flutters each and every time.

"The past no longer matters—only the present and future. You own this thing that has started beating in my chest again, Saraya. It's been cold so long; I didn't think it would ever work again." Nyx grinds himself into me nice and slowly.

Not only am I stunned by his confession, but also by the fact that Phoenyx Beckam, a God of Nyte's Hall, is making love to me. His head dips down, and he starts kissing and nibbling on my neck as he continues to rock his hips back and forth, keeping a leisurely pace. When he hits that particular spot deep inside, I tilt my head back, crying out from sheer pleasure.

It's not long before I feel my climax building, and Nyx must, too, because he picks up his speed just a little and plunges deeper and harder with each of his thrusts. I've never had this before—I've never felt it like this.

"Phoenyx..."

"Come for me, baby. Give me your everything, and I'll give you mine."

I. Come. Hard.

"That's it, Raya. Yes, just like that..." His voice strains as he empties himself into me.

We stare into each other's eyes as we give our everything to the other. I don't even know I'm crying until I feel tears slide down from the outer corners of my eyes. Nyx wipes them away with his thumbs before leaning in and kissing my lips. Before pulling completely away, I feel his breath on my lips.

"I fucking love you, Saraya."

Five little words have my mind in a tailspin, just like every other time I've heard them spoken from his lips. *Nyx loves me.* I'll never tire of hearing him say them to me.

"Had I known I could have stopped the sass just by telling you how I felt, I would have said it sooner," he had teased me at one time.

I've never stopped loving him in all these years. As each year passed, I would torture myself, wondering if that would be the year Phoenyx would marry another. Now that I have him back, and he's confessed his feelings for me, I'll do whatever it takes to never lose him again.

He'll do the same thing for me—right?

A voice on the other end of the call brings me back to the present. "I'm sorry, Ms. Abbott, but we're out of the usual lube packets until next week. We can send you a different brand to get you by until then. I'll even knock off forty percent."

"Yes, that will be fine, thank you. I think that's all for this month. If I'm missing anything, I'll be sure to call you back," I tell the woman on the other end.

Nyx dropped me off at the club, so I could call in the inventory. He had an errand to run but said he would be back soon. Of course, now that I've returned to my senses, I'll tell him as soon as I see him that I love him, too. I can't have him thinking it's only one-sided. I'm so tired of all the miscommunication.

The front door opens when I hang up with the supplier, and two men in suits come in. They exude money, and I can tell they've never been here before by how they look around before greeting me. One has blonde hair with a bit of gel holding it in place, while the other has dark red hair with a splatter of freckles speckling his nose. They're both good-looking men, but far from my type, even if I didn't have the sexiest man alive.

Making sure I'm in hostess mode, I give them a genuine smile and greet them. "Welcome to Club Unholy, where all your fantasies come to life. Pick your poison, and we'll happily see that all your needs are met."

"Well, that was the perfect opening because it's exactly what we are looking for." The redhead grins.

The blonde licks his lips before asking, "How about you? Are you available?"

Before I can say anything, Amara appears from thin air and jumps in to answer our new guests, seductively, "Sorry boys, Raya, here, is taken, but I think I can help you find what it is you're looking for."

"Hm, that's too bad," Blondie states. "She's exactly who I pictured I would have my cock buried in tonight."

It happens so fast that I don't see Mara pulling out her favorite knife and holding it to the guy's crotch. She continues to smile at him, but her jaw is clenched, and her tone warrants no room for argument.

"I said she's unavailable. There is no room for crude remarks towards your hostess. Now, if you want to have fun, I can show you boys around, or we can skip it all and head back to my domain. I have two holes more than willing to entertain you both."

"Hey, is that really necessary?" the redhead questions as he stares down at his friend's crotch.

"Oh, am I threatening your favorite toy?" Amara asks, dragging the knife up and down the bulge that Blondie now sports.

He's turned on.

"Men," I chime in, "Let me introduce you to our little devil. If you're looking for a wild ride, and you don't mind a little pain with your pleasure, she's the one for you."

The redhead speaks up again. "We have a friend stopping by in a bit. Will you show him to our room?"

"Certainly, as long as our little devil is up for it." I look at Mara, and she smiles wickedly.

"The more, the merrier." She removes the knife from Blondie's crotch and licks the blade.

The men are mesmerized by Mara, and I have to snap my fingers to get their attention. "Excuse me, but her time isn't free. I assume you have no membership; are you planning to pay for just one night?"

"Uh, yeah, sorry," Red states.

"It's okay." I hand him two clipboards. "I'll need both of you to fill this form out. It's twenty-five hundred for the night. Which card will you be using tonight?"

"Oh, none. We will be paying with cash."

I study the redhead momentarily and then nod. We usually don't get clientele who pay with cash, so it throws me off a little. It's not that it's unheard of, especially if they're married and don't want the charges showing up on their statements, but typically, they don't care if they keep their rings on. We don't judge them for their infidelities, but these two aren't wearing rings, nor do they bear the marks proving they've been removed.

Once they've finished filling out their forms and have paid their fees, I nod at Mara and hand her their limit lists. She then grabs them both by their ties and walks away, her ass swaying back and forth more than usual. They don't realize what she's doing. Amara Nichols likes to show off her *pets,* and since she has no leashes, the ties work as their replacements. Everybody who is anybody here at Unholy now knows that the little devil will be making both those men her little bitches for the night. Of course, that is if they filled out their limit forms correctly.

I smirk, shaking my head. *Oh, to be a fly on that wall.*

My phone buzzes with an incoming text.

NYX: Staying out of trouble, little lamb?
ME: Always
NYX: Lies
ME: Believe what you want.
NYX: Do you know what I want?
ME: I can only imagine what it is with your perverse way of thinking.
NYX: I want my future bride to FaceTime me.
ME: Why?
NYX: I want to see that gorgeous face that I'm going to mess up by the end of tonight. I want you to cry tonight, baby. Will you do that for me?

Jesus. How does he do this with just his words? My panties are now wet, and we've only exchanged a few words.

I jump when my phone rings. Apparently, I was taking too long, so Nyx FaceTimed me instead. I place my phone upright on the holder attached to the stand and answer the video call.

"I'm working, Nyx."

"Well, it's good that we own the club then. You don't have to worry about getting in trouble with the boss." Nyx gives me his sexy grin.

I see he's outside walking, and then he's getting in his car. He never said what errand he had to run, but he's downtown somewhere.

"Where are you at?" I ask.

"I just finished my errand. I'm heading back to the club now."

"Okay, well then, why did you video call me?"

"Two reasons. Firstly, I wanted to see that gorgeous face like I said..."

"And secondly?" I cock my brow.

"I want to watch you take off your panties and show them to me."

"What?! I'm not doing that!"

"Little lamb, will you please remove your panties and show them to me?" he asks nicely as he starts his car, looks to ensure there's no traffic, and pulls out of his spot before his eyes land on me again, briefly. He's so fucking hot, it's just not right.

I finally give in and bring my hands up and under the hem of my dress after ensuring the coast is clear. Not that it matters; we're in a fucking kink club, for Christ's sake. Hooking my fingers into my panties, I push them down and step out of them.

"Happy now?" I ask as I let the dark purple scrap of material dangle from my finger.

"I want to see how wet I made you."

"Nyx," I say his name in warning.

"Show me, little lamb, or you won't get the gift I have for you."

My heart flutters. It's been so long since I received a gift from anyone. Biting my lower lip, I fiddle with my panties until the crotch is visible to him. There's no missing the wet spot I left behind.

"See, you can be a good girl after all." He grins wickedly.

The front door opens, and I quickly toss the panties inside the hostess stand. Instead of ending the video call with Nyx, I turn to the newcomer and smile.

"Welcome to Club Unholy, where all your fantasies come to life. Pick your poison, and we'll happily see to it that all your needs are met."

"Hello, beautiful," the guy greets, and I hear a low growl come from my phone.

"My name is Saraya. How can I help you, mister?"

He doesn't give me a name, but he does ask about a couple of friends. "They asked me to meet them here. One is blonde, and the other has red hair."

"Oh, yes. Let me call back to the room, and someone will come and take you back with them. In the meantime, can you please fill this out and make your payment?"

"Sure." He seems nervous, but I push it aside because I see a lot of first-timers act nervous.

I pick up the house phone and call Mara. It rings and rings, and then nothing. Furrowing my brows, I hang up and try again. It rings three times, and then she answers, a bit breathless.

"Yeah..."

"Hey, their friend is here. Can you come get him?"

"I was just going to call you as soon as I cleaned all the blood off me—"

"What?" I ask as I turn my back on the guy. "Why are you cleaning *that* off you?"

"They weren't here as customers, Raya. Keep their friend busy, and I'll come to greet him and take care of him, too."

"What do you mean?" I glance back at the man and find him watching me suspiciously.

I smile.

"Just keep him there, I'm on my way..."

Everything happens in slow motion. I'm hanging up the phone when the guy reaches into his jacket and pulls out something resembling a black box. He presses something and throws it into the middle of the room before taking off out the front door. I see the red numbers immediately, and my eyes widen in horror. I first look at Nyx, still on my screen, and then yell, "Bomb!"

I try running to the coat closet, but as I open the door, a loud explosion occurs, and heat licks at my back. The force of the blast propels me into the room, slamming me into something hard. I remember hearing Nyx scream my name just after I yelled bomb, so his voice is what's running through my head when darkness takes me.

THIRTY-EIGHT

I find myself whistling as I leave the store. It was perfect timing that they called to let me know my purchase was ready to be picked up, so after dropping Raya off at the club, I came straight to the store. It's barely been an hour since I left her at the front door of Unholy, but I need to hear her voice.

Is this what it means to be whipped?

I stop to think about what I'm going to do but say fuck it. Too many years were wasted without Raya, so I pull my phone out and text her. When that still isn't enough, I FaceTime her instead.

All is going well until I hear a male call my girl beautiful, and then, I can't get back to the club fast enough. I know I'm overreacting, but I don't like hearing other men flirting with what's mine.

When Raya's voice takes on a different tone after calling Mara, warning bells start to go off. *Something's not right.* My foot automatically presses down on the accelerator; I'm not too far from the club.

"Bomb!"

The word doesn't faze me right away when she screams it, but the second it does, I call out her name just before a loud explosion, and the screen goes black. I think I've gone into shock. I don't remember the rest of the drive to the club. The flames coming out of the front doors immediately catch my attention, along with the crowd standing outside the club.

I see many familiar faces, all in different states of dress or undress. Some were in private rooms at the time, so they have sheets or towels wrapped around them. None of them are the ones I'm most concerned about.

As soon as I exit my car, I hear the firetrucks in the distance. I try calling Raya's phone again, but it goes straight to voicemail. *She was up front.* I stare at the flames lapping outside the building from the front entrance.

"Saraya!" I call out repeatedly, tugging at my hair.

It reminds me of the accident scene I came upon when she left me not too long ago. *She's got to be okay.* I call out again, but I still get nothing.

"Nyx..."

I hear my name and feel a hand on my shoulder. Spinning, I see Cray standing there, worry written all over his face. I ignore him and turn back to the club. I can't stand here any longer, so I start for the front entrance, only to be yanked back.

"What the fuck, Nyx? Are you trying to die, Jesus?" Cray yells over the noise of the fire.

"Let me go; I need to get to Raya!" I scowl at him as I try to break free.

"Zilas!" I hear Cray call out, and suddenly, two of my best friends are holding me down.

I struggle until they take me down to the ground and hold me there. I stare out at the fire, not being able to move—not able to get to my little lamb.

"Saraya!" I scream at the top of my lungs.

I can't lose her. I just got her back! *Please, God, don't take her from me!* I chant over and over in my head, praying to a God I have no business praying to because I don't acknowledge him any other time, but still—I pray.

"Get the fuck off me! I need to get inside; I need to get to her!"

The firetrucks pull in, and immediately, they start running the hoses toward the fire. It's not good enough, though. I need to get inside. However, Cray and Zilas have a firm grip on me as I lay on my stomach. I can feel the tears drip from my nose as I lay here and stare at the burning building that has my little lamb held hostage.

I begin to struggle again as I threaten my friends, "If you don't let me up, and Raya dies, you fuckers better hide, because I'm coming for you!"

My friends look at each other, not only with concern but hurt. I don't fucking give a shit. I was just beginning to live again, and that was all due to her—the love of my fucking life, who could very well be burning to death while they hold me down.

I press my forehead to the cement—and cry.

"Oh, fuck," Cray curses.

"Nyx," Zilas says my name.

I ignore him, not wanting to look at him or Cray, but their hold lessens until they no longer hold me down. It doesn't really matter, though. I remain with my head pressed against the ground.

"Nyx!" Zilas calls out again as he tries hauling me to my feet.

I shove him away. "Leave me the fuck alone—"

"Fucking look!" he cuts me off and points toward the east side of the building.

I don't recognize the sound that escapes me as I see Adrik carrying Raya in his arms. She hangs limply against him, so I know she isn't conscious. My feet feel like cement blocks as I start running toward them, unable to get to them fast enough.

"Raya!"

I pull her out of my friend's arms and hold her to me. I don't waste any time hurrying over to one of the emergency vehicles, shoving a few people with minor cuts and scrapes out of the way. When the paramedic tries stopping me from laying Raya on the stretcher inside the ambulance, I glare at them.

"Do you know who the fuck I am?"

They look me up and down before their eyes land on the skull tattoo on my hand. Everyone knows that only the Gods of Nyte's Hall have this tattoo on our hands. Unless you are a newcomer to Nyte, everybody knows our mark.

"I'm sorry. I didn't realize—"

"Shut the fuck up and help her—now!"

"Yes, Sir. Can you tell me what happened?"

"I don't know. I was on the phone with her, and there was an explosion. The phone went dead after that."

I watch as the young guy puts an oxygen mask over her face before he takes her vitals. I sit on the bench, holding Raya's hand, hoping she will open her beautiful eyes for me. Her clothing is torn and singed from the fire, and soot is covering parts of her face and other parts where there's skin showing.

"I found her in the coat closet. She was partially buried under the shelving unit that became detached from the wall." Mara's comment has me looking in her direction, and it's the first time I even noticed that she was with Adrik when he came out with Raya.

"You found her?" I ask as I look our little devil over.

Amara's leather outfit is torn, and some of her hair is singed. She holds onto her left arm with her right hand as she leans against Adrik for support.

"Yeah, I was halfway to her when the bomb went off. Luckily, I was able to get through a sliver of the room that led to the hostess stand. I saw the door to the coat room open and ran to it since I didn't see her anywhere nearby. It took me a bit, but I finally got her free and dragged her to the back of the room and the door leading to the back hallway."

"I was making sure the building was clear and was heading out myself when I saw Mara dragging Raya," Adrik finishes explaining.

"Thank you—both of you." It comes out as a whisper, but I know they heard me.

I glance at Mara as she stares at Raya on the stretcher. The concern is written all over her face. I know they haven't gotten along in the past, but they were best friends at one time, and I'd like to think that Mara's animosity toward my little lamb has lessened since finding out the truth.

"Sir, we need to get her to the hospital right away," the paramedic states, and I nod.

Looking straight at Adrik, my face hardens as I ask him to do me a favor. When he nods, I tell him, "Find the motherfucker who did this and bring him to me."

"You know we will," he responds right before the doors close and the ambulance drives away.

✦

It doesn't matter who the fuck I am; the medical staff refuses to let me through the double doors they take Raya through. Had I not known the nurse on duty, I would bulldoze my way back there, not trusting a damn soul. Thankfully, Maria tells me she has already called Mahony to come in as soon as the incident came over the radio, and it was announced who was being transported in the ambulance.

It doesn't stop me from pacing the waiting room. When Adrik walks in, I give him a questioning look. "What are you doing here? You should be helping the others find who did this."

"We will—the guys are working on it—but Mara is hurt and refused to come, so I brought her."

I stop pacing and ask, "Is she going to be okay?"

"Yeah. She's got a gash on her arm and leg; both need stitches. Otherwise, she should be fine."

My hands ball into fists even tighter. "They fucked with the wrong people. Their deaths won't be quick. They're lucky that we don't hurt *their* loved ones." My lip curls as I snarl.

"Have you heard anything?" Adrik asks.

"Fuck no! They won't let me back there either. I'm about two seconds away from barging back there and—"

"You need to let us do our job, Mr. Beckam." I whip around to find Dr. Mahony standing in the doorway.

"Mahony, how is she?" I ignore his comment altogether.

"She's still out. Ms. Abbott suffered a few burns on her back, but they're minor. She also has a few cuts, but I'm most concerned about the goose egg on the back of her head. There's no doubt she's suffered a concussion, but we won't know any more until she wakes up. There are no other major injuries, and that's good."

"Can I see her?" I ask the doctor.

"The nurses are taking her to a private room. As soon as they have her settled, they will come and get you." Mahony turns toward Adrik and informs him, "I'm heading to check out Miss Nichols. I'll come out once I have, and you can go back to see her."

I go back to pacing the room.

"You look like shit, Beckam."

I glance at my friend, then flip him off when I see the slight smirk on his face. I know he's only trying to lighten the mood, but until I see Raya for myself, I can't sit here fucking around like all is right with the world.

"The guys told me what you said to them," Adrik states. "Don't you think it was a bit harsh? We've been by your side, through thick and thin, and you threaten Cray and Zilas for trying to keep you from killing yourself?"

I stop pacing again and turn to him. "I love you all like my brothers, but that woman," I say and point in the direction I last saw them take her.

"She's my fucking world, and if anything happened to her because they stopped me from trying to get to her, then yes. I'm sorry you don't understand, but you will once you find the love of your life."

Adrik stands there, staring at me in disbelief, but I don't give a shit at the moment. I'll worry about smoothing things over once I know my little lamb is okay. He's right, of course; they have all been there for me, but that doesn't change the fact that I will do whatever it takes regarding Saraya.

"Mr. Beckam, I can take you back now." A voice breaks the staring contest Adrik and I seem to be having. I turn to see a nurse standing in the doorway, hesitant to come in.

"Let me know how Mara is when you find out," I say as I pass Adrik.

"You just worry about Raya, I've got Mara," my friend growls softly.

I stop walking momentarily, but then continue before I say something I may regret. Thoughts of Raya immediately pushes the issue aside as I follow the nurse back to my girl's room. The sight when I enter claws at my heart. The nurse gives me a small smile and closes the door, shutting me alone with Raya.

Pulling a chair to the side of Raya's bed, I take her hand and sit beside her, determined not to leave until she wakes up. Her head has a white bandage wrapped around it, and gauze covers one of the cuts on the forearm of the hand I'm holding.

"Baby, you need to wake up for me. I need to know that you're going to be okay. It's killing me not knowing." I kiss the top of her hand and keep it against my lips. "I love you, little lamb..."

The hands on the clock tick away as I sit here and wait. I can feel my phone buzzing with notifications, but I'm not interested in what anyone has to say until I see my lamb's doe-like eyes staring back at me. I can't picture my life without her in it any longer. Now that I've had her back, she's become a part of me that I can't live without. People can talk shit all they want. They can say it's not right or that what we're doing is forbidden, but there is nothing wrong with the love I have for my stepsister.

Why can't people get it through their heads that we are not of the same blood? Yeah, we've been family since the fifth and sixth grades, but does that even matter? Fuck it, and fuck anybody who tells me the love I feel is wrong when it's the only thing that has ever felt right in my entire life.

I'm just starting to close my eyes to try to catch a little nap when I feel a pull on the hand I'm holding. My head snaps up, and I gaze at the most beautiful sight. Saraya's eyes are open, and she's staring right at me. I kiss her hand again and smile at her.

"Thank fuck, I've been going crazy, baby. Don't ever scare me like that again."

The look she returns has my smile faltering, and when she pulls her hand out of mine, I frown, but what she says next has me sinking back into a dark abyss. I may have heard her wrong—I couldn't have heard her correctly.

"What did you just ask me?"

Her brows crease, but she speaks louder as she asks, "I asked who you were. Do I know you?"

Hearing this has my world spiraling, and it's about to crash and burn...

THIRTY-NINE

Saraya

My whole body hurts, and I can't open my eyes because they hurt, too. I'm so out of it; I have been for a while now. I want to open my eyes, but then I get tossed into sleep again and again. I've heard a voice the few times I've been somewhat alert, and I want to talk to them. I want to find out why it feels like I've been hit by a bus.

It hurts my head whenever I try to think about what could have happened. Finally, after many tries, my eyes open to a dimly lit room. The low lighting still hurts my eyes, but they adjust after blinking a few times. Realizing I'm in the hospital, I stare at the ceiling briefly until a weight on my hand draws my attention away.

I pull on my hand, but the grip only tightens. My eyes land on a dark head of hair, and then suddenly, I'm staring into a pair of dark gray eyes. The hand they're holding is numb, and as they tell me how they're happy that I'm awake, I try pulling my hand out of their hold again. This time, it's freed.

"Who are you?" I ask after seeing what a wreck they are.

Their smile slowly disappears, and they ask me to repeat myself. So, I do.

"I asked who you were. Do I know you?"

The grogginess still has hold of me, as well as the throbbing in my head. I can hear them saying something, but I'm still too out of it to pay them much attention, much less notice the hurt look upon their face. On top of everything, I'm parched. I bring my hand to my throat and instantly, a cup with some water and a straw in it is held to my lips.

I take a long drink, but they pull it away and say, "Not too much, little lamb, you'll make yourself sick."

I relax onto the pillow and groan, "Hm, what happened?"

"You really don't remember?" they ask.

"No, the last thing I remember is being dropped off at the club, but even that hurts to think about."

"Wait a minute. If you remember getting dropped off, then you must remember who I am; I'm the one who dropped you off."

I'm confused.

"Of course I remember, Nyx. You're the biggest pain in my ass." It hurts too much to smile, so I don't even try.

"But—you just asked me who I was, and if you knew me..."

"Yeah, because you look like total shit, and I've never seen you look like this before."

Relief overwhelms his handsome features, and he runs a hand over his face sighing. "Thank fucking God. Do you know how I felt when you asked me who I was? I thought you had amnesia!"

"Oh, my bad," I say with a little smile. "I'm sorry. My thoughts are all over the place. I didn't mean to make you think that, but..."

"But what?" Nyx narrows his eyes at me.

"It is kind of funny. I could have kept it going to see what you would do to get me to remember you," I reply with a smirk.

"Oh really? You think it's funny to tear my heart out not once but twice in one night?"

"Well, maybe not that part..." I pause. "Did it really hurt *that* much?" I ask. It's still hard to believe that his feelings are that deep.

"I threatened the lives of two of my best friends; what do you think, Raya?"

My eyes widen as I gasp, "You didn't!"

"I did, and I would do it again. I'll threaten anybody who risks your life. Jesus, Raya, you have me so fucked up that I was trying to run into that burning building to get to you."

A lump forms in my throat, and tears threaten to fall, but I keep them at bay. Suddenly, words spill from my mouth that are long overdue.

"I love you, Phoenyx. I've never stopped loving you, and I'm sorry that I didn't say it when you said it—"

My words are cut off by Nyx as he shoots up from the chair he's sitting in and commandeers my mouth. He's gentle yet brutal as he pushes his tongue past my lips. The kiss heats up fast, and soon, I forget all about my head hurting. I don't even realize he's gripping my jaw until he pulls slightly away from me.

"Don't you *ever* fucking scare me like that again, do you hear me? I love you too fucking much to lose you now." His eyes burn into mine as he waits for my response.

His hold isn't tight, but it's enough to know that he means business, so I nod and whisper, "Yes."

Nyx continues staring into my eyes as he again brings his mouth to mine. This time, the kiss is gentle and passionate as we gaze into each other's eyes. It's so intimate, and I can feel the emotion behind his kiss. Who'd have thought that Nyx Beckam could love like this? Phoenyx, yes, but Nyx?"

He pulls away too soon for my liking and presses his forehead to mine. He states in a low, menacing voice, "I will find whoever did this, and I will make them suffer."

"Nyx, don't get yourself—"

"What?" he cuts me off. "Don't get myself in trouble? Do you honestly think that I worry about that? Granted, the Feds frown upon murder, but they don't bother us too much unless the crime is getting out of hand like it was with our fathers. As for the local PD, we're taking care of that. I've told you that I would burn shit down for you, Raya. Don't *ever* underestimate the shit I would do for you."

We're interrupted by the door to my room opening before I can respond to him. A nurse walks in with a cart and starts stocking up a few drawers before turning to us.

"Sorry to interrupt, but I need to get Ms. Abbott's vitals and give her some meds."

I feel the loss of Nyx as soon as he pulls away, but he doesn't get off the bed. When the nurse raises her brow because of this, he sends her a challenging look in return. I start to roll my eyes, but it causes my head to hurt.

"Just ignore him. You won't get him to move, so just save it." I smirk and find Nyx doing the same when I glance at him.

"Oh, he's one of those boyfriends, huh?" the nurse jokes.

"Fiancé," Nyx corrects her.

"My apologies, Mr. Beckam, and congratulations." The nurse winks at me and begins checking my vitals.

She has me take some painkillers, then leaves us alone once again. Nyx doesn't waste any time as he yanks the blankets down my body and pulls up the gown they put me in.

I try grabbing at it, but I'm not fast enough. "What are you doing?"

"Shush. I'm looking you over. I need to see where all your injuries are. Mara said that you were pinned under a shelf in the coat room."

"Mara said that? Did she..." I can't finish my sentence because it's hard to believe that she would have saved me.

"Yes. She was on her way down when the bomb went off. She found you and dragged you out the back door, where she found Adrik, and he carried you out. Mara is here getting stitches now."

"She's here? Why wouldn't she just go back to the Hall?"

"Because you needed to be here, and I only trust Mahony to work on you, so she had to come here if he was to stitch her up."

"Oh, I see."

"Hey." He lifts my chin, making me look at him when he says, "They all care about you—even Mara. I know she has a shitty way of showing it, but give her a break—she's trying."

"Yeah, trying to get into my pants," I say dryly.

Nyx laughs. "Yeah, that, too, but she still cares. And for the record, I will never allow her into your pants." He cups my pussy through the gown. "This is all mine. Nobody, and I mean nobody, will ever touch it again but me."

"I don't want anybody but you touching it," I whisper as I gaze into eyes that have taken on a stormy appearance.

"Good girl."

Those are the last two words I hear him say as I yawn and close my eyes. I'm fighting to stay awake, so I give up and let sleep take me. However, I feel Nyx cover me up and lie down before I fall asleep. He pulls me into his arms, holding me tight against his chest. I just barely hear his soft words as they follow me into sleep.

"Sleep well, little lamb. I won't let anybody else hurt you."

"Will you put me down? I can walk on my own, you know!" I scowl at Nyx as he carries me into Nyte's Hall from the car.

"The doctor said to take it easy, so I'll carry you if I want to. Just be a good girl and take it like you take *other* things." He smirks.

"*Phoenyx!*" I gasp.

"Well, you asked for it." He kisses my forehead as he continues up the stairs. "I'm going to tuck you into bed and have you rest while I talk to Jessica about something to eat. I need to talk to Cray and Zilas—smooth things over with them and see if they've heard anything. I'll bring you some food, and we can hide away together until you're well enough."

"I want you to have the guys come to the room. I need to hear what they've found out as well. Please don't keep it from me." I plead with my eyes.

Nyx studies me, his lips tight, but then he nods. "Okay. I'll have them come here."

I smile, tell him, "*Thank you,*" and then I shut my mouth as he takes me into his room. Well, I guess it's our room now.

Dr. Mahony allowed Nyx to bring me home against his better judgment. One night in the hospital was enough for me. After all, it's just a bump on the head, a massive bump, but a bump all the same. Only once Nyx gave his word that I would not leave my bed did the doctor finally give in. I guess I owe Nyx for breaking me out, even if it means he'll be coddling me for the next few days.

Sleep isn't as kind to me as Nyx is, though. The last few times I've napped, I've had nightmares about me burning alive. The events of last night are slowly coming back to me. I have yet to remember what the guy who came in looked like, and my dreams haven't been any help.

I haven't been asleep all that long when I'm jarred awake once again. This time, I felt like my whole body was on fire, whereas before, it was just my back. Looking around the room, I don't find Nyx, but I'm not alone.

"Amara. What are you doing here?"

This is my first time seeing the little psycho in anything but leather. Mara is sitting in the armchair beside the doors leading to the terrace. She's wearing a cami and booty shorts, showing off the bandage on her forearm and thigh.

She shrugs. "Just thought I'd swing by and see how you're doing."

"Thank you."

She scoffs, "It's not a big deal, I was walking by the wing anyway."

"No. I mean, thank you for saving me. You could have just left me there. You'd be rid of me for good and not by your hand."

"Ha! Do you honestly think I would be able to deal with Nyx had you died? We would all be on suicide watch for God knows how long," she states.

"He wouldn't..."

"Yes, Raya, he would. He loves you *that* much."

The conversation is heading toward uncharted waters concerning Mara, so I change topics. "Are you sure it's not because you wouldn't be able to try getting in my pants any longer?"

She glowers at me briefly, but my smirk wears off on her, and then both of us are amused. Shrugging, she stands and slowly walks over to me. "I think you would be jealous leaving this world, knowing I'd find my place back in Nyx's bed. Of course, only after the bereavement period."

Instead of getting pissed because I know she's just trying to rile me up, I give her a shrug of my own and reply, "I doubt he'd take you back into his bed after knowing what heaven feels like being inside me." I sit up and lean against the headboard as she sits on the edge of the bed.

Amara, being the bitch that she is, runs her hands over the mattress. "I've got some fond memories of being in this bed. Memories of all the dirty and filthy things I let Nyx do to me."

Okay, she almost has me coming unglued with this last comment, but again, I smile. "Oh, that must be why Nyx ordered a whole new bed for us. He had said that he wanted fond memories of just him and me."

Mara's smile drops, but then she bursts into laughter, and I can't help but join in. It feels weird doing so and it looks even weirder seeing Mara laughing the way she is. It isn't her typical evil laugh or the seductive one she uses on the men.

"Did Nyx really say that?" she asks.

I shake my head. "No, but it sounded good."

She laughs even harder. "Well, if it makes a difference, it was seldom done in his room, with me anyway. That doesn't mean he hasn't had subs in it. Maybe you would be better off buying all new." Mara titters.

Once we sober up, I ask, "How's your arm and leg?"

"They're fine. Adrik is just overreacting and making me take the next two days off, but let me tell you—as soon as we find out who that fucker is, my lazy days are over. I'm going to split that fucker from his puny dick all the way up to his puny brain! I—"

"Won't be doing anything, Mara," Nyx cuts her off as he walks back into the room. "That motherfucker is mine."

"But—"

"No! He tried taking my most treasured possession from me. I will handle it," Nyx growls.

Keeping my smile hidden, I say, "I'm not a possession, Nyx."

He puts the tray he's carrying down and then turns to me. His hand slides to the back of my neck, and very carefully, he grips it and states, "You *belong* to me, and I to you. Therefore, you *are* my possession—a most cherished one at that."

"O-okay," I say softly, turned on like no other.

"Mara?"

"Yes?"

"Leave—now."

Nyx's tone leaves no room for argument, and Mara takes her leave but not without turning our way once she's at the door, and grinning back at me. My eyes come back to the man still holding onto me. I lick my lips. Nyx is too delicious-looking for his own good, even if his beard is a bit overgrown, and his hair could use a good trim. He's fucking hot, and he's all mine.

FORTY

Nyx

"Don't look at me like you want to devour me, little lamb. You're hurt, and I won't be able to go easy on you."

The little minx licks her lips as if she's about to consume a seven-course meal, starting with dessert. I'd love nothing more than to have her and show her just how much I need to feel her take me. After the scare, I need it, but even I ain't that much of a dick. At least not to Raya, anyway.

"But you just booted Mara out. I thought..."

"What?" I ask, smirking. "You thought what?"

"I don't know," she replies and shrugs. "I thought you were going to do—something."

"You're right. I am going to do something. I'm going to make sure you eat all your food. Then I'm going to carry you to the bathroom, where we're going to shower and get the hospital stench off you. Afterward, I'll tuck you back into bed and have the guys come to the room."

Raya gives me an adorable, mischievous look, asking, "Can we have shower sex?"

My eyebrow lifts as I give her a warning look.

"What? I'll let you do all the work. I won't strain myself at all. Girl Scout's honor." Raya's expression is one that I will forever keep locked away—it's *that* cute.

Unfortunately, it doesn't have the desired effect on me. "You're not a Girl Scout, Raya, and you *will* strain yourself when you come all over my cock, or have you forgotten?"

Rolling her eyes at me, she crosses her arms in a huff. "Fine, whatever."

I'm on her in a heartbeat, gripping the back of her neck—not too tight, but enough to show her I mean business. Making her look me in the eyes, I watch her melt at my dominance over her. The bratty behavior disappears instantly.

"I will only say this once, Saraya, so listen well. I will never do anything that may put you in danger. That includes fucking that beautiful cunt of yours. If I have to remain celibate to do that, so be it. Your health and your life come first. I will always put your safety above all. Do you understand me?"

She watches me, waiting to see if I'll say anything else, I assume, and when I don't, she nods.

"Yes, Phoenyx," she says softly.

"Good." I press my lips to hers briefly before pulling away. "Now, let's get you fed."

I stand and grab the tray I brought into the room with me. I had Jessica prepare a light turkey sandwich along with a small charcuterie spread for her. I also brought up a cup of her favorite cappuccino and some juice.

We make small talk as she picks at everything on the tray. It's actually really nice having this time with her when we aren't bickering with each other. I love the woman. She has a mouth on her, and she doesn't take any shit from me, which only makes me more in awe of her.

Raya doesn't fool me, though. I know that every time she stands up to me, she's nervous. It's the same when she stands up to Mara; there's a reason to be nervous there. There's no telling if our little devil will gut you, but my little lamb is like me. She stands her ground regardless of what the outcome may be.

Now, we're just talking like a normal couple, and it's nice. I'm not sure where it comes from, but suddenly, I blurt out, "I want to take you away."

"What?" she asks, confused at the change in topic.

I grin. "I want to take you away as soon as we finish up with this business. Once we find who bombed the club and we take care of him, I'm going to take you away for a few days."

"Oh, okay."

"Is that alright with you?" I ask because her response didn't sound like it was.

"Yes," she's quick to reply. "You just surprised me, that's all. I'd love to go away with you, Phoenyx."

My heart races with her response. I haven't felt like this since I was a teenager, and Raya finally revealed that she also had feelings for me. I felt like I was going to burst with happiness, and it's the same feeling I feel now. Of course, I keep it hidden, but I smile at her.

"Good. I wouldn't have taken no for an answer anyway. I would have kidnapped you and held you hostage, while hiding you away and ravaging every gorgeous inch of you."

I run my hand up her thigh over the covers, causing her breath to hitch. I stop right where her thigh meets her hip and graze her mound with the tip of my finger. I said I wouldn't have sex with her; I never said anything about not teasing her. Maybe if I have her panting like a bitch in heat, by the time her body has healed enough, she'll be a wildcat the next time I take her.

"Nyx..." she says my name in warning.

I grin wickedly at her, but I remove my hand. Seeing that she's done with her food, I take the tray from her and place it back on the nightstand before pulling back her covers.

"Come on. Let's get you cleaned up." I swoop down and pick her up.

"I can walk, Nyx!"

"Yeah, but I want you in my arms, and what I want trumps that."

"What? Why do your wants trump mine?"

"Because I want to feel your body against mine, and I can't do that if you're walking, now can I?"

I notice her lips twitch just before she pecks my cheek and says, "You're a sweet guy, Phoenyx Beckam. You can deny it all you want, but I know better."

I set Raya down on her feet as soon as we get to the shower. I reach in to turn the shower on before I start peeling her clothing off. "And if you ever tell anyone about it, I will tie you down and sexually torture you until I feel you have learned your lesson."

"Mm, when you put it that way, it sounds tempting."

I growl and pull her into the shower with me. "Woman, you fucking tempt me every day, especially when you say things like that."

"Is it working? Am I breaking you—at the very least, cracking you?"

"Not even a little."

I say this, but I'm holding on by a fucking thread at the moment. I need to keep her injury in mind, though. So, no matter what she says or does, I'm going to keep my cock out of her sweet cunt.

I'm harder than a rock, but I'll be fine if my little lamb stops bumping into it. She chuckles every time it happens, making me grunt.

"At least let me jack you off," she says as I finish rinsing the conditioner from her hair.

"No. That would be exerting yourself."

She turns and stares at my throbbing length, wincing. "It looks uncomfortable." She reaches out to touch it, but I slap her hand away.

"Well, it sure as hell doesn't tickle."

"Jerk off," she says just above a whisper.

"What? No, I'm fine."

Her brown eyes meet mine pleadingly. "Please? I want to watch you get yourself off."

Raya turns on the puppy dog eyes, and I find my resolve unraveling.

"Raya..." I sigh.

"Phoenyx..."

"Nyx," I tell her.

She looks confused.

Clenching my jaw, I tell her, "If I do this, then I'm going to be a selfish asshole and want to see you swallow every last drop. I'm not going to be nice about it."

I'm pissed that I'm even in this position. I'm trying to do the right thing by her, yet here she is, teasing the fuck out of me.

"O—kay..." she says slowly.

"On your fucking knees, little lamb."

Not being a complete dick, I hold her hands and help her kneel on the floor of the shower. I swear, when she's recovered, I'm taking my favorite paddle to her ass.

I wrap my hand around my cock and begin stroking it. I can come immediately, but I'm going to make her wait.

"You've given me no choice, Raya. Shame on you for acting like a greedy little whore all because you want my cock and can't have it," I tell her. "Hands behind your back and open that filthy mouth."

The gleam in her eyes gives her away. She's loving this, and I'm loving her even more for it, even though I'm pissed. Raya can be an excellent submissive when she wants to be, but I can't say whether I'd rather have her as one or have her fighting me tooth and nail.

"Tell me, little lamb. Are you a slut for my cock?"

"Yes, Nyx. You know this, now stop talking and start coming. I want my dessert."

"Jesus, Raya! You're starting to sound like me..." My hand picks up the pace, pumping my dick faster and bringing me to climax quickly. "Fucking get ready."

Raya's mouth opens wide, and she sticks her tongue out. Just the sight of her waiting on her knees like a needy whore has my seed jetting out. Most of it lands on her tongue, but I want to paint her gorgeous tits with it, too, so I do.

"That's it. Such a good girl..." I groan, watching her enjoy me painting her with my kids.

Once I'm spent, I help her to stand, and then my mouth latches onto her nipple before licking my cum from it and feeding it to her by kissing her lips. I repeat it once more before I wash her off and wrap her in a towel.

I swing Raya up in my arms and carry her back to the bedroom, where I sit her on the edge of the bed and leave her briefly to grab one of my shirts to wear. I don't bother grabbing her panties. I like knowing she's completely naked under my clothing. I'd keep her naked if I had my way, but it's time for answers, and I'm not in the mood to have my friends see her naked at the moment. Maybe next time...

"I had Cale go through the footage from the club, and we got the son of a bitch on camera. There's only one problem. The fucker knew where the camera was in that front area and avoided showing his whole face. We did get a side view of him, though," Zilas informs us.

"Goddamn it!" I growl, but Raya places her hand on my fist, which calms me a bit.

"Cale searched the database and found about six matches to the profile," Cray states. "So, he's going through each one, trying to link any of them to the other two that came to the club."

"Other two?" I ask. I didn't know there were more.

"Yeah," Raya chimes in. "I remember two men coming in wearing suits. They looked like old money, and they paid their fees. Mara took them back with her. She told me on the phone that she would be down as soon as she cleaned the blood off her. I never found out what happened with those two with Mara."

"We did," Zilas answers. "They were working for Pike. Those two men kept mentioning Raya's name, wanting her to join them. Mara finally had enough and tried kicking them out when one got nasty and shoved her against the wall."

"Are you shitting me right now? Did they not know who Amara was?" I ask incredulously.

Zilas only shrugs. "Who knows, but he told her that they were going to fuck her and cut her up, then they were going to take Raya with them when they left."

"Ha! They obviously didn't know who they were threatening." Raya grins.

Cray finishes telling us how Mara killed the first guy and made the other guy tell her who sent them. That's how she learned that it was Pike's men. The fact that he dared send his men to come in and take what is mine tells me he has no respect for the Gods of Nyte. It's about time we show him and others just what we're capable of. The leader of the South Crew drug ring has just signed his death certificate.

A knock on my door frame has us all turning to see Adrik and Mara walking in. I nod at them in greeting and wait to hear what Adrik has for me. I knew he was at the club getting estimates of the damage done, so I'm hoping he has some good news for us.

"Well, the damage isn't as bad as we thought. The fire didn't spread from the front room, but there is some damage from the blast and the smoke in the bar area." Adrik's news is very welcoming to hear.

Now that we don't have to be as concerned about the club as I thought, we can concentrate on the South Crew. This is going to take all of us and then some.

I talked to Jarod on the phone while waiting for Jessica to prepare Raya's food. He informed me that the Bureau bought the story of Clyde's death. The twins confirmed that Ken, along with Giles and Denver, did indeed work for their father. They also gave the Bureau a few more names of people who worked with their father. Since Clyde had his hands in with Pike, the Bureau has taken Raya off their list of suspects.

"We do nothing but recon until Raya is well enough," I tell all four friends.

"Thank you for allowing me to go with you when you—"

"The hell you will, little lamb. You can come to the warehouse if we bring anybody back, but you will not go into their territory with us." I hate to tell her this, but she's a liability for me.

"You can't keep me from taking part in this. That asshole tried to kill me!" she retorts.

"I get that, Raya, but Pike wants you, and that alone puts you in danger. I'll be too worried about you to be able to concentrate. You're staying here."

"Don't do this, Nyx," she says in a warning tone as if it would make me change my mind.

"*You* don't do this, Raya. I have gotten shot for you, and I've gotten beaten down for you. I don't know about you, but I would like to keep my life, and if you come with us, I may very well lose it."

"Fuck you, Nyx!"

"Guys, Amara, I need you to leave now. I need to have a little talk with Saraya."

I don't need to look to know they have all left and shut the door behind them. I continue to stare at my little lamb as I try to remain calm. She glowers at me as she sits by my side. I hate that she's pissed about this, but I'm not budging on it.

"I will never forgive you if you make me stay. I'll call the wedding off..."

"You will do no such thing, Raya. We *will* be married, and you will forgive me—over time—but mark my word, I *am* going to keep you safe, no matter what it fucking takes."

FORTY-ONE

Saraya

"Will you just work with me here, Mara? I'm sorry I choked you out last time; it won't happen again," I plead with the little psycho.

Amara just stands there, looking at her fingers like she's bored, ignoring me altogether. I caught her in the billiard room at the bar, enjoying Nyx's bottle of Johnny Walker Blue, as always. When she turned to me after I said her name, her eyes raked me from head to toe like I was going to be her next meal until I shook my head. She understood my meaning and rolled her eyes.

I need to learn how to fight; Mara is the best one to teach me. It's been almost a week since the bombing, and I've been released from bed rest. Asking her is hard, but I want to learn from the best. Apparently, that doesn't matter because she refuses to help me.

"I'll tell you what," Mara says. "As soon we've taken care of the bastard that bombed the club, I'll start teaching you."

"But I want to learn before that. I want to show Nyx that I won't be a liability." I know it's a long shot, but I must try at least.

Her laugh is a bit cynical, mocking me like I'm some naïve girl. It pisses me off, but if I want her help, I must play nice. However, the fact that she's doing it specifically so I can't go, has me marching up to her and looking her in the eye.

"Wow, you've got some balls of steel coming up in my space like this, uninvited." Mara's brow arches.

"Listen here, *little psycho,* I'm not a little girl who needs others to fight my battles for me. I get these are dangerous people; I'm not stupid, but I refuse to let others get hurt while I sit here twiddling my fucking thumbs!"

Mara comes within centimeters of my face, her dark blue eyes glaring into mine. "You don't fucking get it! It took me years to become this *little psycho*, and it took a lot of killing assholes before these Heirs allowed me to fight in battles. Do you honestly believe that one little session with me will prepare you for what those motherfuckers have in store? They *ruin* women like you. They kill needlessly—and don't think for a minute that our guys are going to have it easy going after the South Crew."

"They're the Gods of Nyte's Hall; they should have an army behind them," I state, not wanting to back down just yet.

"Jesus, Raya! They only took over a year ago. They're still trying to figure out who's a friend and who's a foe after the way their fathers ran this town! They. Trust. No. One! They can't even trust the PD, as you very well know. This town has gone to shit, and the Heirs are doing everything they can to turn it around."

I understand everything she's saying. I do have eyes and ears, but that still doesn't change the fact that it was my life that was threatened, and I should have a hand in dealing with the fucker! I'm tired of having to depend on everyone else to protect me.

"Either you teach me how to protect myself or not. It doesn't much matter, I will not stay behind when the time comes," I warn her.

Mara grins and shakes her head in disbelief. "You won't stop until Nyx finally dies trying to protect you. Let this be a warning, Saraya. If you dare put yourself in danger, and it causes Nyx to have to protect you, and he dies because of it, there will be no place where you can hide where I won't find you. When I do, you will die a very slow and painful death at my hands."

Mara shoves me to the side and walks away, leaving me here by myself. I've got goosebumps popping up because of her menacing speech, and it's finally sinking in just how dangerous this little mission is. Amara is usually a smartass bitch, but I could see it in her eyes, she's worried.

Running my hand through my hair, I sigh and sit on one of the stools in front of the bar. Mara left the whisky bottle on top of the bar, and instead of putting it back in its place, I bring it to my lips and tip my head back. I like my whiskey cold, but this will do for now.

"Well, what do we have here? I leave you alone for a couple of hours, and I come home to an empty bottle of whiskey and a fiancée whose fucking crocked."

I lift my head off the bar and look at Nyx. Does he have a twin? My forehead creases, and the room spins. I go to stand, and I stumble. Thankfully, Nyx is right there to catch me—as always. I yank myself out of his hands.

"I'm fine. At least let me walk myself, sheesh!"

He lifts his hands defensively and grins. "Have at it, little lamb. You're a big girl who thinks she can drink a bottle of whiskey; I'm sure you can walk on your own afterward, too."

I hate his mocking tone. He reminds me of Mara. I don't care if they're right; I still hate it. I take a step and then another before I realize that even the room is against me because it spins, trying to knock me down just like everyone else.

Familiar hands grab me. I fight them, but they hold firm.

"Stop fighting me, goddamn it!" Nyx curses, and the next thing I know, he's tossing me over his shoulder.

If I was dizzy before, I'm really dizzy now, being held upside down. I ball up my fists and beat at Nyx's back. My feet kick out, not caring if I make him fall over.

"Put me down, asshole!"

His hand comes down on my ass hard. "Keep it up, Raya, and I won't wait until you're sober to punish you."

"You will not lay a finger on me, *Phoenyx!*"

"You're right, Phoenyx won't, but Nyx will. You just earned yourself a ride on the Nyx Express, and I'm not talking about my cock, either."

"Pssh, I won't fuck you even if my life depends on it!"

His hand comes down on my ass again, and I squeal.

"I'm about ready to wash that mouth out with soap. I don't like liars, little lamb."

"What am I lying about?" I can't even remember what I just said to him.

"You said you won't fuck me even if your life depends on it, and we both know that you're a slut for my cock."

I start to rebut, but then I groan instead. "I think I'm going to be sick."

All the bouncing as he walks up the stairs while having me over his shoulder is not the best thing for my stomach. The spinning room isn't helping me, either.

Nyx quickens his steps and enters the bathroom off our bedroom, pulling me from his shoulder before spinning me toward the toilet. I feel my hair being pulled back as I drop to my knees and hug the porcelain god.

"Oh God, what was in that whiskey?" I groan as my stomach threatens to empty.

"Oh, I believe forty percent alcohol by volume and eighty proof," Nyx replies smugly.

"Just don't..."

"Don't what? You asked a question, and I answered it."

"Oh, and you just happened to know the alcohol proof volume thingy?"

"Raya, it's what I drink. Of course, I know the volume and proof."

"You're just loving this, ain't you?" I ask drunkenly.

"You're a brilliant woman, Raya. You should know how to use the word *ain't,*" he chuckles.

"You're the reason I'm drunk. You don't get to make fun of me." I try pointing at him, but I don't know which direction I'm even pointing in.

"Why am I the reason for your inebriation, little lamb?" I can hear the amusement in his voice.

When I go to tell him exactly why, my stomach chooses to release its contents, and I retch—loudly, I might add. Once it starts, it doesn't stop, and the whole time, Nyx is sitting behind me, rubbing my back and holding my hair.

I don't drink often; it's no wonder I'm now sick to my stomach. I'm lucky I didn't give myself alcohol poisoning with the amount of whiskey I drank. I blamed Nyx, but I know I only have myself to blame for the position I'm in at the moment.

"Shh, it's okay, let it all out," Nyx coos when I groan.

Once my stomach settles and I can finally remove my head from the white bowl, I lay on the cold floor, my cheek pressed against it, loving how it feels on my heated face. Do you think Nyx can leave me to suffer alone, though? Of course not. He brings a washcloth over and cleans my face like a child. I don't bother swatting him away because he'll ignore it.

"Come on, baby. Let's get you to bed." He lifts me to my feet and helps me stand at the sink so I can rinse my mouth out first.

"Thank you," I tell him once I'm lying down in bed.

Nyx sits on the edge and pushes some of my hair away from my face as he smiles at me. "No need to thank me, little lamb. It's my job to take care of you."

"What if I don't want you taking care of me?"

His brows furrow. "What do you mean?"

"I'm a big girl and can take care of myself. I don't need you always doing things for me—or protecting me," I throw in at the end.

"Ah, well, you better get used to it, because I'll always do both. I know you can do things for yourself, but I enjoy it. I was robbed of doing it for many years."

"Stop." I can't take it when he's being so nice after I've been a complete douche.

"Stop what?"

"Stop being so nice. You should be lecturing me for drinking so much and..." I don't know what else.

"You don't like me lecturing you, remember? You're not a kid, but I will tell you that as soon as you're sober, I'll be punishing that beautiful ass of yours."

My emotions are all over the place. I was just pissed at him, and now, as I look at Nyx, I can feel the love I have for him. I've been difficult and demanding. He's had his club bombed and his girlfriend almost killed. The least I can do is not give him anything else to worry about.

"Nyx, can you promise me one thing?"

"I'll promise you anything as long as it's within my power and it won't cause you any harm." His smile gets my lady bits igniting.

"Will you promise to come back to me and not get yourself killed?"

His face softens briefly but then hardens, but not in a bad way. I've seen it happen before when lust takes over. His hand comes to my neck, squeezing gently as he leans in.

"I will always come back to you, little lamb."

"Good, because I love you—and I don't want Mara coming after me." I slur my words slightly and close my eyes, smiling.

Nyx chuckles. "No worries, baby. I just got you back; you're not getting rid of me that easily."

"Mm—that's nice," I say and curl up on my side, letting sleep take me.

FORTY-TWO

This is no sneak attack. Our entourage of vehicles crossing the border into Tytan, where the South Crew resides, is anything but inconspicuous. We're not a bunch of fucking pussies like people seem to think we are. Yes, we are our father's sons, but we are nothing like those greedy, power-hungry assholes.

Of course, we want power, but not so we can throw our weight around. We want to keep motherfuckers like Pike out of our town. Unlike us Heirs who own the town of Nyte, Pike doesn't own Tytan, but I bet he wishes he did. However, he runs the South side, and the Blackwood family leaves him alone in exchange.

The Blackwoods, which consists of two brothers and a cousin, own Tytan, like we do Nyte. We have an understanding that we won't fuck with them if they don't fuck with us, and it's worked so far.

Adrik called and talked to Byron Blackwood earlier, informing him that we would be visiting the South side. We're respectful like that, but as for Pike, we didn't tell him shit. We just roll right up to his piece of shit strip club that he loves to hang out at, or so we're told by Byron, and walk through the front doors.

No one expects us to be coming to stir up shit since we have the guts to walk right up to him. Our men wait outside until we give them the signal, but first, I want a few words with this motherfucker.

We find Pike sitting in a booth at the back of the club, a stripper riding his cock, and another one licking and sucking on his ball sack. When we stop and stare at him, the motherfucker smirks.

"Gentlemen! What can I do for you today? Did you come to hang out since you can no longer do so at your club?"

"Cut the shit, Pike! You know precisely why we're here," I sneer.

Ignoring my comment, Pike goes on to say, "It's a shame that someone would do such a despicable thing. I hope nobody was hurt." Pike sits on the booth bench, his arms outstretched and resting on the back. He wears a smug look as he drags his eyes over each of us.

Suddenly, our little devil shimmies her way between Cray and Adrik, and I notice the drug lord's smugness falter. It's the typical response whenever Amara walks into the room.

"Oh, well, that looks like fun!" Mara muses. "Can I partake in the oral event?"

Our little devil is dressed to kill—literally. Her outfit doesn't leave room for imagination. As usual, her attire consists of skintight leather pants and a top that looks like the straps will burst at any moment. Her tits are practically falling out where the top *V*s down to the middle of her stomach.

Her Glock is secured to its holster, wrapped around her right thigh. Nobody thinks she'd be fast enough to pull it out in time, but they don't know our girl. That would be her last resort, anyway. Mara loves her little knives and ninja stars that are well hidden within her barely-there clothing. Her stilettos, themselves, are a deadly weapon, which she's used more times than not.

"Sure, sugar," Pike answers Mara. "There's plenty of room for you."

The fucker bites his bottom lip as he peruses our little devil. Mara, being who she is, sits down beside Pike and pulls out her fucking tits. She yanks the female's arm who is riding him and pulls her off Pike's dick.

"I have something you can suck on, honey."

I never take my eyes off the drug lord as he snickers and his attention follows his stripper's mouth as she latches onto Amara's nipple. I could kill him right now while he's distracted, but I promised my little lamb that I would try to bring him back to the warehouse so we could play together again. It was the only way I could get her to agree to stay behind. Well, that and the fact that I fucked her into a coma before we left.

I can still smell her pussy on my mustache and beard. My cock isn't happy with me at the moment because it would rather be embedded inside our sweet cunt. Instead, we have to be here, dealing with these fucks.

"Okay, okay. I see how it is—you want my sloppy seconds." Pike chuckles.

Our little devil glances downward before cocking her brow back up at the smug asshole. "Honey, it's only sloppy seconds when there's something there to work with the first time around."

I look to my right when I hear a muffled snicker and see Cray covering his mouth. The corner of my lips kicks up slightly, but that's all the amusement I show before returning to our girl and the dead man walking.

Anger appears on Pike's face, and my guard goes up. He looks at the woman still sucking on Mara's tit, grabs her hair, and yanks her back. I think he's expecting to get a scream from our little devil, but he's sorely mistaken. Amara *thrives* on pain, and if the wicked grin on her face isn't any indication, then I don't know what is.

"Fuck yes! Do that again with the other one; my girl is feeling left out," Mara states, pulling the woman back to her other nipple.

"You're a fucking crazy bitch." Pike frowns.

"I believe Saraya refers to me as psycho, but I guess crazy bitch works, too." Mara holds her breast towards the woman's mouth, waiting, but the stripper stalls, looking back and forth between her employer and the crazy woman.

I notice the look that crosses the drug lord's face at the mention of my little lamb's name, and I don't like it one bit. He's pissed about the situation, but I don't give a flying shit.

"Enough!" my voice echoes throughout the area as I tire of the bullshit.

Mara continues grinning, knowing that shit's about to get fucked up, while Pike turns his anger on me.

"This is my fucking club," he barks as he shoves the other woman off his dick. "You don't get to come in here and make demands."

I pull on the cuffs of my jacket, already bored of this conversation.

"I'll have to disagree with you there. Little devil, will you explain to your new little friend precisely why I have the right to come here making demands."

"Oh, it will be my pleasure, Nyx."

And in the blink of an eye, Mara is straddling Pike's lap with her razor-edged knife to his throat. Of course, his men jump to surround us, but he raises his hand to stop them as he smirks. *Dumbass move, dickhead.*

"It's okay," Pike states, staring at Mara. "The Heirs are smart men. They know that being outnumbered won't work too well in their favor."

"Is that right?" our girl asks before leaning into him and dragging her tongue from his chin up the right side of his face. "You tried to kill one of our own while bombing the club, you naughty, naughty boy. Do you know what happens when you're naughty?"

Pike subtly shakes his head. Mara has the asshole getting all hard again talking seductively like she is. She looks over her shoulder at his hardness pressed against her ass and smirks. Licking her lips, she gives the drug lord her attention again as she states, "We punish bad boys and girls."

I wince as she swiftly brings the knife around and slices off a few layers of the tip of his cock before placing the knife at his throat again. "And who says we're outnumbered?"

I can no longer see Mara's face from where I stand, but I can see Pike's. The realization of what Mara just did is slow to take hold and the smirk he had on his face ever so slowly disintegrates before he finally cries out in pain. With the knife flush against his throat, he can't move his head, but his eyes move wildly around, looking for what—help or danger—I don't know.

The club's music turns off, and everyone goes silent. You can hear a pin drop by how quiet it is. I look to my three friends, and they return the gesture. Adrik, being the one who's always up for anything and gets off on fucking shit up, shrugs. Cray gives me his mischievous smile, while Zilas shows no emotion, telling me he's in the zone and ready to go.

"Little devil. You remember what we talked about before we got here," I remind her, but it's more for Pike's sake.

"Yeah, yeah, no killing the South Crew drug lord..."

Pike visibly relaxes, thinking that things are going to be okay. I'm about to rid him of those thoughts with what I'm about to say.

"That's a good girl. My little lamb will be very pissed off if we don't bring him back with us like we said we would. Saraya has plans for him, and I'm *dying* to know what they are."

Pike scoffs. "I'm not going anywhere with you assholes!"

"Oh, you say that like you have a choice, *sugar.* I think it's time you go nighty-night," Mara states.

"What the—"

In a two-way action technique, our little devil is quick as she hits Pike just under his jaw, striking in and then back. It causes a neurological knockout that will have him out for the count for a bit. It's enough for her to secure him while we clean house.

Amara's little stunt sets everything in motion. Our men swarm into the club, taking security and Pike's minions by surprise. I pull my Glock out at the same time my friends pull theirs out. I'm not sure who shoots first, but a barrage of bullets erupts, flying everywhere. Dancers and patrons take cover, and some chance running out of the club.

Taking hold of the table in Pike's section, I flip it on its side so we can use it to shield us. Saraya will kick my ass if I get shot again, and I'd rather be here while the place is getting shot up than deal with my little lamb's wrath.

Adrik's beside me with a broad grin on his face; he lives for this shit, the crazy bastard. I shake my head, then peek out from the side of the table and raise my gun. Amara is still securing the drug lord, so she's not quite shielded. Ensuring that she remains unharmed, I look over the area and notice a lone gunman lifting his weapon to point it in our direction. I don't think twice as I pull the trigger, unloading bullet after bullet into his chest.

I prefer an old-school fistfight, but everything is about guns and knives these days. Fuckers hide behind weapons instead of being real men and using their fists. Using my fists is where my adrenaline spikes; Amara is the same way. I can say with one hundred percent certainty that our little devil is just as deadly in hand-to-hand combat as she is with her Glock, knife, or stars.

Once all firing ceases and the club is quiet again, I push the table onto its top and stand. The carnage isn't as bad as I thought it would be, but Pike's men are all dead. One of our men is holding his arm while another limps around, but all are accounted for.

"Arlo, Tucker... take Pike and secure him in the van, will you?"

"Yes, Boss," they say simultaneously and come over to grab him and haul the drug lord away.

"Well, I guess that's it, then," Mara says, standing with her hands on her hips as she looks over the room.

I face her and grin. "Not until Raya gets her justice."

"Oh, right..." Mara grins wickedly. "Whatever could your little lamb have up her sleeve?"

"I don't really know," I tell her as I throw my arm around her shoulders and turn us in the direction of the front entrance. "How about we hurry and get back, so we can find out?"

A moan comes from behind the bar as we pass it. I nod at Cray, and he jumps over the top, landing on the other side.

"Oh, looks like this is our lucky day!" Cray bends over and pulls a body off the floor.

He drags the guy around the bar and brings him over. Adrik and Zilas chuckle before I get a good look at the guy. I don't have to wait long because Cray spins the fucker around, and I stare into the eyes of my little lamb's attempted murderer.

I laugh cynically, then say, "It looks like Raya will be thanking me extra tonight."

FORTY-THREE

"Wake up, little lamb. Your lion comes bearing gifts for you."

The hypnotic baritone voice that seems to hit every nerve going straight to my core has my eyelids fluttering, as well as my stomach. I love the sound of Nyx's voice when he speaks softly. I doubt he knows the effect he has when he does so, but I won't be the one to tell him.

"Mm, a sexy asshole bearing gifts? I'm not sure I want to know what said gifts are," I tease, turning and giving him my back.

"Why, you little..." He pokes me in the side where he knows I'm ticklish. "You have three seconds to get out of this bed, or else you forfeit the two gifts I have nicely wrapped up for you and placed at the warehouse."

My eyes snap open at the mention of the location. Turning, I gawk at Nyx. "Pike is at the warehouse?"

Grinning, Nyx nods. "And the motherfucker that tried taking you away from me."

How I'm so excited over this is beyond me. When did I lose my morals? I'm looking forward to ending the life of two men—two evil men—but men all the same.

Jesus, I'm going to hell, but hey, at least Nyx will be right there with me.

"Oh, my God, what are we going to do with them?" I ask as I slip out of bed.

I don't care that I'm nude as I walk to the bathroom and turn on the shower. I love doing so when Nyx is around because it turns him on. When I glance back, Nyx is leaning against the door frame. He looks sexy as hell in his dark gray suit. The top few buttons on his black dress shirt are undone, letting the ink on his chest peek through.

"You're drooling all over the place, little lamb," he says, smirking. "As for your question, we can do anything your little heart desires."

He pushes away from the doorway and slowly strolls towards me. I'm mesmerized by the sheer sex appeal he exudes in everything he does. I never had a chance to get away from him. Something always kept me from leaving; now, I'm grateful for it.

"You want me to come up with how we're going to end their lives?" I question, worriedly.

The beautiful man stops in front of me, and using his thumb, he softly runs it over my bottom lip, caressing it as he nods. He slides his hand behind my neck and grips my hair, bringing my face inches from his. I gasp at the sudden jolt that shoots through my center as his gray gaze studies every inch of my face.

"It's your gift, little lamb, so it's your decision. I'm hard just thinking about what you'll come up with."

"That's so wrong. You know that, right?"

His full lips tilt up on one side. "Everything about me is wrong, baby. That's what makes me so right for you."

Well fuck...

"Phoenyx?"

"Yes, Saraya?"

"Will you hurry up and kiss me?" I ask in frustration.

The smile that he knows makes me wet appears, and I see the gleam in his eye. "There's no time for that, baby. Now, get your dirty self into that shower so I can take you to your presents. You smell like my personal whore house."

He slaps my ass before spinning and walking out on me. I'm left with my mouth hanging open, staring after him in disbelief. He did not just do that! Narrowing my eyes at the doorway he just went through; I then turn and get into the shower.

After a quick wash down, I lift my leg onto the small built-in bench and bring my hand between my legs. Closing my eyes, I think about *him*—my arrogant stepbrother-turned-fiancé—and all the things he does to not only my body but my mind, too. It doesn't take me long to come all over my fingers when I was already halfway there, no thanks to Nyx.

Making quick work of it, I dry off, throw the towel in the hamper, and walk out. I hadn't washed my hair, so I don't have to wait for it to dry. It's just thrown up into a messy bun.

Nyx is sitting in the armchair by the balcony doors, and I can't resist sliding my finger under his nose as I walk past him. His head snaps in my direction.

"Little lamb..." he says, his tone a warning.

"Hm?"

I rummage through the dresser's top drawer, where I stored some of my clothes. When I can't find any of my panties, I say *fuck it, it's not like they'll stay on anyway.* I close the drawer, going to the next one down to grab some leggings.

Nyx is behind me instantly, blocking me from getting dressed. I feel the warmth of his hard body against my back, and the bulge poking at my ass proves that he's not unaffected. I don't realize I'm taking quick, shallow breaths when he grips my hand and brings my fingers to his nose. I suck in a lung full of air and hold it.

"Tell me, little lamb, why do your fingers smell like *my* cunt?"

Keeping my smirk hidden, I reply, "Because I fucked myself with them. Why else would they smell like *your* pussy?"

"Did I give you permission to touch what's mine?"

I shrug. "Apparently not, but hey, if it bothers you that much, then I'll just keep my hands on what's mine from now on."

"Yes, you do that..."

I reach behind me and cup his bulge, massaging it through his pants. "Aw, it feels like *my* cock needs some TLC."

He groans and pushes into my palm.

I pull my hand away and duck under his arm to free myself. "Too bad there's no time right now."

There's a low rumble that sounds like a growl behind me. I look back while pulling my leggings on, and Nyx still stands where I left him, his head tilted back with his eyes closed. He wears a tight smile and has his hands balled into fists. Do I feel bad that I'm leaving him hanging like that? Of course, but a lesson needs to be learned. Phoenyx Beckam is too used to having his way, and it's about time someone breaks him of that habit. Who better to do it than me?

When we enter, the warehouse is dark. The way the Heirs keep it looking old and dilapidated gives off a creepy vibe, but that's only in the central area. All the rooms behind closed doors are updated and in working order for whatever the Gods and Mara must do.

The Gods—Jesus, they really are in this town. I've seen how people respect them, even when there is a bit of fear in their eyes. Just look at what they can do without others knowing. There's no telling how many people they've killed. Granted, Mara takes care of most of them, but the Heirs also have some blood staining their hands.

I get it; they aren't the Mafia—not really. They kill the bad guys, blah, blah, blah. Killing is killing—and now I can add myself to their little club. I won't lie; I'm ashamed that I get a little joy in getting rid of the trash. It's almost like a high, knowing that their life was in my hands, and I chose to end it as payback for all the victims they've wronged.

I wish I could have been the one to end my stepfather, Layton, and that rapist son of a bitch, Stanton. I don't know how Stanton died, but I hope it was a painful death. I guess burning to death is a gruesome way to go, so at least I can get a little bit of gratification in Layton's death. I hate that my mother was involved; then again, she did nothing when my stepfather married me off to Kenneth.

Nyx takes hold of my hand as we walk down a long corridor. I have yet to go to this part of the warehouse. Goosebumps break out across my skin, but I'm unsure whether it's due to the creepy vibes or the anticipation of ridding this world of more filth.

Nyx replayed everything that went down with the South Crew on the drive over. I'm astonished that I slept the whole time they were gone. Then again, the multiple orgasms Nyx made me have would've made any woman sleep as long as I did. Initially, I was upset that he had planned it that way, knowing I would try and come, but I know it was best that I stayed behind, so I let it go.

"Who's all here?" I ask when I hear muffled voices coming from the direction that we are walking in.

"The whole gang is here, little one. You forget that we all have a stake in Club Unholy. Why wouldn't we want to be here to watch you deliver the punishment?"

"You're serious about having me decide how to carry it out?"

"Of course! They tried to take your life, Raya—tried to take you from me!" Nyx stops and roughly yanks me against his chest. Cupping my cheek, his gray orbs burn into mine as he vehemently states, "No one will *ever* take you from me again."

Nyx's mouth collides with mine, showing me how much he means what he says. The feelings behind the kiss floor me, making me feel like I'm walking in the clouds. My heart pounds violently as stars begin to dance in my vision. It's just a kiss, yet it's so much more.

When he draws back, taking his lips away, mine follow, not wanting the kiss to end. My eyes snap open to see his clouded over. I can't say they are lustful; they're more than that. Raw hunger exudes their depths as they focus on mine, making my entire body tingle.

"You are my fucking life, Saraya. I love you—always remember that."

I'm speechless, so I nod slowly.

I've never seen Nyx in this state. He's told me before that he would burn the world down for me, and I thought that was the most passion I'd get from him, but I was wrong. This? What he's proclaiming? The intensity behind his every word goes far beyond unchecked passion. I don't know if there is even a word for it—untamed, maybe?

"I love you, too, Phoenyx." My voice cracks a little with my whispered response.

Pressing his forehead to mine briefly, he kisses it and steps back, retaking my hand. "Come on, they're waiting for us."

After squeezing his large hand with mine, I nod, and we continue down the dark hallway until we come to a cracked door. Nyx pushes it open, and all eyes turn to us. Looking around the room, I smirk.

"What? No woodchipper or incinerator?"

Mara grins and says, "I thought maybe we'd try something else. This room is filled with goodies that you can play with. I'm interested to see just how creative you can be."

"I'm sorry, I'm not as sadistic as you are, little psycho, so forgive me if my creativity isn't up to par with yours." I roll my eyes.

"Damn, little devil! She matches your attitude to a T," Cray muses.

"Eh, she still has a little work to do, but she'll get there," Mara states.

I stare at her, astonished by her compliment. "Does this mean you won't try to ever kill me?"

"Oh, that thought crosses my mind every fucking day. Then I remember the warning my therapist gives me, and I push it to the back of my head until the next time."

"Hm, you actually see a therapist? Wow..." I tease dryly.

"Yeah, you fuck him every night." I catch Mara winking at Nyx, and a laugh bursts free.

"You take advice from Nyx?" I ask, grinning.

"Not so much advice, but I do tend to heed his warnings—when it comes to you, anyway."

"Aw, do you want to know what I think?"

"No."

Mara walks away from our conversation, leaving me grinning from ear to ear. I look at Nyx and say, "I think she likes me just a little."

Nyx laughs. "Of course she does, but she'll never admit it. Take this as a win, little lamb. Your life is safe around the little devil."

I exhale and nod. "Yeah, okay. Can we get this over with now?" I glance at the two other men in the room.

Although he's hanging upside down by chains, I recognize the guy who bombed the club. Beside him is another guy, a bit older and rough-looking. This must be Pike. He's got tattoos littered over his face and neck, and he looks a bit scary. He's glaring at me as if I'm the one who brought him here.

"So nice to meet you, Pike. I'm sorry it has to be under these circumstances, but you see, had you just accepted my refusal and moved on, we wouldn't be here."

The thought of me marrying this man is repugnant to me. He's got to be in his forties at the very least, but that isn't why I'm turned off by Pike. Life hasn't been kind to him. Well, it was most likely the drugs. Joining the tattoos on his face are scars that coincide with heavy use of meth, coke, or heroin—maybe all three. How could my sperm donor even consider doing this to me, regardless of whether I grew up with him?

Pike's rageful eyes follow my every move, which I find amusing. Wondering what he has to say for himself has me leaning forward and gripping the end of the duct tape. I don't do it quickly to lessen the pain. Instead, I pull it away from his mouth at a leisurely pace. The grunting sounds from his facial hair being ripped out give me enjoyment. Nothing I do to this piece of shit will be easy on him.

"Fucking bitch. You should have died in that explosion!" He spits at me, but it misses.

Suddenly, Nyx is beside me, raining punches down on Pike. "You fucking dare disrespect my woman! By the time she's done with you, you're going to wish she had given you a quick death."

A gurgling chuckle comes from the bloody drug lord. "What's the matter, Beckam? Do you always need a woman to do the job for you? Are you that much of a pansy that you can't do it yourself?"

I shove Nyx aside and grip Pike's throat, digging my nails into his flesh. His arms strain to break free of the bindings, but it's useless. "This is *my* vengeance, not his. You put a hit on *me*, so I'm the one who gets to play. Haven't you ever heard the saying, *Those who kill together, stay together?* Oh, maybe that's just what I say." I shrug. "It doesn't really matter, but you should know something. Killing seems to turn me on. You should have seen the way Nyx fucked me right beside where Kappel's body grew cold. Luckily, there are too many people here to do it again once we rid the world of your pathetic ass."

The mention of Kappel captures his attention, and the asshole grins, saying, "You would have made for a good whore. At least until I had achieved what I wanted, then I would have given you to my men or shipped your ass overseas."

"I saw his cock, Raya. You definitely dodged that bullet," Mara chuckles from a few feet away.

I turn my head to look at her, then glance down at Pike's crotch. Grimacing, I shove myself away from him. "I'll take your word for it. Now," I spin around and ask, "What toys do we have to play with, little psycho?"

"Finally!" Mara claps her hands excitedly. "Have you ever worked with cement?"

FORTY-FOUR

I blink at the little psycho.

"Have I what?"

"Cement, Raya," Mara says in a slow voice.

"I know what you said, but why would you ask me that?"

Mara shrugs. "It's just an idea, fuck. I was trying to help out, but hey, you've got this."

Images of ideas run through my head, and suddenly, I call out to Mara, stopping her from retreating. "I need something that we can put him in, and we will need something big enough to mix the cement in."

If my memory from my high school Science class serves me right, I believe that placing him in something and filling it with cement will begin to crush him as the cement solidifies. I think now would be a good time to test that theory.

Nyx pulls me into him, grinning. "Look at you, little lamb..." His lips brush my ear. "You're making me so hard for you right now; that cunt better be ready to take a good pounding by the time we get home."

"Mm, that's if we make it that far."

A loud rolling noise interrupts our little playful conversation. I look toward the door and watch Zilas roll in what looks like a giant mixing machine. Adrik is right behind him, pushing in a cart with an oversized metal barrel. Cray is carrying over bags of mixing cement and dropping them right by my feet.

I cock my brow at Mara. "I take it you're accustomed to this?"

Her wicked grin gives me my answer.

Nyx and Adrik approach Pike, and each taking a side, they lift the chair he's in. The other two Heirs help lift him high enough to place man and chair inside the barrel. The drug lord is cursing the whole time this is taking place, but it all falls on deaf ears. He won't be getting help from us.

"You can't think you'll get away with this! People will be looking for me!" Pike growls as he thrashes about.

Nyx snickers and comes to stand behind me. His arm snakes around my waist, and he nuzzles my neck briefly before addressing Pike. "Don't you think they had people looking for the three police officers that tried taking Raya away from me? Look—we're still here. You've forgotten who you were fucking with, Pike. We aren't the Gods of Nyte's Hall for nothing. You may have been able to get rid of my father and his wife easily enough, but I'm smarter than Layton Beckam."

I widen my eyes at what Nyx just said and grip his arm. "Are you telling me that this asshole not only tried killing me, but he succeeded with our parents?"

"Why don't you ask him?" Nyx nods toward Pike.

"Doesn't look as if he's denying the accusation, now does it?" Cray states with his arms crossed, watching Pike like a hawk.

In a matter of seconds, I pull Cray's knife out of its holster around his thigh, and I stab it into Pike's shoulder. Snarling, I pull it out and plunge it back into the other shoulder.

Pike laughs dryly before saying, "Had your precious Nyx showed up instead of being too busy having a gang bang with some French whore, he'd be dead too!"

Patting Nyx's chest, I hand him Cray's knife with disgust. "Here, take it," I tell him, and he does.

I leave Nyx chatting it up with the drug lord while I walk over and watch Zilas start mixing the cement. I can't believe we're doing this. The thought of watching a man suffer as his insides get crushed was never part of my life goals, but here I am.

I glance over at the one still dangling and see that he's passed out. Strolling over, I squat, tapping him on the cheek to try and wake him up. "Hey, fucker, wake up. You can sleep when you're dead."

"Here, watch out, Raya," Cray states as he holds the guy's head just before Adrik lets the chain down.

The man drops down hard and had Cray not held his head, he probably would have broken his neck. We couldn't have that. I'm not ready for him to die yet. When he moans, I give him a little shove with my foot.

"Have patience; we'll get to you in a few minutes."

"P-please...h-help m-me..."

My brows furrow as I stare down at the bomber. I look at Cray, and he seems confused, too. Crouching down, I grab the guy's chin and examine him. His eyes pop open, and I can see desperation in their depths.

"What do you need help with?" I ask.

"I h-had no c-choice. Pike h-has my f-family..."

My eyes widen, and I look at Cray. "We need to sit him up—hurry!"

"How do we know he isn't just saying this to save his ass?" Cray scowls.

"Well, that's what we need to find out."

Once we have him sitting up, I go to the sink and fill a glass with water for him. Nyx is over by Cray when I return, and I hold the cup up to the guy's mouth.

"Raya, we can't just take his word—"

"Don't you think I know this? I won't kill an innocent man, Nyx. So, we will figure out what the truth is."

Nyx gives me a warning look for cutting him off, but I didn't mean to. I'm just disturbed by the turn of events.

I have him finish drinking the water, and when he hands the cup over to me, Nyx quickly starts interrogating him. "What's your name?"

"Brandon—Brandon Cabral. My wife's name is Kate, and my boy's name is Eli. He's only four years old—please help me get them back!"

"Okay," I say softly, stepping in, "We will figure it out."

There is no way someone can fake that kind of fear. I turn and tug on Nyx's shirt while nodding at Cray to follow us. The others follow as well. I pace the hallway, chewing on my thumbnail.

"What is it you want to do, little lamb?" Nyx asks, stopping me from pacing and pulling me into his arms.

"We need to find out if what Brandon says is true." I look at each of the Heirs and Mara.

"This is your call, Raya," Nyx states. "We will do what you want, but we can't wait too long."

I nod and focus on Mara. "Do whatever you need to do to get Pike to talk and tell us where he's keeping the wife and kid."

"Oh, I think I can do that." Mara grins evilly.

"I'll talk to Cale and have him work his magic with the satellite footage or whatever the fuck he does," Nyx states as he pulls out his phone.

"I'll get Brandon to give me more information to work with," I tell them.

"What do you need us to do?" Adrik asks as he stands with Cray and Zilas.

Smirking, I reply, "Just stand there and keep looking sexy."

When I wink at him, a growl comes from behind me, and I turn to see Nyx scowling at his friends. I roll my eyes and head back to the room Pike and Brandon are in.

"Keep your fucking mouth shut if you know what's good for you!" I hear Pike sneer at Brandon.

I stop and listen; neither has noticed me in the doorway yet.

"I'm not going to die for you, Pike. They're going to kill you! Where is my family?"

"I'm not going to tell you..." Pike doesn't finish his sentence when he sees me watching them.

I walk into the room and feel Nyx at my back. I'm so attuned to him these days that it's scary, but it also gives me the sense of security and the courage to go on.

"So, you do have his family? You used a wife and child to get someone to do your dirty work for you?" I stare at the drug lord with disgust.

"I don't know what you're talking about. Brandon is my employee. I have no idea who his whore of a wife is," Pike spits.

When Mara comes to stand at my side, I grin at the man before me. "Since you don't want to repent of your sins and tell us where the woman and kid are, Mara's going to play with you for a bit."

"Ah, the crazy bitch is going to play, huh?" Pike blows kisses at Mara, mocking her.

None of us saw the object in the little psycho's hand until she holds it up and says, "I'm really tired of listening to your annoying voice, so until you are ready to talk, let's shut that hole of yours, shall we?"

Cray quickly holds Pike's head in place while Mara squeezes his lips together. She brings the object she's holding up to his mouth and pulls the trigger. She repeats it until she works her way across his mouth as he tries screaming. When she stands back, we all admire her work. Pike's mouth is now stapled shut for the time being.

It's creepy as fuck looking at him like this, so I turn back to Brandon. He doesn't look so good at the moment. Tilting my head to the side, I scrutinize him.

"How long have you worked for Pike?" I cross my arms.

"Going on three weeks," Brandon responds.

"How long has he had your family?"

"They took them the night before I came to your club. I was on another job for him when his men went to my place and took them. I refused to bomb the club when he first approached me with the job." Brandon glances over at Pike but quickly looks away.

"Does Pike's lips being stapled make you squeamish?" I ask, amused.

"I'm not good when it comes to this stuff. I was a construction worker before this, not a gangster."

"You had to have known what the South Crew was about."

"Yeah, but I also thought that if I did as I was told and stayed off his radar, things would be fine until I got other work."

I look over my shoulder when I hear Pike's muffled scream and see Mara slowly cutting one of the tattoos from his face with her favorite knife. I used to be like Brandon when it came to stuff like this, but I'm obviously accustomed to it now. Pike deserves everything coming to him. Brandon, on the other hand, doesn't—if, in fact, he's telling the truth—and I do believe he is.

"What do you plan on doing if we find your family and release you?" Nyx asks Brandon from right behind me.

The guy shrugs and hangs his head. "I'm not sure."

"You say you did construction before?" Nyx questions.

"Yeah, I was the foreman, but the owner fell on hard times and let everyone go." Brandon focuses on me and says, "I am so sorry that my actions caused you harm. Please know I'm not that kind of person but will do whatever it takes for my family."

The corners of my eyes burn, and my throat forms a lump. Those familiar words hit home on so many levels. I turn and gaze at Nyx. I don't have to tell him what it is I want. His mouth tightens into a thin line, and then he nods.

"Well, Brandon. It seems to be your lucky day. My fiancé has a good heart and seems more forgiving than I'd be. So, I have a proposition for you," Nyx states. "We will find your family, and you will help with the reconstruction work with the club. You will not be paid, but I will ensure your bills are paid. After that, I know of a few companies and will put in a good word for you."

I grin at my sexy man as Brandon gives his thanks repeatedly. I knew Nyx Beckam had a good heart, even if it did take me coming back into his life and fucking up all his plans. When I step into his arms, they automatically encircle my waist, and I kiss him.

"Thank you," I whisper.

He leans into my ear and says, "Anything for my little lamb, but now, it's time to end this so I can take my woman home and fuck."

There's bloody flesh scattered everywhere, yet the South Crew drug lord is still fucking alive. Pike finally gave up the location to Brandon's family, but not until Mara sliced away every visible tattoo marking his skin. He probably would have caved sooner, but with his mouth stapled, he couldn't talk, and Mara ignored all the sounds he was making. She seemed to be having way too much fun.

However, her fun isn't over yet. We're now at the stage where Mara feels she needs to give Pike his last meal. Picking up one of the pieces of bloody skin, she dangles it from her knife.

"It's dinner time motherfucker."

"Fuck you, you sick whore!"

"Aw, I slaved over this meal for you, and now you're being ungrateful?" Mara tsks him. "You know what my mama used to say when I didn't want to eat my food?"

"I don't fucking care what the whore said..."

"Hey! Watch your fucking mouth before I cut your dick off and feed it to you, too!" When Pike doesn't respond, Mara continues with her story. "My mama used to tell me, *You can't leave the table, Amara, until you've finished every last bite.'* I would sit at the table until bedtime, and then, when I woke up, my mama would reheat my supper and put it right back in front of me."

"Your mom sounds like a bitch," Pike sneers.

Mara snickers. "Of course, she was. Who do you think I inherited it from?" She holds the piece of flesh to his lips. "Open wide."

"You're fucking sick! I'm not eating that!" Pike gags.

"Oh, my bad—hold on!" Mara hurries over to the little mini fridge and pulls out two bottles. Holding them up, she asks, "Ketchup or hot sauce?"

Pike's given up answering her questions and refuses to even look at her. So, it comes as no surprise when, once again, Adrik holds his head while Cray pries Pike's mouth open. Mara pours the hot sauce on the flap of skin and shoves it into his mouth. He automatically starts screaming with his mouth closed.

I keep close watch and it doesn't take too long before Pike's furiously chewing his own flesh—and swallowing it. Cray lets up his hold on his mouth and Pike starts gagging instantly.

"That's a good boy," Mara states. "Let's have a few more and then we can call it good."

I'm not going to lie, watching this part of the torture has my stomach rolling a bit. I can't imagine eating my own flesh.

"I wouldn't be so nice, Mara. Don't doctor it up with good tasting sauces," I tell her.

Mara gives me her wicked grin. "This is my own special recipe. It's hot sauce because it's made with acid. It starts to eat at their tongue if they let it sit there too long."

Damn! That's a good idea.

After making Pike eat himself a few more times, I put a stop to it. Mara would be at it all night if I didn't. So, I instruct Adrik to start pouring the cement into the barrel. I wasn't kidding about testing out that theory, and we already had the cement on standby, mixing in the machine while we waited patiently for the little psycho to be done playing.

Brandon is being made to watch, so he knows that the Gods of Nyte mean business when it comes to people like Pike. Unfortunately, he didn't make it through the whole show without vomiting.

"Let this be a lesson for you, Brandon," I tell him. "We don't kill the innocent, but we will do what we must in order to keep the residents of this town safe. They are the Heirs' responsibility. You're lucky that I was here to hear you out. I'm sure they would have released you in the end, but not before you felt some pain."

"I'm grateful to you, Ms. Abbott," Brandon states.

"Beckam," Nyx corrects him.

I roll my eyes at the arrogant Heir. "We're not married yet, Beckam. Don't be getting ahead of yourself."

"Legalities, little lamb. You've been claimed by Nyx Beckam, so you might as well get used to it." Nyx yanks me to him and kisses me hard before stepping back.

"I thought you wanted to get this finished. There's no time for any PDA, mister!" I then check the barrel, ignoring the cries coming from the big, bad drug lord, now covered to his chest.

"Please, I'll change my ways! I'll stop selling drugs!"

I chuckle and say, "I suppose you'll go to church, too."

"Yes! If that's what it takes, I'll go to church every Saturday and pray every night!"

I cock my brow at him. "Church is on Sundays, asshole."

"Whenever... I'll go!" Pike swears.

Narrowing my eyes, I cross my arms over my chest. "No, I don't think you will. In fact, I think that if we were to let you go, you would go straight to your little hole in the ground and find more people to try and take us out again. Do you honestly think we were born yesterday?"

His expression turns dark and menacing, making him look like something from a horror movie with most of his face sliced off. "You fucking bitch!"

"Nah," I say, shaking my head. "I'm not a fucking bitch—I'm your fucking nightmare." I glare at him and then nod at Adrik, who shuts the mixer off, stopping the pour, and places the cover over the barrel.

Pike is still alive, for now. He's going to feel himself being crushed as the cement solidifies, and even if he doesn't die from it, the lack of air will end him. I'm so over this day already. I'm ready to go home and climb into bed, but I know it will be hours before I can sleep if Nyx has his way.

Leaving the warehouse, Cray and Adrik remain behind, ensuring the job gets done. Zilas and Mara take Brandon to go get his family. And Nyx? Well, he takes me home and makes good on everything he said he would do to me, keeping me up until the wee hours of the morning.

FORTY-FIVE

Nyx

The weekend is upon us, and I've decided to pack my little lamb up and whisk her away for the duration. There's too much to do to get the club ready to reopen; otherwise, it would be longer. The weather is supposed to stay nice, and I think a little time at the beach will do us good.

So much has happened since Raya re-entered my life, and I want this time with her to renew our relationship. Yes, she's already agreed to marry me—that was inevitable—and deep down, I knew it was always her. But after all these years, we need to reacquaint ourselves with one another. Maybe that's why I never really settled down, because regardless of the pain I felt, I knew that there would never be anybody else for me.

Submissive after submissive tried filling that hole that never seemed to get full, and to be honest, I'm no hardcore Dominant. I'm one of four owners of a kink club, and I've trained to be a Dom—we all have—but Zilas and I have never really thrown ourselves into the lifestyle. It's a means to keep women at arm's length. Adrik and Cray on the other hand—they embrace it, especially Adrik with all his kinks and perversions. To each their own.

My little lamb is a mouthy shit, and I hope she never changes. Although I don't practice the D/s dynamic all the time, I do love punishing her. She needs to answer for a lot, and I plan on catching up on all her transgressions this weekend.

I hear the shower turn off, and I give it about a minute before opening the bathroom door and walking in. Raya is finishing up drying off when her head whips in my direction.

She studies me closely as I slowly prowl toward her. I toss her one of my T-shirts because it covers all the essential parts. Catching it, she examines it and raises an eyebrow.

"Thanks, but I've already picked my clothes out for the day." She tosses it back, only for me to throw it back.

"Put the fucking shirt on, Raya."

Her brows crease, but she pushes her arms through the sleeves and lowers it over her head. "What's wrong?"

"I never said anything was wrong."

"Then why are you acting weird?"

"I'm not."

"O—kay." She glances at the vanity before meeting my stare again. "I was going to ask if you've seen my skincare creams and makeup. They seem to have disappeared."

"I have." I smirk.

"Well, are you going to tell me where they are?"

I shake my head back and forth slowly. Standing before my little lamb, I take in her natural beauty. She doesn't need any of that makeup shit, but she never believes me.

Lifting my hand, I trace her jawline with my finger, reveling in the silkiness of her skin. When it gets to her chin, I tilt her head up and lean in. "I love you," I tell her softly before briefly pressing my lips to hers.

When I pull away, she runs her tongue over her lips as if she's chasing the taste of mine. I notice the subtle movement of Raya squeezing her thighs together, and I smile inwardly.

Once again, she asks, "Why are you acting weird?"

"I'm not. Can't I express my feelings to my fiancé?"

Raya narrows her eyes at me. I'm sure she can see the mirth in my eyes because I can't hide it completely. When she crosses her arms and gives me that sassy look, I lose all control, and I bend over, shouldering her stomach and lifting her off her feet.

"What are you doing? Put me down!" she squeals as I carry her over my shoulder.

"Sorry, no can do, baby. I've got plans for us, and I'm ready to start. Unfortunately, it takes an hour to get there."

"Well, let me get dressed, and we can go. Wait, where are you taking me? Nyx! I'm not wearing any underwear, and my ass is hanging out!"

"Who fucking cares? Let them all see that perfect ass of mine." I reach up and slap it.

"Grr—you're going to pay for this, Beckam!" Her growl is adorable.

"Nah, why would I pay for it when I've been getting it for free all this time?"

"Oh, haha! You're so fucking funny. Seriously, though. Where are you taking me?"

"I'm taking you somewhere private. I plan on making you my dirty little whore for the weekend, and you're going to love every minute of it," I tell her.

"Oh, you think so?" She giggles.

"I know so. I will tie you up if I have to and just have my way with you day in and day out." We make it down the stairs without seeing a soul, but when we get to the bottom, Cray comes around the corner, stopping in his tracks.

He gives a slow whistle. "Damn, Raya! Your ass is fine."

"Whoa." Zilas comes up behind Cray, but he has the decency to turn his head.

"Oh, don't mind me boys. It's just your boy here thinking he's a caveman and not caring who he showcases my hoo-ha to," Raya says dryly.

"It's just your ass, Raya—calm your tits," I tell her.

"Uh, no, it's not, bro." Cray snickers. "She really does have a pretty kitty, Nyx."

I shrug. "Oh well, enjoy it while you can, boys." I salute my two friends and walk out the front door.

"You're truly an ass, Nyx."

"No, wrong animal. I'm a lion, little lamb, and this lion will be devouring his lamb many times over this weekend."

I hear a slight whimper, and being the dick I am, I slip my fingers between her thighs and feel her slickness. Pushing two fingers into her, I finger fuck her until we get to my car, and I set her down in the passenger seat.

She watches as I suck her off my fingers while buckling her safety belt and then kiss her. "Keep those legs open for me, little lamb. I'm not done with you yet."

The drive to the coast has been the most uncomfortable drive ever. I made Raya come twice but refused when she offered to give me road head. As much as I would have loved it, I was not putting her life in danger by having her out of her safety belt just to give me a blow job.

We enter the spacious beach house with its floor-to-ceiling windows facing the private beach. It belongs to the Gods of Nyte's Hall, but we rarely use it. Placing our bags by the front door, I quickly check to ensure the water is turned on and the pantry and fridge are stocked. An elderly couple who lives nearby takes care of the place for us.

Finding everything as I requested, I take the bags to the room I use when I'm here. Raya is taking everything in and has taken it upon herself to get reacquainted with the house. She had come here a few times when we were younger and our parents brought us, but it's been updated since then.

I pour myself a drink and lean against the kitchen island as I watch her look around. When she stops in the middle of the living room and turns in a circle, our eyes meet, and I beckon her over with my finger. The ice in my glass clinks as I take a drink, waiting for her to get her little ass over here. She's teasing me and doesn't realize how much trouble she's already in.

My cock has been hard the whole drive, and now she thinks it's cute that she's playing with me. I'll show her cute when I turn her over my knee and redden that beautiful ass.

Still wearing my shirt, she stands before me with her hands behind her back, acting all innocent. "Did you need something, *Sir?*"

I finger the zip tie that's tucked away in my pocket, and I smirk. "You can say that." Using my finger with the hand holding my glass, I make the motion for her to turn, and she obeys. "That's a good girl. Now, stay just as you are."

I toss back the rest of the contents in my glass and set it down on the island. Stepping up behind her, I grab her hands and lower my voice to say, "You're going to be good and take your punishments without giving me any trouble."

She gasps softly as I tighten the zip tie around her wrists. "Nyx—"

"Sir, for the time being," I order her.

"I'm not a submissive, Nyx. You know this." She turns her head to the side, trying to look at me, I'm sure.

"Did I say anything about you being my fucking sub, little lamb?" I pull on her hands, and she stumbles back into me. "This is about you taking the punishments you've earned since arriving. While I dole them out, you are to call me Sir. Is that understood?"

Sliding my hand around her throat, I feel her racing heart. I bet if I stick my hand between her legs, she'll be soaked. I don't do that, though. Instead, I step away and order her to go to the couch and wait for me. She may not consider herself a submissive, but she does make for a great one when she's not sassing off.

Adjusting my throbbing cock, I follow her and sit in the middle of the couch. "Come here, little lamb. Drape yourself over my lap."

Raya narrows her eyes at me, but does as she's told with my help. Her head rests on the couch's edge to the left of me, while her feet can still touch the floor to the right of me. I slide the shirt up, presenting her juicy ass, and I run my hands over it, squeezing each cheek.

"This is what's going to happen, little lamb. Typically, I'd make you count, but you will receive quite a bit today, so I won't make you. You will ask me to spank you, and you will take every one of them, thanking me once I'm done. After you've taken them all, you will have a clean slate, and we can enjoy the rest of the weekend."

"This sure sounds like some D/s bullshit to me—*Sir.*"

I chuckle. "To an extent, but this is how I do my punishments. Can you honestly say that you don't deserve them?"

"That's beside the point..."

I ignore her and continue, "You may cry if need be. I prefer it because you'll look so pretty."

"Anything else, *oh great one*?" Raya's sarcasm just earned her another five on top of the fifty I plan on giving her.

"Yes. Once I've finished, I'm going to fuck you hard and deep, and I'm going to make it hurt. It's going to be about me this first time, so I'll fuck you how I want until I fill my cunt with my kids. If you don't come before I do, you don't come at all. Do you have an issue with that?"

"No..." She says it so softly that I barely even hear it.

"Good. Then, let's begin. You must ask for it, Raya."

I feel her tense before saying, "Please spank me, *Sir.*"

I can tell her jaw is clenched when she asks, but it doesn't bother me as I deliver the first one. I have to remind her to relax. Once I feel her do so, I bring my hand down, making the slap resonate through the room.

Raya's body jerks, and she tries twisting herself, so I capture her legs between my thighs.

"You can always say 'Red,' little lamb, but then all will not be forgiven. It's up to you."

"I won't safe word, asshole. It just surprised me, is all." Her mouthy response has me grinning.

"Would you like more added for that mouth of yours?" I ask, amused.

"Fuck you, just get it over with." She's demanding, but I'll let it slide because I want nothing more than to be sliding into my cunt, and I can't do that until I'm done.

I bring my hand down again and again, repeating the slaps on each cheek. Her little grunts soon turn into moans, and I can almost feel her trying to grind on my thigh. I'm gritting my teeth, trying to keep from coming in my fucking cargo shorts.

I pause, so I can look at her ass and debate on whether I can continue. Her skin is a pretty pink after the first twenty-five spankings. Squeezing her cheeks, I jiggle them harshly when she moans in pleasure.

"Don't fucking come yet, little lamb."

"Oh God," she whimpers.

"Spread your legs," I order, loosening my hold on them so she can do so. As soon as she does, my hand comes down and slaps her pussy. "You like that, do you? God, you truly are a little whore for me." I slap her pussy a few more times before going back to her ass.

"Please, Nyx. I need you..."

"You need me to do what? This time, address me properly." I smile when I hear her curse under her breath.

"I need you to fuck me now, *Sir.*"

"Well, I think I can manage that since you asked so nicely."

I give her the last of her spankings, and without releasing her wrists, I reposition us so I'm standing behind her. I open my shorts and pull my throbbing length from its confinement. Her head rests on the couch while her body is bent over, waiting to be used. Her gorgeous, greedy pussy accepts my girth as it splits her open. I groan as I sink all the way into her and stop, savoring the feel of her cunt gripping me.

"Fuck, Raya. You feel way too good, baby."

Looking down at her, she looks fucking perfect, with her cheek pressed to the couch and her pretty pinkened ass in the air, waiting for me to own her. I pull out, then push back in, slowly picking up speed. I edge her a few times, stopping and slapping her ass each time she's about to come. When I'm close, I suck on my thumb and slowly push it into her tight little pucker.

"Oh God... I'm coming!" Raya cries out.

This time, I don't stop her. Instead, I grip her hips in a bruising hold, and I fuck her—hard, fast, and deep—until I have her coming again. Her climax rolls right into another one, and I'm a goner. I empty myself deep inside.

"Yes, take it, baby," I coo softly.

All I hear is an exhausted pant from Raya as I finish inside her. My hand runs up her arm and back down, giving her hip a loving squeeze before pulling out. I pick up my shorts that have fallen around my ankles and find the pocket knife I tucked away in the side pocket.

I release her wrists and massage up and down her arms, helping with the circulation and possible stiffness. Reaching down, I help her to stand and turn her to face me. For a moment, I get lost gazing into eyes that remind me of melted chocolate. I can't stop myself from firmly gripping the back of her neck and taking her lips. She returns the kiss with the same fervor, stirring my cock all over again.

Slowly, I end the kiss before pulling my head back, but I don't release my hold on her. I'm not ready to mourn the loss of her soft curves against me yet. With my other hand, I push a few strands of her hair away from her eye, and I smile softly.

"I love you, little lamb."

"Thank you for the spankings, and I love you, too." Her eyes never leave mine.

It never gets old hearing Raya say those words to me. They aren't said often, but they don't need to be; I know her love for me. It's the same love I have for her—the love born so many years ago.

The corners of my lips lift higher until my teeth show, and I see the question appear in her eyes.

"What?"

"Rest up, little lamb—that was only the first round."

FORTY-SIX

Cape Dayne is a small coastal town where the rich come to get away from everyday life. Because Nyx whisked me away early enough this morning, we've been able to do a little window shopping up and down the beachfront. I was nervous when he first suggested it, only because it's so unlike the Nyx Beckam that I have come to know. However, I was worried for nothing. Within the first ten minutes, Nyx had me laughing, and everything became more relaxed.

Nyx and I hold hands as we walk from store front to store front. We look like a loving couple to others, but they don't know the shit we've been through in order to get here. This is how I used to picture our future when we were young and in love before we knew just how cruel the world could be.

"A penny for your thoughts?" Nyx's breath caresses my ear as he asks.

We had stopped to look inside a window of a clock shop when my thoughts drifted. I must have been in deep thought if I hadn't realized he was pulling on my hand.

I smile. "I'm sorry. I was just thinking about how I would daydream about us being older and doing exactly what we're doing now..."

Nyx presses his lips to my forehead then looks me in the eye and says, "Well, we are doing it now. It may have taken us longer to make it happen, but we're doing it. I can't imagine doing any of this without you, Raya. Nobody deserves this side of Nyx Beckam but you."

My lips tilt up. "Careful, Mr. Beckam. You never know who is nearby and may hear you talking so sweetly to me. We wouldn't want to ruin your reputation."

Nyx pulls me into his arms, his tone turning serious as he states, "I don't give a fuck if people see me loving on my woman. I won't hide my feelings for you from everyone, even if it does make me look like a pansy ass. For you, I'll do it."

Jesus! The intensity of this statement has my panties getting wet. Never in a million years did I think I would ever see Phoenyx behind those stone-gray eyes, but he's there, and it's only for me. I'll take all the shit that Nyx dishes out as long as, at the end of the day, Phoenyx is who I say goodnight to.

The bastard knows what his words are doing to me, and he smirks. Caressing my cheeks, Nyx makes it look to others like he's spewing words of love when, in fact, it's the opposite.

"Aw, looks like my dirty little whore wants to get fucked again. I bet you wish I would drag you into the nearest alley and fuck you against a brick wall, huh? Maybe take you into a public restroom and use you on the germ-infested vanity while others wait outside to use that toilet." His smile is deceptively sweet.

His filthy words only dampen my panties more, and he knows it. Nyx Beckam is the devil incarnate, and I'm head over heels in love with the fucker. He continues with the dirty talk even as tourists stroll past us, window shopping themselves. An elderly couple admiring a grandfather clock in the shop's window glares at us then walks away in a huff after hearing him talk about fucking my ass in the voyeur room at the club.

"Don't think I've forgotten. That will be our first act of fucking once the club is open again."

"What if that isn't what I want? What if I don't want others seeing what is strictly yours?" I lower my voice when I ask.

"I think you and I know better than that. Besides, if that were the case, then I'd still want to do it, if only to show the others that I own *every* fucking inch of you."

I stare at him, not knowing how to respond. His wicked words set my heart racing and my body afire and he knows it. It's frustrating, especially when we're out in public like we are.

"Why, Nyx?"

"Why what, little lamb?"

"What do you wish to accomplish saying this to me here? You already know what you do to me when you speak this way."

He smiles wickedly. "I'm just getting you ready for when we get back."

"Can we go back now?"

"No," he states, glancing at his watch. "Now, we go eat because I have reserved a table for us."

I close my eyes, sighing as I lower my head and press it against his chest. "I really hate you sometimes. Do you know that?"

"I know, baby," he says, kissing my head. "I know."

Nyx is on the phone when I come out of the bedroom wearing the swimsuit he must have purchased for me. At least I think it's a swimsuit. It's definitely what you call a string bikini. It's white, and the tiny triangles that are meant to cover my top, only cover my nipples. The bottom is the same, with a small triangular patch covering my clit and slit. I might as well be nude, and the sad thing is that he probably paid an astronomical amount for it.

He wants to be a smartass by buying it; I'm going to tease him by walking by while he's on the phone with the foreman working on the club. I make it a point to stop in front of him and pretend to adjust the strings on it. Grabbing the towel off the back of the chair, I *accidentally* drop it and bend over and pick it up. When I turn to face him, his jaw is tight, and he's adjusting himself.

"I'll be out on the beach," I speak softly, pointing towards the ocean.

I don't wait for his response as I take my leave with a big smile. With the evening fast approaching, I wanted to take a quick dip and lay out for a bit. It's still a little humid, so the water will feel good.

Laying out my towel, I walk into the ocean, feeling the cool saltwater lap at my body until I'm waist deep. I dive in at this point, but I come back up right away. Wiping my eyes and slicking my hair back, I turn toward the shore and see Nyx standing at the water's edge. Small waves crash into his ankles as he stands shirtless, with only his shorts on.

His hands are in his pockets as he waits for me to return to shore. I can't decipher his mood, but whatever it is, I can handle it.

Nyx's eyes move to my chest, and I look down only to see that the bikini is entirely see-through. Narrowing my eyes, I glower at him for buying such a swimsuit. He's just lucky that this is a private beach.

I avoid him by making a wide berth on my way back to my towel. He chuckles, and then he's behind me, wrapping his arms around my waist and tightening them so I can't break free.

"Such a naughty little whore, teasing me when I'm on the phone," he says before biting my ear. "Do you want to know what I'm going to do to my naughty whore?"

Grinning, I rub my ass against the massive bulge in his pants. "You're going to fuck me roughly and teach me a lesson?"

His chuckle is one of sheer amusement. "No, little lamb. I'm not going to fuck you because that's what this slutty cunt wants me to do." He cups my sex, rubbing his palm against the sensitive little bud. He spins me around and says, "Instead, I'm going to lay you down on your towel, and I'm going to love you."

My heart has been racing with anticipation, but I freeze when he announces his intentions. Did I hear him right? He's going to *love* me? As in, make love to me? He's only done that once, right after he fucked me good. Nyx doesn't make love.

Maybe not, but Phoenyx does.

Nyx takes my lips and slowly lowers me down to my towel. The moment my back hits it, his mouth begins to move, kissing other areas of my face, then descending to my neck, and then my chest. He cups my breasts, rubbing his thumbs back and forth over my nipples before devouring one and then the other.

He moves the triangles over and pays homage to both for a while before reaching up and untying the strings at my neck. Once he fumbles with the knot at my back, he tosses it aside, baring me entirely, and continues downward.

His mouth is hot as it covers my sex. Nyx nips and licks at the skimpy fabric before moving it aside and dragging his tongue through my folds. I look down at him, and his eyes are on me, watching and waiting until he makes me fall apart. I open my legs wider, giving him more space, but he removes himself instead.

I whimper, and he chuckles, but then he's dragging my bottoms down my legs, and they end up with their other half in the sand. Nyx stares down at my naked form as he stands and slowly opens his shorts, letting them drop to the ground before stepping out of them. His hand wraps around his beautiful girth and strokes it up and down.

I come up to my knees, and with my eyes burning into his, I open my mouth. A bead of pre-cum forms at the tip, which he rubs over my lips, painting them with salty goodness. Then, ever so slowly, he pushes into my mouth and allows me to pleasure him at my own pace. Although his hand is on my head, there's no pressure added to it as I bob up and down, twirling my tongue around and around.

"Fuck, Raya. I fucking love your mouth," Nyx says softly.

I bring my hands to his muscular ass and grip his cheeks as I take his cock all the way to the back and past my gag reflex. I hold it there, letting him enjoy the feeling of being so deep in my throat before I back off to catch my breath.

"Enough, little lamb," he states when I return for more.

Nyx drops to his knee so we're almost at eye level and takes my left hand. Suddenly, a massive diamond ring appears between his fingers as he holds it up. The setting sun hits it just right, making it sparkle.

"I know it's going to happen regardless, but I didn't want to be *that* dick that doesn't do it properly. I know I can be an asshole, you tell me all the time, but Saraya Abbott, I want to be *your* asshole. So, will you do me the honor of marrying me and becoming my queen? Will you bear my spawns and let me fuck you for the rest of our lives?" He holds the ring at the tip of my finger, waiting for me to answer while his wicked smile works its magic on me.

Tears spill as he says his little speech, and when he gets to the end, I can't stop the laugh that bursts free. I nod vigorously, trying to get the lump from my throat.

"Yes, I will be your queen and bear your spawns. As for fucking me for the rest of our lives, that will have to be negotiated because I'm going to want to be the one fucking you sometimes."

The tears blur my vision, but I don't miss the enormous grin that appears once I'm done answering him. I grab his cheeks and crush my lips to his. I feel myself being lowered back down with Nyx coming above me. He lifts my leg and presses it against his hip, notching the head of his cock at my entrance.

Nyx gazes down at me with a look that I can only describe as captivating and yearning. As his face nears mine, my heart feels like it's going to beat right outside my chest.

"Thank you, little lamb. You've just made me the happiest and the luckiest asshole alive." He pushes inside me at the same time he claims my lips.

Nyx takes it slow but deep, pushing in as far as he can with every slow thrust. I move my other leg, spreading myself open further for him and making him grunt the next time he pushes inside of me. He continues to kiss my lips and my jaw, moving to my neck and then my breasts before claiming my lips again.

I've never known real love as I do right now. The way Nyx moves in and out of me while worshiping my upper body, more tears rolling down my cheeks. Nyx Beckam can fuck, but by God, making love to him is a whole new experience, and I'm not sure which one I love more.

The tingles start off slowly, building higher and higher until I can't hold them back, and I detonate. I'm tossed over an invisible ledge, where stars and flashes of light dance in front of me.

"Oh God, Nyx...yes, please don't stop..."

"Never, little lamb. Give it to me, baby...give me all your love."

My walls clench around his cock as I ride out my climax, trying to milk him of his own release. It feels like mine goes on forever until, finally, it begins to dissipate. Nyx picks up the pace a little when he gets on his knees and holds my legs up and apart. He watches as his length enters me, and I think it's the sexiest fucking thing ever.

"Play with your clit, baby. Come again for me."

I do as he asks and rub my sensitive bud as my God of Nyte takes me over the edge once more, only he joins me this time. We come together, and it feels like something profound is happening.

"You are my world, Raya."

I can't even respond as I cry out with my release at the same time I feel Nyx release inside me. We're left panting and gasping for air. Nyx drops down beside me but brings me into his side as we lay here in the aftermath of whatever the fuck we just did. If that's making love, then damn, I need more of that in my life. We lie in complete silence like this for about five minutes.

"A penny for your thoughts?" Nyx kisses my head.

"I was just wondering when we'll be able to do that again," I reply.

He chuckles and rolls me onto my back as he hovers over me. "How about we go back to the house, shower, and then we can recap."

"Mm, I love the way you think, Beckam."

Stacy Rush

FORTY-SEVEN

Nyx

"I've got something for you, little lamb." I sit on the edge of the bed, caressing Raya's hair, trying to rouse her from sleep.

We spent the weekend shopping, eating, and fucking, so my little lamb is worn out. Once I put the ring on her finger and we sealed it by making love on the beach, something shifted. We returned to our old selves, no doubts or insecurities hanging between us. It's like we were never apart, but we know better, and I know there will be times when the past comes back up. Raya and I have agreed to deal with those times once they present themselves.

I sat here for a minute, taking in her beauty and all that is once again mine, before waking her. She looks like an angel when she sleeps, but damn is she a mouthy one. My life will never be dull from here on out.

"Mm, what time is it?" Raya's groggy voice asks.

"It's time to get your beautiful ass up unless you want me to redden it again."

"Why are you always threatening me with a good time, yet you don't always follow through?"

I raise my brow, giving her a serious, no-nonsense look as I slide my hand to the back of her neck and squeeze. "How about I use the cane or whip on your ass as punishment next time? Then, we'll see if it's still a good time."

She fucking grins at me.

"Keep being a brat, Raya. I know how sore your cunt must be, but I won't let that stop me. Now, be a good girl and jump into the shower. I want to run a little errand before returning to Nyte."

"I thought you said you had something for me?" Her lip juts out in an adorable pout.

"I do, but we need to go get it." I yank the covers away, earning myself a dirty look, but it doesn't bother me one bit. "I'll lay some clothes out for you and take the luggage to the car."

"Please leave my makeup. I'll take it to the car when we leave."

"No."

She stops just outside the door to the bathroom and turns to look at me. "What do you mean, no?"

I walk over and stand before her, cupping her cheek as I look over her bare face. "You're gorgeous as you are. You can wear makeup any other time, but not today. I want to look upon your natural beauty, little lamb. Give me this..."

She lets out a long sigh and then nods. "Okay. I can do that."

"Thank you." I lean in and kiss her, but when I try to deepen the kiss, Raya pulls back.

"Um, hello—morning breath!"

"I don't give a fuck. You will not deny me a kiss, woman..." I yank her back to me and plunder her mouth in a deep, soulful kiss.

Once I feel her relax and start to return the kiss, I end it, grinning. "Go shower—we leave in twenty minutes."

I find it cute that she thinks her scowls affect me. All they do is get stored away for when it's time to dole out another punishment. Raya likes the pain, at least to an extent. She's no pain slut, and that's okay. I just love that she likes it enough to let me color her ass and make her pretty pussy weep for me.

⚜

I'm finishing closing the beach house when Raya comes out of the bedroom. I point to a stool at the island and say, "Sit—eat."

It's not much—just a croissant breakfast sandwich from the deli down the road and a hot cup of coffee in a travel mug. We don't have time to stop anywhere before the appointment I'm taking her to. It was hard enough getting the owner to come in on a Sunday. I had to name-drop, and although this isn't Nyte, people know who the Heirs are for the most part. Besides, it's not my first time receiving services from them.

"Are you going to tell me where we're going?" she asks before taking a bite of her sandwich.

Melted cheese lingers at the corner of her mouth, and I can't help myself. I lean in and lick it off before pressing my lips to hers.

"Nope. You'll find out soon enough."

"O—kay. Then can you at least tell me why you picked this skimpy sundress for me to wear? I prefer shorts and a tank for the ride home."

I answer her question in two simple words.

"Easy access."

She rolls her eyes but continues eating the hot ham and cheese until it's gone. I quickly wash her plate, placing it on the rack to dry. Looking around one last time, I take Raya's hand and walk out, locking the house before we go.

Raya's quiet on the way to the appointment, but that's okay; she'll know soon enough, and then I'm sure she will have plenty to say. I grin, just thinking about her reaction. I'm holding her hand on my thigh, savoring it because, more than likely, she'll be too pissed to hold it later.

Why do I want to piss my little lamb off? It's not that I want to, but this must be done—more for my sanity than anything else.

As I slow the car and pull into a parking spot, there are a variety of businesses up and down this road, but only one with its lights on. Raya stares at the latter and then at me, cocking her eyebrow.

"I know you're not taking me in there," she states with a bit of attitude.

"Have I ever told you that you're even more beautiful when you're giving me lip?"

"Don't try being cute, Nyx! Why are we here?"

"You'll see—come." I get out and hurry to her side, holding my hand out for her.

She takes it, albeit reluctantly, and lets me continue holding it. A bell above the door jingles as I open it and let her go in first. Pictures and artwork hang on the walls, and there's a sitting area with albums placed on a table in front of the couch and chairs.

"Mr. Beckam. It's good to see you again. This must be the lucky woman," the owner states as he holds his hand out for Raya to shake. "Hi. I'm Colt, owner of this fine establishment."

"Hi, I'm Saraya," my little lamb replies.

"Thank you again for coming in today. I do appreciate it," I tell him.

"Yeah, yeah, just remember, you owe me one." Colt shoots me a grin and then clasps his hands together. "So, what are we doing today?"

I hold up my right hand. "I need this made smaller to fit on Raya's inner wrist."

"What?!" Raya exclaims.

Colt examines the Gods of Nyte tattoo on my hand and nods. "I'll take a picture and run it through my scanner."

"Nyx, I never agreed to get a fucking tattoo!" My little lamb clenches her jaw, trying to talk in a low voice.

"You agreed to marry me, did you not?"

"Yes, but—"

"Well, that alone is you agreeing to wear my mark. Besides, people need to know that you are the wife to a Gods Heir."

"I don't want a big tattoo like that, Nyx," she whines.

"It won't be. It's going to be a dainty skull on the inside of your wrist is all. It will look cute," I tell her.

"Cute? Since when are skulls cute?"

"When they are carved into your beautiful body," I say and kiss her.

Rolling her eyes, Raya gives up the fight and sighs. "Fine, but you owe me big time for this, Beckam!"

Grinning, I help her up onto the chair where Colt does his work and bop her on the nose with my finger. "It's cute that you think you can demand things from me, little lamb," I say, then lean in closer and lower my voice. "Now, be a good girl, and I'll make you come on the ride home like I did coming here. You'll like the sting the needle will give you; I promise."

Taking her lips in a forceful yet loving way, I kiss her until she moans against my mouth. Just before Colt returns, I firmly grip her chin and stare into her eyes.

"I love you, Raya, and I want *everyone* to know you are *mine.*"

Saraya

I will never admit to Nyx that I absolutely *love* my skull tattoo. I've always admired his, and when it's shrunk down and given a feminine touch, it's absolutely adorable. Admitting that he was right about the fact that I would like the sting is also off the table. I more than liked it; I'm ready to get another tattoo! There's much catching up to do if I want to fit in with the others.

When we got home and I showed the guys and Mara my skull, Mara snubbed it, saying it doesn't really count because it's so small. If you ask me, I think she may have been a little hurt. Amara has been with the guys her whole life, and she couldn't have the tattoo because she wasn't an Heir.

I've tried bringing this up to Nyx, who keeps saying he will discuss it with the guys, but he's yet to do so. I could be a bitch and rub it in, God knows Mara would probably do it to me, but I genuinely feel bad. It's just a tattoo—I understand this—but doing what Mara does for the Gods of Nyte should be recognized somehow.

It's been two weeks since we've been back, and Nyx has been busy finalizing last-minute details at the club with the guys, so there really is no reason for him not to have a chance to talk to them. I don't know why I'm making such a fuss over this; maybe it's because, deep down, I want to mend things with the little psycho.

The Hall has felt like a ghost town lately. With everyone gone at Club Unholy, I'm mostly home by my lonesome. Nyx hasn't wanted me around all the construction in case any accidents happen. So, when I hear the front door open at almost midnight, and laughter fills the front foyer, I rush out of the billiard room where I was tucked away, reading.

I stop abruptly when I see Nyx and Amara hanging all over each other. Mara is laughing and Nyx has his finger to his lips, also laughing, trying to shush the woman with her arms wrapped around his waist. The picture they make is not a good one. I should know better than to let this get to me because I know Nyx loves me, but it's apparent that they are both intoxicated. I was left home by myself while my future husband was out getting drunk with a woman he used to fuck.

I'm about to clear my throat to make my presence known when Mara stretches up and hugs Nyx around his head, holding him close. Her face is hidden in the crook of his neck as he slides his arms around her waist. It looks like an intimate hug, and I feel the burn behind my eyelids.

What finally does it for me is watching Nyx close his eyes as if he's savoring the hug. I finally come out of my shocked state and head for the stairs. When they still don't hear me as I walk by, my resolve breaks, and I sneer at them.

"Get a fucking room, will you? I don't want to see that shit!" I'd laugh at the sight of the two jumping apart, but I'm too devastated.

"Raya," Nyx slurs my name a little as he pushes Mara away and holds his arms out to me. "Come here—I've missed you."

"Fuck you, Nyx. It didn't look like you were missing me that much. If you were, you could have come home to *me* instead of getting drunk with *her*."

Mara snickers as she stumbles where she stands.

"Jesus! How much did you drink? Who drove..." I stop and scoff. "You know what, I don't give a fuck anymore."

"Little lamb..." Nyx calls out.

"Just let her go, Nyx. Talk to her in the morning," Mara giggles.

I spin around to face Mara, anger radiating from every pore. "I can't believe I've been feeling sorry for your ass! You just can't help picking up my sloppy seconds, can you?"

Mara seems to sober up a bit as she stumbles forward, sneering, "What the fuck did you just say to me?"

"The fucking truth, Mara! Have him because I no longer want him..."

Pulling my engagement ring from my finger, I throw it at Nyx, watching it bounce off his chest. I turn and run up the stairs before he can see the tears fall.

✦

I'm huddled in a corner in my old room after locking myself in when there's a sudden crash, and the door splinters into pieces. A crazed-looking Nyx stands in the doorway, his chest heaving heavily. He looks around wildly, and when he doesn't see me, he storms to the bathroom, only to walk back out a second later. I'm in a dark corner of the room, and I almost get away with him not seeing me, but then his stone-gray eyes land on mine.

He jerks back abruptly, and the wild look in his eyes fades and then softens. When he starts towards me, I hold my hand up to stop him. I don't want him anywhere near me.

"Don't. Just leave me alone..."

"Fuck that! I will never leave you alone, Raya. You. Are. Mine."

"No, I *was* yours."

"What the fuck is your problem? How could you even think that Mara and I..." He doesn't finish.

Finally, something snaps, and I no longer give a shit if he sees the state I'm in. I jump up and stalk him, poking him in the chest when I stand in front of him.

"For the past two weeks, I've been left home alone while you've been off getting the club ready. I was okay with it because I knew it needed to be done. But to find out that while I'm here bored out of my *fucking* mind, you're out getting plastered with your old whore?!"

I expect him to yell back at me, but he doesn't. Instead, Nyx drops to his knees and pulls at his hair. "You can't leave me, Raya. It's not what you think—I need you to trust me."

I scoff, "I'm done trusting people..." I start to walk away but his words stop me.

"I was doing it for you. I wanted it to be a surprise—I didn't realize how long you were left alone. We drank tonight because we were celebrating its completion. Well, I was celebrating that I was finally finished with your surprise." When he looks up at me, his eyes are bloodshot and they're glistening.

"A surprise—for me?" I ask wide-eyed.

"Yeah. I wanted to give you our own private room at the club, one that's just ours and not used by others. I needed it to be perfect because you're perfect, and you deserve nothing less."

My feet bring me back to Nyx and I drop to my knees, so we are face to face. "So, you and Mara aren't..."

"No! Of course not! It's only you—it's only ever been you."

"I'm so sorry..." I tell him just above a whisper.

Nyx gazes at me, and then cups each side of my face, saying, "No. I'm the one who's sorry. I've neglected you and made you doubt my love for you. I don't ever want you doubting my love. You have my heart, Raya—I can never give it to anyone else."

A loud sob slips past my lips, and I crash them against his. I'm not sure how long we're here kissing, but when we finally pull away, Nyx slips my ring back on my finger.

"If you ever take this off again, I'm going to have it implanted into your finger." He kisses the ring, and I chuckle.

"I'll be sure to get the whole story next time," I tell him.

"There will never be a next time, little lamb. From now on, you'll go where I go, no matter what."

We walk back to our room, my arms wrapped around his waist, mainly to help him avoid stumbling. I'd like to say that we spent the night having hot and kinky makeup sex, but the truth is, I barely got his shoes off his feet before he passed out. I lay beside him, thinking about everything, knowing I was in the wrong. Admitting it is only the first step. Tomorrow, I will have to beg for Mara's forgiveness if she doesn't *off* me first.

EPILOGUE

Nyx

Life has a funny way of playing out. I thought I would spend the rest of my life in a dull, boring, loveless marriage. I was tempted not to marry at all, but I needed to have something constant in my life—something that would say a big *fuck you* to my father. He ruined many lives during his time on this earth, and I was determined to do the exact opposite.

Fuck no, I'm not a saint and never claimed to be. I know I'm going to Hell, but before I go, I want to undo everything my father had worked so hard to do. Nyte may not be the safest or cleanest place to raise a family yet, but the Heirs of Nyte's Hall will stop at nothing until we fix that.

It's by sheer luck that I got Saraya back in my life. If anybody remembers that we are stepsiblings, then they haven't made it known, and quite frankly, they can eat a bag of dicks if they have a problem with it.

After that awful night a week ago, when I came home drunk with our little devil, I've been doing everything I can to show my little lamb that nobody could ever replace her. I know she still has her doubts, but I'm going to fix that tonight. I'm going to take control, and I'm going to dominate my little lamb for the first time at the club.

We've had lots of makeup sex during this past week, but that's different. I'm in charge tonight, and for once, Raya has gifted me her submission, if only for tonight. She will see how nice it is to give control over, but whether she allows it again is anyone's guess.

At the moment, I'm watching her through the camera I have installed, so we can watch our scenes at a later date. My little lamb struggles as she remains draped over and cuffed to the spanking bench. A beautiful silver plug with a ruby gem peeks out of her pretty little ass.

For now, an open-mouthed gag is strapped to her head, which will be removed when I'm ready to take her ass, so I can hear her moans. I just want to see the beautiful picture she makes as she's restrained, cuffed, and plugged with drool dripping from her mouth. I can tell you from looking at one of the other camera's views that she loves this if the wetness glistening on her pretty pussy tells me anything.

This is our own personal playroom with almost everything you can think of at our disposal. The room is located smack dab in the middle of the building with a hall on each side, so naturally, I had installed viewing windows on all four sides of the room for an all-around view. Of course, we won't use them all the time, only when my little lamb is in the mood. Tonight will be the first night. It's a night of firsts since I'll also be taking her ass for the first time.

When I think she's had enough time to lay there and be humiliated, knowing that others are watching her, I return to the room. She can't see me enter the room; the collar attached to the bench doesn't give her room to move her head. She jerks when I run my hand up her leg but then relaxes when she realizes it's only me.

I don't say anything to her yet as I massage her ass cheeks before pulling them apart to show the voyeurs how pretty her ass looks at the moment. *I'm about to fucking ruin it.*

I round the table and gaze down at her, her eyes strained to look up, tears already glistening in their depths. "Do you want to use your safe word, little lamb?" I caress her cheek as she tries to shake her head. "That's my good girl. You know," I start, as I undo my jeans and pull my cock out, stroking it a few times. "I'm not big into dominance, but I must say, little lamb, seeing you like this, a needy little whore just laying here waiting to be used by me—well, a guy could get used to it."

I slide my hardened length into her mouth, taking it slow and continuing until the tip is down her throat. She only gagged a little until I got past the reflex; then, it was easy sailing.

"Mm, you deep-throat me so well, baby."

I hold both sides of her head as I slowly move in and out, sinking all the way in each time. I don't want to come yet, so I remove my cock and stand out of the way, ensuring everyone can see what a drooling mess she is before I remove it.

"Thank you, Sir," Raya says once it's removed.

"What are you thanking me for?"

"Thank you for choking me with your cock, Sir." She doesn't say it sarcastically, but I can tell she's not a fan.

"You're welcome, little lamb. I'm now going to remove the plug and fuck your ass. Remember to use your safe word if you need to." As I've said before, I don't sugarcoat shit.

I kiss the crown of her head and move to where her ass and pussy are waiting to be used. I'll be using both tonight. Gazing at her beautiful backside, I admire the soft silky skin that stretches from head to toe. It's already flushed a tinge of pink from me using her mouth—it's fucking gorgeous.

Working the plug out from her tight pucker, I then drizzle some more lube around it and work some into her hole. I grab a condom from the nearby bowl and rip the packaging open with my teeth before rolling it on. I hate using these fucking things, but if I want to fuck my favorite cunt later, I had better use one for her ass.

Once everything is nice and lubed, I bring my hand down and slap her ass. She moans while I groan as I spread her cheeks open; never seeing an ass so fucking perfect before. I spit on it for good measure and start working my cock into her. She's so tight that it's taking me longer than I'd like to get my full length into her.

I have to pause a few times, otherwise I'll come too soon. Once my balls slap against her clit, indicating her ass is taking me so fucking deep, I take a deep breath, and shudder. Her warmth wraps me in a cocoon, and I don't ever want to leave it.

"You're ass takes me just as well as your mouth does, baby." I pull out and thrust back in, working on picking up the pace.

I reach around and work her clit until she's about to come. "Hold it—don't come—not yet." I strum her clit a few more times, making her hold her climax before I give her a break.

I want to work her into how not to come when her body is so overstimulated. Gripping her hips, I start fucking my little lamb harder as she moans and whimpers.

"Fuck yeah, look at my sweet little lamb acting like a whore. You're fucking perfect for me, baby."

I slap each cheek before spreading them and watching as I fuck into Raya's forbidden hole. Soon, we'll be married and having kids, and I'll still be craving every fucking inch of this beautiful woman. I hope our parents are watching me as I drill into my *stepsister*. They did what they could to keep us apart, but it ultimately made no difference. Saraya was made for me and I for her. No motherfucker will ever pull us apart again.

I feel the tingle in my spine as my balls begin to pull up. Removing my cock, I yank the condom off and direct my aching shaft to her slit. Running the tip up and down through her folds, I push into her sopping-wet cunt and groan.

"Damn, did you like having your ass fucked, baby?"

"Yes," she pants, but it sounds strained.

I grin and ask, "Do you need to come?"

"God, yes...please!"

"Not yet little lamb. Tell me—does it get you off that so many people are watching your holes get railed?"

"Nyx...stop."

"Say it, Raya. Tell them that you love having them watch—be honest with your sexuality. I'm not trying to be an ass, I swear."

"Fine! Yes, them watching me turns me on—please, Sir!"

Thank fuck she finally admitted it. I didn't know how much longer I could hold out. Reaching around, I play with her clit and insert two digits into her ass. Now she is stuffed. Readjusting my stance, I get deeper and pick up the pace, pounding into her as my climax closes in.

"Come for me, baby—fuck—come now!" I roar and let loose an army of my little soldiers. I thrust and jerk, emptying everything I've got into my little lamb.

"Oh, Nyx—yes—uh, ohh!" Raya comes hard, squeezing my cock so tight I can't pull out.

"That's it, baby. Let it all out—there we go."

I spit on her ass again and keep fucking it with my fingers, taking her into another orgasm, because she deserves it. She was so good tonight. I couldn't have asked for a more perfect night with her.

Only after her body shudders with the end of her release do I pull out. I let my cum seep out, and as the crowd watches, I swipe up some of my seed and push it into her ass. As the voyeurs watch me fuck my cum into my little lamb, I make it known to all.

"Saraya is mine. She wears my mark, she wears my ring, and as you can see, she wears my seed. Let anyone know who asks who this fucking perfect woman belongs to. She will be my wife and a queen of Nyte's Hall!"

I don't need to see their responses because I don't give a shit what they think. I uncuff Raya and lift her off the bench to stand before me. Wiping her matted hair from her face, I ask, "Are you okay, little lamb?"

She nods.

"Come on. Let me take care of you now."

I pick her up and carry her to the bed that takes up a good portion of the room before picking up the remote and closing the viewing windows. This is a private moment with Raya—I will not share it with anybody. I know—it's fucked up—but for me, sex is sex. You don't touch my woman, but you can watch as *I* fuck her, and you don't watch when I do aftercare on her because these moments are going to be my favorite ones if she ever allows me to do this again.

❖

"A penny for your thoughts?" I ask a very quiet Raya as we lay in our own bed.

"Hm? Oh, sorry, my thoughts seem to be everywhere at the moment." She snuggles into me.

"Anything that I should know about?" I kiss her forehead.

After a moment, Raya asks, "How often will you want to do that? I mean, what we did tonight."

I shrug. "It's not something I need to do regularly, just whenever we're in the mood for being a bit adventurous. Why?"

"No reason. I guess that's okay. Don't get me wrong, it's apparent that I get off on that sort of thing, but then I feel so exposed afterward."

I tilt her chin so I can see the silhouette of her face in the darkened room and say, "We don't ever have to do that again, baby."

"But you made that room for us..."

Well, shit.

"Are you telling me that you never want to play in the room with me? We don't have to have an audience, but I would love to be able to play in the future."

"Hm, what will we do with the baby?" she asks.

"We have time to figure that out. At least we have a fun playroom to practice making one in." I chuckle.

"Phoenyx, we don't have to practice anymore," Raya states softly.

389

"What? Not practice? That's crazy..." I cut my sentence short when her words hit me.

I jump from the bed to turn on the bedside lamp. My heart is racing, and goosebumps invade my body.

"Are you fucking with me? What are you saying, Raya?"

She sits up, blinking her eyes against the sudden brightness. She's gorgeous with the after-sex glow, and my dick stirs once again. Fuck, I already took her again when we got home—I need to let her rest.

"Should I start calling you Daddy now or wait?" Raya smiles softly.

I crawl back onto the bed and take her face in my hands. "Are you for real? Are you pregnant, little lamb?"

Raya bites her bottom lip and nods. "I found out this morning." She giggles. "Apparently, that's why I've been so moody for the past week."

"I thought you were on birth control?"

"Yeah, about that. It seems you have to remember to go back and get another shot."

My smile slowly grows as I stare into the love of my life's eyes. I pull her in and kiss her, giving her everything I've got. She opens for me, and our tongues tango. Saraya has just given me the best gift she ever could. Not only is she marrying me, but she's bearing my spawn, just like she said she would.

I'm so fucking ecstatic that I want to shout it from the rooftops, but then something comes to mind, and I stare at Raya as so many thoughts run through my head.

"What is it?" she asks.

"We need to get married, like right away!"

My little lamb laughs. "This is 2024, Nyx. It's okay if we aren't married when the baby is born."

"Yeah, I know, but *I* want us to be married before they're born." I flatten my hand over her stomach, and tingles shoot through me. *I'm going to be a father.*

I retake her lips, unable to get enough of her or thank her. Saraya gave me life when she came back to me, and now, she's giving me another one—I'm just blown away.

When I pull back, I can't seem to stop smiling. "Thank you, Raya. Thank you for giving me your love and trust, but most of all, for giving me the family I've always wanted. I love you, little lamb."

"I love you, too, but you know—you will have to stop calling me little lamb at some point. We don't want to confuse the baby."

"Fuck that! I've reclaimed you as mine, Saraya. I'll never give up calling you my pet name. You will always and forever be your lion's little lamb.

Acknowledgment

First and foremost, I want to thank my family. Putting up with my long hours and my being absent a lot is not easy, but they take it in stride, knowing what my writing means to me. Thank you for loving me enough to put up with me while I'm in the 'zone.'

Next, is my small PR team of my favorite smut ladies lead by my Head PR and PA of Sweet Magnolia Author Services, Elizabeth A.K.A. Lizzy Sue, who help me get my titles out on social media, but above all, they keep me somewhat sane... most of the time. Brittany, Cierra, Kindra, Kristen, Kristie, Linnea, Natalie, Nicole, Stafanie and last, but certainly not least... my assistant, Stephanie. I love all of you bunches.

I want to thank all my ARC readers for taking the time to read this title and give me their feedback, they truly are an amazing bunch!

Sky, my proofreader, who has also become a new friend of mine. As always, always lots of laughs with her throughout the proofing and I will cherish all of them. I am so blessed to have you on my team, and I hope you know that you are truly appreciated.

More by Stacy Rush

The Elite Series
The Vampire's Hellion
The Vampire's Angel
The Vampire's Salvation
The Vampire's Mate
The Vampire's Rebel
The Vampire's Saving Grace
The Vampire's True Love
The Vampire's Chosen
The Vampire's Forsaken
Book #10
Book #11

The Bully Series
My Bully's Love
Addicted To My Bully's Love
My Bully's Best Friend
Loving Them: Our Happily Ever After

The Choice Duet
Aria's Choice
Aria's Choice: Choosing Them

The Twisted Duet & Novella
Twisted Hunger
Twisted Lies: A Twisted Novella
Twisted Bonds

Standalone
Saints and Sinners